APOTHECARY

Peter Cawdron
thinkingscifi.wordpress.com

Copyright © Peter Cawdron, 2023

All rights reserved. The right of Peter Cawdron to be identified as the author of this work has been asserted in accordance with the Copyright, Designs and Patents Act 1988. All the characters in this book are fictitious, and any resemblance to actual persons living or dead is purely coincidental.

Cover Art: Composite image created from NASA ISS027E012224 image of sunrise and Robotic Hand Making Contact by Guillaume.

Disclaimer: No Artificial Intelligence (AI) was used in the creation of this story. Some would argue, no intelligence was used at all.

Imprint: Independently published

ISBN: 9798376848692 — Paperback
ISBN: 9798388297402 — Hardback

For you, the reader.

Without you, none of these stories would be possible.

Thank you.

Notes on Language

As *Apothecary* is set in the United Kingdom, this novel has been written using British English. To give you some context, the first act takes place several years before Shakespeare was born. Initially, I used dialogue from the 1550s, but after a few chapters, I realised it was too cumbersome for the modern reader. I had to find a balance that helped readers immerse themselves in the period without the prose becoming unreadable. To this end, I've used modern sentence structures while avoiding modern terms like, '*Okay.*' The dialogue in critical moments, though, such as during the executions at St. Paul's have been lifted word for word from historical records to ensure authenticity.

Act I

16th Century

Blue Skies

Anthony hops up on the stone window ledge at the front of the apothecary. He shuffles in beside Julia without saying a word.

"What do you see?" she asks.

Unlike everyone else bustling between the stalls, her head remains still. She stares blindly into the distance. Flies buzz around fish laid out on drying racks in the sun. Crates full of medlar, mulberries and crabapples sit beneath a canvas awning. A mule neighs softly, pulling at its reins as it stands before a hitching rail. It's trying to reach a tuft of grass growing beside the village trough. Its hooves stamp impatiently at the cobblestones.

A cock struts in the dirt, ignoring the crowd. Its feathers are proud, arching high above its back. It's a patchwork of conflicting colours. Black tail feathers, orange wings and a brilliant red comb on its head make it a delight to watch as it scratches at the dirt, looking for insects. For Anthony, it seems cruel to enjoy a sight Julia is forever deprived of seeing.

Julia is patient.

Anthony wonders how he should respond to her. She nuzzles against him, imparting some warmth on a cool October morning. He looks down at her arm rubbing up against his. For him, it's intimate—inviting. But he understands that's not her intent. For her, sound takes the place of sight, while touch is how she connects with the unseen world immediately around her.

A breeze blows across in front of the bakery, causing the smell of fresh bread to drift on the wind. Sunlight breaks through the clouds, resting on his cheeks. Water drips from the eaves of a thatched roof with a steady rhythm. An autumn storm rolls on, grumbling and complaining as it wanders off into the distance. These are all things she can sense. He could tell her about them, but she already knows they're there. She's far too perceptive to have missed any of the subtle hints drifting on the wind.

"I see the white of the clouds," he says. "The blue of the sky, the green of leaves swaying in the trees, shifting like waves lapping at the shore. The yellow of hay being thatched into the roof as workmen clamber up and down their ladders."

Julia nods. She's been blind since she was six. Sometimes she sees bursts of light in the darkness, although she thinks it's random. She has no idea what these '*ghosts,*' as she calls them, mean—if anything. Maybe those flashes are like the crackle of wood burning in the hearth, sending sparks drifting into the chimney. Sometimes, on the darkest of nights, she'll swear she can see the faint outline of a man similar to her father, but Anthony suspects she's remembering rather than seeing him. It breaks his heart to know there's no recourse for her, no recompense to ever recover her sight. She's been robbed of a joy few ever deeply consider. One day, the world was full of sights and shapes, bursting with colour—and then it was gone—only it wasn't. It was still there. It is still there. Try as she may, she opens her eyes each morn, but her eyes never wake for themselves.

Rather than watching the crowd, Anthony turns to look at her. Admiration lights up his face, although she won't know that. Perhaps she suspects as much as a slight smile reaches her lips. She must be able to feel the motion of his body through the subtle change in the way his leg rubs up against her thigh. Anthony wishes she could see the world as he does. If only wishes came true.

Julia faces the sun, bathing in its light, listening to the cacophony of sounds around her. Her fingers reach for him, missing his arm. Her hand brushes lightly against his shirt, so he shifts his arm, allowing her hand to rest on the back of his wrist.

She nudges him with her shoulder, wanting more detail. For Anthony, the challenge is how to describe something so mundane and yet utterly astonishing.

"Tell me more, Ant. What does it look like today? The sky?"

"Blue is still blue," he replies, unsure how to describe something so radiant. "It's the same as yesterday."

No sooner have those words left his lips than her visage drops. He's being lazy. He can do better.

"Blue is… it's cool, but not cold. It's soothing, like dipping your feet in a creek on a hot summer's day. Blue is somehow light and dark at the same time, but mostly light. And it's vibrant. It's as though the sky is alive. When I see the blue of the sky, I think of the promise each day holds."

Julia smiles, and he wonders what she sees in the depths of her imagination, perhaps memories from before the pox.

"In the distance, it's faint," he says, pushing himself to describe the sky in more detail. "Down low by the horizon, it fades. It's almost as though the sky is vanishing over the chimneys."

He cranes his neck, looking up past the scattered clouds.

"But above us, it's vibrant. It seems to curl overhead like the canvas of a tent."

"A tent?"

"A vast tent. One that reaches hundreds of miles above us."

"Hundreds?"

"Hundreds."

"And?"

"And it's deep."

"Deep?" she asks. Her soft voice is lost in the clatter of a cart rolling past on the cobblestones. Merchants call out to the crowd, plying their wares. Buyers barter with traders, haggling for produce. Coins clink in purses being rattled to torment the sellers.

"Beyond the clouds," Anthony says, ignoring the markets. "The sky is deep like the sea. Down here in the village, it is as though we're sitting at the bottom of the ocean. Up there, it seems as if there's no end."

Julia looks up, not that she can see anything, but she directs her gaze there anyway.

"Perhaps there is no end," she says. "Perhaps we imagine an end where there is none, and it just goes on and on."

"Perhaps."

Anthony's curious. What can she see within the darkness? Is there a glimmer of warmth? A hint of colour? When Anthony shuts his eyes, he sees a muddy mess of ruddy colours swirling behind his eyelids, a cacophony of pinks and purples along with a smattering of brown and red that seems to pulsate. Is that what she sees? Or is her darkness eternal? Is it broken only by the heat of the radiant sun on her forehead?

"And the clouds?" she asks. "Tell me about the clouds, Ant."

"They're scruffy," Anthony says, taking a good look at them. "Some of them are dark, almost dirty underneath. It's as though they've scraped along the mountains, scrubbing the slopes clean as they laid down their rain and snow. Others are as white as cotton. They're like tufts of wool drifting across the sky. They're bits of fluff that have fallen on the shearing room floor. They're the froth of milk swirling within a pail, the churn of cream before it becomes butter."

"What about there?" Julia asks, pointing randomly into the market. Anthony knows what she's doing. He's supposed to be at work, but she's stalling. She doesn't want him to leave. Not yet. He smiles, not that she would know. As much as he'd love to sit here telling her about the world around them, that won't earn him a pretty penny, and yet he can't bear to leave her. To do so would be cruel.

"Coal," he says. "As black as the night. Packed in sacks. Stacked on pallets. Staining men's hands and faces with soot."

Black is a colour Julia knows all too well—and she hates it—as he well knows. Her hand swivels, pointing elsewhere just as he knew she would.

"Game," he says. "Birds and deer felled fresh from the forest, hanging from the butcher's stall."

"Tell me about them."

Anthony picks his words with care, thinking about what he sees.

"Well, there's a pheasant. It's beautiful. With feathers that paint a dark rainbow. The tones are earthy. There are browns and reds with black stripes on the tail and white dots on its chest. Oh, and it has a white collar ringed around its neck."

"Just like a priest?"

"Yes. And its head is adorned in a red as rich and as regal as anything set before the queen."

"And?"

Anthony's not sure what else to say as the vision before him is one of heartache rather than celebration.

Blood drips from the head of a pheasant. The dead bird hangs from a decrepit wooden rack. Its plumage, so regal in life, is now destined for quills and the adornment of hats. Its flesh will be roasted before the sun sets in the even. Golden feathers give way to an iridescent blue, catching the light and glistening like oil on water, revealing hints of a blue-green as deep as the sea. He wants to tell her about these colours, but he can't. Amidst the chatter and bartering within the market, the pheasant's eyes have long since glazed over. Like Julia, the pheasant stares blindly at the mud in the gutter.

In the rear of the stall, a small crate rests on the cobblestones. It's hidden in the shadows, being barely visible from where Anthony's sitting on the other side of the street. A soft cluck carries on the wind, followed by the cry of a hen calling for her fallen mate. Having been spared for laying, she cannot conceive how life has been wrung from her partner. She can see him. She calls to him, longing for an answer that will never come.

As Anthony opens his mouth to speak, a hand clips him on the back of his head, catching him just behind his ear. Instinctively, he lets out a yelp, leaping from the window ledge. Like a mongrel being kicked from behind, he turns, desperate to protect himself. His boots slip on the muddy road. He scrambles to keep from falling over.

A voice bellows, "What the smithing hell are you looking at?"

Master Dunmore is gruff and haggard. His face has been pitted by the pox. Julia has her hand over her mouth, trying not to giggle, knowing how mean the old man can be. To him, she's nigh on invisible; she's just another beggar in the market.

"Didn't yah hear me calling? Away with the fairies, are yah?"

Master Dunmore raises his hand, making as though he'd gladly hit the teen again.

"What in hades were you looking for out there? A knight in full armour?"

For a moment, Anthony assumes the master's question is sincere. He stutters, trying to offer an explanation, struggling to articulate his thinking. His ear hurts, which makes it difficult to concentrate.

"I was looking at colours," he says, correcting himself with, "Looking at life!"

Master Dunmore leans forward with his hands resting on his knees. His face is mere inches from Anthony. He's so close the teenager can smell his putrid breath. With his belly protruding from beneath his dirty shirt, the master bellows, "Life? Git to the port, yah slackard, or I'll wring the life out of yah!"

Master Dunmore swings his calloused hand, swatting at Anthony, but being seventeen years of age, Anthony has the agility of a cat. A wooden crate sways as he darts into the crowd, weaving his way between surprised patrons.

"I want that shipment secured," the master yells after him, pointing toward the docks.

"I'll get it. I'll get it," Anthony says, backing up and bumping into an old woman carrying a piglet under her arm. She recoils. The animal squeals, kicking with its legs and trying to escape. Anthony apologizes profusely and peels away, dancing through the crowd as he makes his way down the street. Julia laughs at the chaos she's inadvertently unleashed.

"I'll be back," Anthony yells, more so for her than the master. "Soon."

She yells, "Have fun, Ant."

Anthony waves, not that Julia can see him, but knowing she can hear the emotion in his voice. For all he's told her about the world around them, she's taught him more about the subtleties of human affairs.

Julia divines much from acts as small as a sigh, a huff, or a pause in a conversation. For her, silence is a hymn sung in a cathedral. Even though she's imprisoned in darkness, she sees more of the human soul than anyone he knows. Julia has shown Anthony that words say far more than their owners ever intend. He's learning to hear as she does—with the care of a mouse outwitting a cat. Master Dunmore, with his gruff voice and frustration boiling over into anger, must speak volumes to her. He's anxious. Frustrated, but not by Anthony. He's a good man at heart and has extended an apprenticeship to Anthony when many a village lad would leap at the opportunity. He might sound angry at indolence, but something else has him on edge. He feels under pressure. There's a weight of expectation bearing down on him that Anthony can't understand. Perhaps it's the value of the shipping. Should it be stolen, it might cripple his business. Maybe it's the uncertainty around finding buyers for items from the Levant. Perhaps it's all that and more.

As Anthony leaves the market, he takes one last look. Master Dunmore disappears back into the apothecary. Julia's still sitting perched on the window ledge. Her legs dangle over the water running through the wide gutter. Her head turns, being attuned to the call of a bird flying overhead. She instinctively picks up on its direction, height and speed. She's smiling, tracing its motion as it wings its way across the sky, singing now the rain has passed.

Anthony makes his way down a cobblestone alley to the main street.

Westminster is both a village on the outskirts of London and the seat of parliament, with the House of Commons being located on the bank of the Thames. Why the House was positioned outside the walls of the capital is a curiosity. It seems the electors wanted to be close but not too close to the monarch's sharpened pike. It's not uncommon to see farmers and gentry passing along the same road. Horses trot past proud and tall, pulling stately carriages. Top hats stare out of narrow carriage windows, watching as the avenue passes by, talking incessantly.

Chimney sweeps wander the streets, dragging their brushes and poles in handcarts, calling out for work. They're sullen, lacking enthusiasm even though the day has only just begun.

A Spanish caravel sails down the Thames, heading out toward the channel. Sailors hang from the rigging of the ship, repairing the mainsail. They hoist sections, working on the cloth ribs that make up the vast square sail. Several sailors perch themselves on the crossbeam, gathering loose folds and fixing tears. Two triangular lateen sails have been raised at the front of the caravel. These carry the vessel on at a walking pace. Gulls flock around the caravel, looking for scraps. The river twists and churns in the wake of the ship, leaving a muddy trail through the water.

Anthony climbs onto the river wall. He scrambles along the carefully hewn rocks with his arms outstretched, keeping his balance. As much as he needs to watch the gentle rise and fall of the wall, he doesn't want to take his eyes off the foreign ship. With its shallow draft, the captain is confident even during the changing of the tide. He stands proud beside the helmsman, talking excitedly and pointing at the landmarks of London. Several sailors sit on the forecastle rising high above the river. A thin prow forms the bow of the caravel. Most of the crew sit on the gunwales, dangling their feet over the edge of the wooden hull, laughing and jostling with each other, enjoying a break as they sail the quiet river.

Oh, how Anthony longs for the sea. Adventure calls to him. It was a couple of caravels that found the Americas, along with a carrack. Everyone remembers the *Santa Maria*, but *La Niña* survived a hurricane that would have sunk many a ship twice her size. She may have been *a little girl*, as her name reckons, but she was feisty. *La Pinta* was the fastest ship in the fleet. It's no surprise that it was from her decks the New World was first sighted.

Anthony jumps down from the river wall and scrambles across a narrow wharf. Fishermen unload their catch, emptying their crates. Seagulls call, fighting with each other for scraps as they drift on the wind. Anthony darts through a makeshift stall where an old woman is selling vegetables. She scolds him, shaking her fist as he vaults a basket full of cabbages. The day is too bright and full of life to be sour, and he simply laughs, climbing back on the wall and continuing on his way.

The Thames curves, following an S-bend as it meanders through the countryside. Anthony's on the outer bank. Despite his efforts, the caravel outpaces him. The stern of the ship teases him, threatening to leave him in its broad wake.

What wonders must there be in the New World? Anthony longs to escape London. He wants to strike out on his own and search for exotic lands. He's seen sketches from the Americas of savages with their naked chests and feathered headdresses. They paint their faces, but why? Oh, to explore an alien continent. For him, it would be worth the hardship of all the Atlantic storms.

With that thought, Anthony's boot slips on a moss-covered rock. He falls from the wall. The wind swirls around him, catching his long hair. He tumbles onto the steep, rocky embankment leading down to the Thames. Anthony scrambles with his legs, grabbing at the blur of rocks rushing past. He lashes out with his boots as he slides down the sloping wall, desperate not to land in the muddy river. Loose pebbles and shards of rock embed themselves in his soft palms.

Barnacles and limpets line the inter-tidal shore, clinging to the lower rocks. Anthony kicks to avoid them, pushing with his boots, wanting to slow his descent. Skin is torn from his knees as he tumbles, trying to come to a stop before he lands in the putrid mud.

Anthony comes to rest inches above the waterline. He rolls onto his back, shocked by the sudden onset of pain surging through his hands and legs. Blood seeps from the torn skin on his palms. Reality is cruel. Why should a momentary lapse cause such agony? For all of God's mercies, pain isn't one of them. What is there in agony but the linger of regret? Blood drips from his knee. His pale white skin turns flush, forming welts that are a brilliant red. Anthony looks up at the clouds drifting by so serene in the sky. They're unmoved by the tears welling up in his eyes. Birds circle high above him, ignoring his anguish.

The caravel sails on with its flags fluttering in the breeze.

For a moment, Anthony just lies there on his back, breathing deeply, trying to soothe his nerves. He wants to block out the pain, but he can't. He's shaking. He focuses beyond the moment, listening to the water lapping beneath his boots, trying to rid himself of the agony pulsing through his fingers. The sun is warm. The wind is cool. Although the Thames stinks at low tide, it's somehow refreshing, distracting him, helping his mind move on. Slowly, he opens and closes his hands, gingerly pushing through the pain wracking his body.

From somewhere above him, a woman calls out. Her words carry on the breeze, but her inquiry is clearly directed at him.

"Are you well?"

A dumb question prompts a polite but equally dumb reply.

Without looking up, Anthony says, "Yes, all is well."

Whoever she is, the woman pauses for a moment before saying, "You don't look well."

Anthony leans back, looking up the sloped rock wall, surprised to see a lady peering over the edge. Her ornate headdress marks her as nobility. Tiny pearls have been embroidered into a dark blue bonnet. She leans forward, exposing the furs wrapped over her arms.

"You are not in good form."

He laughs. "No. I'm not."

Given she's at least three classes above his station, Anthony figures that's the end of the conversation. He closes his eyes, shaking his head, still trying to block out the pain. He's not interested in being her curiosity. What good can come from being the idle amusement of a rich patron on a fine Sunday morning? At dinner, she'll no doubt recount his fall and her surprise that he wasn't covered in mud. She'll pass him off as a point of gossip with her sisters, using him as a means of socially navigating an otherwise dull, boring, overly stuffy meal with people she only pretends to care about. Family can be like that. As a poor boy, Anthony's stared through plenty of windows, hidden in the shrubs, watching how the upper class lives. Unlike his peers, he doesn't see anything to envy, just the trappings of a different kind of prison.

Above him, swords clatter in their scabbards. Shields are laid to rest on the rock wall. Anthony leans back, opening one eye and peering up at the lady. Two soldiers clamber onto the wall. They're not wearing armour, but they are in military dress. A brilliant blue crest adorns each tunic. To his horror, they begin descending the steep slope, only they're much bigger than him and more prone to slip and fall. With their leg greaves and leather boots, should they land in the mud, they'll get stuck. Anthony springs back into life. He turns and climbs, using his hands to guide him up the quarry-hewn rocks.

"That's it, boy," one of them says, holding out a gloved hand. Anthony reaches out to take his hand. No sooner have their fingers touched than he's hauled up and over the wall. In the blink of an eye, he finds himself plonked on his ass on the other side of the rock wall. The soldiers clamber back over the edge, picking up their equipment.

"You're certainly not fine," the lady says, crouching beside him and examining his wounds. "Anyone can see that."

To his surprise, her voice is kind rather than stern. She's genuinely concerned about him.

"I—slipped," he says as though a description of what happened provides any kind of actual explanation. To say he was distracted by a foreign ship with its broad wooden hull and white sails adorned with a scarlet red cross seems silly.

"She is beautiful, isn't she?" the lady says, looking down the river as the Spanish caravel rounds the bend.

Anthony gets to his feet, following her gaze and watching as the flag at the stern of the caravel flutters in the breeze.

"Magnificent," he says.

It takes him a moment to realize the soldiers have fanned out, forming a semi-circle around them, keeping passers-by at bay even though there are only a handful of people walking through the dockyards. The soldiers stand firm with gloved hands resting on hilts, peering outward, looking for an enemy that doesn't seem to exist. Anthony is on the verge of saying something when the lady beckons to a well-dressed gentleman carrying a carpetbag.

"Do we have some balm?" she asks him.

"Certainly, m'lady."

Anthony is bewildered.

A swallow swoops down on the other side of the wall, dropping low as it snatches an insect from the air. It dips one of its wings, causing it to peel away out across the river. Several other birds follow, flying in unison behind it, curving through the air as though drawn on by a string. They glide rather than beat their wings, making the impossibility of flight seem leisurely and mundane.

"You're easily distracted, aren't you?" the lady says, turning his hands over and looking at his injuries.

"Sorry, m'lady," Anthony says, bowing slightly as the gentleman examines the bloody skin on his palms.

"This is going to hurt," the man says.

Anthony lets out a solitary laugh. "Everything hurts."

Gently, the man rubs a salve on Anthony's palms.

He flinches, catching the scent of rotten garlic along with the pungent tinge of onions lashing his nostrils.

"You need to keep your cuts clean," the strange man says. "It's very important. Far more so than you know."

Anthony nods, fighting back tears as the balm bites. He looks around, wanting to distract himself as the man works on his wounds.

Ropes strain as labourers work on a pulley, lifting bales of wool from the back of a horse-drawn cart into the nearby stores. A carriage trundles past with its wheels scraping on the cobblestones. Horseshoes drum a steady beat on the road, mimicking the rhythm of a drummer marching by.

Strips of cotton are wound around Anthony's hand, binding his injuries. A spot of salve is applied to his knees. Blood is wiped from his leg.

"Why did you say you were fine?" the lady asks, genuinely concerned. "I saw you trip. I felt sure you had fallen into the Thames."

"Oh," Anthony replies, unaccustomed to such kindness from a stranger. "I—ah. I didn't want to impose upon you, fair lady."

"And the ship?" she asks. "Why does it fascinate you?"

"The caravel?" he replies, surprised she picked up on his interest in the Spanish vessel as the cause of his fall. "For me, it speaks of new lands."

She smiles, saying, "A fine ship will do that."

"One day, I'll set foot in those lands."

"Why would you want to leave the country of your birth?" the lady asks. It's a question that takes him off-guard. His friends have only ever asked *how* he intends to get to mainland Europe or the New World. No one's ever asked *why* he wants to go. To them, the journey seems impossible. But *why* is the real question. Is it wanderlust? No, it's something more.

"I want to know," he says. "To learn."

"You can learn here in London," she replies, gesturing around her. "We have universities."

Anthony laughs at the thought of attending college. Does she not recognize his station? There's compassion in her eyes. She's serious.

He says, "The knowledge I seek requires more than mere rote learning. 'Tis more than facts I desire."

Anthony's not sure why, but he feels he can confide in her.

"And what knowledge is it you seek?" she asks, clasping her petite gloved hands in front of her dress.

Anthony points at the birds flying over the Thames, saying, "It's to understand the way a swallow flies, the way fish swim, the gait of a horse as it gallops through a field. I want to know how trees grow in a forest. I want to understand the way flowers bloom in a meadow. There's a harmony in nature that is not unlike music."

Ah, now he sounds like Julia. To speak such words to a stranger is liberating. He'd never talk this way in front of Master Dunmore. Perhaps that's why he seeks new lands. There's freedom to be found in stepping away from the old. The lady, though, doesn't seem to agree.

"And you think you cannot learn here?" she asks. "You think you need to travel to the New World to see it? We have swallows and fields, flowers and trees."

"I think we're too close to them," he replies. "We don't see them for what they really are."

"Which is?"

"Extraordinary."

"And how did you come to such a grand conclusion?" the lady asks.

"My friend, Julia. She's blind," he replies. "She cannot see, so it is I who must see for her."

"And what do you see?"

"When I see for her, I see all that I missed. I see that we take the spectacular for granted. The magnificence of a swallow is hidden by its familiar sight in the sky."

The lady smiles, nodding in agreement.

"There is a freshness to knowledge not found in books," he says, getting excited. "Julia taught me that. She cannot see, and yet she sees more than anyone I know."

"Julia sounds wise."

"She's seventeen," he says. "And I think it's funny."

"You think what's funny?" the woman asks.

"That neither of us can read. Not me with my sight nor her with her wit. I can but recognise the characters and piece together a word. I can discern the numbers in a ledger and see that an entry is for lavender or jasmine, but to read and calculate with fluency escapes me. 'Tis like magic when one reads to me from a book."

"And yet?"

"I don't lament my lack. I think it a boon."

"How so?" the lady asks, looking inquisitive.

"To read a scroll of Latin philosophy seems a mistake to me as there is nothing to be gained. It is to learn only that which is already known. Out there, there's so much more waiting to be discovered. That is why I long for the new world."

The woman nods, smiling affectionately at him. "You'll make it there one day. I'm sure of it."

"Do you think so?" he asks. "Mostly, I doubt the future."

"Stay curious, young Anthony," she says, ruffling his hair with her gloved hand. She turns and walks off, adding, "And don't let anyone talk you out of your learning."

"Wait," he calls out as her entourage closes around her. "How did you know my name?"

"I've seen you at the apothecary," she says, peering back over her shoulder. She turns for a moment, walking backwards for a few seconds. The lady addresses him as no one else ever has, stretching her arms wide as though she were encompassing the sky in all of its entirety. "Curiosity is a gift, Anthony. Never forget that. Reason is the cure for all that ails this world!"

With that, she spins around, causing her dress to swirl in the breeze. She skips for a few steps, keeping pace with the soldiers. The lady leaves him standing by the rock wall, befuddled. As she disappears into the crowd with her escort, he yells out, "Who are you?"

There's no reply.

Fire

For Anthony, the quickest way to the main docks is to follow the road into London, skirting the edge of the Thames as it snakes its way back and forth through the land. Spanish caravels and fine ladies notwithstanding, he needs to pick up a shipment of spice from the wharf. Ordinarily, Master Dunmore would commission a wagon, but a single crate from Persia needs only a good pair of hands and some sturdy legs. Besides, theft is a tax his master would rather avoid. Oh, they call it breakage and sometimes spoilage, but there's implicit meaning behind the act—debts must be paid. It's never more than the tithe. Rarely less. Spoilage is surprisingly consistent but requires a markup to recover.

Although numerous villages have sprung up along the banks of the river, further inland farms dot the landscape surrounding London. Hedgerows define the various tracks and roads leading north, segmenting the fields. Sheep dot the hillside. Dogs bark in the distance. Farms give way to forests.

Markets line the intersection at Charing Cross. Anthony pushes his way along to The Strand. As he moves closer to London, the crowd swells. Sellers compete for attention while buyers mill around, blocking the road. He should have taken one of the back alleys. A silk banner blows in the wind, advertising a stall outside a weaver's cottage. Pottery is on sale by a set of factory gates, with a young man of similar age to him calling to the crowd, advertising his wares.

"Penny for a pot. Glazed and fired. Finest in all of London," he yells over the bustle in the street. Their eyes meet and they exchange a nod, sharing the same cause. Neither is wed to their profession, but whether it's out on the street, trapped in a factory or crawling through a mineshaft, there's unity to be found among the youth. Besides, fresh air ain't so bad.

As Anthony passes by, he lends his voice to the cause, calling out, "Pots for a penny. Penny for a pot," and his brief acquaintance smiles in appreciation, joining in on the chorus. "Finest in all of London."

Soldiers walk rather than march along the cobblestones. They're resplendent in their scarlet dress, with swords hanging in their scabbards. The troop is led by yeomen with pikes raised. Tassels flutter in the breeze, but the guard is relaxed. It's unusual to see them easily a quarter mile outside of London town, no doubt doing the bidding of the Queen's Council. Anthony thinks nothing more of them. Out of prudence, he gives them a wide berth, crossing the road and continuing on his way.

Once he's in London proper, pedestrians keep to the edge of the road as carriages carry Tudors through the streets. Gentry ride on horseback behind them. A scruffy villager such as he isn't despised so much as ignored. Like the beggars in the side alleys, he's all but invisible.

Saint Paul's looms large over the city. Its sharp spires and vast steeples seem to intimidate rather than persuade the masses, rising high over the church grounds. Newsmongers stand on boxes in the park, yelling at no one in particular, bellowing as they announce the latest decree. They compete with each other for the fleeting attention of a crowd that neither knows nor cares about their pet causes.

Monks of the Dominican Order busy themselves stacking wood to form a fagot, with sticks aligned vertically, falling inward on all sides to form an orderly heap. They set the makings of several bonfires in the middle of the gravel yard in front of the church. Their dark cloaks are both mysterious and menacing.

Anthony has never understood the allure of religion. There's freedom, they say, but only in surrender, which doesn't make sense to him. For them, conformity is the highest of morals. The world is full of sin and demons—if they're to be believed. Any deviation from the doctrine is to be punished. His father likens their obsession to walking along a dreary road on a beautiful summer's day, seeing only the fall of each foot on the dusty cobblestones and not hearing the call of songbirds in the trees.

Anthony ignores them, following Old High Street to Watling. He continues on to All Hallows, making his way toward the docks by London Bridge. Muckrakers push sewage through the streets, working with poles to direct effluent into a creek leading to the Thames. As the storm has passed, the excrement lining the roads has lifted with the runoff. The city smells particularly pungent today, like that of a rotten corpse. From what he can tell, the flow is coming down from Bishop's Gate, washing through the streets. Most of it trails in the gutters, but at those points where there are bends in the road, it pools. The stench there is overwhelming, making his eyes water. An elderly man works with a shovel, flicking horse dung into the gutter. Anthony picks his way along the side streets, avoiding the worst of the stink as he approaches the river.

Ropes creak, straining as loads are raised from the hold of a Dutch fluyt resting at port. With its sails furled, a solitary flag flutters at the stern of the European trading vessel. Sailors work a series of pulleys, heaving in unison as they raise a pallet loaded with sacks of flour. They lift it out of the hold and high above the deck. A longshoreman leads a guide rope, swinging the pallet across the water and over a cart waiting on the dock. Workhorses neigh, knowing from experience the weight they're expected to drag through the streets of London. They stomp their hooves in protest as the wooden flatbed groans under the load resting upon it. The master has a good hold on the reins of his team, keeping them in check.

Anthony makes his way to the *Comte Maurice*, a galleon regaled with flags of the Ottoman Empire. Unlike the English, Dutch or Spanish vessels, it's an extravagance of colour. Dozens of flags adorn the four masts, each being easily twenty to thirty feet in length, tapering to a fine point and forming streamers that dance on the wind. Streaks of red, blue and purple bring the docks to life. Julia would want to hear about each of them individually, and yet it's seeing them as a whole that's breathtaking.

The gun ports on the galleon are closed, hiding a dizzying array of thirty-six cannons. Their shuttered windows are a gesture of goodwill on a merchant mission, but no doubt, deep within her hold, there lies shot and powder aplenty.

A banner has been unfurled and draped over the side of the hull next to the plank leading to the dock. Ornate Arabic letters glisten in gold, being set on a scarlet background. Their styling is entirely alien. Instead of the tight curls and loops of the English language, they're long and thin, with hooks and dots and squiggles that, to Anthony, seem indecipherable. He may not be able to read well, but he knows numbers and letters. He understands basic words, if not the sentences they form, but this is different. To him, the Arabic words appear more like art than literature. There's a rhythm and beauty to the way they flow together with a flourish of passion. They speak of foreign lands, telling him there's adventure beyond the horizon.

A squad of English soldiers has been stationed beside the vessel, but it's unclear whether they intend to protect London from the Turks or the reverse. Even they seem uncertain of their assignment. They sit on crates, relaxing in the sun. They joke and smoke rather than stand at arms. Several of them laugh with sailors from the galleon, exchanging small goods and coins for trinkets from faraway lands.

After clearing access with the duty guard, Anthony makes his way up the plank, paying strict attention to every detail on this exotic vessel. Rather than having wooden treads, the gangway is coated in tar with grit embedded in the surface, providing grip. A latticework of carefully drilled holes and drainage channels lines the sides of the ramp. Instead of being single file like those planks he's walked when boarding English ships, this plank is wide enough for three or four men to walk abreast, carrying cargo. It's far more practical, and he wonders why the English haven't adopted this custom.

The plank leads not to the main deck but to the lower cargo hold, entering a door on the side of the vessel. A Persian sailor escorts him on board the midships. They pass beneath thick timber beams. From there, internal stairs lead from the hold to the main deck. With a brush of his hand, the sailor signals for him to wait as he speaks in Arabic to an officer, who smiles in response to what's said before disappearing into a cabin below the quarter deck near the stern of the galleon.

Anthony wants this moment to last forever—the feel of the ship rocking softly as the keel moves with the change in tide, the flex of ropes reacting to the shifting tension, the smell of spices wafting from below deck as a meal is prepared. He's in awe of the order around him, from the way hundreds of nails fix the boards on the deck, evenly spaced in row upon row, to the balustrades lining the forecastle deck and the way various ropes have been coiled, ready for action. Given the chance, he'd spend hours working his way from bow to stern, carefully observing and considering the design. It seems to him that order is used to negate the chaos of a busy, cluttered deck, and he longs to stow away on board.

"Tell your master we're even," an officer says, taking Anthony by surprise as he walks up behind him. He's smiling, joking with him, speaking in broken English. "Except for your ale. He owes me ale. A lot. Tell him that."

"I will, thank you," Anthony says, taking a crate from him and holding it by a set of rope handles positioned at either end. The crate is almost three feet long and a foot wide, but far less than a foot thick. It feels light, almost empty by comparison to the heavy stock he normally hauls from the basement in the apothecary. As he walks, a slight sway betrays vials rocking within straw padding.

"Next time, bring the old fart with you," the officer says as Anthony makes his way down the internal stairs and into the dark of the galleon.

As he crosses the gangway, he looks back, calling out, "Oh, I will."

With a cheerful heart, Anthony starts out toward the apothecary, cutting back through old London town, oblivious to the piss and shit in the streets that caused such an affront to him on entering the capital. To his surprise, a throng of people presses toward St. Paul's. Ordinarily, the streets are a crisscross of traffic, but rumours are swirling of an execution.

"They're being held in New Gate," one fine gentleman says to another as Anthony passes by. "Accused of blasphemy."

"Heresy," the other replies. "I heard he cursed the pope. Called him the antichrist."

"Damn fool."

Both men are gentry, wearing tight-fitting doublets—dark brown jackets with dozens of carefully spaced, polished brass buttons running up either side, joining mid-chest. Their breeches are puffed, with deep red pleats showing beneath the black material. They stride on ahead of Anthony, pushing their way through the crowd. He follows close behind them, using them to clear the way through the crowd as a plough cuts through clods of dirt in a field.

The last Anthony hears from them is the older man saying, "Queen Mary will not be trifled. She has no time for insolence."

On reaching the grounds surrounding St. Paul's, Anthony keeps to the outer wall, wanting to trace his way to the far side and exit by the Lud Gate, which was first established by the Romans back when the city was known as *Londinium*. The cobblestones there date back well over a thousand years. Wide grooves have been worn in the stone over the centuries, marking the passage of innumerable carts. Anthony finds the depth of time conveyed by those simple stones surreal. The rain from tens of thousands of storms has given them the smooth appearance of river stones. They represent a timescale that dwarfs not only his life but the lives of everyone he's ever known, regardless of their age.

Soldiers line the street to the north, keeping the crowd at bay. Two men walk between a squad from the Queen's Guard. Their heads bow low. The chains shackled to their wrists cause their shoulders to stoop. Their clothes, though, are crisp and clean. The younger man is barely out of his teens. The skin on his arms is still soft and supple. He's followed by a thin, grey-haired man that could be his father. With freshly-shaven faces and neatly combed hair, they're pushed on by the sheriff. Waterfowl run across the road behind them, oblivious to what's going on but taking advantage of the lull in street traffic to get back to the creek.

For his part, the sheriff is dressed in formal attire, with a ruff drawn around his neck. Hundreds of carefully folded pleats of pure white cotton form the high collar of his uniform, while his black robes are solemn and austere.

Beside him walks Bishop Blaine, an elderly man balding on top. He's wearing a black headpiece and mantle of sackcloth covering his fine linen garments, symbolising his humility. He carries what's supposed to be a shepherd's crook—only the wooden pole is dead-straight and glistens with fresh polish. The tip of the staff is embossed with gold leaf. It's barely seen daylight beyond the thick church doors, let alone sheep in a field.

Without him realizing, Anthony's brisk walk slowed to a crawl before coming to a halt entirely. Like all those in his village on the outskirts of London, he's heard of executions in the capital, but he's never seen one. The pomp and ceremony accompanying the slaughter of two men seems incongruous. It's an affront to the sanctity of life.

The sheriff reads the charges. "By the grace of Her Majesty and in accordance with the dictates of the Holy See, Morris Alexander and William Mace have been found guilty of heresy in that they have defied the sacrament of Holy Communion."

As the sheriff speaks, the men are released from their shackles. They shed their shirts. From within the crowd, women weep, being held at bay by guards with pikes and soldiers resplendent in their formal colours. The condemned fold their clothing with meticulous care before handing them off to attendants. They remove their rings, placing them on top of their clothing before the attendants convey their effects to the women.

To Anthony's surprise, the bishop addresses the crowd rather than the condemned men, saying, "For the unity of the church, all must accept the consecration of the priest and the power of his words to deliver the body of Christ in the bread and wine. He who was born of the Virgin Mary is present to deliver us in corporeal, of that there can be no doubt. Communion is most sacred."

"It is nothing but bread and wine," the young prisoner yells, only to be struck on the back of the head by a wooden club. He falls to the mud, landing on his knees. Two soldiers drag him to his feet. Blood seeps from his matted hair.

As the men are led to the bonfire fagots, additional wood is stacked around each base. The younger man tries to wrestle free, wanting to flee into the crowd, but the old man calls out, "Be of good cheer, my friend, for tonight we shall dine in heaven with our Lord."

The young man breaks away from the executioner, but he advances no more than a few steps before soldiers block his path. The sheriff wrestles him to the ground and, with a clean blow, one of the soldiers severs the man's right hand, cutting through skin and bone with his sword. Blood sprays across the woodpile.

The murmurs within the crowd cease as the man screams in agony, clutching at his wrist, desperately trying to stem the flow of deep red blood as it splatters in the mud. The women cry out in anguish. One of them faints and is carried away. A soldier binds a length of ribbon around the young man's forearm and ties it tight, preventing blood from running out of the stump. Whether it is out of cruelty or kindness, Anthony cannot tell. The young, condemned man holds his severed hand, having picked it up out of the mud. He stares at it with astonishment, unable to comprehend what has befallen him. Blood drips from dead fingers he can no longer feel.

"On and on," the sheriff yells. "Bind them. Sentence has been passed. Punishment must be met."

Both men are chained to their pyres, albeit with loops of additional chain being wrapped around the young man to fix him to the stake, lest he tries to escape again.

"Oh, that this were a cross," the older man yells, lamenting that his execution cannot mirror that of Christ's death. He looks up at the clouds in the sky. Tears fall from his cheeks.

Heavy chains are draped around both of their necks, along with collars full of gunpowder resting on their shoulders. The leather pouches are packed with fresh powder and crimped with steel caps, ready to explode at the first spark. There's not enough to decapitate the men, but the blast will tear through soft skin. It'll sear flesh and break bones. If the fire doesn't complete its gruesome task first, this grim necklace will ensure they die in bitter agony.

"Into thy hands, O Lord, I commit my spirit," the younger man yells with rich, dark blood dripping from the stump at the end of his arm.

"Morris Alexander and William Mace," Bishop Blaine bellows. "I offer you one last opportunity to recant. Admit your sins, and you can pass from this world into everlasting peace with the love of our Lord. Refuse me, and it is into the furnace of hell you will descend."

Anthony shakes his head. Either way, they're going to burn, which seems utterly heartless to him. He's unsure which of them is Morris Alexander and which is William Mace. Such a detail may be trivial, but to him, it's important. People are important, and yet the sheriff doesn't care. Neither does the bishop. They may be Christian, but the example of Christ is nowhere to be seen.

Torches are lit. Women weep. Children hide behind their parents, burying their heads into their mother's skirts. Burning tar drips from the torches as the soldiers thrust them into the base of the fagots, lighting the pyres.

Flames leap from the dry wood. Fire licks at the prisoners' bare feet. Smoke rises into the air, and yet neither man cries in agony nor calls for mercy. A calm has descended on them the likes of which Anthony has never known. Instead of yelling in pain, they recite Psalms, calling out above the crackling, burning wood.

"O my God, I trust in thee: let me not be ashamed, let not my enemies triumph over me."

For Anthony, such courage is incongruous with reality. When it seems as though all is lost, they rejoice. Never before has he seen such cruelty met with such grace.

Some of the wood collapses as it burns. With blackened legs, the older man slumps forward, having succumbed to the heat and fumes. His head bows as he gives up the ghost. The fire under the younger man hasn't taken as well. The torch smoulders, having fallen into the mud. Flames leap from the fagot but only on one side of the pyre. Perhaps some of the wood is damp. He squirms, shifting away from the flames rising out of the woodpile. Several soldiers add more timber to the fagot, crouching to avoid the searing heat as they poke at the fire. With their pikes, they spread glowing coals throughout the base of the pyre. The blood dripping from the young man's severed arm sizzles on the burning wood.

He's delirious, calling out, and saying the same phrase over and over, "Lord, receive my spirit. O Father, receive my soul."

He wants to die, of this, there is no doubt, and yet death seems reluctant to come for him. Murmurs ripple through the crowd. Tears fall. Women wail at the agony unfolding before them. Men hang their heads in anguish.

The wind shifts, coming from the port and causing the flames to flare, rising up the stake and reaching the chains binding his neck. Without uttering a word, he flinches, flexing against the chains, moving as one with the fire. The gunpowder in his collar ignites with a flash and a thundering boom. White smoke billows into the heavens. With that, bloodied and burned, the young man's head falls to his chest. He sinks into the flames, kneeling as though lost in prayer. Blood drips from his torn neck. His skin turns as black as coal. Dark fluid runs down his charred body.

Seconds later, the explosive collar around the older man ignites. He's already dead, but seeing his head being thrown violently to one side by the blast is sickening. Black, burnt flesh sizzles as the powder burns.

Anthony is aghast at what he's seen. His heart pounds in his chest, threatening to break through his ribcage. Sweat runs down his brow.

Bishop Blaine has his back to the executions. To Anthony's surprise, he's watching the crowd, not the men burning at the stake. He's yelling. His voice bellows through the yard, echoing off the buildings, but Anthony can't hear what he's saying, such is the shock of seeing raw flames consume these men. Just moments ago, they were alive. Now, their seared flesh blackens, leaving them as nothing more than a burnt carcass. Anthony's seen cattle afforded more dignity than these men.

The bishop singles out people from the crowd, pointing at them and challenging them. Before Anthony realises what's happening, the bishop is barely ten feet away from him with spittle flying from his lips. He's interpreted Anthony's horror as defiance against the church.

"All have sinned," Bishop Blaine yells, locking eyes with Anthony. "Repent or be damned. Turn from your wicked ways."

Guilt strikes at Anthony's heart for no other reason than that he's been singled out from the masses around him. Mere existence is a sin. Whereas he'd like the opportunity to defend himself, the authority of the bishop is absolute and beyond question. *Thy will be done* is the bishop's will at that moment, and the fiery wrath of an angry god descends within the church grounds with each of the bishop's words.

The bishop bellows, "You will be tried and hung in a balance!"

He steps toward Anthony, reaching out his hand and pointing at him. He's directing the attention of his guards. Whether he intends to grab Anthony or simply scare him is unclear. For all the talk of conspiracy, it seems the bishop is far more insidious than those that died. Anthony's terrified of being snatched and dragged into a dungeon.

As he backs up, mud squishes beneath his boots. Anthony wants to run, but he can't. His feet feel like lead weights. He's on the verge of dropping the apothecary crate. Were he to turn away, the bishop would be upon him.

A hand grabs him, pulling at his shoulder and dragging him to one side. Soldiers rush around him, but not from the Queen's Guard. They've come from behind rather than in front of him. A shadow passes over him.

Bishop Blaine steps back, surprised, straightening as he's challenged by a stranger.

"Ah, Lady Elizabeth de Brooke," he says, with bitterness thinly veiled as respect. "And what business have you with a peasant?"

"There has been enough bloodshed today, don't you think?"

Sunlight catches the lady's hair, making it impossible to see her face, but there's no mistaking the dress. This is the noblewoman that called for Anthony to climb up from the Thames. He recognises the guards forming up around them. They have their hands by their sides, resting on their scabbards, ensuring their swords are plain to see but not drawn. The sheriff and several of his guards rush to the bishop's aide, sensing conflict.

"You have no authority here," the bishop says. "None."

"Neither do you," she replies, goading him.

"Mine is the highest authority," he says, indignant, holding his shepherd's crook as though he were Moses commanding the Red Sea. He plunges the end of it into the mud not more than a foot from her. "I could have you arrested."

"And how would you explain that to my beloved Philip and Mary?"

The bishop stamps his boots, clenching his fist, enraged. "You cannot call upon them forever. There have been rumours. People are talking."

"Of what?"

"Of unnatural practices. Of witchcraft."

Lady de Brooke laughs. "And I have heard rumours as well. Of you and little boys."

The bishop's eyes go wide. Anthony is sure that, if he could, Bishop Blaine would strike her down. He can see it in the man's clenched jaw and the flare of his nostrils. There's no pretence anymore, only bitter hatred.

"Go," the lady says, turning to Anthony.

He needs no further encouragement. With his heart racing, Anthony turns and pushes through the crowd, determined to get out of London. He pauses by the Lud Gate and looks back through the masses, but he can no longer see either the bishop or the lady.

The Apothecary

"Where in Jupiter have you been?"

Master Dunmore snatches the wooden crate from Anthony. In what seems like a contradictory motion, he then places it gently on the stone benchtop at the back of the apothecary.

"What in hades happened to you?" the old man asks, looking at the scrapes on Anthony's arms, his bloodied knees and the bandage wrapped around his right hand.

Sheepishly, Anthony says, "I fell."

"Fell where?"

"From the rock wall."

"Watching ships on the Thames again, were ye? 'Tis your own fault then, lad. I pay you for chores, not daydreams. You were to go straight to the docks. You should have gone straight through old London Town and not skirted the river. And why did ye take so long to return?"

"Th—There were executions," Anthony says. That seems to soften the master's disposition, but only slightly. The old man's eyes narrow. His shoulders drop.

"Stay away from the church," he mumbles. "No good can come from either side of religion. To damn or to be damned is equally flawed.

Both fools stand for piety, and neither can stand the other. 'Tis like combining sunflower oil with water. Try as you may to mix them, there will always be separation, for they are of different kinds."

Anthony isn't sure what to think about the horrors he witnessed this morning outside St Paul's. He's still reeling from the image of two men burning alive. What crime could justify such harsh punishment?

"It was... It was..."

"Cruel," the master says. "Two fires consume the land. And us. We, who would have none of either madness. We must needs refrain, or we too will burn in flames."

"These things should not be," Anthony says.

"No, lad. They shouldn't. They speak to our frailty. They insult our smarts. They reduce us to mongrels scrapping in the streets." Master Dunmore seems to understand Anthony's anguish as he adds, "Take your time, my boy. Take your time."

His head bows as he turns away. Enough has been said.

The master leaves the crate and attends to a customer. Anthony steels himself. It seems wrong to go on with life as though nothing has happened, but sanity demands routine. He sweeps the floor. Several minutes later, once the master has completed a sale of rosemary and coriander, he glances at Anthony and nods. He knows. At some point, he, too, was first confronted with the abject brutality of this world and had to let go of his notions of fairness. What had seemed carefree and joyful as a youth was an illusion as an adult. Anthony can see it in his eyes. And now he's living through the same heartache his master once felt. Anthony's chest aches. Is this his lot in life? To accept the disparity thrust upon him? To ignore the plight of the innocent even though it could easily be him dragged before the crowds and burned on a fagot? But what can he do? The master is right. To stand up against the madness would see him chained to a stake with fires set at his feet. Anthony laments the helplessness he feels.

As the afternoon grows long, patronage wanes, and the master turns his attention to the crate. Anthony joins him, curious about the contents.

"Let's take a look, shall we?"

It seems they both need a distraction. Master Dunmore uses a crowbar to open the wooden lid, prying out the nails. Inside, straw protects a series of earthen vases and jars, but these are unlike the smokey glass vials on display within the apothecary. They're larger, being almost a foot in length.

"What do they hold?" Anthony asks, curious about their exotic contents.

With the care of someone handling a cracked egg, Master Dunmore picks up one of the vases and hands it to Anthony. The teen cups his hands, examining it as it rests in his palm. The master holds one of the jars up to the light streaming in the window. To Anthony's untrained eye, it looks like smokey glass, but he knows it isn't as it's been carved from some kind of stone.

These jars are like nothing he's ever seen before. Whereas the bottles and vials in the store have flat bottoms, allowing them to be stacked on shelves, these are long, thin and pointed. Handles curl outward near the neck. The heart of each vial is no thicker than a clenched fist. The base tapers to a point. Master Dunmore stands them in the straw but not on the bench. If he were to place them there, they'd lie on their side and likely roll off the edge and break.

"Turmeric," the master says, releasing the cork on one of the tiny vases and sniffing its contents. He offers Anthony a chance to smell the dry, musty spice.

Twine binds labels to the neck of each jar, but the words are ornate, having been written in cursive Arabic. As basic as Anthony's reading may be, he thought he'd at least be able to distinguish a few letters. He's seen calligraphy in Latin scrolls, but the sweeps, curls and flourishes before him are indecipherable, representing an alien language. Seeing their beauty on paper, he'd love to hear each word pronounced in its original tongue as he's sure it would resonate like a song.

For all his bluster, Master Dunmore has a soft spot for the young man. He enjoys his curiosity and points at each of the vases, saying,

"These contain cumin, saffron, afghan lavender and cardamon."

He closes one earthen jar and opens another, sniffing, "Ah, this is a cinnamon mix. This one is a secret of the Arabs. They won't tell me what concoction they've used, but it's heavenly."

The master holds the vase up, allowing Anthony to smell its contents. Anthony is determined to make his master proud and uses the same technique Master Dunmore employs when sharing scents with buyers. He holds his index and middle fingers together, wafting them gently over the open top, swishing them through the air time and again to draw the subtle tones from the vase. To his nose, cinnamon smells neither sweet nor savoury but rather intense. It's pleasant but seems to singe the edge of his nostrils. If he were to describe it in a single term, he'd call it autumn as it reminds him of leaves falling and the onset of winter.

"And this one is clove of the orient," the master says, swapping one vial with another.

Anthony would love nothing more than to grab Julia and allow her to sniff each jar. Master Dunmore, though, would worry she'd drop one. Even now, he won't let Anthony hold any of the more exotic containers for more than a minute. He returns each to the straw with care. Julia, though, would look with her fingers. She'd run her hands all over the curious shapes, marvelling at how impractical they are. Anthony's only ever seen pointed jars like these once before, but that was holding liquor. The narrow base allowed sediment to settle with the least amount of spoilage. These spices, though, are dry. They could have been sent in wrappings or glass jars, and he wonders about the strange cylinders. No doubt Julia would love them. It's the novelty of holding something from faraway lands and imagining all that brought them to this point in time. She'd be delighted by the smells. With her loss of sight, all of her other senses are heightened. She'd appreciate cinnamon far more than him. Anthony's only ever eaten pap-bread dusted with cinnamon once before and wasn't sure what to make of it. Rather than being delicious, it tasted strange to his palate.

"The lady will be well pleased," the master says, putting corks back in the neck of the delicate vases.

"Lady?" Anthony says as the master steps past him.

"And here she is."

Anthony turns, seeing Lady Elizabeth de Brooke stepping over the threshold. The sun is high overhead, flooding the market outside and darkening the shadows within the store. Her profile is unmistakable.

Master Dunmore bows slightly, taking her hand and talking softly to her.

"As always, it is a pleasure to see you, m'lady."

"Thank you, kind master."

The soldiers stay outside. As Lady de Brooke moves down the aisle, her dress brushes against the edge of the benches, threatening to but not catching any of the glass bottles on display.

"This is my boy," Dunmore says.

"We've met," the lady says, smiling as she nods. Anthony feels a lump well up in his throat. She was following him, trailing him to the docks and back, but why?

"Ah," she says, lifting one of the vases from the straw and examining it carefully. Her white-gloved fingers handle the vase with a sense of reverence. She steps toward the rear of the store, where sunlight falls on a windowsill, and holds the vase up, examining it in the light. "Wonderful."

"This one is made from alabaster," the master says, offering one of the other vases to her, but she's not interested, politely waving him away. She returns one thin vase and retrieves another. Anthony's expecting her to pull off the corks and smell each of the spices, but she doesn't. It's then he realises she doesn't care about the contents. It's the vases themselves she's after.

Lady de Brooke turns one of the jars over, examining the carefully hewn stone. There are imperfections. Swirls mar the smooth rock. Hundreds of shells have somehow become embedded in the rock, only these are not sea shells or barnacles. They're as coarse and rough as the rock itself. It's only now, on reflection, he realises they're unlike anything he's seen before.

"Yes. Yes. This is good. I want more of these," she says, holding up the vase carved from shells stuck in the rock. "And anything else you can procure that looks like this. Tell your traders to look for anything where rocks and bones appear fused together. I will pay, and I will pay well."

"You want bones?" the master asks, confused.

Lady Elizabeth de Brooke is quite clear in her reply. "Not bones. I want stones that look like bones. There's a difference. Do you understand?"

"Yes, ma'am," he says, scratching at his beard. "And this is what you want? Not the spice, but the stone bone?"

"Only bones embedded in stones. Bones that have become stones."

Anthony says, "I think I know where you can find more of them."

Master Dunmore glares at him, but Anthony is undeterred.

"I've seen these before."

"Where?" the lady asks.

"Ah, Low Hauxley in Northumberland. Lulworth in Dorset. There are a few places along the coast."

"Aye," the master says, wrestling the conversation away from Anthony. "There are spots around the country where bones that appear as stones can be found."

"Mostly by the seashore," Anthony says, wanting to be helpful.

"Oh, yes," the master says, trying not to show his aggravation with his young apprentice. "Mostly along the seashore. They are found where the cliffs fall. Among the rocks thrashed by the waves."

"And they look like this?" the lady asks, holding up the vial. As the jar has been fashioned by hand, being cut out of stone, the various shells mixed into the rock have been shaved at different points, forming intricate patterns that reveal their outer husk and smooth insides. The jar has been polished, making it glisten in the light.

"Aye," the master says. "But they're of no use. They have no value. The folk I've seen with them treat them as oddities. They're ornaments. A curiosity to sit on a shelf."

"They're valuable to me," the lady says, examining another vial with black leaves impressed on the stone.

She opens her purse and pulls out a gold sovereign. She holds it between her thumb and forefinger, turning it slightly, so there's no doubt about its authenticity. The master's eyes light up. Anthony's never seen a sovereign before. Latin words weave their way around the edge of the coin. On one side, an ornate rose symbolises the authority of the Crown. On the other is the Queen's crest of arms.

Lady de Brooke gives both of them a few seconds to take in the sight.

In practice, sovereigns are useless as a form of currency. They're so valuable that changing just one for shillings and pence would consume all the money within the apothecary. Gold sovereigns are largely ceremonial as they need to be exchanged for common currency at the royal mint.

Lady de Brooke pushes the sovereign into the master's palm. He looks down at it in awe.

"And there's more," she says, pressing another sovereign and another and another into his hand.

"F—Four," he stutters.

"Five," she says, placing one more in his trembling palm. "I will have stones that once were bones." She tips her head toward him. "Consider this a downpayment—a show of good faith to fund an expedition to retrieve them for me."

"Oh, m'lady, you shall have a cart full of stones that once were bones."

"And there is more where these came from," the lady says, surprising Anthony with her generosity. "Find me those stones, and I will reward you with a dozen gold sovereigns in all. I need variety. Lots of different types. No duplicates. Are we clear?"

"Clear we are," the master replies, jingling the gold coins in his hand and watching as they clink into each other. He seems impressed by their weight. "I'll send word, ma'am. I'll have the boy convey your instructions to my regular traders on the northern and southwest routes. They'll get your bone stones."

Lady de Brooke turns to Anthony, saying, "Stay clear of the town. Follow the river. Don't cut through the church grounds."

"Aye," Anthony replies, in no rush to see any more executions, let alone to witness his own.

"You heard of the burning?" the master asks.

"I was there," the lady replies. "As was he."

"No good can come from all this. It's been barely a month, and already over a hundred people are dead." The master addresses Anthony. "Mind what the lady is telling you. Take the long way around the river."

"I will," Anthony replies, even though this instruction contradicts the one given to him earlier by Master Dunmore.

"Fear not heretics," Lady de Brooke says, addressing Anthony. "Fear those that would burn heretics at the stake."

"Everyone's a heretic to someone," the master says.

Lady de Brooke says, "When they kill in the name of their Lord, there's no foul to which they will not swoop. 'Tis not about right and wrong. 'Tis about enslaving others."

Master Dunmore says, "It is as Gregor of Wurzburg spoke, *Unwissenheit und selbst—I have seen the enemy. They have but two battalions arrayed against us: ignorance and ego.*"

"You speak German?" the lady asks, turning to him in surprise.

"I was raised in Tübingen."

"I've been there," Lady de Brooke says. "We stayed in the castle Schloss Hohentübingen."

The master bows slightly, saying, "It's beautiful."

"Yes, it is."

Anthony can see what Master Dunmore's doing. He's deferring to the lady's social class and politely bringing the conversation to a close. He understands her kindness is a measure of pleasantry rather than friendship. She's being polite and not solely focused on business matters as that would be inappropriate, but someone of her station would never condescend to Master Dunmore's level, or Anthony's—and yet she did help him when he fell. Perhaps her kindness is worth more than words.

Lady de Brooke returns the earthen jars to the small crate, making sure there's straw between them.

"Oh," she says before she picks up the crate to leave. She reaches back into the purse hanging from her forearm and pulls out another gold sovereign. Rather than handing it to the master, she flicks it. The coin tumbles end over end through the air before being caught by Master Dunmore. "Thank you for these. They're a fine start to my collection."

"It's my pleasure," the master replies.

"Farewell to you," she says, taking the crate.

"And to you, ma'am."

Anthony steps back against the wall, allowing the lady to pass. She doesn't say anything else to him, but she smiles, nodding her head slightly. For someone of her stature to make such a gesture to him is beyond reckoning. Most gentry won't acknowledge his existence. As an apprentice to a master, his duty is to serve and not be seen, to listen and not be heard. He nods in reply.

Master Dunmore is called away to another customer. She seems irate, which distracts him. The lady lingers in the doorway. One of her guards takes the crate from her, but she doesn't follow him out onto the street. Instead, she stands there for a moment, consumed with thoughts Anthony cannot begin to imagine. Her dress fills the entrance, touching both of the jambs. She reaches up, tapping the lintel above the open doorway, which is a curious gesture. She's lost in thought and not at all aware she's blocking the doorway.

Lady de Brooke turns. Anthony feels embarrassed at being caught staring at her. She reaches out her gloved hand, beckoning him to approach. Master Dunmore has his back to them. He's several rows away, crouching as he shuffles through items on the lower shelf, looking for something for the angry customer. Anthony walks over to Lady de Brooke, unsure of himself.

"Come to the estate," she says, briefly taking his hand. "And I'll teach you to read."

"But—"

"It's true. Books are the mind of the past," she says. "And yet they're stepping stones to the future."

Anthony nods. He reflects on his comment to her earlier as they stood by the river wall. Back then, he was dismissive of reading, but only because he couldn't read that well. To him, it seems to be a cruel example of class division. He can't read properly. But can't ride a horse or parry with a sword either. Standing before her, words are not enough to convey how he feels. When he said *but* in response to her invitation, it wasn't out of doubt or ingratitude. Deep down, he'd love to be able to read. Oh, he might complain about Latin being a dead language—the bloated corpse of priests and politicians—but he'd love to know what secrets lie on each page. Saying *but* was a reaction to feeling out of place with someone of her high stature.

The lady is kind. Her eyes are full of compassion.

"It's not what you read that's important. It's what you *think* about what you've read that can change your life. That's the secret to learning—to reflect on the meaning of all that's discussed on the page. Books allow you to live beyond the moment. They compress a thousand lifetimes into just one—yours."

"Yes, m'lady," Anthony replies, lowering his gaze.

And with that, she's gone. Lady de Brooke joins her entourage on the street. Her guards march behind her, which is something Anthony has only seen with princes and princesses. As she's part of the royal court, being only once removed from the Queen herself, she's above even the gentry. Why would she extend such an offer to him?

Julia is sitting across the road, basking in the afternoon sun. She's perched on a crate beside a farmer selling grain to merchants venturing down from Covent Gardens for a bargain. Julia may not be able to see Lady de Brooke, but she can sense her presence, of that, Anthony is sure. He can see the way her head moves in response to the rustle of leather belts rubbing against cloth. Normally, the apothecary only attracts those wanting balm or spice from the middle tier of society. Master Dunmore doesn't cater to high society, let alone royalty. The march of soldiers and the soft clatter of scabbards hanging from their hilts must ring loud to her. Anthony can see her poised like a cat, ready to cross the road behind them to talk to him.

"Listen carefully, boy," the master says, placing his hand on Anthony's shoulder and dragging him away from the doorway, back inside the apothecary. "I have errands for you."

"Yes, sir," Anthony replies.

Without making it obvious, the master pushes the sovereigns into Anthony's hand.

"Four to the hide. Two for the traders. One to Bill Baxter in the old abbey. He knows the Low Hauxley well. One to Jamieson at the Bailey Stores. He does the circuit to Dorset twice a year. Tell them I'll pay one sovereign in advance and another when they return with a full cart. But their curiosities must look well. I won't be paying for all of the same rock. I'm paying well because I'm expecting well—you tell them that. If the lady wants shells and bones in rock, we'll give her as much variety as we can, but don't you mention her name. They'll ask. Don't you say a word. Understand? I don't want them stealing my customer from me."

"I understand."

"And no foolery. No mistakes. Talk to them in private. This is important. If we get this right, we could open within London Town itself. I'm trusting you, boy. Guard these with your life."

"I will."

"Then get to it," the master says.

Another villager walks in, asking for a poultice to bind over an open wound. Master Dunmore shifts his attention to him. He gathers herbs and meal flour as Anthony clutches the sovereigns, hiding them in the palm of his hand. The master casts him a quick glance before measuring herbs into a mortar. He makes small talk with the customer as he grinds the herbs with a pestle to form a fine powder.

Julia stands on the edge of the doorway peering in with blind eyes. She has a grin on her face. She may not have heard what was said, but she recognised their voices. It seems she can sense Anthony's standing not more than ten feet from her over by the front window. Anthony desperately wants to tell her about all that's transpired with Lady de Brooke, but he dares not raise the ire of his master.

"Wait there," he says quietly. He heads to the store room, knowing the master's watching him. The old man may be attending to customers, but he's not one to tolerate insolence. Anthony hurries along the stone corridor leading down rough-hewn stairs to the storeroom.

The apothecary is an old stone building backing onto the abbey grounds on the outskirts of Westminster. Whereas most of the stores in the village are wooden with plaster walls and thatched roofs, the apothecary was once a toll gate on the western road to Eaton. The rise of Covent Garden as London's market and the fire of 1512 saw the Tudors move into London proper. Westminster retained the Commons and the Houses of Parliament, but the inland village lost its lustre. Sojourners preferred a more direct route to London, bypassing Westminster for Mayfair in the northeast and the toll house fell into disuse.

The walls of the apothecary are thick. The doors are made from heavy oak. There are bars on the windows at the rear, but not to keep thieves out. Once they had to be kept in as the building was a toll booth. The storeroom was originally a gaol cell used to hold merchants that tried to defy the local tax collector. Now, it's packed with wooden shelves and crates.

Anthony crouches at the rear of the basement. He shifts a wooden box to one side. From where he is, he's out of sight from the store and the window. He slips his fingers into the cracks around a large block on the bottom row of the rear wall and works it out. It takes a few seconds as it's heavy and a tight fit. Master Dunmore has him perform this task regularly as the old man's fingers are too big to fit into the gaps. Anthony struggles to slide the stone out, but behind it, there's an old drain from the days when this room was a prison cell. The master has filled the pit with rocks and placed wooden slats over them. Several purses sit next to each other, holding shillings, pennies and farthings. There's a ledger and a pencil.

Anthony takes a plush velvet purse and adds four of the gold sovereigns to the silver coins. He flips the ledger to the page for deposits and writes '*Lday 4-gs.*' For a moment, he stares at what he's written, realising it should be *Lady* rather than *Lday*. Too late. It's now forever *Lday*, which to his ear, sounds correct anyway. He wonders who will read this in the years to come and if they'll think it's some exotic spice from the Levant.

Master Dunmore trusts Anthony with his wealth, which is something Anthony prides himself on. He'd never steal from the old man. Honest work begets honest pay. Despite the odd clip across the ear, the master is good to him. Besides, Anthony has no desire to flee the city and run through the countryside for the rest of his life, always on the move, waiting for the day when the hangman's noose finally catches him. He returns the purse and slides the rock back in place. Before pushing the crate back in front of the wall, he scoops up some grit from the floor and pushes it into the cracks around the brick. The wall looks intact.

From behind him, a girl's voice says, "Are you going to tell me what's going on?"

"Julia," he says, getting to his feet. "What are you doing in here? If the master catches you..."

"He's out in the garden gathering coriander for one of the priests."

"Come," Anthony says, taking her hand and dragging her up the stairs and out the front of the store.

"Why the left hand?" she asks as he leads her down an alley, away from Westminster and toward the river. This far from London, there are no docks or walls on the Thames. They take a path through the trees growing along the bank.

"Are you going to answer me?"

"What?" he says, not because he doesn't know what she means. He's desperately trying to ignore her. He was hoping she'd give up on her question.

"You're holding my left hand," she asks. "Why? What's in your other hand? And where are we going?"

"Oh, questions, questions," he replies. "Why so many questions?"

"Questions are all I have," Julia replies. "To me, questions are sight. Answers are a ray of sunlight breaking through the clouds."

Anthony brings her to a halt in the long grass just off the track, saying, "You can't tell anyone."

"I swear, I won't."

He takes her hand and opens her fingers to the sky. With a grin lighting up his face, he pushes a single gold sovereign into her palm.

"A coin?" she asks.

"Not just any coin."

She tosses the coin slightly in her hand, feeling the weight of it.

"A sovereign?"

Anthony leans forward and whispers by her ear, saying, "I have two of them."

"Two!" she cries, half yelling, trying to be quiet as excitement wells up within her. "Where did you get them? Why do you have them?"

"Ah, questions," he says, laughing.

"Go on. Tell me," she says, reaching out and tickling him.

He jumps back, landing in the bushes on the side of the trail and saying, "Oh, you win. You win."

Julia smiles. The wind catches her hair. Sunlight falls on her face, coming through the leaves in the trees. Her eyes stare past him, looking blindly across the river. She holds the coin in her left palm while exploring the letters and grooves with her right hand, running her fingers over the bumps and indentations.

"This is soooo much money. And all in one coin!"

"I know. Lady de Brooke gave two of them to Master Dunmore."

His voice wavers but only slightly. Anthony doesn't mean to lie to Julia, but he has to protect the master's interests. If anyone were to realise there was a purse full of gold sovereigns hidden within the apothecary, they'd tear the building down stone by stone. It's not that he thinks Julia would betray his confidence, but rather that he feels he needs to avoid the possibility of anyone overhearing something they shouldn't. Julia, though, doesn't seem to notice his hesitancy. She's too excited. She might not be able to see the shine of gold in her hand, but she can feel its weight.

"She *gave* them to him?"

"They're a downpayment."

"On what?"

"On bones that look like stones."

"Bones that look like stones?" Julia asks, screwing up her face.

"I know. It's crazy. The lady—she's crazy. But she's got plenty of coins, and that's what she wants."

"What do these bones look like?" Julia asks, furrowing her brow. "Don't all bones look like stones? I mean, they're white and, once dry, they feel like rocks."

"Ah, not these ones," Anthony replies. "The master received a shipment from the Ottoman Caliphate, but it wasn't the spices she wanted—it was the jars they came in."

"The jars?"

"Several of them were carved from stone, but the stone had hundreds of tiny shells embedded in them."

"And that's what she wanted?"

"Yes. She looked very closely at them."

"I don't understand," Julia says. "You can't get the shells out, right? It's not like they're stuck in mud or clay. They're set in stone."

"Yes," Anthony says. "That's what seems to intrigue her—that they're part of the stone."

"Weird."

"Hey, listen," Anthony says, taking the gold sovereign back from her. "I've got to run errands for the master, but Lady de Brooke invited me to her estate."

"Oh."

"Come with me."

"When?"

"Tonight."

The Estate

A carriage trundles past in the dark. The clack of hooves and the noise of wheels riding up over rocks on the track mask the words spoken from the bushes.

"I'm not sure this is such a good idea," Julia says. "Venturing outside the village after dark is not smart—and that's coming from someone that only ever sees the darkness."

"We're close," Anthony whispers, watching as the carriage rounds a corner, moving away from them. Its lantern is visible through the trees. It crosses a wooden bridge, which changes the way its wheels sound in the dark.

Anthony grabs Julia's hand and leads her out of the weeds and back onto the trail.

"You know," she says, "when most people get invited somewhere, they go during the day. We could run into robbers."

"We've nothing to rob. What could we lose?"

"Our lives."

Anthony laughs.

On the other side of the bridge, the road forks in two. Water sings over the rocks in the brook. The birds have fallen quiet with the onset of night. Crickets take up their song.

"Down here," he says, leading her along the left fork. Within a hundred yards, they come to a brick wall reaching over six feet in height. Shrubs and bushes crowd the edge of the track, obscuring the wall. Moss clings to the stone. Ahead, Anthony can see a dark patch marking a gap in the wall. There's movement. A soldier paces in the shadows.

Anthony whispers, "We're going to have to jump the wall."

"I thought you said you were welcome here," Julia replies in an equally soft voice.

Anthony ignores her comment. He leads her off the path and backtracks, looking for a way over the wall. His hands skim the stone, testing it for handholds.

"Here," he says, placing Julia's hand on a rough-hewn stone protruding from the wall.

"Oh, no," Julia replies. "You first."

Quietly, Anthony scrambles up on top of the wall. He leans down, reaching with his hand for Julia. Their fingers touch. She climbs up next to him.

"Remind me never to do this again," she says.

Anthony drops from the wall, landing in the long grass. His ears prick, listening for the slightest sound from the guard house, which is easily four perches further along the wall. If he was back in the village, it would be two or three storefronts from the front door of the apothecary. The night is still, allowing him to watch for the rustle of bushes.

Oak trees line the driveway, leading to the estate home almost a furlong away.

Anthony's dropped into an orchard. Crab apple trees have been planted at regular intervals, forming rows reaching back toward the house.

"Ready?" Julia asks.

"Come on down," Anthony replies, still watching the driveway for any movement.

Two feet strike the centre of his back, followed by a body crumpling on top of him. Hands grab at his shoulders. Julia flattens him, knocking his breath from him. She sprawls out on the grass.

"Oof," he says, rolling over and groaning. "What was that?"

"You were supposed to catch me," she whispers.

"You weren't supposed to land on me."

"I'm blind, remember?"

"Ah, yeah," he says, getting to his feet and reaching out a hand to help her stand. Their fingers touch once again. As soon as she knows where he is, she grabs him, but she doesn't grip his hand. Instead, she reaches for his wrist. Julia hauls herself up, almost pulling him on top of her.

"There had better be fresh food scraps at the back of the kitchen," she says.

"Sweet pastries," he says, imagining what they might find. "Bread and pudding."

"Roast lamb," she replies, playing along with him. Anthony leads her through the orchard. They creep up the gentle rise leading to the stately home. Horses neigh softly in the stables. The wooden doors leading to the mews are open. A cat creeps past in the darkness, which is a good sign as cats are scroungers. If the cats are out hunting, they're looking for mice. And mice won't emerge until long after the servants have gone for the night. Cats are sleepers. They won't start prowling until they're confident of a catch. If they're expecting mice this early in the evening, then this is a quiet part of the estate.

Anthony peers in through a window leading to the basement, confirming his suspicions—there's no one in there. The sunken kitchen is clean and tidy. The benches have been cleared. The candles have been doused. If anything, it's early for the kitchen staff to have finished for the evening, but it means they'll have retired to their quarters for the night.

The two of them creep along the front of the wall leading to the main house. They cross the forecourt. Pebbles crunch beneath their shoes, but that can't be helped. Besides, the sound won't carry far without any wind.

"There's light at the far end of the home."

Julia says, "Aren't you going to knock?"

"No."

"Why do I get the impression you weren't invited here at all?"

"I was. I promise."

"But?"

"But I want to see them first."

"You want to see them?" Julia asks. "You can see them once a maid has answered the door."

"No, I want to see them before that."

"Why?"

"Because seeing is more than looking with one's eyes. You taught me that."

"I taught you to stalk the grounds of an estate?" Julia replies as they cross beneath the portico and follow a low garden wall beneath the windows of the three-story house.

Under his breath, Anthony replies, "You taught me to see beyond mere sight. You taught me to see what others miss."

"Ah. And you want to see them before they see you."

"Yes, before they can tailor their words and actions."

"You're weird. You know that, right?"

"Thank you," Anthony says, coming to a halt below the only window with candles flickering within. "Wait here."

Anthony climbs up on the flower bed. A trellis has been mounted by the window, allowing vines to wind their way up the side of the building. He tugs on the wooden slats, making sure they're secure before taking hold of the slats and hauling himself up.

"What can you see?"

"A long, wooden table with a silver candelabra at both ends. Oh, there's got to be a dozen candles burning in there."

"Is there anyone in the room?"

"Yes," Anthony whispers. "Lady de Brooke is standing by the fireplace with her husband."

"Okay, can we knock on the door now?"

"Hang on," he replies. "They're not moving."

"What do you mean, *they're not moving*?"

"I mean, they're standing still. Like statues."

"Are they talking?"

"I don't think so," Anthony says, trying to see them more clearly.

"Well, they've got to move."

"They're not."

"They must be talking."

Anthony is silent. After almost a minute, he says, "Their arms, their legs, their hands, their faces—they're all still. And..."

"And what?"

"The floor is covered in coloured ropes."

"Ropes?"

"I think so. Lots and lots of rope. Some of them are thick, others are thin, but they're everywhere. You couldn't walk in there without tripping over them. They run under her dress and over to his boots."

"I don't like this," Julia says. "We need to go."

"The fire," Anthony says. "It's not real."

"What do you mean, *it's not real*?"

"I mean, there are flames in the hearth, but the logs are not being consumed. They should have blackened by now."

"I don't like this," Julia says.

"Me neither."

"Can we go?"

"Sure," Anthony says. He starts to climb down.

A sharp *crack* echoes through the night. The trellis comes loose from the brick wall. It swings out, falling back toward the ground. Anthony loses his grip on the wooden cross-frame. He falls. Air rushes past, catching his hair. He knows what's coming, but there's not enough time to brace himself. His back slams into the pebbles, knocking the wind out of his lungs. A split second later, the trellis comes crashing down on top of him.

"Anthony!" Julia yells. Although she's blind, she scrambles over, feeling her way with her hands. She drops to her knees and pats the ground, searching for him.

"Here," he says feebly, struggling to free himself from beneath the trellis. Anthony rolls to one side, pushing the wooden frame away from him. Julia's hands run over his body, squeezing his arms and legs.

"Are you well? Is anything broken?"

"I'm fine," he says. "Just sore. We need to—"

The sound of a sword being drawn from its scabbard sends a chill through him. Lying there on his back, he looks up over his head at the moonlight reflecting off a polished steel blade barely inches from his throat. A guard stands poised to attack, but like Lord and Lady de Brooke, his features are set like stone. He neither speaks nor moves. His eyes fail to blink. Not so much as a word is uttered from his mouth.

The tip of the blade menaces, threatening to plunge into his neck. Anthony squirms, wanting to wriggle away, but the blade follows, poised to strike.

"I'm sorry. I didn't mean anything," Anthony says.

From the look on her face, it's only then Julia realises there's someone else there with them. How could the guard come upon them with no sound save that of his sword being drawn? If he ran over, they would have heard his boots crunching on the pebbles. Perhaps he'd seen them and cut across the grass. He must have been on his way to nab them when Anthony fell. The sound of the trellis falling would have masked his last few steps.

"Please, mister," Julia says, appealing to the soldier but looking in the wrong direction. She's staring across Anthony's chest, peering over toward the mews.

Footsteps pound on the carriageway. There's yelling. Lady de Brooke runs toward them, holding her skirt up so she doesn't trip on the long fabric. Lord de Brooke points and yells at his soldiers. A squad fans out around them. Several other guards run into the orchard, looking for anyone else that may have come onto the grounds.

"Anthony?" Lady de Brooke asks, surprised by his presence on the estate.

"I'm sorry," he says. "I didn't mean any harm."

Lord de Brooke comes up beside her. "What did you see, boy?"

"Nothing. I swear."

"Don't lie to me," he says as the guard's sword inches closer. The tip of the blade is less than an inch from Anthony's exposed neck.

"I—I saw you and Lady de Brooke standing by the fireplace, talking—but I couldn't hear what was being said. I heard nothing. I promise."

Anthony's lying, but it's all he can think to say. Lord de Brooke, though, seems satisfied by his answer. He looks at the guard looming over them and nods. The guard sheathes his sword and walks off toward the grass, barely making any noise on the pebbles. Anthony wants to turn and look in that direction, but he dares not take his eyes off the lord and lady lest he arouses their ire.

"Oh, Anthony. What are you doing here?" Lady de Brooke asks, crouching beside him. She reaches out, offering her hand to help him stand. He accepts. Her fingers are as cold as stone.

"We—We were excited about learning," Anthony says.

"This is the blind one?" Lord de Brooke asks, grabbing Julia by her jaw and turning her to face him. Julia doesn't resist. She looks up at his face even though she can't see him. His gloved fingers turn her jaw one way and then another. It's as though he can see through her.

"They mean us no harm," the lady says.

"You cannot do this," the lord says, but he's addressing her, not them. "We need to limit contact. With each approach, there's the danger of exposure."

Lady de Brooke says, "It's not commoners that are our concern. 'Tis the bishop that threatens us."

"Keep your distance, my dear," her lord says. He turns to Anthony and Julia. "And you two. Be gone and never return, or it's the steel of my blade you'll feel."

"Yes, m'lord," Anthony says, taking Julia's hand and rushing along the driveway back toward the gatehouse. Julia overtakes him, pulling him on even though she can't see where she's going. Anthony increases his stride, coming alongside her and steering her toward the entrance to the estate. Behind them, soldiers march up, escorting them off the grounds.

Once they're on the muddy road, they turn back toward Westminster.

"Read," Julia says, sounding displeased. "And you thought you were going to learn to read. Hah."

Julia

Sunlight streams in through the wooden shutters of the apothecary. After yesterday, Anthony is determined to prove his diligence to Master Dunmore. He arrives early and closes the door behind him. It's not often the apothecary has customers before the markets open, but he wants no distractions.

Anthony's first task is to set the fusee on the mechanical clock hanging next to the counter. Master Dunmore is particularly fussy about his German clock. Accuracy is important. Wind the spindle too tight and the mainspring will release uneven torque and the hours will race by too quickly. When Anthony first started his apprenticeship, it took six months before the master trusted him with this task each morning. *'Wind until the resistance feels like the weight of an empty cup in your hand and no more,'* the master said. And he knew. Each noon, Master Dunmore would stand out in the garden courtyard behind the apothecary, watching the shadow cast by the sundial. On reaching noon, he'd check to see if his clock registered the same time. If it had raced ahead to one or two in the afternoon, Anthony would be reprimanded for winding too hard that morning. If it fell more than half an hour behind, Anthony would face the disappointment of his master with a knowing glare. Over the years, Anthony came to pride himself on his precision. Now, even after several overcast days where the sundial cannot be read to calibrate the clock, it'll stray by no more than fifteen to twenty minutes. The slight nod he gets from the master when that happens is worth more than gold.

Anthony would love nothing more than to dismantle the clock and examine its inner workings. He can see the mainspring and spindle, the gears and cogs, the rotating cam and collars through the ornate faceplate. Perhaps one day, when Master Dunmore purchases a newer clock, he'll allow him to open it up.

Anthony sweeps the aisles and restocks the bottles. There's a commotion outside. The yelling of guards apprehending someone reaches his ears, but he's at the back of the store and can't hear what's being said. After mopping up some spillage from yesterday that seeped under the counter, he gets the store ready to open.

Anthony removes the bolts on the windows and opens the shutters wide, allowing sunlight and fresh air to stream into the apothecary. As the store is set in an alley leading from the main road to the market square, buyers are already starting to walk past outside. They chat with each other, laughing and joking.

Anthony looks around for Julia. Normally, she's here before him, sunning herself on the ledge.

He opens the heavy wooden door and arranges portable shelves in the open window, staggering the wares to entice customers to enter the store. A drainage ditch runs below the window. To enter the apothecary, customers step across a paved stone walkway. Many a drunk has stumbled into the ditch on either side only to be dragged out by Master Dunmore the next morning. It's not deep, but it is wide. The channel is two feet in width and runs along the front of the buildings on the western side of the lane. A smooth curve marks where water has wound its way through the centuries. Anthony stacks the display bottles on the windowsill without fear of them being stolen. Anyone game to try would find themselves slipping on the moss that lines the drain.

It's a beautiful day. It's the kind of day when Julia would quiz him for hours about the comings and goings within the markets. She loves to have the sounds she hears interpreted as images by him. The steady, rhythmic squeak of a wheel—a farmer pushing a barrow of pumpkins toward the market. The laughter of children—either a family using all hands to carry their produce home or a gaggle of kids skipping through the streets, chasing a cat. The clomp of boots in unison—soldiers making their rounds, resplendent in their red dress jackets and dark trousers. At the cluck of birds, she'll train her ear, leaning forward and listening for the subtle clues that tell her whether these are chickens, ducks, pheasants or quail.

Although he shouldn't leave the store unattended, Anthony decides to harvest some lavender from the garden at the back of the apothecary. So far, no one's entered the store. He'll be quick. Lavender will freshen up the displays—and Julia loves the perfumed smell. He grabs a sharp knife, unbolts the back door and rushes out into the garden. Anthony cuts a large swathe from the bushes growing against the far wall of the courtyard. Within a minute, he's back inside and separating the lavender into six vases. Visually, lavender is stunning with its purple flowers and long stems, and the scent will drown out the smell of stagnant water pooling in the drain.

Where's Julia?

Anthony pokes his head out of the door and scans the market at the end of the alley. Normally, by this time, she's chatting with the cooks in the bakery across the way, scrounging for crusts or loaves with a burnt base.

Anthony has left a spot for her on the windowsill. As grumpy as Master Dunmore may be, even he has a soft spot for the blind girl. Besides, having her sit by the door means the wares on display are out of arm's reach to those crossing the paving stones to enter the store. Both he and Anthony angle the shelves toward her, making it as though she were part of the display, and in many ways, she is. Her cheery countenance and chatty nature are welcomed by customers. Julia makes the apothecary more friendly.

Only once has Julia toppled into the drainage ditch. It's a mistake she's never made again. Although instead of sewage, the ditch normally has runoff from the thatched roofs further up on the main street.

The presence of the abbey nearby means there are no nearby homes, only businesses. The cloister is on the other side of the abbey, making this alley more of a thoroughfare between the main road and the markets. The House of Commons lies on the far side of the abbey. Although it's always busy, gentry tend not to stray too far from the House, meaning it's only buyers and sellers that venture this far.

Anthony keeps a few stems of lavender with lush flowers aside for Julia. He places them on the windowsill where she sits, knowing she'll find them by smell alone. After their late night, perhaps she's slept in. He hopes she's not angry with him for endangering her. Being blind, it must have been terrifying hearing soldiers running in toward them and knowing swords were being drawn. She would have felt helpless, unable to flee.

Master Dunmore comes down the lane, walking from the abbey toward the market. A cart full of firewood trundles past him with its steel-rimmed wheels clacking on the cobblestones.

"I'm so sorry," the master says as he steps on the paving stone spanning the gutter. "I really am."

Anthony stutters. "I—I."

Anthony's greatest fear is that he'll be dismissed before completing his apprenticeship. He knows being discharged could happen for any reason, be that a lack of performance, a complaint from a customer, or the master wanting to cut costs. It's not just the loss of income that worries Anthony but the prospect of being blackballed. Even the perception of being sacked is enough to deter other masters from picking him up. Anthony knows apprentices that have struggled to find work after an abrupt discontinuity. They've ended up sweeping chimneys, binding ropes or working in the mines for a living.

He grabs the broom, wanting to reinforce his diligence to the master.

"She was a good lass," the master says.

"What?"

Master Dunmore wags his finger, adding, "You need to stay

away. You understand that, right? Let justice take its course. You can't interfere. They'll take any pretence they can to draw more fish into their net."

"Julia?" Anthony asks, still confused.

"Bishop Blaine took her."

Anthony stutters. "But wh—why?"

He knows it's a pointless question. There is no reason—not in the sense of one that's justifiable or proportional to any wrong that has been committed. Hate rules the church. Defiance is a sin, only defiance is framed by the whim of the bishop rather than liturgy or scripture.

Anthony protests. "But she's innocent."

"Everyone's innocent," the master says, hanging his head.

"It's a mistake. It must be. Julia's no heretic. She'll tell them, and they'll let her go. They must."

The master is brutal in his reply. "This is the Holy Roman Church. They'll admit no mistake in taking her. Her only hope is an appeal to mercy. Given she's young and blind, they may offer forgiveness."

As much as Anthony doesn't want to admit it, he knows Master Dunmore's right.

"I have to see her."

"No, boy. Don't you see? He's casting a broad net. He'll take all the catch he can. You. Me. Anyone that stands in his way. It matters not what is already done but what comes next. You can't give him the satisfaction of adding you to his haul."

"But—But."

"But nothing. There is only ill in their eyes. While Mary is queen, they'll take their revenge on the reformists."

"But she's no reformist."

The master quotes from the New Testament. "*Qui non est mecum contra me est. He who is not for me is against me.* They see only light and darkness. They see none of the colours of the rainbow nor any of the shades in between. In their eyes, if she's not devout, she's a heretic."

"It's not fair."

"No, it's not. We can only pray she finds mercy in their sight."

Tears well up in Anthony's eyes. He doesn't want to cry, but he can't help it. Julia's his dearest friend. He wipes his cheeks, sniffing, struggling to hold back more tears.

"I can't abandon her," he says, bolting between the aisles within the apothecary and making for the door.

"No!" the master yells, running after him but stopping on the edge of the threshold.

Anthony sprints out into the street. He runs as fast as he can, ducking between people and pushing his way past both buyers and sellers. He sprints along the main road heading north.

As much as he wants to, Anthony can't run forever. He's barely reached Covent Garden when his lungs start to ache. His heart is beating so hard it feels as though it's about to break through his chest.

Anthony stops on the side of the road and leans forward, pressing his hands against his knees. Around him, the world continues on as it has for each and every day of his brief life. Chimney sweeps drag their carts behind them. They call out for work, but they're stooped and weary. Soot lines their arms and faces. Women sit in the shadows of an awning weaving cloth. Kids run naked down the laneways, kicking a bundle of rags tied together with twine as though it were a ball. A dog pisses on the corner of an alleyway. Gentry ride past on horses, elevated above the muck and mire of the day, ignoring all but the riders next to them. They're obnoxious, refusing to acknowledge the poverty around them as they boast of the latest fox hunt. Rats keep to the shadows, scurrying through the gutters. An elderly woman throws dirty wash water out of a window. It splashes across the road and runs into the cracks between the cobblestones, curling back toward the ditch.

The sky is radiant and full of promise. Clouds dot the horizon, but the vast expanse overhead is clear. The azure blue speaks of another world—one other than this dirty, filthy, smelly abode.

The brickwork on the wall beside him is chipped. Flies buzz around a dead bird. Wet mud clings to his shoes, and yet the sun warms his face. The contrast couldn't be more stark and yet no one notices. Perhaps that's what upsets Anthony. Everyone's going somewhere. No one's arriving anywhere. They hang their heads, looking at the fall of each foot on the cobblestones. Regardless of how beautiful it may be, the day is ignored. Everything else is more important—only it isn't. And somewhere out there, Julia is languishing in the sheriff's gaol. Somewhere in old London Town, Julia has been wrongfully imprisoned. He imagines her staring out through the bars of a window at a sky full of beauty she cannot see.

Anthony walks through the Lud Gate and past the cathedral. He heads up the hill to the barracks and makes inquiries after Julia. No one knows anything. No one cares. It takes several hours before he learns she's being held in the cells on Chancery Lane. He walks up to Bishop's Gate and past the Holburn Conduit. Guards have been stationed by the entrance to the prison. Like the apothecary, it's been built with stone rather than brick. Bars line a series of basement windows set level with the laneway. Several women crouch by the windows, talking to those imprisoned there. As visitors are not allowed inside the prison without magisterial approval, this is an informal way of giving them access. It's tacitly rather than formally recognised. Anthony crouches beside one of the barred windows and peers into the darkness. Although the window is level with his feet, within the prison, it aligns with the roof, being easily seven feet off the ground.

"Julia?"

Shadows flicker in the basement beneath him. Rough hands snatch at the bars in front of him, causing him to recoil in fright. White knuckles grip the thick iron. Rotten teeth snarl from the darkness. A face presses hard against the bars, trying to squeeze between them.

"Who you looking for, my spring gosling?"

"A friend," Anthony says, shocked to see the pale, plague-ridden skin of someone that hasn't seen sunlight in years.

"The new girl? The blasphemer?"

"She's no heretic."

"That's not what the bishop says. Not that the bishop's ever said anything that doesn't line his own purse."

"Do you know where she is?"

A hand wriggles through the bars. Fingers point down the alley.

"The condemned are kept in the corner cell."

"Thank you," Anthony says.

"What of me, boy? What kindness have you for me?"

Anthony pauses, unsure of what he means.

"Food? Water?" the convict says. "Recompense me for what little I have done to help thee. Have pity on the forgotten, I beg you."

His fingers reach through the bars, appealing to Anthony for mercy. They're thin and boney. He's lost several fingernails. Those that remain are chipped and blackened. They resemble the claws of an animal more than those of a man. Pus-filled scabs cling to the prisoner's knuckles. On one hand, Anthony is repulsed by the diseased state of the man. On the other, he pities him, knowing time and chance are all that separate them. What Anthony wants to do is recoil from him and leave in a hurry. He'd love nothing more than to erase the memory of this interaction from his mind, but he can't. That wouldn't be honest.

Anthony reaches into his pocket. He hands the man a crab apple he was saving for lunch. As soon as his hand is within reach, the apple is snatched from his fingers.

"Ah, you're a good lad," the man says. "Look for your lass down there."

Anthony backs away and walks further along the lane. The alley slopes down toward the distant river while the building has been built level, meaning the windows that were at ground height rise higher the further he descends on the cobblestones. As he walks on, the windows align with his chest height. Soldiers watch him with interest. They're leaning against the wall on the other side of the alley, but their casual manner is a bluff. They smoke, whispering to each other as they watch all those talking with the various prisoners. There's an unspoken rule that informal visitations are allowed, and food can be given.

Without saying anything, Anthony peers into the corner cell. It's no wider than the broom closet in the apothecary, but it reaches ten feet in length. A bed has been pressed up against one wall. There's barely room enough to stand next to it. The thick oak door has a viewport barred with an iron grate. From the angle Anthony's peering into the cell, all he can see is a pair of dirty legs and a torn dress.

He whispers, "Julia?"

"Anthony?" is the curious reply from the darkness. Julia stands on her bed, but even with the extra height afforded by its legs, she can't reach the window. Her hands cling to the edge in front of him. Her fingers touch the bars. Anthony reaches in, touching her fingers.

"I can't see you," he says.

"I can't see you either," Julia replies. She might be behind bars, but she's irrepressible. Her comment brings a smile to his face. He's tempted to say, "You haven't seen me in over a decade," but the words that come out are, "You see more than anyone I know."

Julia is silent.

"What happened?" he asks.

"Bishop Blaine. The angry bishop from St. Paul's. He's accused me of defying the sacrament."

"How? Why?"

"He's saying I refused to attend Holy Communion. He's got witnesses testifying that I stood on a church pew and read from Ecclesiastes—in vile English, not sacred Latin—and then refused the bread and the wine."

"And he knows you're blind?" Anthony asks, astonished by what he's hearing. "He knows you can't actually read because you can't see?"

"Oh, he knows. It makes no difference. Lies are nought to him. He clings to what he wants to be true. And he will have blood."

"No, no, no," Anthony says. "I'll get you out of there."

"Oh, no," Julia says, cutting Anthony off before he can say anything else. "You must leave, or he'll burn us both."

"I'll talk to the sheriff."

"No. The sheriff is a hawk swooping on a squirrel. He cares not for anything beyond the reach of his talons."

"There must be another way," Anthony says. He grips the bars in front of him, pulling on them to no avail. His knuckles go white.

Anthony's not the only one to languish outside the prison as a loved one rots in a cell. The cobblestones he's standing on have been worn smooth by those that have visited here over the centuries. Actual visitations within the prison are rare. From without, few questions are asked of those stopping by to find someone. A guard stands not more than fifteen feet away, watching various friends and family crouching by the windows. Dangerous prisoners are kept on the upper floors. Those kept in holding cells like these are offered more lenience. Should a knife be passed, a guard would intervene. Otherwise, they watch with the interest of someone waiting for fish to dry on a cloudy day.

English law is simple. It's not justice that's sought, only conformity. Innocent or not, the law is a deterrent to others. Its role is two-fold: to punish and to warn. Mercy serves neither of those goals, so it is seldom found among any but the wealthy.

Anthony hangs his head. He pushes his forehead against the bars.

"It's okay," Julia says, hearing him sigh. "They're not going to kill a blind girl. I don't think even Bishop Blaine could justify such cruelty. They'll make an example of me, of that, I'm sure. Besides, it's the men they hate. Anyone that threatens the supremacy of the church is burned, but I'm lowly. I am but an ant to them."

Anthony says, "Even ants are crushed underfoot."

"Hey," Julia says. "You're supposed to give me heart. You should agree with me."

"I'm worried."

"Don't be. All will be well."

"Is there anything you need?"

"Water."

"I will bring you some," he says, reaching out and touching her fingers again.

"I thank you."

Reluctantly, Anthony steps back, watching as her fingers fall from the bars.

"I'll be back."

"I know," her soft voice says from the darkness. Julia doesn't sound scared so much as alone.

Anthony wanders rather than walks through London. He's lost in a daze. The sounds around him seem harsh and amplified. A raven squawks, screaming at him as it flies low overhead, causing him to duck. Kids laugh. Their laughter, though, shouts at him in staccato. To Anthony, it's caustic. It's like burnt lime eating away at bodies in a plague pit. They're not laughing at him, that much is clear from the way they jostle with each other, but they sound inhuman. They're like donkeys neighing for straw or geese honking in defence of a nest. There's no intelligence, no compassion, only a reaction that's guttural.

A lord rides past on a horse. His trousers are navy blue with a red stripe running from his ankle to his hip. A sword hangs from a scabbard on his waist. His jacket is open. The breast guard rocks with the swaying of his horse. His riding hat is elongated. It has a large white swan feather that catches the wind like the flags of a caravel.

Sweat has formed on the animal's long neck. White foam seeps into its rugged mane. The lord has ridden his charge hard to reach London. The horse flares its nostrils, still gathering its breath. In any other context, they'd appear regal. To Anthony, though, the clack of steel horseshoes is like the beat of a drum announcing war.

Anthony fiddles with his purse, feeling a collection of half-farthings rubbing together. An upper-class woman brushes past, and he snatches at his purse, pulling it tight to his chest as though he were fending off a robber. She glances back, surprised by his reaction. With long, flowing hair in a colourful bonnet, she's pleasant to behold. Her dress is black with an ornate silver trim catching the sunlight. She's baffled by Anthony. It is her rather than him that ought to be protective. She quickens her pace, wanting to get away from him.

Anthony walks into the market beside the docks. Prices here are inflated, being almost twice the asking price in the villages approaching London. Convenience is a tax in itself. The incessant chatter of buyers and sellers is overwhelming. Anthony holds his hands to his ears. His purse dangles from his fingers. He turns, trying to focus but there's too much happening at once. His mind struggles to distinguish individual words in the cacophony of conversations unfolding around him. He stumbles to a stall selling black bread. It's stale, but he's past caring. He buys some along with a water bladder and slips them into the pouch slung over his shoulder.

With his head down and his eyes cast only on the fall of his feet, he pushes through the crowd, heading back to the prison. Within the wall of noise reverberating around him, he hears a woman calling his name. Anthony can't stop—not here. The chorus of voices around him is painful to his ears. He needs to get out of the market. He turns down a side alley and cuts back toward the centre of town.

"Anthony," a kind voice says. Laced, gloved fingers touch his shoulder from behind. He turns, looking at Lady de Brooke with bloodshot eyes.

"I need to get back," he says. "Julia needs me."

"Anthony," the lady says, slowing him down. "It's you they want, not her."

"Me? I—I don't understand," he blabbers. "Why me?"

"I'm sorry. I sought to protect you from all this. I never meant to draw attention to you but the bishop, he's a bitter man."

"Why would his ire be set against me?"

"He's a brute beast," Lady de Brooke says. "He seeks to punish me, but my cousin is a handmaiden to the queen. She's trusted. She gives me access to Queen Mary's court."

Anthony's no fool. "He can't touch you."

"No."

"But anyone close to you?"

Lady de Brooke hangs her head.

"And this morning?" he asks.

"He dispatched guards to arrest you at the apothecary, but they couldn't find you, only her."

"Why take her?"

"Because she refused to tell them where you were."

"I—I was inside," he says, shaking his head. "I was cleaning. I kept the door shut while I swept the floor."

"I'm sorry."

"One day?" Anthony asks. "I've known you for a single day. Is but one day enough to warrant such cruelty?"

"I didn't mean for any of this," the lady replies.

"I do not understand. I know you only from your kindness by the Thames. But what is that to him? Why would he seek to punish me in place of you?"

Lady de Brooke ignores his question, saying, "I've sent entreaty to the queen, but she is in the northlands. I fear my courier won't reach her in time. Bishop Blaine seeks to conduct his executions with haste."

"Julia doesn't deserve this."

"No. She doesn't."

"We have to save her."

"I can't intervene," the lady says. "Not without the consent of the queen."

"I won't leave her."

"You must," the lady says, gripping his hand in hers. "You need to leave London while you still can."

"I can't."

"If he catches you—"

Anthony has tears in his eyes. "If he catches me, then I'll die chained beside her."

Burned Alive

Anthony crouches in the alleyway beside the prison. He whispers, directing his voice through the bars.

"Julia?"

There's no movement within the cell. He strains, trying to see her within the shadows.

"I've bought food and water. I have some bread."

A feeble hand reaches for the edge of the window. Bloodied fingers grab at the torn loaf he pushes through the bars. Three of Julia's fingernails have been ripped off, exposing the tender flesh beneath. Her fingers weep blood along with drops of clear fluid.

"What happened?"

"A confession," she replies. "I—I confessed. I had to."

Anthony's heart races. "Lady de Brooke. She's petitioning the queen for mercy."

"It won't matter."

"Why?"

"It's her he's after," Julia says. "Someone must have seen us going there last night. They told him we were there. That's why he came for us—for both of us."

"But why?"

"The bishop wanted to know what heinous witchcraft we saw at the estate."

"But you didn't see anything. You couldn't. You're blind."

"He knows that, but it doesn't matter to him. He wants slander, not facts."

"And he wouldn't listen to you?" Anthony asks.

"He blabbered on about seeing with spiritual eyes. I tried to appeal to common sense, but he hears only the sweet dulcet tones of his own voice."

Anthony whispers, "I'm sorry."

"Don't be. He's but the braying of an ass refusing to pull a cart. I won't give him the pleasure of hearing me bleat like a hog being led to slaughter."

"Oh, Julia," Anthony says with tears running down his cheeks.

"Don't cry for my loss," she says, sensing but not seeing his tears. "I'll embarrass him before he lights my pyre. I'll have him rue the moment he dragged me from the alley."

Metal jangles on the far side of the door behind her. A steel key scrapes against the opening of the lock. Within the metal panel, gears grind as the door is unlocked. The rusted parts within the lock grate and click.

"It's time," she says. Her fingers drop away from the window ledge.

Julia turns to face her gaoler.

Anthony squints. It's bright in the alleyway, making it difficult to see within the darkened cell. Like Julia, he's blind to all that's transpiring. The heavy wooden door is pushed open. Hinges groan as the door slams into the wall. Boots thump on the hard stone floor. Three guards rush into the narrow cell. Batons strike soft flesh time and again for no reason beyond utter cruelty.

"No!" Anthony yells. One of the wooden batons strikes at his hands, smashing several of his fingers against the bars and splitting the skin. Anthony cradles his hand against his chest. Blood pools in his palm. Julia is dragged out into the hallway, screaming as she's pulled by her hair. Within barely ten seconds, it's over. The cell is empty and the door's left open.

Anthony runs up the hill and around in front of the prison. Blood drips from his fingers. The sheriff is standing outside with an execution detail. Guards surround them. An elderly prisoner reaching up over six feet in height stands there in chains. His shoulders are stooped. Blood runs from a cut on his head, turning his grey hair a brilliant red and staining his puffy white shirt. Next to him, a younger, shorter man stands proud with his head held high. He's been stripped of his shirt. The torn remains hang from his waist, exposing fresh scars on his back where a whip has ploughed his flesh like the fallowed fields in spring.

Women, both young and old, cry out for mercy, wailing within the crowd. Julia is dragged down the steps of the prison to join the men on the street. Heavy chains bind her hands. She's wearing a linen nightdress. Her new clothing is noteworthy for how clean and white they appear. Even from afar, it's apparent the dress has been pulled over her own scruffy clothing while a pair of white stockings have been tugged up her legs. For some reason, the bishop is obsessed with ensuring the condemned appear pure even though they look dejected.

Julia hangs her head and shuffles along with the men as the procession marches down the street. The bishop and the sheriff lead from the front. The prisoners lag behind them with troops bringing up the rear. A stiff shove in the back with the wooden shaft of a pike gets the old man to walk faster. Julia keeps pace with him, staying close by his side, using the fall of his heavy boots as a guide.

Anthony pushes through the crowd following them. He squeezes past the guards flanking the condemned, wanting to get in front of the march.

As he pulls level with the bishop, he calls out, "Jules!"

Even though she's blind, their eyes meet. She shakes her head, not wanting him to reveal himself. Although he understands her intent, it leaves him feeling like a coward. A knot turns in his stomach, churning and threatening to make him sick. He wants to scream at the injustice. If he could, he'd shout profanities at the bishop, but Julia's right. It would accomplish nothing.

Town criers flank both the sheriff and the bishop, calling out to city folk and drawing in a crowd. "Come all. Hear all. The Lord our God is holy. All who partake of the blood and the body shall be saved. Those that deny the sacrament deserve their eternal damnation."

The main cobblestone road leading to the Lud Gate is broad, being a major thoroughfare. It runs past the low stone wall surrounding St. Paul's and the attached grass field. The buildings on the near side of the road are practical, being those of a blacksmith, a wood turner, a bakery and a communal stable for those visiting London. On the far side of the road, the cloister backs onto the church grounds. An alley beside the church provides pedestrian access to London proper. A carriage trundles past, oblivious to the parade marching toward the bottom of the hill.

Anthony pushes past the glassworks at the top of the rise. Heat radiates out through the open doors, coming from the winged furnaces inside. Coal is shovelled into the fires. Apprentices work with molten glass, glowing in reds and yellows. At the bottom of the hill, the church courtyard is being prepared with ten fagots of wood, even though only three will be used today. Thick wooden poles rise out of the kindling and logs stacked around each base. Blackened chains hold the firewood in place so it doesn't fall away as it burns.

A crowd has already formed five to six people deep. Commoners stand almost thirty feet away from the fagots, back by the outer wall of the cathedral grounds. Ash and burned wood have mixed in with the mud in the open yard, making it look more like a factory entrance than the hallowed grounds of a church. What little grass there is has been trampled.

Guards surround the entrances and alleyways leading to and from the church grounds. Their parade dress is resplendent. They've been adorned with threads of gold and purple. They're wearing dark stockings with puffy, pleated pants leading down to their knees. Fitted jackets have been pulled taut across each chest, being buttoned with a row of polished brass knobs. Their velvet headdresses rise for several feet, being adorned with the feathers of a pheasant. Each guard has a pike in hand, reaching up twelve feet beside them. The polished wooden shaft leads to a shiny metal spike. Rather than being symbols of divinity or even authority, they conjure up images of cruelty disguised as ceremony. The reaction of the crowd as they form ranks by the doors to the cathedral is clear. The people cower before the guards. There will be order during the execution, but only because the crowd fears them.

The bishop addresses the gathering as the sheriff prepares each of the prisoners, weighing them down with heavy chains and binding explosive collars about their necks.

"The gospel of Jesus Christ is one of simplicity," the bishop says, gesturing with his arms as he parades himself before the crowd. "Heaven awaits those that honour the sacrament. We're all sinners, but our Lord is gracious, forgiving us and offering us entrance into paradise—if we repent!"

Julia is proud. Her body language has changed now she's chained to a stake. She has nothing left to lose. She refuses to shrink in fear. She holds her head high. She may have been subdued during the march, but she's at peace with her fate now. With her shoulders back and her chin raised, she's defiant. As the guards wrap chains around her, she yells at the bishop, "Liar!"

The bishop turns on her. As she's on the third stake, he marches down toward her, calling out, "And what does this young wench cry? What lies does she espouse? Would she curse the Lord's anointed?"

"Only cowards hide behind lies," she yells, spitting at him but not reaching further than the base of the fagot beneath her feet. Several guards pack additional dry wood around her legs. With her arms locked behind the stake, she tugs at the steel cuffs holding her bound, wanting to break free.

The bishop parades before her as though he were an actor on stage.

"But my child, I offer you a chance for forgiveness before you depart this world. Will you not embrace the love of Christ?"

Julia replies, "Christ loved the poor. He healed the lepers and cured the blind. What love are you showing to a blind girl? What love is there in burning us at the stake?"

"Heretic," the bishop yells.

"Honest," she yells in reply.

Julia looks past him at the crowd. She can't see them but she knows they're there. She can hear their murmurs. She bellows, "They know. You may parade lies before us, but they are not fooled. They see you for what you are—cruel and unjust. A coward among men."

The sheriff speaks to the bishop, saying, "Do not answer her. You owe her nothing. What communion is there between an apostle and an apostate? What debate can there be between angels and demons?"

He turns to one of the guards saying, "If she speaks again, thrust your spear into her side. That will quell her spirit."

The bishop nods, agreeing with the sheriff's sentiment. The guard readies himself, positioning the point of his pike mere inches from her side.

"No!" Anthony yells, stepping out of the crowd and confronting the bishop. "This is wrong. She's innocent. Let her go."

"And why should I let her go?" the bishop asks. "She has blasphemed in the house of the Lord, reciting the scriptures in the tongue of the crude instead of the language of the church."

"She can't read," Anthony says, holding out his arm toward her. "She can't *see* to be able to read. And you say she's blasphemed? You're not making any sense. All of us assembled here know the truth: one without sight cannot read from the Bible. 'Tis not possible."

"Take him," the bishop says, recognising Anthony with a gleeful look in his eye. "Bind him to a fagot."

The sheriff signals with the flick of his gloved hand. Before Anthony can react, he's flanked by two guards. They grab him by the upper arms. Their fingers are like iron tongs, squeezing the muscles on his arms so hard the bones beneath them ache. He squirms, trying to free himself as they drag him to the fagot next to Julia.

"Stop," a woman yells from behind Anthony. Although her voice is gentle and easily lost in the rumblings of the crowd, a hush comes over those gathered before the execution. Every word she utters can be heard with clarity. "Let him go. Let them all go."

"You," the bishop says, turning on Lady de Brooke.

"This madness ends now," she says, stepping forward as the crowd parts around her. The lady has four of her own guards, but they're vastly outnumbered. They rest their hands on the swords hanging from their scabbards, watching the approach of the sheriff's men.

Anthony is pulled away. The soldiers on either side of him lift him off the ground. His feet swing between them, unable to touch the dirt. Their ability to snatch him from the crowd and lead him to be executed is frightening for its speed and brutality. He's gone from feeling he had command of his own life to being powerless in barely the beat of his own heart. They raise him up on one of the fagots.

Lady de Brooke addresses Bishop Blaine. "This is between you and me—not them. Release them!"

The bishop raises his hand. He points at the blue sky above, yelling, "Light the pyres!"

Attendants in black cloth rush forward with torches already burning. Flaming tar drips onto the ground. Women wail within the crowd, crying out for mercy.

A cloud passes in front of the sun. Dark shadows descend on the churchyard. Within seconds, the brilliant, bright sky is covered by a storm. Thunder rumbles overhead. The wind picks up. Bits of straw swirl through the air.

"No, no, no," Anthony says as his arms are jerked behind him. He's lashed to the stake next to Julia. He tries to pull away, but the ropes holding him in place are tight. Heavy chains are draped over his shoulders. The links have rusted. They rub against his clothes, leaving the appearance of dried blood on his tunic.

"You can't do this," Julia yells, hearing but not seeing the commotion beside her. "Let him go. He's done nothing. He's confessed nothing. He's innocent."

"Aren't we all?" the condemned man on the other side of her says.

Julia reaches out her arm, stretching her hand toward Anthony. He leans to one side, pulling against the chains and ropes. He holds his arm out to reach her. Their fingers touch, but they're unable to grip one another's hand. A soldier strikes Anthony's forearm, knocking his hand away. Tears run down Julia's cheeks. She sobs.

"This is madness," Anthony says as a monk dressed in black lowers his torch, preparing to light the pyre. Anthony yells at the crowd, calling out, "Stop them. Don't let them do this. You don't have to stand idly by. You know this is wrong. All of you. Not just the lady."

Throughout the crowd, heads hang in shame.

Bishop Blaine and Lady de Brooke stand barely a foot apart on the dusty ground, yelling at each other. Neither can nor wants to hear the other. Fingers are pointed. Spittle flies. Around them, nervous guards clench the hilts of their swords, but no blades are drawn. Additional soldiers arrive, having run down from the barracks. Unlike the guards that have gathered for the execution, they're carrying muskets with bayonets attached. Some of them have their weapons shouldered. Others ram wads into barrels and cock their flintlocks. A captain looks on nervously. Should the squad fire, they'd almost certainly miss at least some of their marks, striking the crowd instead.

"Stop this insanity," Lady de Brooke yells, stamping her boots in the dust. "The queen will not stand for such insolence and injustice."

With spittle hanging from his beard, the bishop replies, "The queen understands the need for purity. The church must be cleansed. Heretics must be punished."

Burning torches are thrust into the fagots. Flames lick at the dry wood. Smoke rises as the kindling crackles. The old man squirms, wriggling on a stake, trying to avoid the waves of heat rising from the fire. The younger man cries aloud, "Mercy, Heavenly Father. I beg you for mercy."

The executioner moves down the row, prodding torches deep into the fagots, making sure their flames have taken hold. The heat from the flames rises in waves. The bottom of Anthony's feet hurt. The exposed skin on his hands stings so he tucks his fingers beneath his tunic. It's feeble, but it's all he can do to spare himself for a few more seconds.

Rain falls from the sky. At first, it's refreshing, barely spitting. Anthony turns his head to the heavens and embraces the cool, wet air on his face. Within seconds, the rain is coming down in waves, washing over him in a torrent, soaking his clothing and dampening the wood beneath him. The flames still burn from the tar on the torches but the fagot itself is extinguished.

"What sorcery is this?" the bishop says, turning to Lady de Brooke. Rain mats down her hair, soaking her dress.

"It's called a storm," she replies. "Some days it's sunny. Some days it rains." She points up at the clouds, smiling as she adds, "Don't you know? Those that sow seeds love the rain!"

"You witch," he says, pointing at her.

The bishop backs away from the lady and her entourage. The guards present for the execution appear confused. They seem unable to decide whether they should focus on restarting the fires, quelling the unrest within the crowd, or supporting the bishop.

The sheriff barks orders, wanting to establish a clear perimeter. The crowd has begun milling around on the forecourt in front of the fagots, blurring the line between the matted grass strip and the back of the yard. They're cheering, looking up at the rolling storm in awe of what they perceive as divine intervention.

Rain comes down in sheets, washing over the church courtyard, but no one cares. Women dance in the rain. They swirl around, rejoicing and calling out that their prayers have been answered.

Julia laughs. Raindrops have supplanted her tears. She looks up at the sky, unable to see the clouds that have brought her salvation but smiling at them anyway.

"We're okay," Anthony says, feeling a rush of emotion. "We're going to be okay. Lady de Brooke will get us out of here."

"Ah, the floodgates of heaven," Julia replies, still looking up. Her hair is wet, sticking to her neck and shoulders. Water runs down her face.

The old man on the next fagot calls out, "Oh, how beautiful are the clouds that floated Noah and his ark, rescuing his family from destruction."

Lady de Brooke addresses the bishop, saying, "It looks like the weather has turned. This storm has settled. Foul winds like these can last for days, which gives my beloved Queen Mary plenty of time to return to London. And when she does, I will demand a full account of you and your actions. Your transgressions shall be read before the court. Then we shall see what justice purity demands."

The sheriff comes up beside the bishop. He whispers something in his ear.

"Yes, yes," the bishop replies to him. "If not with cleansing fire, then purge their souls with steel forged in fire."

"What? No!" the lady calls out.

The sheriff signals with his hand and the guard standing in front of the old man lowers his spear. He angles the tip so as to thrust through the man's torso. The guard aims to plunge his spear into the man's stomach, passing from his sternum up into his heart and lungs. The soldier braces himself and lunges.

Lightning strikes.

The flash is blinding. From Anthony's perspective, it seems to come out of nowhere, following a jagged path into the dirt just a few feet away. The crack of thunder is almost instant, rattling his bones. The boom is like that of a dozen cannons being fired from the Tower of London. Anthony closes his eyes, wanting to ward off the influx of light, but the lightning strike has seared itself in his vision. From behind closed eyelids, he can still see the outline of the soldier and the way the lightning struck the tip of his spear. The guard's body glows on the back of his eyeball. Although the man has already fallen to the dirt, for Anthony, it's as though he's still standing there, ready to strike.

Women and children scream, running for the gates surrounding the church grounds. Steam rises from the body of the guard lying inert in the mud. The wooden shaft of his spear is on fire. The steel tip glows red.

Two more guards come running down the hill from the reinforcements on the main road. Lady de Brooke points at them with an outstretched hand. Another bolt of lightning strikes, coming down from the clouds and landing between them. The guards are knocked off their feet by the thundering boom. Swords and muskets scatter across the cobblestones. No sooner have the soldiers fallen in the mud than they're up and scrambling back the way they came. They leave the sheriff and the bishop with only a handful of guards by the line of fagots.

"Witchcraft!" the bishop yells, backing away from Lady de Brooke.

"Be gone," she says, staring him down.

Already, the remaining guards run back up the hill, away from the church grounds. The sheriff is out in front of them, sprinting for the supposed safety of his reinforcements. The yard in front of the cathedral is almost empty. The only people remaining in the courtyard are the lady and her guards, the condemned still bound to their stakes, and a few brave women desperate to reach their loved ones stranded on the burnt fagots.

The bishop reaches out to steady himself. His legs are shaking. He touches the low stone wall surrounding the churchyard as he retreats. His fingers guide him, allowing him to walk backwards without turning his back on Lady de Brooke. He reaches the open wrought-iron gates by the main entrance.

"You'll burn for this," he yells, having retreated almost twenty yards from her.

"You're welcome to try," Lady de Brooke replies, spreading her arms wide and inviting him to strike. A snarl crosses his face. He clenches his fists. Several miles away, out beyond the Thames, lightning ripples through the darkened clouds. Jagged crackles of blue/white light rush in toward them, rolling through the clouds and coming from behind her. It splits into multiple tongs overhead, briefly lighting up the sky. Thunder rumbles through the air as though it were bellowed by an angry giant.

On hearing that, the bishop turns and runs to join the sheriff.

"Get them down from there," the lady says to her guards.

Although the chains binding the prisoners to each stake are locked, they're old and worn, having been used for numerous executions. Decades of exposure to flames and heat have tarnished the iron. The sharp tip of a dagger springs the lock. Anthony feels an immense sense of relief as the heavy chains fall onto the wood and into the mud. The rain soaking his clothes and washing over his face has never felt more refreshing.

Julia is free of her chains, but the guard releasing her doesn't seem to realise she can't see. She reaches with her hands. Anthony jumps down from his fagot and lands in a puddle of water.

"Here," Anthony says, reaching up and taking her by the waist. She leans forward, trusting him. Julia pushes off and falls toward him. He's gentle, lowering her to the ground.

"What was that?" Julia asks. "The bang. Was that a cannon?"

"It was the lady."

"Lady de Brooke did this?"

"Yes."

The courtyard is eerily quiet. The other two men set to be executed along with them have already fled with their families. The bishop and the sheriff watch from a distance. They're on the slope of the hill. The Queen's Guard cowers from the wind gusts, taking shelter on the side of the road. The sheriff and the bishop, though, are defiant. They stand in the middle of the cobblestone street, but neither they nor the soldiers with them dare return to the church grounds.

The body of the dead guard lies not more than fifteen feet from Anthony and Julia. Quietly, Anthony takes Julia's hand and leads her around the body, being sure to stay well clear of the man's legs so she doesn't trip over them. Smoke rises from the soldier's smouldering clothes.

Raindrops splash in puddles.

Lady de Brooke talks in hushed tones with one of her guards. He rushes off. The others remain between her and the soldiers further up the hill. They have their swords drawn, but they seem almost like statues. The intensity of their focus is something Anthony has never witnessed.

"We need to get you out of here," the lady says.

"But where can we go?" Anthony asks. "Nowhere is safe."

"He'll come for us," Julia says. "Again and again and again."

"For now, we'll get you out of the city," the lady says, leading them to a side alley. Anthony knows it well. This particular alley runs down to the Thames. Lady de Brooke rushes along the cobblestones with the front of her dress held high so she doesn't trip. Rain continues to fall but it's no longer torrential. Faces peer out of doorways and partially closed shutters, watching the three of them with a mixture of fear and curiosity. Anthony has no doubt these people will point the way for the sheriff and the bishop to follow.

Escape

Lady de Brooke's guards are nowhere to be seen. Anthony felt sure they would follow along behind them, but it's just the three of them fleeing toward the river. The guards must be stalling, wanting to deter the sheriff from following, but as there are only a handful of them they could be easily outflanked.

Whistles are blown on distant streets. Dogs howl, straining against leashes. Anthony knows the sound. This is how soldiers round up common street gangs. They herd them like sheep, cutting off avenues for escape and funnelling them to a point where they can be captured. Lady de Brooke quickens her pace from a fast walk to a run.

Anthony drags Julia along with him. She tries to run but she can't. Her feet trip on the uneven cobblestones and she stumbles. Anthony grabs her. He swings his arm up over her back and holds her beneath her armpit, helping her along. Julia leans into him as she runs, using his body as a guide.

"This way," the lady says, reaching the riverbank.

Anthony's expecting her to flee the city for her country estate, but she turns toward the docks. Bewildered workers pause while unloading hay from the stores. They sense panic. They can hear the calls of soldiers closing in and realise these three are the quarry. They watch on with sympathy, knowing that regardless of what justice is meted, it will invariably be disproportionate and heavy. Little do they know, these fugitives are fleeing execution.

Anthony locks eyes with a teenage girl of a similar age. Without uttering a word, his eyes plead for mercy. The furrow of his brow cries for compassion. Anthony can see compassion in the girl's eyes. Although they don't know each other, she can see the way he cares for a blind girl. She sees how helpless and dependent Julia is on him in a crisis. And she knows that one day, this could be her running from the righteous anger of authority. And she hopes someone else will show her the same kindness.

Four men stand on the wooden flatbed trailer. Two more crouch on the open upper floor of the warehouse, hauling up hay for the winter. The girl grabs the reins of the lead horse and calls out in a loud voice, startling it out of its lethargy. She wheels the lead horse around, forcing the other three horses in the team to follow. Nostrils flare. Hooves stomp on the cobblestones. As the street is flanked by the river on one side and storehouses on the other, there's not enough room to turn the team of horses around. Anthony's seen them working here before. They normally come in from the south, pulling their elongated wagons behind them, and exit by way of the old gate to the north. This girl, though, has turned her team across the road, leaving the horses facing out across the Thames. The men on the flatbed wagon sway, struggling to keep their balance as the broad cart turns, blocking the road behind Anthony. Bundles of hay fall from the open back. They split open, breaking apart on the road. Straw scatters with the wind.

"What in the bluebells are you thinking, girl?" one of the men asks, jumping down from the wooden tray. He marches up to her cursing. His hands fly through the air, pointing in different directions and threatening to strike her as he cusses. She shrinks, preparing to take his blow. Further back, soldiers rush onto the embankment by the river. They turn both ways, looking for the fugitives, but they can't see them through the confusion of wagon wheels and horses stamping their legs, snorting in anger in the cool air. The hay bales stacked on the wooden deck obscure the view further along the docks.

Anthony wants to stop and thank her, but she knows. For all the faults of the class system, it ensures that like protects like. She'll laugh about this tonight, recounting her exploits with friends and telling them how she helped another young apprentice get away from a bunch of brute thugs in fancy jackets. Uniforms may please the upper class, but the lower see them for what they really are—nothing more than licensed goons.

Anthony turns away, following Lady de Brooke between stacks of crates. As he slowed while passing the wagon, she's easily thirty feet ahead of him. She pauses, looking back and beckoning him to hurry.

Julia says, "W—What was that commotion?"

"A friend helping out."

Whereas most of the stores bordering the river are built on the embankment with only a narrow passage for horse-drawn carriages to pass, the dockyards are extensive. Timber beams stretch over the river, forming broad piers and allowing ships to sit in the channel while unloading their wares.

Ahead, a squad of soldiers rushes toward a sailing ship resting against the dock. Given all the other activities, with produce being unloaded and teams of horses carting crates away toward the town, the soldiers don't notice the three of them.

Lady de Brooke says, "I need fog."

"Understood," is the reply but there's no one beside her. That one word seems to linger, hanging in the air. Julia may not be able to see that the lady's alone, but Anthony can. He's puzzled. Who replied? And what does she mean by asking for fog? Who wants fog? No one can command the weather. And even if they could, why would they want fog?

"I don't understand," he says, deliberately setting his reply in contrast to that sole mysterious word.

"Patience," the lady says, reaching out and taking his free hand. She leads them across the pier to a coastal fishing boat docked behind a galleon. As the vessel only clears the waterline by a few feet, only its mast is visible from the dock. The three of them will have to climb down a ladder to reach the narrow wheelhouse.

"I'll go first," Anthony says.

"Go where?" Julia asks.

Lady de Brooke places Julia's hand on the side of the ladder, saying, "I need you to climb down to a waiting boat."

"I'll go in front and help you," Anthony says, turning around and backing down the ladder rungs in front of Julia. Gulls squawk, being disturbed and taking flight from where they were nesting on a cross-member beneath the pier. Soldiers look at the commotion, but their eyes glance up as the flock of birds takes flight. Julia follows. Anthony stays three rungs below her, matching her pace. As it's low tide, the mud flats are visible beneath the pier.

"What's that smell?" Julia asks, screwing up her nose.

"It's the pungent waft of freedom," Anthony replies, joking with her.

"Ah, well. I could get used to that."

One of the lady's soldiers waits at the bottom of the ladder. He helps each of them step off onto the gunwales of the fishing boat and down into the hull. The boat is tiny compared to the galleon. The wheelhouse is barely big enough for the shipmaster to shelter behind during inclement weather. The raised deck hides a hold. Given the covers are low, it seems they're intended for a fishing catch and not for the comfort of the crew.

An elderly man works with ropes by the bow. He raises the mainsail. As soon as the lady steps aboard the boat, the soldier helping them climbs onto the ladder. He uses his boot to push the boat away from the pier.

"He's not coming?" Anthony asks, seeing the soldier returning to the dock.

"He'll execute a ruse," the lady says. "He'll distract the guards and lead them away."

"But he'll get caught."

"Oh, no, he won't," she replies, but she doesn't offer an explanation as to why.

The tide is turning. The current draws the fishing boat out into the channel, but they're drifting upriver away from the ocean. They need to sail against the incoming tide to reach the sea, which will make for slow progress.

Above them, soldiers from the Queen's Guard call out to each other. They're searching the docks with the care of a cat pouncing on a new brood of chicks. Carts are dragged to one side. Wooden crates are broken open. A woman screams.

The old man works with the sail, wanting to catch the wind, but for now, the boat drifts back the way they came.

Anthony and Julia crouch behind the gunwale, trying to stay out of sight. To anyone peering down from the dock, they've huddled together like the fugitives they are. A curious young lad looks at them from beside one of the pier footings but he doesn't say anything. Like the girl earlier, he seems keen to help them escape for no other reason than to spite the authorities. Being cruel doesn't engender loyalty so much as frustration from the common folk—and from the look in his eyes, he relishes the opportunity to help.

The lad turns away from them and points further down the docks, past the galleon, yelling, "There they are! They're over there!"

Having added to the confusion, he sneaks away.

Julia nudges Anthony as he peers over the gunwale. "What can you see?"

A squad of soldiers marches along the bank with muskets shouldered. The sheriff has mobilised the London barracks, probably with rumours of treason or rebellion being fomented against the queen or some other convenient lie. Officers prance past on horseback, holding their steeds at a semi-trot as they yell at their men. Flags flutter at the end of pikes. Soldiers ransack the stores along the riverbank searching for the condemned.

Julia nudges him, wanting a response.

"A lot of angry men," he replies.

Fog sweeps around the boat. At first, it's annoying as it obscures Anthony's view of the shore. Within a minute, it's so thick he can no longer see the dock a mere twenty feet away.

From the embankment, someone yells. "Shut down the port! No one leaves until we've found them."

Lady de Brooke stands at the stern with a steady hand on the rudder, guiding their fishing boat on down the river. The sail is full even though there's barely any wind down low near the water. Anthony can't see anything beyond the gloom. The rain has stopped but clouds still rumble overhead, blanketing the city with darkness. Out of the fog, Anthony sees the wooden side of the galleon drift past as they sail down the Thames. They're so close he could reach out and touch the curved planks that form the galleon's hull. Looking up, he can see the battened hatches closed over the gun ports.

The incoming tide reduces their speed to barely a walking pace but the fog hides them from sight. After a few minutes, they've cleared London itself, having drifted past the Tower.

The further they sail from London, the more the fog dissipates.

Fields stretch across the hills. The landscape is dotted with clusters of thick woodland. The wind picks up. Now they're sailing through the countryside, Anthony can see torrential rain still pouring down on the stone buildings within the city. To anyone back there, it must seem as though the storm stretches across the entire land, but it's only over the heart of the city.

Anthony turns to say something to Julia only to notice she's gone from his side. In a panic, he looks around the boat, surprised to see she's ventured to the stern and is sitting beside Lady de Brooke.

As he walks up to them, he hears Julia ask, "Is it magic?"

"No."

Anthony picks up on the conversation, saying, "But you have mastery of the elements. You command the heavens. Is that not witchcraft?"

"To you, it must seem as though I've struck a bargain with the devil, but I haven't. People fear that which they don't understand, but don't—don't be afraid."

"I'm not afraid," Julia says.

Lady de Brooke is silent. It seems she doesn't want to elaborate. For Julia, this is an affront. Being blind, she expects people to accommodate her and answer her questions. She's strident. She crosses her arms over her chest, leaning against the stern of the boat. Like Lady de Brooke, she's seated behind the wheelhouse, which is inset, being half below deck. In fair weather, the shipmaster can sit up on the gunwale and peer over the waist-height cabin. In foul storms, they can retreat and steer from a sheltered position.

Anthony holds onto the side of the wheelhouse as the boat sways, saying, "Like Adam, I know to pick between good and evil. And today you saved us from evil. Witchcraft is the wrong term for whatever it is you wield. What this is, I know not, but 'tis not evil."

"No, it's not," the lady replies.

"Besides, good and evil lie with intent, not type," Anthony says. "A knife can be used to cut lavender or a man's throat. 'Tis not the knife that's evil."

"No, it's not," the lady says, repeating herself and still not elaborating on the way she took command of the storm and lightning, the wind, rain and fog.

Julia says, "It seems to me, evil is a term of convenience for someone like Bishop Blaine. And that's evil in itself."

"And perhaps that's the problem," the lady says, finally opening up, "Perhaps it's the labels we use that are misleading."

"I've seen this in the apothecary," Anthony says.

"You have?" the lady asks. She sounds genuinely surprised by his comment. With a gentle touch on the rudder, she corrects the course of the fishing boat.

"Yes. Sometimes we'll get shipments of curcumin only it'll be labelled curry. It looks the same, but it's not. You have to sniff it to be sure. 'Tis not the label but the contents that determine character."

"I like that," the lady says. "Labels are useful. But labels don't change what's on the inside."

"No, they don't," he replies.

"Watch this," Lady de Brooke says, standing up. She keeps one hand on the tiller while resting the other on top of the wooden wheelhouse. She looks past the full sail, beyond the mast and over the distant fields at the point where the river curves. Anthony is fascinated. She has that same distant look in her eyes as she had back on the dock. Her lips are pursed, ready to speak, but he knows these won't be words intended for his ears.

"Give me a broad low-altitude pressure drop at one mile on this heading."

Anthony can't shake the feeling they're being watched, but who is she talking to? Where are they hiding? Whoever it is, they're a guardian angel.

Julia seems to sense something's about to happen as her knuckles go white, gripping the edge of the gunwale beneath her.

"Ready?" the lady asks, raising her hand and pointing at the sail. As she's facing the bend in the river, Anthony's expecting something to happen in front of them, but instead a gust of wind rushes past from behind, pushing them on. The boat skews sideways slightly as the sails adjust. Waves ripple in their wake.

"Was that witchcraft?" the lady asks.

"No," Anthony says, delighted but not surprised.

"What was it then?"

"I don't know. All I know is it's something I don't understand."

"You are wise beyond your years," the lady says, offering him a smile. "When faced with the unknown, we have a choice: to be afraid or to be curious. Most people are afraid."

"I'm curious," Julia says, releasing her grip on the edge of the boat.

"How do you do these things?" Anthony asks.

"Through knowledge, not magic," the lady replies. "The Latin term is *scientia*. Sir Thomas More calls it science in his writings, but what it means is knowledge applied."

"I know much," Anthony says, "but I cannot apply that to move a ship."

"Can't you?" the lady asks. "Are we not moving according to science? Ships sink all the time, but this one floats. Why?"

"Um. I—I don't know."

"You may not know, but the shipbuilder does."

"He does," Anthony concedes, nodding.

"And this is important," the lady says. "It matters not who knows but that someone knows. No one can know everything. But together, we can know enough to sail the oceans."

Julia says, "So your mastery of the storm is no different from sailing a ship?"

"No. They're the same. In both cases, it's the way we exploit what we know that makes a difference."

Anthony laughs. "And now I want to know how a boat floats."

"This is why you should read," the lady says, shaking her finger playfully at him. "Books are the building blocks of past generations. They're stepping stones across the stream of ignorance."

Anthony is impatient. "So why do some boats float while others sink?"

"The Greek philosopher Archimedes figured this out well over a thousand years before you were born. He discovered a simple principle: buoyancy. He knew that if a ship weighed less than the same amount of water in the same space, the ocean beneath the ship would try to rush in and push it up, keeping it afloat. As soon as it's heavier, it sinks."

Anthony looks at the deck of the fishing boat and then at the water rushing past as they sail on, saying, "Huh."

"He knew," Julia says.

"He did. People had sailed in boats for thousands of years, but no one understood why they worked, only that they did. Once Archimedes explained the process, others could make bigger and better boats."

Julia says, "They used that knowledge."

"Yes. And it exposes a flaw in our reasoning process. Most people think gold is valuable or that kings and queens rule the world. Nothing could be further from the truth. Your world is governed by knowledge. It's those who harness what they know who have mastery over nature. Knowledge is worth more than all the riches of the world."

Anthony says, "And you know how to bend the wind to your will."

"I do, but it's not that extraordinary. Think of all that surrounds you, all the things you take for granted. Think about how remarkable they are. How is it that rocks dug out of the ground can be melted in a furnace and transformed into steel? How is it that wind can be caught by a mill and used to grind flour without the need for a workhorse? Or consider how a spring and gears can be used within a clock to count out time."

Anthony likes her logic. Rather than questioning her further, he adds to her examples, showing he's embraced her point. "And how is it that fires can be struck from a flint but not a river stone? Or that black powder can propel an iron ball from a cannon?"

"Indeed," the lady says. "It all comes down to knowledge."

Julia says, "And you know more than we do."

"I do."

"So you can do more with that knowledge," Anthony says.

"Yes. The so-called witchcraft the bishop fears is nothing but the mastery of all that can be understood about this world."

"But... but..." Julia says, "this is marvellous! Why wouldn't he want to learn from you?"

"Those in power fear nothing but change," the lady says. "The bishop fears losing his hold over the people. Questions are more dangerous than a fixed bayonet or a loaded musket. Remember, it takes but a single spark to ignite a keg of gunpowder and destroy an armoury. The bishop knows this. He cannot allow sparks from the flint that is your questioning minds. He has no choice. If he is to continue in his authority, he must snuff you out before you snuff out his ideas."

"He's cruel," Julia says.

"His cruelty has a point," the lady replies. "He seeks to deter even the simplest of doubts for these are the sparks that will set the church alight."

"But why us?" Anthony asks. "What reason could he have for capturing us? We're nothing and no one."

"His authority rests on obedience, not reason. As soon as someone thinks for themselves, he must act or he'll lose what little hold he has over them. Fear is his only weapon. He needs the populace to be afraid. If they're not, they'll find the courage they need for change."

The old man has been sitting near the bow, tending to the sail. He rises on weary legs. Wooden planks creak beneath his boots. He's noticed something moving along the shore behind them. He points. He's spotted a rider long before either Anthony or Julia heard the clomp of hooves or saw the flicker of shadows rushing through the forest. A dark horse gallops along the path following the riverbank. It passes in and out of a thicket of trees.

"There be news coming," he calls out to the lady.

"I see him," Lady de Brooke replies, steering the boat in toward shore. She sails close to the bank. The rider pulls up ahead of them and dismounts.

As they sail past not more than twenty feet from shore, he throws a leather purse, calling out, "Fare thee well, m'lady. Safe sails to you and your kin."

"Thank you, Mark," she replies.

The old man catches the purse. He undoes a thin leather strap and pulls out a crumpled sheet of paper.

He approaches the wheelhouse, reading from it as he says, "M'lady. The estate is in flames. They know we've fled by water. The sheriff has petitioned the lords for charges of insurrection against the House of de Brooke. He's forged the writs for pursuit."

The old man points behind the boat, adding, "And they've dispatched a galleon. We'll have their measure in the river, but once we reach the sea, they'll be able to unfurl their full sails and overtake us."

"And the *Santa Cruz*?" the lady asks, looking back over her shoulder at the galleon several miles behind them.

"She's sailing under the Spanish flag of Guipúzcoa."

"Has she made landfall in England?"

The old man scratches his balding head, saying, "No. I was told she's carrying cargo from Rotterdam to Bilbao and then on to Lisbon. Once there, she departs for the Indies."

"And she's in the Channel? You're sure of that?"

"Aye. Mackelraven and I smuggled brandy from her on her northward passage four weeks ago. We have an agreement to meet again, exchanging wool for wine to avoid port taxes."

"And she'll wait?" the lady asks, sounding worried.

"Aye, they want that wool. It'll fetch a fair price in Portugal."

"And my lord?"

The old man glances back down, looking at the paper in his hands. "Lord de Brooke is riding south. He's heading for Hastings where he'll commission a vessel to bring him to the *Santa Cruz* as we pass through the Strait of Dover."

"Very good."

He hands the sheet of paper to her. Anthony is curious why she didn't read it for herself. As she takes hold of the page, he catches a glimpse of the text. There are no words or letters. Various symbols such as squares, rectangles, triangles, stars and arrows adorn the page. There are dozens of shapes he doesn't recognise.

"What language is that?" Anthony asks.

The old man beats the lady to her reply, saying, "That, m'boy. 'Tis the smuggler's code. Most of it is gibberish, meant to confuse anyone not in the know."

"Knowledge, huh?" Anthony replies.

"Knowledge is the key that unlocks prison doors," the old man says. He turns and heads back to the bow.

The lady says, "There are hundreds of local variations of the code. They're used to thwart the authorities."

She tears the sheet of paper into tiny pieces and scatters them on the water as they sail on.

Galleon

The sun is setting in the west as they reach the mouth of the Thames in the east. Shadows stretch across distant hills. The riverbank, so close beside them for most of their journey, is now easily a mile away on either side of the Thames. They sail out into the bay. Waves rise around them. The sea is choppy. The point at which the river meets the ocean is turbulent. Their small boat rocks on the growing swell. The old man pulls on the main line, trimming the sail.

"The Red Lion is gaining on us," he yells, pointing over the stern.

The galleon looms behind them, gaining on them. Dozens of sailors climb the rigging, rushing up the sloping rope ladders that flank each mast. While it was in the river, the galleon only had its lower course sail set. Now the captain means to unfurl the topsails and topgallants on all three masts. Once they're up in the rigging, dozens of sailors work their way along the yards, dangling easily fifty feet above the deck. Working in unison, they swing on the foot ropes beneath each yard and release the heavy canvas sails. Down below, more sailors work with block and tackle to set the stays and bow lines.

With its square-rigged sails unfurled, the galleon rides through the waves with ease, sending out a wake before it. Their pursuers have reduced the distance to within half a mile.

"They're getting close," Anthony says, turning and peering over the gunwale. He's nervous. Julia squeezes his hand. She may not be able to see, but she can feel the fishing boat struggling in the deep water. Lady de Brooke works with the tiller, watching their heading and seeking to maximise their speed.

Anthony asks what to him seems to be an obvious question. "You can control the wind. Can't we use that to escape?"

"They're too close," the lady says. "Any wind we create will benefit both ships. Don't worry. We'll lose them in the dark. They might be bigger and faster, but we're more nimble."

An errant wave crashes against the side of the hull, sending salt spray washing across the deck. The boat rocks.

"What about a storm?" Julia asks. "Like the one during the execution?"

"It'll hinder us more than them," Lady de Brooke replies. "They're big enough to ride the waves. No, we need to focus on reaching the *Santa Cruz*. She's waiting for us out in the Channel."

"I fear we won't make it," Anthony says.

Thunder rumbles in the twilight, but the sky is clear. Anthony peers back at the galleon. The sun sits low on the horizon. A puff of smoke drifts from the bow of the warship. Seconds later, a column of water erupts several hundred yards behind them, rising like a geyser from the depths of the ocean.

"They're firing on us," Anthony says, feeling panicked.

"They're ranging their culverins," the lady says. "If anything, they're firing short and heavy. They won't reach us."

Julia whispers, "What's a culverin?"

"A cannon," Anthony replies. "A cannon with a really long barrel for accuracy."

Julia grips Anthony's hand, interlocking her fingers with his. Her knuckles go white. She shakes her head. It's subtle. Most people would miss her slight motion, but Anthony knows what she's signalling: *this is not good—we need to get out of here.* But there's something about her posture that tells him it's not the culverins she's worried about. It's the way her head tilts slightly, listening to the slap of water against the hull.

Back at the apothecary, Julia could ferret out a rat in the crowd. Sitting there on the windowsill, she'd pick out a thief with little more than a few words drifting on the wind. It didn't matter that she was blind. It was their confidence. Unlike other buyers, they'd have a little more resonance in their voice. She'd nudge him and point without making it obvious. Anthony would then describe what he saw: a young man in a cream tunic with a black waistcoat. "Watch him," she'd say. "He's after the carpet seller's purse."

Anthony never asked her how she knew. For him, it was nigh on impossible to pick out individual voices in the bluster of the market, but Julia would twist her head slightly, picking up on the direction and blocking out the cacophony of other noises. And she was always right. With a few boisterous words, a bit of misdirection and a kind-but-fake smile, the thief would lift a purse without the seller noticing. On that particular occasion, Anthony dropped down onto the edge of the gutter and pushed through the crowd. He came up behind the young man with a shiv in his hand. Taking him by one shoulder, he gently rested the point against the man's hip, saying, "Wouldn't it be nice to walk away intact?" In a flash, the trickster's confidence was gone. With stooped shoulders and a trembling hand, he returned the purse and rushed off through the crowd—and all without turning to face Anthony, such was his shame.

In the same way, Anthony realises Julia's got a sense of what's about to happen out here in the bay. To him, there's a rough swell rocking the boat, but nothing more. He's been to sea before. Never quite this far, but he's been out far enough to vomit with the unrelenting motion.

Gulls circle overhead, looking for fish scraps as they fly around the boat. The galleon is still well behind them and struggling with the shifting winds within the bay. Their fishing vessel is lighter than the galleon. It rides up over most of the waves, but Julia's worried. She senses something the others can't. It would be easy for Anthony to dismiss her concerns because she's blind and vulnerable, but he knows her too well. For Julia, blindness isn't an impediment. Others may look on her with pity, but he understands her strengths. Being blind has heightened her other senses.

Lady de Brooke stands in the footwell of the wheelhouse, yelling over the wind as she directs the old man on how she needs the sail set. Julia sinks below the edge of the gunwale. She slumps down and sits with her back against the wooden hull, keeping her legs up close to her chest. Anthony sits beside her.

"How far are we from shore?" she asks.

"Ah," Anthony replies, craning his neck as he looks to either side. "On our left, it's several miles. To the right, maybe half a mile. Maybe more. Why?"

"Can you swim?"

"What? No. I mean, I can frolic in a lake but not out here. The waves are too big."

"We need crates. Empty crates."

"Crates?" he asks, confused. "I don't understand."

"To keep us afloat while we make for shore."

"You want to jump overboard?" Anthony asks as the fishing boat is pushed roughly to one side by another wave coming at them from starboard. Spray washes across the deck. The stern skews in the water. Lady de Brooke turns the tiller in toward the wave, but it's already passed. She returns the fishing boat to its heading as the swell rolls beneath them. Waves break across the bow.

Julia says, "No, silly. But when this boat turns over—and it will—we'll need something to hold onto while we kick for shore."

"How do you know we're going to sink?"

"The waves," she says. "The ones that hit from the side. Most of the waves come from in front, but those that slap the side of the hull, they're getting stronger."

"And you think they're going to tip us over?"

Julia ignores his question. "I've been counting them. I can hear them slapping against the wood. There are twenty against the bow and then there's one from the side. Every third wave from the side is bigger than anything that came before."

"And you think—"

"Listen," she says, pointing at the hold even though she can't see the hatch. "Can't you hear the water sloshing around down there? With each wave that washes over us, we sit lower in the water. It's only a matter of time before we're swamped. Time is the only factor. Nothing else."

"So you're not worried about the galleon firing at us?"

"No. The lady's right. We're too small to hit. And we're able to turn faster than the galleon. The waves, though..."

"I've got to tell Lady—"

Julia cuts him off, gripping his forearm with her thin, boney fingers. "Crate first."

"Yes, of course," he replies. Being blind, Julia needs the assurance of knowing she can survive being tipped into the sea. The fishing boat has seats running along both the port and starboard sides of the hull. When they first boarded the boat, the seats made it easy to step down onto the deck. Most of the seats have hinges, which is a sign they're used for storage.

Anthony gets to his feet. He's unsteady. He shifts his legs wide and staggers over to the nearest storage seat. On lifting the wooden lid, he sees a crate full of knives, ropes and some netting. He pulls it out and swings it upside down, dumping its contents back into the storage hold. The lid slams shut with the rocking of the boat. With one hand on the gunwale, Anthony reaches over, giving the crate to Julia. She senses it's near and grabs at it, clutching it to her chest.

"M'lady," Anthony says, holding onto the wooden surround of the wheelhouse as he approaches her.

"Not now."

Behind her, the galleon rises on the swell. Its bow crashes down, sending spray rushing out across the ocean. Two shots break over the wind. Thunder reverberates across the waves. The first shot strikes the ocean not more than fifty feet behind them, sending up a water spout that plummets back into the waves. The second strikes not more than ten feet to port, sending up a wall of water. The spray catches the sail. Had that shot struck their boat, it would have plunged through the hull, sinking them in an instant.

Behind him, Julia's counting aloud. Anthony hears her reach twenty. She calls out, "Brace!"

Anthony leans into the side of the wheelhouse with his legs spread wide behind him. A wave strikes the side of the hull. Water crashes over the gunwale. Foam rushes across the deck before draining away. Salt spray hangs in the air.

"You're missing the problem," Anthony says as seawater runs down his cheeks.

"The problem," Lady de Brooke says, correcting him. "Is we are about to be overrun by a galleon."

"That's not the real problem."

"And what is the real problem?" she asks, staring at him.

"The waves striking our starboard hull. They're swamping us. They're slowing us down. And soon enough—"

"We have to outrun that galleon," the lady says, snapping at him. Waves rock the boat. Wet hair clings to her cheeks. The lines of her face have hardened with determination. Her eyes stare dead ahead, watching the line she's sailing. At the bow, the old man has stripped down to his undershirt. He works with the lines, tightening ropes and trimming the sail.

"No, we don't," Anthony says, not afraid of contradicting her. "We have to stay afloat."

"What?"

She looks at him bewildered. To her, the idea of running from the galleon must seem obvious. They're being chased. They need to escape. The problem is—that's not the most pressing problem. Julia figured it out, and Anthony's been around her long enough to trust her judgement.

He says, "We can't outrun them. And we're taking on water. We'll sink before we're hit by their iron shot."

Lady de Brooke looks at him as though he's mad—and he is. He's no sailor. He's taking advice from a blind girl. He must look ridiculous standing there soaking wet. It's then she laughs. Her clothing is dripping wet as well. Damp cotton sticks to the pale skin on her arms.

"Right you are," she says, smiling. "And what would you have us do?"

"Face them," Anthony replies.

"You want me to turn around?" a bewildered Lady de Brooke asks. "And square off against a galleon?"

"We can't keep sailing into rough water. Whether by wave or culverin, we'll never make the *Santa Cruz*."

"And you would have us turn and surrender?"

"Not surrender," he replies. "You said it yourself, our advantage lies in being nimble. We need to use that advantage. At the moment, they have the advantage of size and speed. We need to take that away from them."

Lady de Brooke bellows at the top of her voice. "Prepare to come about!"

The old man looks at her as though she's mad, but she repeats her command, saying, "Make the rigging for beating upwind. I mean to tack toward the galleon."

He responds, yelling, "Aye, m'lady."

"Coming about," she yells, pushing hard on the tiller and pointing the bow into the waves. The fishing boat rides up on the swell. Water crashes around them. Julia clings to the crate, still holding it close to her chest. Waves splash against the hull. Salt spray hangs in the air around them.

Once he's fastened the lines, the old man makes his way to the stern, asking Lady de Brooke, "What compels you, ma'am?" He points. "We're no match for a warship."

The galleon is barely a quarter of a mile away, cutting through the sea with its sails billowing in the wind. The sun has set. Clouds dot the sky. They're being lit up in golden yellows, pinks, reds and blues as they catch the last rays of sunshine.

"Denying them opportunity," the lady replies to the old man. "We'll cut back in toward the lee of the shore where the waves are slight. That galleon is in full sail. It'll take them at least an hour and several miles to execute a turn in pursuit. By then, we'll be under the cover of darkness."

"We'll be within range of their culverins, m'lady!"

"We will, but the two they've dragged on the forward deck will be useless. They'll range long."

"But a broadside?"

"A broadside needs to be prepared," the lady says, pointing past the bow of the fishing vessel at the bow of the galleon thundering toward them over the ocean. "We'll feint to their port side and tack to starboard, leaving them staring out at the waves as we sail past on the far side."

"Aye."

Ahead of them, the warship rocks and sways, crashing through waves as it charges at them. The lady's assessment of their tactics is correct. In the dim light, Anthony can see hatches being opened on the port side as that's where their current setting will take them. Bronze barrels extend from the darkened interior. Sailors line the deck, keen to see the action. Within a matter of minutes, the galleon is looming ahead of them, threatening to crush them.

"On my command," the lady yells, pushing the tiller even further over and ostensibly committing her boat to pass on the port side of the warship as it bears down on them. Waves crash against the hull of the galleon. Its bow rides up and down as its captain steers a course to crush their fishing boat.

The lady yells, "Tacking!"

The old man scrambles, releasing lines and pulling on ropes as she swings the fishing vessel around. In those precious few seconds, they're caught dead in the water with the wind rushing past their flaccid sail. For a moment, it seems as though the galleon is going to ride up over them. The fishing boat, though, has momentum. The lateen rigging swings across and catches the wind on the far side. Immediately, their vessel is drawn the other way. The fishing boat cuts across the bow of the galleon, passing within ten feet of the warship as the old man rushes to secure the lines. The wake coming off the warship pushes them on, brushing them past its broad hull. For a moment, they're riding the wave pushed up by the galleon itself. It sweeps them on.

The wooden hull of the galleon rushes by mere feet from their fishing boat. The warship towers over them. There's yelling from up on deck. Muskets are fired, but the shots are futile. With the rolling of the sea and the motion of both vessels, accuracy is not assured. Four shots are wasted, splashing harmlessly in the sea. One shot punches through the sail, but they're already racing past the stern of the warship by this point and heading to dark water.

Lady de Brooke smiles at Anthony, nodding her head in appreciation.

The old man says, "You've done us well, lad."

Julia smiles. Anthony wants to say something and credit her, but he knows her too well. She'd shy from any attention.

As the galleon drops away behind the fishing vessel, Anthony spies sailors rushing up the rigging, desperate to gather their sails and come about. The fishing boat catches a fair wind, whether that is by means of nature or the lady, Anthony is unsure, but it carries them on at a fair pace.

With the moon rising over the horizon, the galleon is easily visible in the distance. It's already side on and coming about, albeit slowly.

"I need cover," the lady says. Anthony is wise enough not to ask to whom she's speaking. Within minutes, thick clouds blot out the Moon, allowing them to hide in the darkness. Lady de Brooke makes as though she's turning north toward the coast before cutting back to the south several minutes later. She means to mislead anyone watching through a spyglass on the galleon.

The Santa Cruz

Hours pass like entire nights spent listless and languid.

Lady de Brooke sails close to the southern coast leading out into the English Channel, where the sea is calmer and the waves are more consistent. The ocean swell still rocks the boat with a steady motion. Occasionally, choppy waves send up a fine mist as the bow crashes against them, but the fishing vessel is no longer being swamped.

Anthony and Julia huddle next to each other at the back of the boat, staying low and out of the wind. Their clothes are damp.

Boredom sets in.

The sky above is clear, allowing the stars to shine down on them. Lightning crackles in a storm several miles away off the port side of their vessel, out in the middle of the bay. Large clouds billow in the moonlight, stretching along the horizon.

"Is that you?" Anthony asks.

"Yes," the lady replies. "I'm using a storm to drive them northeast, away from us."

"How are you going to find the *Santa Cruz*?"

Lady de Brooke points slightly to one side of the mast, saying, "She's roughly forty miles that way."

"You can see her?"

"Not I, but I know someone who can."

Anthony lets that comment slide, knowing any answer she might give would lie beyond his understanding.

"Where are we going?" Julia asks. The meaning of her question is curious. It's not the *Santa Cruz* that concerns her, it's the ship's destination.

"Where can we go?" Anthony asks.

"To the new world." When neither of them replies, the lady adds, "To the Indies of the west. There is an island there. Cuba. Its principal is Havana, a small Spanish port, but there are French, Portuguese and English settlers on the land. You will be able to start a new life there."

Julia is conspicuously quiet. Anthony may have wanted to sail the oceans and explore new lands, but that's his dream, not hers. They've talked at length about his wandering desire. Julia made it clear she felt no such compulsion. She was content sitting on the ledge of the apothecary, dreaming about the comings and goings of the markets. For someone that's blind, there's more to fear than hope for in a new land. Lady de Brooke must sense this as well.

"You'll have a purse, I promise. You won't have to beg."

Rather than nod, Julia hangs her head. Anthony puts his arm around her shoulder and pulls her in tight. He doesn't offer any words of consolation. What could be said? The future is a fog descending on a strange town. Without a map, it's impossible to know what lies out there in the mist.

"Try to get some sleep," the lady says.

As they sail into the lee of the Kent hills, a fair wind rolls down from the forests surrounding Canterbury. The wave height subsides. The sea becomes unusually calm. Anthony suspects the lady is weaving her magic again. He's about to ask her about it when he corrects himself, remembering that what seems like sorcery to him is merely another, higher form of knowledge.

Anthony remembers the first time he saw black powder burning. Sparks leaped into the night. Master Dunmore imported some powder for a local blacksmith and wanted to entertain his young charge. He waited until after dusk and then sprinkled a trail on the pavement, weaving a line several feet long that led to a pile not more than an inch in height. He mixed a few other powders in with the black but wouldn't say what they were. He told Anthony it was a waste, but it seems even he wanted to see the powder burn naked for himself; such is the novelty of fire even for adults. The master used a candle stem to light a wick leading to the powder and stood back.

Anthony expected the black trail to flash like a musket firing with a thundering boom to follow, but it sizzled. Seeing black powder burn freely on the cobblestones was a surprising delight. There was something magical about watching a flame dance its way along an uneven trail. Grey smoke billowed from the glowing tip of the flame as it advanced along the path. Flickers of yellow and red shot into the air. The smell was pungent, lashing his nostrils, but he didn't care.

After several seconds, the flame reached the pile. Green sparks leaped into the air. Like falling stars, dozens of thin red embers shot out across the alley. A yellow flash glowed like the sun, even if only for a fraction of a second. Anthony watched in awe as a vast cloud of smoke folded in on itself, rising into the night air.

But it wasn't magic.

It looked like magic, but it was elemental. There was a prescribed process that could be followed to replicate the effect. Far from being an illusion, it was an unveiling of all that lay potential in the powder all along. A spark was needed, not magic. Sitting there in the back of the fishing boat, Anthony realises the same is true now. Whatever mastery Lady de Brooke has over the weather, it's not because she's in league with the devil but rather because she understands how the weather forms. Like Master Dunmore, such mastery isn't the result of angels or demons. It's knowledge that unleashes power.

Julia leans into his shoulder. After a few minutes, her body goes limp. The gentle rocking of the boat has lulled her to sleep. Anthony shifts to get comfortable. He lies on a crumpled heap of canvas and, within minutes, falls asleep as well.

Water laps gently against a wooden hull. Ordinarily, a soothing sound wouldn't wake Anthony, but he's suddenly aware their fishing boat is at rest. He opens his eyes. The sail has been lowered. The Moon is high overhead, meaning the night is long. He's been asleep for hours. The lapping of the water, though, is not coming from the fishing boat as it is riding high on the gentle swell. A dark wooden hull looms beside him. His first thought is one of alarm. *The galleon!*

A sailor up on the aft deck of the ship throws a rope over the gunwale. It unravels and splashes in the water by the bow of their boat. The old man gathers it and ties off the bow. He uses an oar to position the fishing vessel along the hull of the vast ship, bringing them gently alongside. Lady de Brooke reaches out for a rope ladder hanging over the hull. She pulls on it, making sure it's secure. Before stepping up, she looks back, seeing the concern on Anthony's face.

"It's the *Santa Cruz*," she says. "We made it."

Julia sits up, stretching as she yawns.

"Come," the lady says. "Let's get on board."

"We're here?" Julia asks.

Anthony looks around, staring out across the still, moonlit waters. If they're near land, it's on the far side of the *Santa Cruz* as he can't see anything beyond a warm glow on the horizon. He leads Julia across the deck and places her hands on the rope ladder. She climbs up as Lady de Brooke is helped over the railing by her husband.

Before heading up to join them, Anthony turns to the old man, knowing he risked his life to help them.

He says, "Thank you, kind sir," even though the elderly fisherman is roughly in the same social station as both he and Master Dunmore. Sir seems appropriate.

"I wish you fair weather and following winds," the old man says, smiling. He reaches out, taking hold of a cargo net being lowered from the ship on a wooden crane swung over the gunwales. Several crates sit in the net. Once the net is resting on the deck of the boat, he's able to remove the crates. Anthony helps him as Julia climbs out of sight. The two of them stack the crates on the deck as the boat sways beneath them.

"Ah, you've got a good heart," the man says, opening the hold. "And a hand with these, if you don't mind."

"Sure."

Waterlogged bales of wool lie beneath the deck. They'd be stupidly heavy when dry. With seawater dripping from them, they might as well be blocks of clay. There are only four, but it's exhausting work to lift them. Once they're in the cargo net, the sailors on deck haul them up. Anthony and the old man shift the crates of wine down into the hold.

Anthony jokes with him about the alcohol, saying, "Your fish are pickled."

The old man laughs as he replaces the cover over the hold. "Aye. These will fetch a sweet penny in the markets."

Anthony steps up onto the rope ladder. He's expecting the old man to follow him up to the deck of the *Santa Cruz*, but once Anthony's halfway up, the old man releases the guideline. He calls out to the captain, thanking him for the haul. Then he uses an oar to push away from the *Santa Cruz*.

Anthony pauses on the ladder. Out of necessity, he's facing the wooden timber forming the hull of the *Santa Cruz*, which is frustrating. He feels compelled to turn around on the ladder and watch the old man depart. Anthony and Julia's lives have been irrevocably changed in the space of a single day. When soldiers and priests sought to kill them, the old man showed them kindness, helping them escape.

Anthony knows his life will never be the same. Everything that felt so normal and routine is gone, never to return. He knows he'll never see Master Dunmore again or the apothecary with its courtyard garden in full bloom. What will the master think of him fleeing the city? He'll be glad he's escaped, but he'll worry about him being tracked down and captured. The bishop has a long memory, and the sheriff a long reach.

By now, a bounty would have been placed upon the three of them. Who can they trust? And for how long? Someone they trust today could betray them tomorrow—and all for a pretty purse. Standing there on one of the rungs of the rope ladder, watching as the fishing boat drifts away on the current, Anthony sets his eye on the old man as he raises his lateen sail. The ageing man tugs on a line running up the mast and back down to the heavy canvas. His is a hard life. It takes all his effort to raise the sail.

Anthony can't help but think this is his last chance to return to England. He wonders about the future. It's impossible to know what he should do. Part of him wants to call out to the old man and beg him to take them back to land. He and Julia could head to Wessex or even as far as Cornwall. The bishop would be none the wiser. They could disappear in their own land rather than that of the Spanish or French. As for the Indies, what awaits them there? Good or ill? It's not possible to know what the future holds.

For all Anthony's talk of escaping to the new world, now he longs for home. His mother will be worried sick about him. His father will no doubt make discreet inquiries, but he too will be saddened by his son's sudden departure. Anthony wonders if he could sneak back into his home to gather his belongings and into the apothecary to collect his wages. Would the sheriff pay someone to watch for his return? How long would that last? At some point, the bishop will move his ire along to the next poor soul.

"Ant. Are you there?" Julia asks, sounding worried as she leans over the side, looking for him with blind eyes.

"Coming," he replies, swinging around and continuing up the outside of the hull. One of the sailors offers him a hand, helping him over the gunwale.

The captain issues the command to weigh anchor. Six men lean into the wooden beams protruding from the circular capstan on the foredeck. To Anthony's mind, the capstan looks like a purpose-built wooden barrel not unlike those Master Dunmore used to ship wheat in bulk. The men heave, pushing their way around the capstan as they wind in the thick rope securing the anchor. The last ten yards are dominated by a heavy iron chain. As the anchor is drawn out of the depths, it scrapes against a metal guard on the side of the hull. Once the links are wound around the massive wooden spindle, the men use a locking pin to secure the anchor.

Dawn is breaking.

Sailors climb the rigging, scrambling up rope ladders to unfurl the sails from the horizontal yard. The mast creaks. Ropes groan as the sails fill with wind.

"Talk to me," Julia says, clutching his arm and leaning into him. "What can you see?"

"Ah," he replies, unsure where to start. "The sails are being lowered on the fore, the main and the mizzen."

"All three masts?"

"Yes. And I can see sailors climbing out over the water to lower the bowsprit."

"And the lines?"

"Oh, there are rope lines running everywhere. I—I have no idea what they do, but sailors are working to tighten some and release others. They're careful to coil their loose ropes and stow any batons and braces. It's chaotic and yet it isn't. There are men everywhere working on the rigging, but it's with purpose. They know their role. They work with block and tackle to set the sails."

"I can feel the breeze on my cheeks," she says. "And I can feel the ship starting to move."

"Yes," Anthony says. "We're underway."

"And our patrons?"

"Lord and Lady de Brooke are standing beside the captain on the poop deck. The helmsman is working the wheel, wanting to catch more of the breeze."

Julia's face lights up. "Can we go there?"

"We can go anywhere," Anthony replies, leading her on.

He steps up onto the gangway linking the decks, knowing she'll feel him rise and realise there are steps in front of her. She follows along half a step behind, hanging on to his arm. If at any point, a crate or bits of rigging block her path, he gently guides her around them, whispering the name of the obstruction. Gulls soar on the wind, barely flapping their wings as they circle the ship. Several of them land on the cross-tree at the top of the main mast. They seem content to stow away with them on this voyage.

"Are we near land?"

Anthony looks around. "No."

As the two of them approach Lord and Lady de Brooke, the tone of their patrons' conversation changes. Whatever they were talking about in hushed whispers, it was intense.

"You two—again!" the lord says, but he's not angry. He's smiling.

Based on the sound of his voice, Julia offers a cheerful wave with her free hand. Her other hand, though, clenches Anthony's arm. She's nervous. For her, all this must be unsettling. What little control she had over her life has vanished. Being blind, she's at the mercy of those around her.

"I'm sorry, m'lord," Anthony says. "Neither of us meant for this to happen."

"Oh, it's not your fault," Lord de Brooke says. "Once, the sheriff could be reasoned with. Now that the bishop has his ear, he's convinced righteousness is only found in obedience to the church. Only the church is swayed more by sovereigns than scripture. Few have the courage to stand against either man, so I commend you for your hearty spirit."

Anthony nods, surprised by the lord's generous assessment.

"We were preparing to leave England anyway," Lady de Brooke says. "Perhaps not so soon, but our stay was coming to an end."

Anthony says, "I'm sorry about your estate."

Lord de Brooke looks confused. His brow narrows. His head twists slightly as he turns toward his wife, wanting clarification.

"The house was razed to the ground," Lady de Brooke says.

"Ah, yes. Of course."

For someone that just lost an entire estate to fire, Lord de Brooke doesn't seem bothered at all. From what Anthony saw through the windows, there were landscape paintings, exquisite mechanical clocks, gilded candelabras and dainty polished furniture spread throughout the home. The trappings of just one room within the mansion would have been worth more than Anthony could earn in a lifetime working at the apothecary.

"Be sure to accustom yourself to the *Santa Cruz*," Lady de Brooke says. "We have two ports of call before we cross the Atlantic. This will be your home for the next four months."

"Thank you, m'lady," Julia says, offering a curtsy. On seeing her motion, Anthony bows.

"The stairs on the quarter deck will lead you to the Orlop deck three levels down. I've secured you a steward's room. You'll find it at the point the mizzen mast passes through the deck. You'll need to acquaint yourselves with the head and the galley, but for now, go up to the bowsprit. We have dolphins leading us on."

"Thank you, m'lady," Anthony says, taking his leave of her and guiding Julia away.

"What's a dolphin?" Julia asks as he leads her down the stairs.

"I don't know. Let's find out," he replies.

On reaching the bow, Anthony sees a canvas weather cover bunched up against the gunwale. It makes for a comfortable seat. He sits so he can look past the bowsprit mast at the sea below. Water rushes past. A wake is kicked up by the ship as it cuts through the ocean.

"What are they like? These dolphins?" Julia asks, still holding him by the upper arm, although her grip has relaxed.

"Um, I don't see... Oh, how wonderful."

"What? What is it you see?"

"Ah, just a flicker. A flash of grey rushing along beside us. There are several of them. They duck and weave through the waves."

"What do they look like?"

"I can't see them."

"What do you mean you can't see them? You can see."

"They're too fast. They're a blur within the waves. They rise and sink out of sight. All I can see is—oh!"

"Oh, what?" she asks, squeezing his arm.

"They jump."

"They jump?" Julia asks, confused. "How can they jump? Aren't they fish? They don't have legs, right?"

"No. I don't think so."

"And there's nothing for them to push off."

"Nothing but the sea itself," Anthony replies. "And yet they do. They jump out of the water, clearing the surface entirely before plunging back into the ocean. And, oh, their bodies. They're slick with water. They have tails and fins but not those of a fish."

"What do you mean—not of a fish."

"Fish have scales. Their fins have ridges, and they flex. These are fixed. They're smooth. And they're thick. They're muscular. These dolphins are much bigger than any fish I've ever seen in the market."

"How big are they?" Julia asks.

"Um, the size of a goat," Anthony replies. "Or perhaps a horse. But they're much faster."

From behind him, a familiar voice says, "They have far more in common with a horse than you think."

Anthony turns to see Lady de Brooke leaning against the gunwale with a smile on her face.

She says, "Dolphins may look like fish. They may swim like fish and feed like fish, but they're not fish. Like deer, they suckle their young. And their bodies are warm, not cold like a fish. They—"

A hand takes hold of her elbow from behind, causing her to stop mid-sentence.

"Enough," Lord de Brooke says. "We cannot do this. We can't

interfere."

"I was just providing observations," the lady says.

"Observations they and their kind should make—not us."

"Of course," she says, lowering her head and walking away.

Once the two of them are gone, Julia asks, "What was that about? Why did he not want her to tell us about dolphins?"

"Because of knowledge," Anthony says. "I know not who they are, but the lord and lady thrive on knowing more than we can dare imagine."

The Stars

The day is long.

A warm breeze carries their ship on as the night descends once more.

The *Santa Cruz* sails along a rugged coastline. The land looks dry. Windblown cliffs give way to woodlands, but they're nothing like the fertile fields of Kent or the brilliant green forests that dot the coast near Dover. When they departed England, dry land lay to their starboard side. Now, it is to port. At a guess, they're sailing close to France.

After dinner, Anthony and Julia sit on the wooden cover of the main hold, looking out across the ocean at the stars. Lady de Brooke joins them. She doesn't say anything but Julia seems to recognise either her footfall or the scent of her perfume as she turns toward her. The lady sweeps her dress beneath her as she sits on the raised hatch.

"What can you see?" Julia asks. She's not talking to Anthony, so he remains silent.

"The depths of an endless ocean dotted with islands," the lady replies, but her voice is distant. Her gaze is toward the heavens, not the sea.

"What of the constellations?" Julia asks. "Which can you see?"

"The constellations are an oddity," the lady replies, facing Julia even though she knows she can't see her.

"What do you mean?"

Anthony says, "They're specks of paint. There's no lion of Leo or woman of Virgo. The constellations exist only in our imagination."

"This is true," the lady says, "The stars suggest nothing but their own majesty."

"What are they?" Julia asks.

"You wouldn't understand."

"They're far away," Anthony says. "Like a lighthouse on the horizon."

"Up close, they're big," the lady says. "Bigger than anything you could imagine."

"Bigger than the apothecary?" Julia asks.

"Bigger than the ocean on which we sail," the lady replies.

"But they look so small," Anthony says.

"They are a very long way from us. And they're bright."

"How bright?" Julia asks.

"As bright as the sun. Some are brighter."

Julia is curious. "They're as bright as the sun, and yet they've been banished into the night?"

"It sounds strange, doesn't it?" the lady says. "How can something so bright be surrounded by darkness?"

There's no doubt in Anthony's mind that the lady understands far more about the stars than he'll ever know, but he wants to contribute. He wants to grasp ideas greater than his own. He pushes himself to imagine how this could be possible.

"They're like candles in a window," he says. "Within a cottage, there's light enough to read, but from the road winding through the fields, out far from the village, they're but tiny specks of light."

"That they are," Lady de Brooke says, resting her hands on the wooden hatch on either side of her and pressing against the lid. She gets up. Anthony knows she's probably already said more than she should—more than she would if her lord were here, but Anthony must know more.

"Wait," he says, getting her to pause but unsure how to continue.

Anthony has heard Master Dunmore talking about the Prussian scholar Mikołaj Kopernik and his heretical views so despised by Bishop Blaine in his liturgies and sermons. If the ideas of Mikołaj infuriate the bishop, perhaps they would please the lady.

Anthony struggles to recall the name of the book Master Dunmore showed him. It was written in German. Anthony recognised letters but not words on the delicate, yellowing pages. The sketches, though, captured his imagination. There were concentric circles and spheres. Lines crisscrossed the page, evoking his imagination. Mikołaj dared to describe the stars and planets in terms of mathematics. Up until that point, Anthony had only ever thought of math as the rudiments of economics. A box of cardamon that cost fifty pence from the docks could be divided into ten vials, each of which would sell for a shilling, bringing a return more than twice the original value. It was the offset Master Dunmore sought. He'd even go so far as selling bundles of lavender for as little as a farthing if they were purchased with a pouch of cinnamon for the going rate of a groat. To the villagers, it was a bargain, but the master would get entire crates of cinnamon from the Arabs for as little as a gold noble. To Anthony, mathematics was the language of trade—and here was a Polish polyglot declaring that math was also the language of the heavens. For Anthony, the idea was intoxicating. Although he didn't understand what Master Dunmore read to him from the book, he was thrilled to realise the incomprehensible wandering of the planets and comets could be reduced to a calculation like that of profiteering from nutmeg or turmeric. What seemed cryptic was predictable. It's no wonder the bishop hated Mikołaj and his drawings. While he sought to confound and subjugate, Mikołaj Kopernik wanted only clarity.

Anthony blurts out, "*On Heavenly Spheres*. It's like that, isn't it?"

Lady de Brooke looks at him with delight, speaking at first in

Latin and then English. "*De revolutionibus orbium coelestium*? You know of *On the Revolutions of the Heavenly Spheres* by Nicolaus Copernicus?"

"I've seen his diagrams. My master. He could read it. He read the original German. On a winter's eve, he'd tell me in English of the eight spheres with the sun at its heart. He said our world was no more or less than a ball spinning as it circled the sun. He swore it was Earth and not the Sun that moved during the course of a day."

"And you believed him?" she asks.

"Bishop Blaine called Mikołaj an upstart and a fool. He said he wanted to reverse the common knowledge found in scripture. He lectured how Joshua commanded the Sun to stand still, and not the Earth."

The lady smiles, asking, "So which is true? Which stands still? Earth or the Sun?"

"I—I," Anthony says, stuttering. He wanted her opinion. He feels exposed, expressing his own fledging thoughts. "I see the sun rise. I see the sun overhead. And then I see the sun set."

"But?"

"But mathematics says otherwise."

"Mathematics?" the lady asks. "And not scripture?"

"Aye. It's knowledge again, isn't it? His calculations say 'tis the simplest solution we should cling to. He speaks of predictions that math makes, predictions the church cannot make. And then his math is observed in the heavenly sphere."

"And you believe this?"

"Math is exact," Anthony says. "Mathematics can be trusted. It's precise. You divide a pound into twenty shillings yesterday, today and tomorrow. It's reliable."

"But the scriptures?"

"I know not what knowledge with which they were written, but it wasn't the language of mathematics."

She steps in front of him, crouching slightly as she tosses his hair affectionately. "You never cease to surprise me, young Anthony."

"So it's true," he says, pulling away, not wanting to be treated as a child. If anyone knows the truth, it's Lord and Lady de Brooke, of that he's sure.

"It's true," she says. "And more."

"More?" Julia asks. She's been conspicuously quiet, which Anthony knows means she's intensely interested and measuring every word that's spoken.

Lady de Brooke says, "The Moon swings around Earth like a maypole, but rather than once every few seconds, it takes a month. And they two swing around the Sun like Morris dancers exchanging hands. But Nicolaus has only glimpsed a fraction of all that holds true. Even the sun is in motion. The sun and the stars are all swinging through the endless night, only they're so distant their motion isn't obvious. If you were to look at star maps from the Greeks and Babylonians, from thousands of years ago, you'd see subtle differences as everything everywhere is in motion."

Julia says, "Like ships on the ocean."

"Like ships on the ocean," the lady says, nodding. She likes that analogy, which makes Anthony feel proud of Julia. "Now, get some sleep. Tomorrow, we make port in Bilbao."

"Yes, m'lady," they both say in unison.

Having been up since dawn, they're both tired. They walk to the stairs leading beneath the quarterdeck. The steps are set at a steep pitch, one far too steep to proceed down while facing forward. Whether sighted or blind, it makes no difference as it's too easy to fall. A rope has been set on either side of the ladder-like stairs, acting as a handrail. Anthony turns around and backs down ahead of Julia. On reaching the bottom, he holds out his hand, steadying her by touching lightly at her waist as she comes down.

"I'm fine," she says. Whether she's indignant or offended, he's not sure, but she doesn't want to be touched. Out of necessity, though, she needs his help. Perhaps that's what she resents. Back in the village, she could run across the cobblestones without fear of crashing into anything, knowing the alleyway was kept clear for carriages. She's told him that, on sunny days, she can sense shadows. If she crosses the alley, she can feel the shade of the buildings on her skin as she approaches them. Knowing her, she's probably memorised footfalls and patterns on the stones. Here on the *Santa Cruz*, she's not only blind, she's been robbed of the mental maps that allow her freedom.

Once she's down, he stands silently facing away from her along the corridor. He has his hand resting on his hip with his elbow out from his side. Without saying a word, she turns, reaches out and takes his arm. From just the subtle sounds around her, she knew precisely where he was.

As soon as her fingers grip his bicep, he walks forward, staying to one side of the narrow corridor. There are a few more stairs to traverse, but he'll keep his distance. How can she learn the layout of the *Santa Cruz* if he's crowding her? He needs to give her the opportunity to map their new home. He has no doubt that, by the time they reach the Indies, she'll be able to run and play and skip through the passageways with ease.

A board creaks in front of her, and she instinctively falls in behind him, allowing a befuddled sailor to squeeze past going the other way.

"I need to go to the head," she says, referring to the long-drop bathroom located near the galley.

"We went before dinner," he says, surprised by her request to backtrack through the hull of the sailing vessel.

"I learned the way from the galley but not from our cabin," she says. "I need to know how to get there at night."

"Wake me," he says.

"I will not."

"You shouldn't be alone below deck."

"Because I'm blind?" she asks. "Or because I'm a girl?"

"Both."

"Well, aren't you a gallant knight on a white steed? Shall I offer you my handkerchief as a token?"

"I—I just don't want anything to happen to you," he says.

"You can't always be there for me," she replies. "Life doesn't work that way."

"In the morning," he says as they reach their cabin. "We'll map the entire ship tomorrow. I promise."

Anthony pulls on a heavy wooden bolt and opens the door.

"I'm not using the privy bucket," Julia says, pointing into the far corner of their cabin. The smell alone singles it out. When the previous occupants departed, they failed to rinse it, leaving it to the flies. The cabin is narrow, being barely wide enough for them to enter single-file. The bunks are set on the wall backing onto the stern.

"Top or bottom?" Anthony asks, ignoring her. Julia reaches out and takes hold of the wooden bunk frame.

"Do you really have to ask?" she says, hoisting herself onto the top straw mattress. A thin cotton sheet separates her from the padding.

Moonlight creeps into the cabin from around the weather hatch on the far wall. Anthony props it open with a lever, allowing fresh air to circulate within the cramped space.

"Can you see them?" Julia asks, leaning over the top bunk as though she were watching him.

"Yes," he replies, knowing she means the stars. Someone's placed fresh blankets on the bed. Anthony lies on his bunk, feeling the cool air on his cheeks as he looks up at the stars. Within minutes, he's asleep.

Another Crate

"Ant. Ant! Wake up," Julia says, shaking Anthony by the shoulder. He's facing the bulkhead with his back to the narrow cabin. Normally, Anthony wakes with the first call of the birds, but out at sea, the rocking of the ship has sent him into a deep slumber.

His eyes open. He rolls over, feeling groggy.

Looking out through the hatch, the sky has a pink hue. Dawn is breaking. Julia continues shaking him, urging him to wake. Even though he's turned over, she has no way of seeing his eyes are open. He has to say something for her to realise he's been raised from his sleep.

"Julia, what ails you?"

"They're gone."

"Who?"

"Lord and Lady de Brooke."

"How is that possible?"

"I woke to the sound of a longboat being lowered. Curious, I went up on deck. I could hear them talking—the sailors."

"What did they say?"

"That madness has taken his lordship."

"I don't understand," Anthony says, pulling a shirt over his head.

Julia says, "We're in the Bay of Biscay, between France and

Spain. There's no land. Not for hundreds of miles."

Anthony sits up, tossing his hair. He's struggling to believe what she's saying. "And they left in a longboat? They don't even have the use of a sail? How is it possible to reach land?"

He slips on his shoes.

Julia takes his hand, saying, "Come. Quick."

They rush along the passageway, up several ladders and onto the quarterdeck. The sun breaks over dark clouds on the horizon. Long shadows are cast around them. Ropes creak with the swaying of the ship. The ocean is as still as a lake, but somehow, the *Santa Cruz* continues on. Its sails catch a light breeze.

"What do you see?" Julia asks.

Anthony looks around. "Nothing but the ocean. No land. No longboat. Nothing. Are you sure of what you heard?"

"I'm sure."

The two of them rush along the gangway past the hold and back toward the stern. It's too early for the captain to be raised. The night watch is in the process of changing shifts, meaning there are two men on the helm instead of one. They're talking about their passage through the bay. Several other sailors point up at the rigging, handing over details of the settings that were used through the night and making recommendations for the day.

"Lord and Lady de Brooke?" Anthony says, rushing up to the helmsmen. "Where are they?"

"Oh, you're the London boy," the older man says, reaching for a bag on the shelf beside the wheel. "They asked me to give this to you."

Anthony takes the pouch from him. He slings it over his shoulder. Coins rattle.

"And they are?"

"Mad," the helmsman says, pointing at the wake trailing behind the *Santa Cruz*. Several hundred yards back, a longboat drifts with the current. Two figures sit at either end. Oars are lowered, stroking the water but without much effect.

"And no," the helmsman says. "We're not going back for them. The captain's issued orders."

"He knows?" Anthony asks, rushing to the gunwale at the stern and peering out across the smooth water.

"He said they've done this before."

"They have?" Anthony asks, confused.

The helmsman chuckles. "As Saint Christopher is my guide, I'd much rather make landfall at port than row to shore. For a lord, that man is of narrow build. He has nigh shoulders. I doubt he'll make the coast, but it's his gold that says we leave him be."

"We've been... abandoned," Julia says, feeling at the railing as she comes up behind Anthony.

Anthony's palms go sweaty. His heart races with the onset of anxiety. "Why? I am at a loss. Why flee when there's no one in pursuit? What good can come from being set adrift in a longboat when land is nowhere in sight?"

"And us?" Julia asks. "Are we to continue on to the Indies?"

Anthony unwinds the leather strap wrapped around the clasp of the satchel and peers inside. Dozens of gold sovereigns stare back at him. They slosh around, sliding over each other and revealing even more coins as he peers into the shadows. He closes the bag, winding the strap tight.

"We'll be fine," he says, but his eyes aren't on Julia or the ornate wooden carvings that adorn the stern of the *Santa Cruz*. Julia doesn't believe him. For that matter, neither does he. Anthony stares out across the water trailing away behind the *Santa Cruz*. He watches the longboat as it turns away from the breaking dawn. Lord de Brooke is rowing away from land, out toward the open ocean.

"We'll be—"

"No, we won't," Julia says, expressing what Anthony feels but can't admit.

Anthony's about to reply to Julia when a wooden crate is shoved into his back. It strikes him above his buttocks, causing him to flex and lean backwards. He's in no danger of falling over the stern of the *Santa Cruz* as the gunwale reaches up above waist height. The polished armrest runs the width of the ship.

He turns.

Julia stands before him holding a crate in one hand and a rope line in the other. She's tied the line roughly around the wooden slats that form the base of the crate. The other end is looped around her wrist.

"What are you doing?"

"What are *we* doing?" she asks in reply, reaching out with her free hand to grab the gunwale.

"You want to go after them?"

"Don't you?" Julia asks. "What weather would ever be as fair as the winds we have encountered with Lady de Brooke? Without her, I'd be ash. And so would you."

"But they're... We can't..."

Julia's already grabbed the railing. Her knuckles go white. She raises a leg, getting ready to straddle the gunwale.

"No," Anthony says. "If we are to go, we jump from midships where the fall is less."

Julia swings her leg back down. She grabs his hand and pulls him on as though she's the one with sight. The helmsmen have their backs to them. If the old man heard their discussion, he doesn't let on. He laughs as they pass by, but it could have been in response to something someone else said. He seems more concerned with the clouds billowing on the horizon to the south, pointing them out to one of the seamen.

Julia rushes down the steps to the main deck. She holds the crate in front of her. The rope she's used to tie herself to the crate is easily twenty feet in length. It drags on the wood, threatening to trip her. If she feels the rope swinging against her leg, she doesn't care. For once, she pulls Anthony on.

"We're jumping to our deaths," he says.

"We're jumping *from* our deaths," she replies, countering his argument. "For we will surely die in the Indies, be that in months, years or decades to come."

"What if they don't see us?"

"Then we die by water and not by fire."

Anthony laughs. "But we die, huh?"

"Eventually, we all die."

"Then let us die chasing knowledge," he says, impressed by her spirit and finding courage where only insanity should lie. Jumping from the deck of a sailing vessel is intoxicating to him. It's taking a chance. It's freedom.

"Better to die with knowledge than to live in ignorance," Julia says.

Anthony brings her to a halt. He stops at the point the deck begins to curl up toward the bow. As it's early in the morning and the ship is sailing under a fair wind, the deck is empty of all but a handful of sailors. Those that are present go about their duties, ignoring the two of them. Anthony releases a bolt on the side of the gunwale, opening a hinged door used to secure a gangway when in port. He swings the waist-high door to one side. Julia steps up to the opening. She releases his hand and holds onto the railing.

"Is it far?"

"It is far."

She jumps, leaping out into the air. The crate tumbles beside her as she plummets toward the dark water. The rope unravels, allowing the wooden crate to fall away from her. The ship glides on. Julia lands several feet further back, splashing as she plunges into the sea. The crate floats. She disappears into the depths. Seconds later, her head appears in the wash coming off the bow. She grabs at the rope, pulling herself toward the crate.

"Back from the edge, lad," a sailor says. He grabs Anthony's arm, pulling him away from the opening.

"No," Anthony yells, realising that with every passing second, Julia is drifting further away from him. He wrenches his arm, desperate to break free, but the sailor's grip tightens, squeezing his bicep so hard the muscle compresses against the bone. Pain surges up his shoulder. He can't pull away. The sailor is too strong. As it is, he towers over Anthony. And Julia? By now, she must have already drifted beyond the stern of the ship. In the perpetual darkness of her blind world, she must be terrified. She'll be confused. She won't understand why he hasn't followed her. She's alone in the ocean.

Anthony does the only thing he can. He can't pull away from the old salt, so he turns toward him, taking the sailor by surprise.

"What the blazes do yah think yah doing?" the sailor asks. His beard is unkempt. Several of his teeth are missing. The skin on his cheeks has been marred by the pox, but his eyes speak of kindness. He doesn't understand. In his mind, he's saving a young boy from certain death—only he's condemning Julia to die alone.

Have Lord and Lady de Brooke seen her? Do they know she's in the water? Can she reach them? Without sight, she has no way of knowing where they are. From where Anthony is on the deck, he can hear her calling his name. Her cries are faint, but they carry on the wind.

"Ant? Ant! Where are you?"

The sailor is easily six feet tall with square shoulders and muscular arms. Although his complexion is pale, the skin on his arms has been tanned by the sun.

"Please," Anthony says. "Mercy."

With kindness in his voice, the sailor says, "You'll die, boy."

"But not alone."

With that, the sailor's grip eases. For him, this must be perplexing. What foul miasma must have infected these poor souls to have them leap into the ocean? And yet, for all that, he must sense a deeper truth in Anthony's eyes. It's too much to explain. Given Lady de Brooke's command of the sky, the clouds and even lightning itself, Anthony believes there's hope. Her knowledge of the elements has empowered her beyond any bishop or sheriff or ship's captain. What seems like suicide to this sailor is trust to him.

Anthony steps back. His heel hangs over the edge of the deck. As tempting as it is to turn and look at the fall, his eyes are on the old sailor. The man is aghast. He holds his hands wide, appealing for reason one last time. Anthony simply smiles.

Although he intends to fall into the water, Anthony hasn't accounted for the curved hull of the *Santa Cruz*. He steps off the edge. Wooden planks rush by inches from his face. The wind catches his hair, but before he reaches the waterline, his feet clip the side of the vessel. He tumbles, falling head over heels. Rather than splashing into the sea, his body slaps the waves.

Water rushes around him. The ocean closes over him. The bright of day fades to night as he sinks into the depths. He kicks with his legs, but his clothes weigh him down. The satchel hanging around his neck is like an anchor, dragging him into the depths of the sea. Anthony presses toward the surface, swinging with his arms and kicking, but the gold sovereigns have a mind for the darkness beneath him.

Bubbles slip from his lips. His lungs scream for air. He drives hard, wanting to break the surface. It seems so close, and yet it's forever out of reach. The *Santa Cruz* sails on. Its rudder passes by, cutting through the water like a knife. Waves curl behind the vessel.

Darkness descends on him, but it's not from the failing light. His sight is fading. With every ounce of his body crying out for air, he wriggles free of the satchel. The purse sinks into the depths. More gold sovereigns than he could ever imagine fade from sight. He pulls off his shirt, wanting to free himself of the weight and kicks for the surface. His fingers break the water. His head rises above the waves, and he gasps, drawing in a long breath. He's alive.

After flailing around for a few seconds, he calls out, "Julia!"

There's no reply. Up on the deck of the *Santa Cruz*, it all seemed so simple. Julia was floating along, holding onto her crate. Lord and Lady de Brooke may have been a way off, but he could see them. Now that he's in the water, Anthony is shocked to realise he can barely see an arm's length in front of him. He splashes with his hands, propelling himself on, wanting to look around him. As he turns, he catches a glimpse of the ship, but he can only see the top of the sails and the tip of the three masts with their flags blowing in the breeze. The *Santa Cruz* sails out of sight, but it gives him a point of reference. He's drifted to one side. Lord and Lady de Brooke, and presumably Julia, are somewhere to his right. He pays attention to the way the sunlight falls on his face, knowing this will be his compass. He kicks toward them.

Although the swell is gentle and the waves are few, Anthony feels as though he's making no headway. Like most boys his age, he learned to swim in the lakes that dotted the nearby forest on a hot summer's afternoon, but back then, he could easily reach the shore. He and his friends would take turns jumping off the rickety wooden pier used by the fishermen from the village. With a holler and cry, the teens would plunge into the muddy depths and turn, making broad strokes for the bank before climbing out and doing it all again. Back then, it was fun. Now, it's about survival. Now, there are no rocks beneath his feet to give him respite.

Anthony splutters. Water splashes on his face as he breathes in. Suddenly, air can no longer fill his lungs. He coughs, desperate to clear his airway and breathe deeply. The sea takes hold of him, pulling him under. He reaches with his arms, trying to break the surface, but he's been robbed of strength by the lack of air. Bubbles slip from his nose. His hands grab at the water, desperate to take hold of something, anything so he can pull himself out, but the ocean slips between his fingers. His throat constricts. His body screams at him, demanding he does more, but he's losing against the weight of the ocean bearing down on him.

A hand grabs his wrist. At first, he thinks he's imagining being rescued, but there's someone in the water next to him. The ocean churns as he lashes out with his legs. A wooden crate bobs before him. Anthony reaches out and grabs at the slats, hoisting himself up and spitting water as he gasps for air.

"Ant," says the kindest voice he's ever known.

"Julia," he replies. For now, names are all that need to be

exchanged. Anthony swings an arm up over the crate so he can rest on it and catch his breath. Julia retreats from it. She holds on but is content to float next to the crate as he recovers.

"How did—How did you find me?" he asks the blind girl.

"You were flailing around like a drowning rat," she says. "I swam toward the noise."

Waves lap around them. The sun beats down on them from a cloudless sky. The storms on the horizon aren't visible from this low in the water. Anthony takes a moment to breathe. The air filling his lungs is as sweet as a meadow full of wildflowers.

A woman's voice carries on the wind.

"Are you well?"

Anthony laughs. Julia looks confused, but for him, it's as though he's skidded to the bottom of a stone wall on the banks of the Thames once again. Far from being a dumb question, this time, it's playful.

"Yes, all is well," he calls out in reply.

"What are you saying?" Julia asks, nudging him. She calls out at the top of her lungs, yelling, "Here! We're over here!"

Julia waves with one hand held high above her head. There's silence, then they hear the sound of oars dipping in and out of the water. Anthony turns to see the smiling face of Lady de Brooke as the longboat pulls alongside them.

Lord de Brooke has a scowl on his face. He lifts his oars out of the water. The longboat drifts next to them. Lady de Brooke kneels on the wooden seat. She leans out of the longboat and grabs Julia under her armpits. Dripping wet and squirming in surprise, Julia flops into the bottom of the boat. Anthony puts the crate over the edge of the longboat and then hoists himself up on the rim. The boat sways in the water but is in no danger of capsizing.

"What were you thinking, boy?" the lord asks.

"I want to know more," Anthony replies. "We both do."

"You know not what you ask."

"But we do," Lady de Brooke says, addressing her lord as she clears wet hair from Anthony's eyes.

"You should have stayed on the *Santa Cruz*," the lord says. "And what of the sovereigns? Did the crew not give you the gold?"

"They did," Anthony says.

"Where is it then? Was it not enough?"

"It lies at the bottom of the ocean," Anthony replies. "It was much, but not worth all we could learn from you."

Lord de Brooke nods. He seems strangely satisfied by that answer. He turns to his lady and asks, "What are we to do with them?"

"Take them with us."

"What? No. We can't. It is forbidden."

"All is forbidden at some point—and then it isn't," she says.

"You would take them as part of the collection?"

"Not in the collection. As aids to us in our exploration."

"No. We cannot."

"The boy," Lady de Brooke says. "He knows where we can find evidence of ancient life. Isn't that right?"

"Ah, yes," Anthony replies, unsure of what she's referring to. He's distracted. Anthony's looking around for the *Santa Cruz*. He spies the tip of the mast on the horizon. Far more time has transpired than he thought. Lady de Brooke lowers her gaze, wanting him to say more. He guesses. "The shells. The stones that look like bones. You want to find more of them."

"Yes, yes," she replies.

"You can lead us there?" the lord asks, "to Low Hauxley in Northumberland and Lulworth in Dorset? You can find them on a map without markings."

"I'm from Dorset," he replies. "I grew up along the coast before taking my apprenticeship with Master Dunmore."

"And you've seen them?"

"Aye. The rocks there are unlike anything seen elsewhere.

They're layered like clothing after it has been washed and dried in the sun and stacked for return to the manor. 'Tis as though some giant crumpled the land just as you or I would stack a pile of paper on a desk."

Lady de Brooke claps her hands in excitement. "Uplift. It sounds perfect." She looks to her lord, saying, "I thought we'd lost deep time to the motion of the crust. We have to see this. We must."

"You need to understand," the lord says, leaning forward and raising his index finger barely an inch from Anthony's face. "If you come with us, there is no going back. If you follow us any further, you can never return to your world. Never. For it is not possible once you leave."

"I understand," Julia says, beating Anthony to a response.

"I don't want to go back," Anthony says.

"Never," the lord says. "Once we depart, there is no opportunity to ever see your home again. It will be forever a memory."

"A nightmare," Anthony says.

Julia nods.

Lord de Brooke looks to his lady. Before he can say anything, she says, "Then so be it."

She snaps her fingers and the water around the boat ripples. Hundreds of tiny waves spread out from the hull, but they're perfectly uniform, forming a circle around them on the smooth ocean swell. To Anthony's mind, it makes no sense. The longboat is long, for lack of a better term. He expects any ripples to match its shape, but the concentric circles vibrating in the ocean form a perfect circle spanning easily thirty feet around them, rushing outward.

Something hits the bottom of the hull. Julia clings to the seat. The longboat rocks sideways, resting on whatever lies beneath it. Lord de Brooke stands up and steps out of the boat. Instead of sinking into the depths, he wades through knee-deep water.

"What's happening?" Julia asks.

Lady de Brooke says, "Just as you sail between countries on the ocean, we sail between stars."

"Stars?" Anthony asks, looking up into the clear blue sky.

"Oh, they're out there. They're always there. It's just too bright to see them during the day."

"Venus," Anthony says. "The bright and morning star. It can be seen during the day."

"And the Moon," Lady de Brooke says. "The brightest day is still as the darkest night. Your world floats on a sea of stars whether you realise it or not."

Julia has a grin on her face. She's looking up at the sky, feeling the warmth of the sun on her cheeks even though she cannot see what they're describing.

"You're not from this world?" Anthony asks, shocked at the notion.

"No more than the sailors from that caravel were from England."

"And you have a ship?"

"We have a ship. Although it uses not the currents or tide, nor the trade winds to sail."

"It uses knowledge," Anthony says.

"Yes, it does," the lady replies, beaming with pride.

Anthony steps out of the longboat, following Lady de Brooke. Her husband is fifteen feet away from them, seemingly walking on water within the depths of the ocean. He crouches, reaching beneath the now shallow surface as he fiddles with something beneath the ripples.

"What's happening?" Julia asks, reaching for the gunwale of the long boat to steady herself as it rocks with the motion of the others stepping out.

"I don't know," Anthony replies, and he doesn't. From the look on her face, his comment doesn't inspire confidence. He adds, "Something wonderful," wanting to assuage her doubts.

Now he's out of the longboat, he reaches back, taking her hand

and helping her. She's unsure of herself. She searches with her feet, wanting to test the ground beneath the water before committing her weight.

"It's sturdy."

"What is it?" she asks. "Have we reached the shore?"

"No."

"What do you see?"

Lady de Brooke is quiet. She's smiling. It seems even she's interested to hear what Anthony describes.

"Ah, we're standing in the middle of the ocean. There is no land for miles around."

"But?"

"But their vessel lies beneath us, hidden under the waves."

"What does it look like?" Julia asks as both their longboat and the now ankle-deep water rise above the surrounding ocean. At first, it's only by a few inches and barely noticeable. Within seconds, it's a few feet. Water cascades over the edge of the ship.

"Ah, we're standing on top of their vessel. It's rising from beneath the sea."

"I can feel it," Julia says with childlike enthusiasm.

"The water around us is caught as though held in a horse's trough."

"What shape is it?"

"Circular. Like a pond. I'd say it's a good perch from here to the rim."

"And beyond that?"

"More. Much more."

Anthony takes her hand, leading her over toward Lord de Brooke.

"We're higher now," Anthony says. "Higher than the deck on the *Santa Cruz*. And we're getting higher still. Perhaps higher than even the masts on the *Cruz*. The sides of this ship slope away. They're curved.

They fan out around us like a skirt or perhaps the awning on the entrance to the church. And the water beneath us. It's moving."

"The sea? It's moving?"

"Yes. It's as though a squall has descended on the ocean, only instead of blowing to the east or the north, it's spreading out in all directions, blowing away from us."

The seawater around their feet drains, leaving them standing on a grey metal platform. The longboat lies on its side not more than ten feet away.

Julia asks, "How big is this ship of the stars?"

"I—I don't know. I can't see all of it yet. Down low, there are spikes. Out on the fringe, it is as though thousands of pikes have been arranged pointing outward."

Lady de Brooke answers Julia's question. "It's not quite as big as London, but it's close."

"A ship as big as a city?" Julia says. Her face lights up with excitement.

"Big enough to sail between stars," Lady de Brooke says. "Besides, London is still quite small. It'll grow over time."

A circular hatch opens in the floor. It's unlike anything Anthony's ever seen before. The opening started as small as a coin and expanded out to the size of a table in barely a few seconds.

Lord de Brooke walks down the circular staircase leading inside the strange ship. His lips are moving, but no sound comes out. Lady de Brooke follows him. She pauses halfway down the stairs and turns, asking Anthony, "Are you well?"

"Yes, I am well," Anthony responds once again. He steps forward, but Julia remains where she is. She has hold of his hand. She pulls him back, whispering, "Are you afraid?"

"No."

For a moment, she dares not speak. For all their bravado, it seems she knows this is the point at which everything changes. Anthony respects her for that. He'd bumble on regardless, only to think about the consequences of his actions later, but she's always been forward-thinking.

She squeezes his hand, saying, "Then, neither am I."

Act II

Into the Void

Out of Darkness

Julia steps down through the darkness, following Anthony's lead, squeezing his hand for reassurance. From the gentle way his arm swings, she can detect the fall of his steps ahead of her, allowing her to anticipate the distance between stairs.

For over a decade, darkness is all Julia's known. At first, being blind was confusing. She understood she was surrounded by light, but she was barred from sight. Life was cruel. Tears still ran from her dead eyes, but no light could pass beyond that thin fleshy veil. Julia could feel the heat of the sun on her cheeks or a fire radiating from a hearth—she knew there was light—but nothing could penetrate the darkness. Being blind was frustrating as light seemed to be within her grasp and yet it wasn't.

Within a month, the darkness turned to frustration. Julia understood she was surrounded by people and various items at the markets or in her home, but they remained hidden in the darkness. Even when she was engaged in conversation, she felt utterly alone, as though she were talking to the ghosts of family and friends.

Nothing was easy. A glancing touch with the tip of her fingers would send a cup tumbling from the bench and into oblivion as far as she knew. Even though she could hear it bounce across the floor and could feel the spilt water on the wooden boards while searching on her hands and knees, finding the cup was nigh on impossible.

Colours became abstract. Although she knew colours were vibrant and exciting, filled with differences that pleased the eye, green and blue held no meaning to her any more. Red seemed to be grey. She remembered white, but only because it was the antithesis of the inky black darkness that surrounded her every waking moment.

In her dreams, Julia could see again. Dreams offered her an escape, and she'd dream of horses and birds, trees and flowers, but never in colour. Hills and forests were only ever shades of grey. Over the years, her dreams became blurred. The faces and places within her dreams grew dull and vague. Then she stopped dreaming altogether. Darkness consumed her day and night.

Stepping down behind Anthony, walking into a sailing ship that traverses not the ocean but the very stars of heaven, Julia feels dread. The darkness hasn't changed. It's still impenetrable, but somehow it seems different. She feels as though she's stepping from one world to another. Perhaps she is.

Julia's heart beats madly against the inside of her chest. She can feel her ribs beneath her shirt. Blood pulses in her neck.

Julia's been blind for eleven years. Not since those early days, when her sight first faded and dread seized her mind, has she felt this sense of foreboding. Back then, she could see fine one day, only to wake the next with a headache and blurred vision. It was terrifying. She felt helpless because she was helpless, and that terrified her even more.

Seeing is easy—until it isn't. After Julia recovered from the pox, for about a month, her sight would surge and wane. Some days, it felt as though all would be well with the world. Colours would flood her vision. Wildflowers had never seemed so pretty. Then, the next day, she'd wake to utter darkness and lie in bed crying.

Sight forms the basis of all motion—until it doesn't. As the darkness descended, Julia found herself becoming more and more withdrawn. Touch became sight, but she could only touch things at arm's length, and she could only touch a small part of an item at any one time. That caused the world to shrink around her.

At first, Julia struggled to identify even simple objects. Wooden plates would slide out of reach across the table, being pushed on by fingers fumbling in the dark. The edge of a window frame felt like an open door. The cool breeze would beckon her outside, only she'd stumble against the wall and stand there confused for a moment, unsure where she was within her own home. Then she'd feel along the dried mud wall, trying to orient herself. It was as though the world had shifted around her without her noticing, twisting and turning into a dark prison.

Over time, Julia became familiar with the common areas inside the village of Westminster. She could find her way from her home to the market and the apothecary with ease, but should she stray or accidentally turn down the wrong alley, terror would seize her mind. Being just a few steps beyond the safety of a known path would fill her with angst and leave her feeling as though she were hundreds of miles from home. She'd search with her hands and backtrack, desperate to feel the large stones of the village wall or the rough wooden planks that lined the tannery next to the apothecary.

The markets taught her how to use sound as a guide. Before she lost her sight, Julia had only ever thought of the bustle within the stalls as annoying. Now, that commotion was a compass. She'd listen for familiar voices floating on the breeze, giving her a clear indication of where she was within the village.

Farmer Miller had a deep, gruff voice and would oft complain when haggling over produce. His voice carried best, rising above the din. Miss Massey had a sweet tone that could only be heard when Julia approached to within twenty yards of the market square. Even though she'd call out to the crowd with as much vigour and passion as Farmer Miller, her voice was lost by the end of the alley. Master Dunmore wasn't one to yell—except at Anthony. Whenever Julia heard his voice, she knew she was close to the apothecary. Even though she couldn't make out sentences at a distance, hearing words like jasmine and coriander or olive oil and lavender would guide her on to Anthony.

Whereas touch became sight up close, sound became staring into the distance. Being in the middle of the ocean somewhere off the coast of France and Spain, though, was unsettling. Lady de Brooke said they were descending into a ship that could sail between stars rather than continents. Not only was that unnerving, the smell and sounds around her were foreign and left her feeling lost.

Being able to see, Anthony probably ignored the clues that screamed caution to Julia. Each footfall echoed beneath her. Not only did that speak of the depth of the cavern into which they were descending, but the sound was one she'd only ever heard at the blacksmith. This wasn't the clump of boots on stone as she might find in the doorway to her home or the echo of wooden stairs that lead to a loft. The two of them were walking on metal, and that confused her.

And she could feel how thin the stairs were. With each step, a slight shimmer resounded beneath her. Nothing about this was familiar, and that scared her. Mentally, Julia wanted to embrace this journey with Lord and Lady de Brooke. Emotionally, she was struggling to trust Anthony as her guide. It wasn't that he wasn't trustworthy, but rather that she understood he, too, might as well be blind, walking inside a vessel from another world.

And what did that even mean? Another world? Lady de Brooke had spoken of her origin among the stars as though it held no more significance than another city or another country. Julia had her doubts.

Anthony speaks softly to her, saying, "The steps curve like those in a castle turret."

"But it isn't a castle turret," she says, reaching out with her free hand, wanting to touch an outer wall that isn't there.

Anthony squeezes her fingers gently, saying, "Stay close to the inner edge and follow as the stairs turn."

"And the fall beside us?"

"Twenty. Maybe thirty feet."

"Onto what?"

"Silk," he says, with doubt lingering in his voice. "The floor. It seems to be moving. It's like a flag billowing in the wind, only it lies flat beneath us. There's furniture, but it is like nothing I've ever seen."

"What is it like?"

"There are benches and tables made from light."

"From light?" she asks. For someone confined to darkness, the idea of a magical kingdom created out of light itself is appealing. Anthony's comment awakens a sense of wonder within her. Julia wishes she could see as he does. With each step they descend, she grows more confident. Her fear fades. Far from walking down into a cave, it feels as though she's stepping into a fairy tale.

"Lights rush around. They curve over chairs, couches, workbenches—at least, I think that's what they are."

"What colours are there?"

"Blues. Whites. Yellows. Pinks. Reds. Greens."

Lady de Brooke stands at the bottom of the stairs. Julia's not sure how she knows, she just does. Perhaps it's the way Anthony slows his descent. Perhaps it's the soft rustle of the lady's clothing or the scent of her perfume.

"Look up," Julia says to him. "Tell me what you see."

"Ah, it's like a cathedral. It's as though we have come down from a high ceiling in the House of the Lord, but there are no cold, dreary stones, no pillars or columns to support the roof. And no windows to allow sunlight in. And yet the chamber is bathed in light."

"Welcome," Lady de Brooke says.

"And we've reached the bottom," Anthony says, escorting Julia down the last few steps. No sooner has she walked beside him than the stairs retract. She can hear the mechanical motion ticking over like the gears in a clock. The central pole retracts, drawing in each of the steps as it rises into the air. The sounds are soft and subtle, but with her keen sense of hearing, she can detect not only that they are retreating but that they're doing so sequentially, from the bottom to the top. She can hear each one as the pole rises behind her.

The hatch above them is already closed. Whether Anthony realises that or not, she's unsure, but Julia can tell because the sea breeze has been replaced with what smells like crisp, clean, clear mountain air.

Lord de Brooke seems frustrated. From the change in pitch in his voice, it seems he's doubting the decision to bring them on board.

"I don't think this is wise. It may all be too much for them. The shock. They might not be able to cope."

Lady de Brooke is upbeat. "They're young. And they're keen of mind."

"Of their intelligence, I have no doubt. But what of the future? Their future? This is fine for today. 'Tis a lark. It's a splendid thing for them to escape persecution, but they have their whole lives ahead of them. Have you thought of that?"

Although his lordship is addressing Lady de Brooke, it's Julia who answers. She can feel it in the air. The sense of change implicit on entering the hull of this unusual ship of the stars. What at first scared her now excites her. His lordship would not be debating this decision were it not noteworthy on a scale neither she nor Anthony can imagine. Julia can sense the magnitude of the moment. For her, it is as though she's standing on the edge of a cliff, looking down at the waves of the sea, feeling a tremble in her legs at the great height and the jagged rocks below.

"Life is more than breathing," she says. "It's more than waking and eating and working and then sleeping. It's about change. Being better today than yesterday. It's about caring. Thinking deeper today than yesterday. It's about making the world a better, brighter place."

"But which world?" the lord asks. "I admire your passion, young lass, but you cannot know what lies ahead. And 'tis not excitement or danger or even change that drives life—'tis mastery of the mundane. 'Tis boredom that must be reckoned with. Repetition gives life rhythm. Today's adventure is tomorrow's tedium. And what then?"

Anthony says, "Then we will have time to learn."

Lord de Brooke is dismissive. It seems he's backtracking on his initial decision. "We should offload them in the Caribbean as planned."

"No," Lady de Brooke says in unison with both Julia and Anthony. "Once they learn who we are—who we really are—and what we are—"

"They're not meant to know these things," her lord counters. "You know how dangerous this is for the future of their kind. Should word of our mission leak, it could alter the perception of their people and catapult them to oblivion. Maturity must emerge naturally. It cannot be forced. And they are most certainly not ready."

"We're ready," Julia blurts out.

"Oh, not you, lass. Your kind. The kind that allows Bishop Blaine to stand in a pulpit on Sunday, speaking of truth and love to both Queen and congregation, and then execute the innocent on a fine, sunny Monday morning."

Lady de Brooke says, "But it is not so with these two."

"And 'twas not so with Blaine. Not at first. Nay, he learnt to delight in such cruelty. He learnt that power is a tankard of ale to be sculled on a whim. 'Tis not power that corrupts such as he. 'Tis power that releases the bond of his chains. 'Tis power that says, '*Drink your fill and have merriment with whomever you please.*'

"Drunkards need not reason, only will. For them, to be pleased is the greatest of virtues. And you. You two. You are not as dissimilar as you may think. Oh, you have seen excess and been repulsed, but if power were laid in your hands, what would you do? Of that even you do not know."

Julia and Anthony are silent.

Lady de Brooke says, "Even drunkards sober with the coming of dawn."

"And yet the broken glass remains in the streets."

"If we have offended you, m'lord," Julia says, bowing her head.

"No, no, no," he says, resting his hand on her shoulder. "For us, debate is healthy. To discuss is to resolve. I seek only clarity to avoid a mistake."

"What is our mission?" Lady de Brooke asks him. "What is the point of visiting a world like this if not to bring light into the lives of others?"

"We're collectors."

"We're observers," the lady replies, correcting her husband. "Our mandate is to learn all we can about life on this planet."

"We are way beyond our mission mandate," her lord says.

"But think of all we could still learn. You must sense it. They're different."

"Would you take them as specimens? Would they become your pets?"

"I would take them as equals."

"Equals?"

Lady de Brooke asks, "Why cannot they stand at the Convergence? Why cannot they represent the rise of intelligence on their world?"

"You assume much. Too much."

Anthony says, "Oh..."

There's something about the pitch in his voice that tells Julia his comment has nothing to do with the discussion between Lord and Lady de Brooke.

"What?" she asks, squeezing his hand.

"I can see."

Being blind, Julia doesn't find Anthony's comment helpful. If anything, it's grating. "See what?"

"Everything. The ocean. Even the *Santa Cruz* off in the distance. The coastline of France. The mountains of Spain. We're so high, above even wisps of cloud."

"Do you want to see?" Lady de Brooke asks, crouching before Julia.

"B—But of course, and yet I cannot. Darkness is my domain."

"I can help you. We can help you."

"M'lady," Lord de Brooke says, but Lady de Brooke cuts him off.

"You need to trust us."

"I trust you."

"This will hurt," the lord says.

"You'll experience pain," the lady says, "but I promise—you will see again."

To Julia, Lady de Brooke's words sound like the incantation of an ancient spell. She should be frightened of such sorcery, but she isn't.

"I want to see," she says. "I want to journey with you to the stars. I want to see them for myself."

Lord de Brooke sighs. He walks away, but not out of disagreement. Julia can hear him working with the controls of the starship. There are no creaking boards or straining ropes, no flapping canvas or gulls calling on the breeze, and yet she can feel them sailing through the air.

"Are you sure about this?" Anthony asks Julia quietly as Lady de Brooke fiddles with something on a nearby workbench. "We know not what power she wields."

Julia replies, "She commands the rains, sails to the stars, and now we find she can heal the blind. What is there to fear?"

Anthony releases Julia's hand, allowing her fingers to drop from his. Her arm falls by her side, leaving her alone in the darkness, but for once, she feels at peace there in the emptiness. There's not much talking for the next few minutes. Anthony backs away from her and then turns and walks over to join Lord de Brooke. She can tell that from the way his shoes move on the floor. There's a slight squish to their motion that changes depending on whether he's stepping on the balls of his feet or his heels.

Lady de Brooke is busy working with something that has the rhythm of a loom weaving away in a stone cottage. After several minutes she comes over, saying, "Hold out your hand."

The lady places a clunky piece of heavy metal in Julia's palm. Immediately, Julia runs the fingers of her other hand over the device, feeling the different textures, the bumps and grooves, the smooth surfaces and rough. The strange device is in the shape of a crescent. It's roughly the size of her forehead.

"What is this?"

"A machine. In the same way you use a hand pump to draw water from a well or a pulley to raise bales of wool, this will allow you to see. Only to work, it must be set into your skin. It must be one with your flesh and bone."

Julia swallows the lump rising in her throat.

"Don't be afraid. It's how we see, only adapted for your body. If anything, given the way your brain is so acutely adapted to sight, you may see even more than me."

"And it'll work?"

"It'll work. But you need to understand. Once attached, it can never be removed. Never... Are you ready?"

"I'm ready."

Lady de Brooke leads Julia over to a waist-high counter. Her hand is cold. "Lie here."

Julia reaches for the bench top, wanting to hoist herself up, but it moves, reacting to her motion and forming a soft, curved surface, not unlike that of a bed. She backs up to it, and the edge slides beneath her, raising her up, which is something she finds delightful.

"Now, lie back."

Julia does as she's told. She'd feel better if Anthony was with her, and she's tempted to call out to him when familiar fingers take hold of her hand. The warmth radiating from Anthony's palm is in contrast to Lady de Brooke's icy-cold fingers touching her forehead.

The bench she's lying on curves to support her body. Around her head, hundreds of thin tendrils reach up and over her face. Although she can't see them, she can feel the tiny pads working their way beneath her hair, behind her ears and over her face. They bite, cutting through her skin, causing her to flinch.

"Steady," the lady says. "Try to lie still."

Julia feels the metal device closing in over her eyes, lying across the bridge of her nose and wrapping around her skull above her ears. Fire sears her skin, burning into her face, following the contours of the device. She screams. The device reaches from the top of her cheeks to her forehead, completely enclosing her eyes. Julia clenches her teeth. She squeezes Anthony's hand, wanting to ride out the waves of pain washing over her.

Flashes of light break through the darkness. Like sparks rising from a bonfire, they drift before her as though floating on a breeze. The pain is still there. If anything, it's more intense, but the light gives her hope. It feels as though her skull is melting, yet she's not filled with dread.

Thousands of tiny pinpricks reach deep inside her head, but her fascination with the light overwhelms the discomfort. She can see. She's not sure what she can see, but she can. Streaks of thin white light rush past, all coming from a single point high off to one side. They cascade past her like golden raindrops. The size and shape of the sphere from which they emanate is strangely familiar. She's looking at the sun. As a child, Julia was told not to look at the sun. If she ignored that admonition, the glare would hurt her eyes. Back then, a perfectly round sphere would become impressed on her eyeball for a matter of minutes. She'd blink and close her eyes, and it would still be there. She'd turn away from the sun, but the glare would follow. This, though, is different. She can see streams of light rushing out from the sun as though it were a fountain or a rain cloud bursting high overhead. But how can she see the sun? She's inside the ship. The hatch is closed.

"How do you feel?" Lady de Brooke asks.

Julia looks at Lady de Brooke's hands and recoils at the sight. This is no lady. The apparition before her is ghostly. She can see teeth and eyes, but they are not veiled by flesh. Beyond them lie thousands of tiny boxes and curls of string, or is it wire?

"Are you well?" Anthony asks.

Julia turns to him and sees a skeleton. The shock of seeing bones in motion causes her to creep back on the bench, wanting to get away from the horror.

Although she's seen animal bones at the butcher, Julia's only ever seen a jester's sketch of a human skeleton before, laughing and dancing, announcing the arrival of a fête. On reflection, she remembers seeing human skeletons on a tarot card as well. Anthony looks like one of these images was brought to life.

A thin transparent membrane wraps around Anthony's bare skull. To her, it looks like the mucus that drips from an egg white. His eyes are perfectly round, while his jaw moves up and down as he speaks, losing the nuance of lips flexing and cheeks shifting. She can't see his lips or his nose, just a series of holes where his nose should be. Beyond his skull lies a lumpy, fleshy pulp at the back of his head. It has curves and undulations not unlike those found inside a melon. Stringy cords reach down into his spine. Inside his chest, a grotesque muscle beats with a rhythm that is both familiar and unsettling. Julia has felt this beat herself when resting her fingers on her neck or checking her wrist. The internal thumping of the body is a novelty the kids in the village point out to each other while trying to grasp reality, but they're unable to say what drives it on. Now, though, she can see the source of this pulsating drum beat.

"She's not well," Anthony says.

"What can you see?" Lady de Brooke asks.

"Everything."

"And that can be overwhelming," the lady says. Julia sits up on the bench and looks down at the bones in her own arms and hands while Lady de Brooke says, "If you reach up and twist the right side of the device, you can control the sensitivity."

Julia touches the point where once her temple lay and feels what could be the smooth curve of an eggshell. As her fingers glide over the surface, the view changes. Without moving, she can make objects appear closer or farther away. Twist her fingers, and she can see solid objects. Twist a little further, and she can see through them as though they were made from glass. She looks down at her feet, through the floor, and through several more floors of the starship. Her new eyes are drawn to an unusual form of motion in the distance. She watches as an octopus swims between rocks on the ocean floor. It appears transparent, almost ghostly, lacking bones, but the shape is familiar. Back in the markets, Julia felt the boneless, squishy shape of these extraordinary creatures on sale alongside fish, but they baffled her. How could anything exist without bones? How could such a creature support itself? Now, she giggles, amused by the way it propels itself through the water.

"Are you well?" the lady asks.

"I've never been so well," she replies. "I can see it."

"See what?" Anthony asks.

"An octopus."

Anthony looks confused. He turns his head, looking around the inside of the vessel, although all Julia sees is the outline of his hair and his skull twisting on its spine.

"Where?" he asks.

She points just beyond the bones in her toes, saying, "There. Not here. Outside. Beneath us."

She moves her finger, keeping pace with it as the starship glides on through the air, hundreds of feet above the surface of the ocean. She can zoom in and out, seeing it as a tiny speck beneath the waves and then as big as her hand.

"You can see that? An octopus?" Lady de Brooke asks, surprised.

"They move backwards," she says.

"Backwards?"

"It's madness, but they do. To go forward, they must go backwards. They push their arms back. They squeeze themselves like a parasol being opened and closed." She laughs. "Imagine running backwards everywhere. It's so silly."

Anthony shakes his head—or his skull from her perspective.

Lady de Brooke says, "Oh, this is wonderful. It's taken better than I expected."

"But there's no colour," Julia says.

"Because there is no colour," the lady replies.

"I don't understand," Julia says, bringing back the sensitivity so she can look at them more clearly.

"Neither do I," Anthony says, pointing at the lady's waist. "I see colours. You have a red sash around your waist."

"You see an illusion," Lady de Brooke says. "No two species on your planet see the same colours. You see a red sash. A dog sees this as brown, while a snake would see green and a cat would see grey. Bees can see colours you cannot begin to imagine."

"What?" Anthony says, shaking his head. "And Julia?"

"She sees all colours for what they are—shades of grey."

Anthony says, "No. That's not possible."

Lord de Brooke joins them, being interested in the discussion. He lowers his gaze, looking at Lady de Brooke. The poise of his body speaks without the need for words. Julia scales back her vision so she can see his face rather than see through him. She feels as though she can read his mind.

"This is what you meant, isn't it?" she asks, addressing him. "This is one of those things you thought would be too hard for us to grasp."

"I can see colours," Anthony says, insisting on that point. "They're real. Red is real. Blue is real."

Both Lord and Lady de Brooke are quiet. To Julia, this seems like an unusual point for Anthony to become hung up on. Perhaps the shroud of darkness that descended on her for more than a decade has made it easier for her to accept colours as an illusion. Anthony, though, is upset by the notion.

"If colours aren't real then why can I see them?" he asks.

"That is something that baffled us," Lady de Brooke says. "It took us a long time to unravel the mystery of what you call colour because they're different for each animal."

Lord de Brooke poses a question. "How do you speak to someone that cannot hear?"

"Ah, we point, or make signs and gestures."

"What if you need to speak to something other than a person, like a tree or a bee?"

Julia laughs. "That's silly. No one can speak to trees or bees."

"Why not? They speak to you."

Anthony laughs. "Insects can't speak!"

"Can't they?" Lady de Brooke asks. "What do you do when you see the yellow and black of a wasp buzzing nearby?"

"I move along."

"And just like that, the wasp has spoken to you, but not with words. It's used light and sound to get you to react. You—who are hundreds of times larger. You—who could kill it with a single swat."

"But I don't want to get bitten."

"And that's what it's telling you. The coloured stripes on its body are a warning. They speak to you of danger. The wasp doesn't want to bite you because you could kill it in response, so it has developed a way of warning you with colour. And it works. You keep your distance."

Anthony says, "So colours are words made of light?"

"Yes."

"And plants?" Julia asks.

"The beauty of a flower isn't meant for you—it's there for the bees."

"The bees?"

"Flowers attract bees, luring them in with sight and smell, offering them nectar if they'll visit. And by dancing from flower to flower, bees spread life. Plants can't move, so they're faced with a dilemma—how can they spread across the land? Some drop seeds that twirl and soar in the wind. Others attract insects, allowing them to spread their seed. As pretty as you may think a flower is, they appear even more spectacular to bees. There are patterns on the petals you'll never see. Although, now, perhaps you will."

Julia says, "I really want to see some flowers now."

Lady de Brooke goes on to ask her, "How do you know when fruit is ripe?"

"By its colour," Anthony says.

"Precisely. Your world hinges on the subtle difference between shades of grey you interpret as colour. But they're a convenient illusion. They're no more real than a court jester pulling flowers from a hat. Colours speak to you. And your kind has learned to respond to them, but they're not real."

"But they look real."

"The best illusions always do," Lady de Brooke says. "But answer me this. If colours were real, would your eyes ever tire of seeing them?"

"No."

"And yet they do. Stare at a red square for less than a minute and when you turn away, you'll see the reverse. You'll see the ghostly image of a green square still impressed on the back of your eye because it's hard work making up something that doesn't exist."

Anthony slumps onto one of the stools rising out of the floor. Reluctantly, he concedes.

"I—I've seen that."

"Your sight is wonderful," Lady de Brooke says, consoling him. "While our science may seem magical to you, your ability to enjoy colours like red and blue is magical to us. It's something we'll never experience."

The Convergence

"We're running out of time," Lord de Brooke says as they approach the southern coast of England, having spent the night conducting repairs in the Bay of Biscay. "There are too many other worlds to harvest before the Convergence. Time we use here, we lose there. As it is, we spent too much time integrating within their society."

"But they have a society," Lady de Brooke says with enthusiasm. "Among our seventy surveyed worlds, that is unique. That is notable for the Convergence."

"Aye, 'tis, but they're hundreds of years away from the stars, if not thousands. My fear is they'll destroy themselves long before they break the chains that bind them to their past."

Julia is silent. She wants to contradict him, but she can't. Anthony grits his teeth. He has to be thinking the same thing as her, that although she wishes them to be wrong, she fears they're right.

Lady de Brooke ignores her lord's comments. She's standing in front of a bench covered in an array of lights that form lines and squiggles. There's meaning there, but Julia doesn't understand it.

"This, though," the lady says. "This is too good an opportunity to pass up. Uncovering ancient life forms could tell us so much more about how life unfolded on this planet."

Lord de Brooke says, "We already have the internal evidence

from within the building blocks of their bodies. That they share the same base instruction set reveals their common origins."

Lady de Brooke isn't satisfied with that answer. "But we have no idea how different life was back then. Seeing ancient body shapes alone will tell us about their different modes of life. With this, we can capture not just life as it is now, but as it was throughout time on this remarkable planet."

"We don't have time," the lord replies.

"There's always time. We can make time."

"By burning through our reserves at a horrendous rate," he counters.

"Just a few samples, that's all I'm asking. I want to understand the preservation process as well as compare body types, then and now, to see what has progressed and what has been snuffed out for eternity."

Julia's not entirely sure what all that means, but Lord de Brooke seems satisfied with Lady de Brooke's answer. He nods and begins working on one of the benches. Rather than working with tools as a carpenter would, he presses his hands against the bench and seems to meld with it, joining it.

Julia is fascinated. To her, standing on the deck of the starship is akin to being on a sailing vessel minus the sails gathering the wind. There's no swaying deck or guide ropes secured by block and tackle, but the essence is the same. For a ship that sails among the stars, it spends a lot of time in the water. It's late afternoon, and they're sitting off the Dorset coast about fifteen miles from Lulworth Cove. The strange craft is once again submerged, with just the hatch above them exposed to the air.

While they were in flight, soaring like a bird but without flapping wings, Lady de Brooke took Julia and Anthony on a tour of the vessel, showing them the cargo hold. It was not filled with exotic spices, rum, wine or bales of wool, but rather with animals of all types suspended in an amber fluid within glass vials that stretched from the floor to the ceiling. She recognised some of the animals, like sheep and cows. Others were vaguely familiar, appearing like goats but with long twisting horns akin to those on the fabled unicorn. Still, others were mystical to her, like what Lady de Brooke called the elephant. It was a gigantic beast larger than a house with a nose longer than any of its four legs. The giraffe seemed impossible. It was a creature with a neck longer than its already elongated body, including its legs. The rhinoceros had a buttress-like horn that seems as though it could assault the fortified doors of a castle. The sheer variety of birds surprised her, with the vulture being the most grotesque. There was even what looked like a beaver with the beak of a duck. Julia questioned Lady de Brooke about it, but she insisted it was real, saying they'd retrieved it from the other side of the world.

With her newfound vision, Julia was able to see within each animal and observe their similarities rather than simply focusing on their differences. In particular, the rib cage, shoulders and arm bones fascinated her most. Creatures such as bats shared more in common with humans than she ever dared imagine. Julia was fascinated to see birds, bats, humans and even the mighty elephant all share the same basic bones, albeit in different proportions.

Humans had their fingers clustered at the end of their arms. Birds had stunted bones, but the archetype of the wrist and thumb were still visible in their wings, while fingers formed their wingtips. But it was bats that fascinated Julia most. The wing of a bat was leathery rather than covered in feathers. The bones within were little more than an arm with stretched, elongated fingers. It was as though someone had stuck sticks to the end of the fingers, making them five to ten times longer than they should have been. Although Lord de Brooke didn't elaborate on it at the time, this must have been what he was referring to when he said life on Earth shared the same basic instructions. Rather than being different, the bones of the animals she saw were variations on a common theme. It reminded her how the same timber beams could be used to build a barn, a ship, or a home. It wasn't the materials that differed, only how they were used and how they were combined.

"What can you see within the cliff?" Lady de Brooke asks. "As remarkable as it must seem, the light collector works better for you than either of us. Your mind is more keenly adapted to process sight.

We could deploy multiple probes, but I suspect you can already see what we're looking for and probably with greater clarity in a fraction of the time we'd need."

"The cliffs?" Julia says, raising her hand and touching her now metallic temple. "They're beautiful. The layers within them are folded like fabric packed for sale at the markets, or canvas sails stacked by the docks."

"Look closer. Look for things that shouldn't be there."

"Um, oh," she says. "There are shells, only they're huge. They're the size of a dinner plate."

Lord de Brooke says, "I can capture what you're seeing and display it here so we can all see it."

"Look for bones," Lady de Brooke says.

"I can see teeth," Julia replies. "Lots of them. They're arranged by size and set in a curve. Oh, there's the jaw bone. It's part of the stone. Ah, and a long, slim body, and flippers and a tail, but all of it is rock."

"It's rock now," the lady says, "but once it was alive."

Lady de Brooke smiles. She's looking at the projection in front of them, watching the section Julia's focusing on.

"But they're the same," Julia says. "The stone and the bone. There's no difference between them and yet I can see the density differs. I don't understand. How can they be the same?"

Anthony asks, "And how did they become stone? Was Medusa's cruel gaze cast upon these creatures?"

"We've only ever seen this on one other planet," Lady de Brooke says. "Almost everything that dies rots or is eaten by scavengers, but sometimes, on rare occasions, a dead body will be smothered by mud and silt during a flood. Once buried, over hundreds of thousands of years, the flesh and bone are replaced bit by bit with stone, making a perfect copy of the original. 'Tis marvellous. Splendid. It gives us a glimpse into the past as it was millions of years ago."

"Millions?" Anthony asks.

"A thousand thousand," Lord de Brooke says.

"There are numbers that big?" Anthony asks.

"There are numbers that make a million sound small," Lady de Brooke says. "The void is bigger than anything you can imagine."

"Bigger than Earth?" Anthony asks, surprised by the notion. "Bigger than a million Earths?"

"Way bigger than a million Earths," Lady de Brooke says. "The sun looks small in the sky, but it alone is bigger than a million Earths. As big as Earth may seem, it is but a speck of dust floating in a sunbeam when compared to the void."

Neither Anthony nor Julia reply to that comment. Everything they've ever known has been compared to a piece of dirt caught in a breeze. Julia finds that both terrifying and exhilarating.

The lord says, "We don't have time to employ local labourers and excavate."

"You're going to go out in the open? What about the hidden protocol?"

"We can go direct and still remain hidden. There's a farm two miles inland, but it's separated from the coast by a dense forest. If the ship stays low, no one will see us. We can extract your samples and leave the cliff looking as though it suffered from erosion. We'll use Julia's imagery to plot a course for our amplified light rays to carve out the echos of ancient life."

As he speaks, the craft rises from the ocean. Water runs off the hull, cascading down the sloping sides of the vessel, forming waterfalls that plunge back into the sea. The thousands of spikes lining the underside of the craft reach out thirty to forty feet from the hull. Julia has no idea what their function is, but she understands they propel the craft on. These are the sails that allow them to move through the air and to the stars. They hum and glow with energy surging through them.

"Oh, it's beautiful," she mumbles.

"What is?" Anthony asks.

For once, Julia pities him. Back in Westminster, sitting in front of the apothecary, it was Anthony that described the world to her. Now, she's the one that sees with clarity. As wonderful as his eyes are, they're bound to only one view of the world around him. Julia can roll through the different forms of light that surround them, each of which has different characteristics. She can see the warmth of his body in contrast to the cold bodies of Lord and Lady de Brooke. And that's something she wants to talk to them about. Although to Anthony, their hosts may seem human, Julia can see they're not.

Julia's seen the sun at night, which is something she would have never thought possible. Earth itself is transparent to her if she looks hard enough. When she stared down last night, she could see the sun on the other side of the planet. It looked different, being fuzzy, but Julia understood that was because she saw it differently from everyone else. She's not even sure it was light she saw as the haze suggested something else was radiating from the surface. Whatever it was, though, it passed clear through the Earth as though it wasn't even there.

Lady de Brooke was right. The brilliant blue skies of Earth hide a lie. Like a cork on the ocean, the entire planet is floating on a sea of stars. And not just stars. Julia has seen clusters of stars that shine like fireflies in a field, even whirlpools of stars that seem to contain not millions, but perhaps thousands of millions of stars. Julia's sure Lady de Brooke would have a name for that number, but for her, it is enough to know the lady is right about the sheer size of the void and the number of suns glowing in the darkness.

Julia finds the distant swirls of stars beautiful. They remind her of cream being churned. She can't see any movement within them even though it's clear from the shape that the stars are all in motion, swinging around each other like children playing with ribbons hanging from a maypole. And that leaves Julia wondering about the sheer distance between her and those fine pinpricks of light.

Anthony nudges her. "What can you see?"

"The void," she replies, distracting herself. "And it's beautiful."

"Can I get you looking back here?" Lord de Brooke says. As both Julia and Anthony have their backs to him, neither has realised her view is still being projected.

"Oh, of course."

Quietly, Lady de Brooke says to her lord, "Still easier than deploying a dozen receivers overhead."

"Maybe," he replies.

The tide is out. Waves break on the rocks. The spacecraft drifts over the debris that's fallen at the base of the cliff. The craft slowly gains height. It hovers over the forest lining the clifftop, but the hills inland hide it from view.

To Julia's surprise, people drop from the underside of the spacecraft. Although she can't see colour directly, Lady de Brooke has shown her the positions that relate to various colours like red, green and blue. As those dropping to the rocks dominate all of those regions, they must be white. If she squints, she can see through them, noting they have the same inner mechanics as Lord and Lady de Brooke. Julia desperately wants to ask them about the nature of their bodies, but for now, she focuses on identifying the stones that look like bones. She scans both the base of the cliff and the inside of the cliff itself. Lord de Brooke highlights anything out of the ordinary. The twenty naked men work to excavate the relics, but they're not using pickaxes or spades. They use a device that reduces the rubble to dust, clearing away the rock as though it were ice melting in the sun.

Julia thinks back to the executions. She remembers hearing Lady de Brooke had soldiers around her, but they never spoke. From what Julia could tell, their motion was almost mechanical, like the turning of a millstone by a water wheel with its sluice gate, pinion, spindle and gears. Although she was blind, Julia would sit and listen to the running water at the local mill. She marvelled at the rhythmic crunch as all the pieces within the machine worked together to grind grain. From what she can see within the men on the ground, something similar is at work, but the moving parts are few. She can see sparks of what looks like lightning pulsing through their bodies.

"The rocks," Lord de Brooke says. "Focus on the rocks."

"Yes, sir," Julia replies.

The men or soldiers or whoever they are, seem to drift back and forth between the ground and the starship, flying through the air but without the need for wings flapping against the breeze. They arrange the haul of once-were-bones on benches spread throughout the vast open deck of the starship.

Julia scans the beach, the rocks and the cliff for several hundred yards on either side of the craft, and as she does, the projection in front of them seems to come alive. It identifies hundreds of remnants, highlighting and targeting them individually.

"Ah, well, that is a lot easier," the lord concedes to his lady. "She's a natural. That level of detail would take several hours to gather manually."

Lady de Brooke smiles.

Various fragments are laid out before them by the white men. To Julia, the remnants appear as though they were made out of moulds of mud or plaster. It's difficult to believe these things were once alive, but the black leaves pressed into the rock in front of her are not crystal. She's astonished to think she's looking at life that perished millions of years ago and yet has been preserved in stone.

"This one looks like five snakes tied together," Anthony says, running his fingers over the rock. The strange-looking creature appears mounted on a flat stone. All of the surrounding rock has been cleared away, revealing an animal that looks impossible to Julia.

"I've seen starfish in the markets," Anthony says, "but this is as though snakes have bitten each of the limbs."

"Oh, it's one creature," Lady de Brooke says. "And it's related to your starfish in the same way you're related to your parents and your grandparents."

"And look at this one," Julia says, moving between benches now her sight is no longer needed. "It's like a snail shell, only much bigger. It's bigger than my head."

"Is this a dragon?" Anthony asks, examining the remnants of a jaw and skull bone with teeth the size of his fingers. The stones are laid out on the bench forming the shape of a spine and ribcage. As more of the workers come in, they lay down fragments that form flippers on this ancient sea creature.

"For you, it might well be," Lady de Brooke says. "But there is no overlap. You and your kind never encountered these beasts. They lived and died millions of years ago."

"I'm glad they died," Anthony says. "This one is longer than the boat in which we fled from London. If it were to swim in the Thames, I'd fear being eaten."

Lady de Brooke smiles. "You would have made a nice snack."

The look on Anthony's face shows he's not sure what to make of her comment, but it gives way to a smile as he realises she's joking.

"I don't understand," Julia says. "What purpose could there be in such magnificent creatures?"

"Life needs not purpose. Life has its own purpose."

"Which is?" Julia asks.

"To live is purpose enough. From our perspective, as those that journey between stars, life gives meaning to the void. Just as the stars provide relief from the darkness, life turns rocks into something glorious. And then, once their time has passed, life becomes stone again."

"*Dust thou art*," Anthony says. "*Unto dust thou shalt return.*"

"And 'tis true," the lady says. "We only see our lives in the context of now, but all that makes up these bodies of ours was once a cloud of dust drifting between the stars. And in eons to come, it will be dust again."

"And life?" Julia asks.

"Life is a moment to rejoice. Without life, your planet would be meaningless, just another lump of rock adrift within the empty darkness. But with life, Earth shines brighter than any star."

"What are you?" Julia asks, changing the tone of the conversation.

"Me? Us?" the lady asks in reply. "It will be difficult for you to understand."

"And yet we must understand," Anthony says. "For trust need flow both ways."

"Indeed," Lady de Brooke replies.

She removes her gloves and holds out her right hand before them, turning it slowly. The skin on her hand dissolves. Her fingernails, her petite knuckles, the lines on her palms and the fine texture on the back of her wrists become as smooth as marble.

"White," Julia says.

"Colourless," the lady replies.

"And 'tis not magic but knowledge," Anthony says. "Science."

"Of a kind that is long advanced beyond where your world now lies," the lady says. "We are alive, and yet we are not, but this is true of us all."

"How so?"

"You look at your body as though it were one, but it's not. You are a conglomeration. Your fingers are not your toes, and yet they share similar characteristics. Your arms are not your legs, and yet—"

"Birds and bats," Julia says, not meaning to cut her off but becoming excited by the concept. "Horses. Cows. Their bones. They're the same as those found in our arms and legs, and yet for them, they only function as legs."

"This is a wise observation," the lady says. "And it runs deeper. All of life is related. You see a dog and a bird and think they're different, but like a tree with branches that twist and turn in different directions, they all stem from the same trunk. Millions of years ago, neither dog nor bird existed but rather the ancestor to both."

"Parents and grandparents," Julia says, remembering the lady's earlier comment.

"Yes. The bones of bats, birds and humans are the same. They vary only in size and length. It's as though they were stretched and squished to suit each species."

Anthony says, "But they're so different."

"Just as the upper branches of a tree differ from the low boughs that sway close to the ground, and yet they're all connected to the same trunk and roots. Your bones are the same because the instructions that made those bones are the same. The tiny packages that form your bones are the same."

"Packages?" Anthony says.

"Consider the apothecary. It's made of stone, and yet it is more than stone. No one stone is any more significant than any other, and yet when combined, those stones become a wall, the frame of a window, the stairs leading to the basement or the lintel above the front door. In the same way, a house made of brick is more than the bricks that line its walls. A cottage is more than the wooden planks that keep out the weather."

"And you? Us?" Julia asks.

"We may differ from you, but we all follow the same principle. Your skin. Your hair. Your lips. Your heart. Your bones. Each of these is made of millions of tiny packets joined together to create something greater than the individual parts. Like the stones of the apothecary, they form your body—and mine."

Anthony holds out his hand, wanting to touch the lady's smooth, white fingers. "These packages."

"They're smaller than your eye can discern."

Immediately, Julia touches the device wrapped over her eyes. She rubs her finger over the control surface and stares at Anthony's hand rather than the lady's.

"Oh, they look like fish scales," she says.

"What do?" Anthony asks, confused. He turns his hand over, looking at the fine lines on his palm, and the wrinkles and grooves that form his skin.

"The outer layer is still, but beneath, there's movement, motion."

"Life," the lady says.

Lord de Brooke says, "Each package is alive. And together, they bring life to you."

"It's beautiful," Julia says, taking Anthony's hand and holding it still.

"Imagine a city bustling with life," the lady says. "Carriages come and go. Horses trot down the avenue. Cats hunt mice. Dogs scavenge in the alleyway. Merchants sell their wares in the market. Ships arrive at the port. Ravens fly over the castle walls."

"And that's my body?" Anthony asks.

"That's one tiny package within your body. Your body is more like the country as a whole with all its cities and towns linked together by tracks and roads. It's covered in farms and forests, rivers and lakes, mountains and fields, and together provides you with life."

"Then I am the queen," Julia says, proudly, sticking out her chest.

"And I am the king of my country," Anthony says, pretending to place an invisible crown on his head.

Lady de Brooke smiles.

"And you?" Julia asks.

"Life is fleeting. Your lives are measured in decades of four, five or six. Ours are measured in hundreds, reaching to perhaps a thousand at most."

"But?" Julia says, sensing something more.

"The void is measured in thousands of *millions*. 'Tis a number so vast it defies mere words, a number so vast it mocks life itself."

"You're not alive," Julia says as the realization hits.

"Not quite," Lady de Brooke says as her fingers turn into rectangles and her wrist forms a square. She twists her deformed hand and it transforms into a bouquet of roses and then a mallet before changing back into a pale, white hand. "Our bodies are machines. They work like your clocks."

"With springs and cogs?" Anthony asks.

"With something akin to that, being able to take any form we choose, but our brains are alive. Like you, we need air to breathe. Our clockwork bodies allow us to cheat death but not forever."

"Not for thousands of millions of years," Julia says.

"No."

"And the Convergence?"

"Imagine you have but one opportunity to meet with your friends and family or you'll never see them again. It's not the place you meet that's important so much as the place *and* time. Arrive too soon and you'll die before they get there. Arrive too late and you miss the party. That moment in between is the Convergence."

Lord de Brooke says, "Long ago, our kind set out to explore the stars, but the stars are so distant it's impossible to journey to more than a handful within even our extended lifetimes. It's like sailing to islands you can see from shore when what you really want is to reach the Americas. What to do then? Are we doomed to only explore a few nearby worlds? Even if we reach afar, how can we share the results of our exploration with our kind?"

Lady de Brooke says, "Imagine you need to coordinate the arrival of people from all around the country. One person is walking from London to the coast. Another is riding a mule from Wales. Someone else is rowing down the Thames. But they all need to meet a ship passing through the English Channel."

"Like the *Santa Cruz*," Anthony says.

"Yes, only this ship won't wait. It can't wait."

Lord de Brooke says, "You need to time when everyone leaves so they all arrive at the same moment in the future. That's the Convergence."

"And once gathered," Lady de Brooke says, "we can share the exploration of a *thousand* different worlds teeming with life, of which yours is just one. Instead of only being able to visit a few worlds, by spreading out and later converging, our kind can gain insights into worlds beyond imagining, tens of thousands of them. Our ships have gone everywhere, knowing they'll be reunited all at once."

Julia says, "But it only works if everyone arrives back in time."

"Yes, and just like here on Earth, if a storm arises and slows progress, we must rush to make up for the lost time."

"And you have more worlds to explore," Julia says.

"Yes. And we're constantly recalculating and recalibrating to make sure we'll arrive on time at the Convergence. Rather than travelling to a place, we're travelling to a time and place set far into the future."

"And we're going to go there with you," Julia says, smiling.

Flight

For the first month, life onboard the starship was a novelty. Having jumped from the deck of the *Santa Cruz,* Julia and Anthony found themselves reaching impossible heights. Whereas once the clouds and the blue sky overhead seemed to mark forever, now it's the darkness of the void that reaches toward eternity.

Julia's not entirely sure how time is measured on this ship from the stars, but she takes to counting her sleeps. Even though some days are longer than others that gives her a rough approximation of days, and having reached thirty, she's happy to call it a month—a month in which she's lived more than in the past decade. Lady de Brooke helped her with her monthly cycle, which came around day ten.

For Julia, life in the void is a fairytale brought to life. She was delighted to learn she could fly like a bird free from the clutches of a planet or moon. Anthony felt sick for the first few days after leaving Earth and vomited a couple of times, but not her. For her, sailing on a ship among the stars is a dream come true.

Thinking back about their time onboard this exotic ship, Julia has already formed fond memories. She was fascinated by their brief sojourn on Earth's moon, where Anthony insisted on hopping along the dusty ground, bouncing over divots on the pale, grey surface. Lod and Lay, as Lord and Lady de Brooke have taken to calling themselves, took pains to explain how the landscape was hostile. Looking at the desolate, barren plain, they told him those regions in the sunlight were hotter than coals on the edge of a fire. Drop water on them and it would boil in an instant. In the shadows, the reverse held true. The dark regions were colder than the coldest snowstorm ever to sweep across London. Then there was the air, or the lack thereof. Lod said it was worse than being underwater and unable to breathe. He told Anthony what little air there was in his lungs would be sucked out in an instant by the void, but Anthony wanted to stand on the Moon and look up at Earth. Lod said it was a waste of time, but Lay said anything that encouraged curiosity encouraged learning and that made it worthwhile. Within a day, they'd constructed a clear dome, balanced the temperatures and atmosphere, and Anthony got his wish. As much as Julia didn't want to admit it, she enjoyed jumping around on the moon as well. She felt as light as a feather.

Lod wanted to leave the sun and its planets far behind, but Lay insisted on showing them Jupiter and Saturn before they departed. Julia knew of these planets only as distant specks of light in the sky from her childhood. They were novelties. They were stars that moved with the seasons. Up close, though, they were more magnificent than anyone on Earth could have ever dared imagine. Master Dunmore would have been astonished by the sheer size of these planets and their beauty. Even Bishop Blaine would have been left speechless before them. All the woes that trouble Earth seem insignificant when faced with such majesty.

Although Lod, Lay and Anthony loved the golden planet with its splendid rings, it was Jupiter that captured Julia's imagination. Lod took them so close to the planet that the clouds appeared as a wall without end before them, stretching above and below their spacecraft. Although Anthony couldn't see through the clouds, Julia was able to peer beneath the curls and swirls and into the depths. To her surprise, there was no surface as such. Rather than having solid ground, Jupiter became increasingly dense. There was a point where the light from without faded while another radiated from within the heart of the planet itself. Heat flowed outward, causing the tapestry of clouds to entwine themselves. To Julia, the patterns were not dissimilar to braiding hair. There was a beauty to them that couldn't be defined.

And then there were the moons of these massive cloud planets. Both Jupiter and Saturn had dozens upon dozens of moons, which was something that fascinated Julia. Coming from Earth with only one moon, and seeing so many bright dots swinging around these vast planets, was a sheer delight. And they weren't all the same. She thought they'd all be as blank and desolate as Earth's moon, but they weren't. Perhaps that was the most surprising detail of all. Most of them were round, but some were shaped like pea pods from her garden after they'd been ravaged by snails. All of them were covered in dents, but some had scratches and scars. Several had mountain ranges that erupted with fountains. These sprayed out high into the void. Snow fell back to the surface, encasing these moons in ice and causing them to sparkle like the finest crystal. Among all this, though, was an impatient Lod complaining that there was no life so they needed to move on. He complained about losing time only for Lay to remind him they could vary their outbound speed to compensate for days and even years spent exploring. For him, it seemed the prospect of missing a potential future opportunity was too great. For her, the real opportunity lay with Anthony and Julia, and Julia appreciated her kindness.

It was several days before they left not only Jupiter and Saturn but the sun itself far behind them. Over the next week, the sun faded like a lighthouse on the headlands as a ship sails on toward the horizon. Whereas once the sun lit their way, now it was just another star in the heavens. It was the brightest star, but Julia saw it for what it was, a star and a star alone in the darkness. What had seemed so grand and powerful and all-consuming on Earth, giving light and life to forests and streams, was commonplace among the heavens.

With not a lot to do on the starship, Lay keeps them busy with studies, telling them learning is its own reward. Julia and Anthony talked all the time. The darkness scared Anthony. It should have scared Julia as well, but it didn't, not anymore. In the quiet times, Anthony confessed to Julia how he longs for the blue skies of Earth, even though Lay told him they were an illusion caused by the way light scatters in the air. Lod showed him the yellowish skies of Mars, which seemed to be locked in perpetual twilight. He said the darkness was normal. It was the blue of Earth and the dusty orange of Mars that were the exceptions.

For Julia, though, there was no darkness—not until they accelerated close to the speed at which light itself rushes through the void like an arrow in flight, having fled an archer's grasp as it races toward a deer in the woods. While Anthony saw a scattering of stars peppered across the dark void, Julia saw innumerable stars reaching out into the seemingly infinite distance. She could dial up her vision to see the sky speckled like a quail's egg. And stars weren't all that lay within the void. There were bubbles and clouds filling what would otherwise be empty. Lod would project her vision onto the inside of the craft so Anthony could see what she was describing, but it wasn't the same as what she felt within the depths of her mind.

Before she fell blind, the darkness scared her. It seemed to hide evil behind a dark cloak. Now, though, she understands that darkness is nothing but the backdrop for light. She understands that with enough patience to peer into the shadows, there were delights waiting to be discovered. What looked like a blurred, hazy star in the midst of the mythical chained woman of Andromeda appeared far larger than the moon when Julia increased the sensitivity of her eyes. Untold stars swirled around each other like leaves circling a drain, but they were frozen in place. It was as though they were but a painting on the sky. They formed a disc not unlike a shield, but instead of a crest of arms in the centre, the heart bulged, glowing like the flame of a candle in the dark of night. What had looked like a single, blurred star was innumerable stars packed so closely together they could not be separated. Like grains of sand on the beach, they appeared as one even though they were never one to begin with.

Then there were sights that seemed twisted and skewed. Thinking back to her childhood, Julia found the novelty of water fascinating. She loved to take a straight pole and stick it into the lake to watch it bend—only it didn't actually bend. It was an illusion. She would try to poke a rock beneath the pier or tap a fish darting around the support girders, but the stick would look as though it had a crook in it. On pulling the pole out, the bend would disappear. It was a simple trick played on the eyes, but one that fascinated her nonetheless as it seemed to hint at deeper truths left unspoken. Now, out in the depths of heaven, Julia sees something similar. What should be discs of stars swirling in the distance bend to either side of a vast star in the middle, only the star in the middle is no star. On closer examination, she can see it too is an illusion. Like the heart of Andromeda, there are so many stars drawn together they appear as one from a distance. There must be thousands upon thousands of millions of them by her reckoning. And like her pole plunged into the water, they bend light around them. To her, it's magical to see her childhood memories played out in the heavens, although she has no doubt Lay would have a knowledgeable explanation for what she sees. For now, Julia's content to know such beauty as she might find in a field full of wildflowers also lies deep within the void itself. Back on Earth, as a young girl, she never dreamed the heavens could be so magnificent.

Julia only remembers a handful of constellations in the heavens. Her mother loved to talk of Virgo and Aries, but Julia could never distinguish between them as a child. She never saw a woman in the sky or a set of scales or a lion. To her, the stars were randomly scattered like a bag of lemons being dropped on the floor. It was only those constellations with clear shapes she could recall. Now she sees with newborn eyes, she's told Anthony that Orion the hunter hides treasures no mere mortal could ever guess at, with slight smudges revealing vast nurseries in which hundreds of new stars are being born. Lay told them Earth and the Sun emerged from a similar cloud thousands of millions of years ago.

Julia learned to look at the void without seeing darkness at all. There was even a setting that allowed her to see streams surging in different directions like the thin, long flags at the top of a galleon's mast, caught blowing in the breeze. Lay told her these were caused by the same phenomena that turned a compass north. She said the void was empty of stuff but not of energy—never of energy.

When their ship of the stars accelerated, Julia and Anthony lost their ability to fly through the air. Now, with their feet set firmly on the floor, it feels as though they're carrying around rocks on their backs. It reminds Julia of the lazy days before she lost her sight when she and Anthony would compete in piggyback races within the village. The rules were simple. Each team had to take turns, alternating who carried whom through an obstacle course. There were hay bales to circle, crates to climb, and fences to crawl under. Anthony would sprint with her on his back and flop into the mud when squeezing under a fence. Julia tended to crumple and stagger under his weight, but she was nothing if not stubborn in a race. Here, though, there's no respite from the weight on her shoulders. Sitting brings some relief while lying down is the only way to get comfortable.

Now that a month has passed and the sun is but a speck in the sky no brighter than any other star, Julia feels at home. It's strange. She doesn't miss the village, perhaps because she never got to experience it through more than touch and sound for so many years. Anthony may seem at a loss, but Julia is at peace.

The Bible

"Why do we have to read the Bible?" Anthony asks, complaining to Julia when he should be taking his disagreement to Lod and Lay. Julia doesn't know the answer. She looks at the thick, bound book lying on the table in front of her with its sealed spine and rough-cut pages.

Anthony says, "Was not Bishop Blaine and his sermons torment enough for us?"

Julia shrugs. She's more concerned with the continued acceleration crushing them. At night, it's difficult to breathe. Anthony probably can't be bothered with the effort required to stagger up to the bridge to talk to Lay. Complaining to Julia is easier, and he knows he'll find a sympathetic ear with her. Julia, though, is distracted.

For Julia, approaching the speed with which light itself traverses the void is unnerving as once again darkness closes in around her. And it's not just some darkness, but *The Darkness*. She can see a darkness as absolute and impenetrable as when she was blind. At first, the effect was subtle. Each morning, when Julia arose, she made a habit of looking to observe something new in the heavens, but since they began their acceleration, she's begun noticing something unusual—the complete absence of everything. There's no light, no waves, no ripples, no stars, no planets, no clouds, nothing. And the darkness is increasing in size. It's chasing them, surrounding them on all sides.

Back when they were circling the Moon, everywhere she looked there was light. Granted, most of it was faint, but she could see distant islands of stars spread out in all directions. Now, though, the bitter, pitch-black darkness she's known most of her life has returned. As their speed increases, darkness closes in around them, suffocating them. The void, once teeming with stars, narrows in front of them.

"Good morning," Lay says, walking into the spacious lounge set between their bedrooms. Neither Julia nor Anthony has ever had their own room, let alone rooms with the luxury of a waterfall in one corner that can be turned on and off with the wave of a hand. Bathing beneath the warm water is heavenly, but Julia has other things on her mind this morning.

"Why the darkness?" she asks, taking Lay by surprise. The lady, with her porcelain skin and ornate dress, raises an eyebrow, which is a nice gesture even though Julia knows it's not real.

Since they departed Earth, all pretense has been dropped. Lod and Lay revealed what was once their true form, which to Julia seems to be a cross between a gigantic spider and a crab. These celestial sojourners didn't have claws, as such, but their outer shell was hard and curved, protecting their backs. They had eight legs, like a spider, but propelled themselves using only six while the front two acted as arms. They had three fingers on each hand with which to manipulate things. Like humans and actual spiders, their sensory organs were clustered around their heads and included eyes, but their hearing was so acute they could hear Julia swallow along with the soft beating of her heart. It was a mirage, of course. Lod and Lay were using their astonishingly flexible, clockwork bodies to simulate what they once looked like many centuries before. For Julia and Anthony's sake, they maintain the form of humans but their skin is pale. There's no need to maintain the appearance of flesh. If anything, they look like dolls brought to life.

"What darkness?" Lay asks.

Julia gestures with her hands, casting them out wide and over her head, tracing the line that, for her, marks the leading edge of the darkness and the ever-shrinking void with its innumerable stars.

"It's impenetrable," Julia says. "No matter what I do, I cannot see anything in the dark. It's as though I'm blind once more."

Lay nods, thinking for a moment. "Have you ever ridden a horse in the rain?"

"No."

"I have," Anthony says.

"When it rains, the droplets fall on your head and shoulders. Start riding and what happens?"

"They hit your chest and arms," Anthony says.

"You're riding into them," Lay says. "Leaving everything else behind."

"And?" Julia asks.

"Look closely at what you can see ahead of us," Lay replies. "Look at how the stars are shifting in front of us."

"I don't understand," Julia says, peering through her and the starship itself at the vast expanse of the heavens. "How is this possible? It is we who are moving, not the stars."

"Like rain falling from the clouds, we're charging into the droplets. Only these droplets are made from light. Being light, they carry all we can see. As we speed up, we see the light that would have come from all around us approaching only from in front, just like those raindrops back on Earth."

"And the darkness?"

"It's nothing. 'Tis what it has always been—the absence of light," Lay says. She picks up the Bible from the table, opens it and lays it before them. She touches the first line. "This is the Geneva Bible, translated not more than a year ago. This is one of the experimental prints. Here. Read this and think about all that surrounds you."

Julia and Anthony have been learning to read using several primers, but, after over a year in the void, this is the first book they've attempted to read. The thick spine, containing thousands of pages, is intimidating.

Anthony reads aloud, running his finger beneath the words as he speaks. "*In the beginning God created the heauen and the earth. And the earth was without forme and void, and darkenesse was vpon the deepe.*"

"Think about what it's saying," Lay taps the page, wanting Anthony to continue reading. Julia, though, reaches out beside him. She touches her finger beneath the words and reads aloud, taking over from Anthony.

"*Then God said, Let there be light: And there was light. And God saw the light that it was good, and God separated the light from the darkenes. And God called the Light, Day, and the darkenes, he called Night.*"

"I don't understand," Anthony says. "Is it true? Did the Divine do all this?"

"Bishop Blaine would say so."

"But Bishop Blaine is evil," Julia counters.

"That he is," Lay says, sitting at the table opposite them.

"And you would have us subscribe to his values?" Julia asks.

"I'd have you think for yourself."

"So it's true?" Anthony asks.

"It's intriguing," Lay replies. "Truth is not static. Truth is more than facts. It's not enough to say this or that is true. Truth seeks what lies *beneath* mere facts. Truth seeks to understand rather than define. Truth expands upon facts, shedding more and more light upon them as time goes on."

Anthony replies, "Master Dunmore says there are no gods but those made by men."

"Is he right?" Lay asks.

"I know not," Anthony says.

"And that's the beauty of learning," Lay replies. "You don't need to know. You need to think, to reason, to debate, to consider, to understand for yourself. Certainty is the crown of a fool. Knowledge should be the beginning of thought, not the end. Understanding is what's important, for it alone is the goal of knowledge."

"Our mass was held in Latin," Julia says. "No one understood what was being said. To me, it was gibberish."

Lay says, "Understanding is more important than any tradition—and that's what you need to realise about the Bible."

Anthony asks, "So we should believe it?"

"Oh, no, for there's no poison so deadly as belief. To have settled on one view alone is folly. Belief is not thinking. It's blind acceptance. We think of knowledge as something static, but 'tis not so. Knowledge grows over time, while beliefs shrink."

"But two plus two always equals four," Julia blurts aloud, being clever and thinking she's caught Lay in a trap, using an example that is static. "It never grows or changes. 'Tis always true."

"Are you sure?"

Anthony laughs. "I'm sure. Two plus two equals four."

"What if sometimes it doesn't?"

"But it does. It has to."

"Does it?"

Julia asks, "When doesn't two plus two equal four?"

"On paper, it does. In the real world, there are assumptions that must be properly understood."

"Like what?"

"If you add two fish to two crab apples, what do you have?"

Julia says a nervous, "Four?"

"Four what?"

"Two," Anthony says, contradicting Julia. "You still only have two of each because they can't be added together."

"Exactly. And so two plus two doesn't always equal four," Lay says. "It's an oversimplification."

"Because you're counting different things," Julia says,

understanding her point.

"Sometimes, but this is true even of things that seem the same," Lay replies. "If you have fish—if you have two minnows and two cod, how many fish do you have?"

"Four," Anthony says glowing with confidence.

"And yet, an adult cod is bigger than three or four minnows. You couldn't trade two minnows for two cod because they're not equal. Your two cod are the same as seven or eight minnows. Add all of them together and you've got the equivalent of ten minnows in four fish."

"So two plus two equals ten," Julia says, laughing and shaking her head.

"Exactly. Life is rarely simple. Often, there are assumptions that need to be properly understood before you can arrive at the correct answer."

"And the Bible?"

"People look for simple answers," Lay says. "They don't want to think too deeply. They *want* two plus two to equal four."

"And you?" Julia asks. "What do you think of the Bible?"

"I think it's fascinating. Regardless of what anyone says about its contents, the Bible has shaped the way your civilisation has progressed."

"Do you believe in God?" Anthony asks.

"I find it interesting that every civilisation on your planet—every single one—and there are a lot of them, all at different stages of development—all hold a belief in God. Only no two cling to the same god. They all differ. And to me, that's telling."

"Telling? How?" Julia asks.

"Telling in that, regardless of your differences, you all share a longing for something more, something beyond here and now."

"But you?" Julia asks, liking Anthony's question and realising Lay has avoided answering him directly. "Do you believe in God?"

"Many among us hold beliefs in a creator, but not I."

"Why not?"

"Because, as on your world, there's no evidence for God. Such a belief can only be made based on conviction and feeling. And I need more than that."

"Why?" Anthony asks, and to Julia, this is a far more penetrating question than perhaps it seems.

"Because stars shine regardless of my feelings. Because planets form regardless of my convictions. Because life arose on your world regardless of my beliefs. To me, these things—feelings, convictions and beliefs—are not the basis for reality."

"So you don't believe," Anthony says.

"No."

"I don't understand," Julia says. "If you don't believe the Bible, why read the Bible?"

Lay smiles. "Because you should never close the door on learning." She swings the Bible around to face her and begins flipping through the pages, skipping large chunks as she searches for something specific. "Let me show you my favourite Bible verse. The light and the darkness, right? That's what we're all fascinated by. You. Me. Us. Our worlds are separated by distances that defy the imagination and yet, in our imagination, we have reached the same conclusions about life. That's quite profound."

She turns the Bible back to Julia, pointing at a verse in Isaiah.

Julia reads aloud. *"Woe vnto them that speake good of euill, and euill of good, which put darkenes for light, and light for darkenes, that put bitter for sweete, and sweete for sowre."*

"Labels don't change the contents," Anthony says, recalling a similar conversation they had while sailing the Thames.

"Intelligence isn't so intelligent," Lay replies. "We flatter ourselves, but your people and mine have struggled with this. We're too willing to believe. All too often, we'll accept what someone says as true when it's a lie. This was written thousands of years ago. And it won't change for thousands of years to come."

"Light for darkness," Julia says.

"Bitter for sweet," Anthony says. "That's Bishop Blaine."

"That it is," Lay replies. "Beliefs are dangerous. They blind people."

Anthony says, "All most people want is to read the labels, they care not to sniff the contents."

Julia addresses Lay, saying, "And yet you see a universal desire for such beliefs not only among the tribes of Earth but on your own world."

"At the Convergence, your Bible will be of immense interest to my people—both believers and unbelievers. Our scholars will look at its internal consistencies and contradictions while lining it up with our own scriptures."

"And?"

"And they'll be fascinated by how the Bible opens by talking about light and darkness, as these are concepts that have preoccupied us as well. They'll be intrigued by the tales of battles and wars, and the way the wholesale slaughter of entire nations was justified as righteous by the victors. That, too, is a trap into which we fell.

"They'll see reason struggling to emerge in the various fables that pepper the scriptures, like Noah and the flood, Jonah and the whale, the pillar of salt, and the talking donkey. They'll see these myths giving way to the rise of strict rules and edicts to govern society. And, like King David, they'll realise heart triumphs over law.

"They'll enjoy the songs and psalms. I can already see parallels between your proverbs and our own ancient writings.

"The advent of the New Testament overturning the Old will perplex them. They'll see it as your species emerging from savagery to compassion. You see, it matters not whether it's true, but that it's a record of your culture spanning thousands of years. They'll see the way the Bible has shaped your consciousness."

"For better or worse," Julia says.

"Blaine is for worse," Anthony says.

Lay replies, "And you... you are for the better."

Cracks

Months become years.

Stars become distant candles in the window of an inn or an estate set on a hill. To Julia, it's as though she's in a celestial carriage, gliding through some ethereal night past farms and villages dotted across a darkened countryside. Planets become like pebbles in a stream. They're familiar. Each is interesting. Each is different. And yet each is also somehow the same.

Over time, Julia has learned to see colours. At first, it was by accident. While exploring a moon with fish hidden beneath miles of ice, the device wrapped around her head flickered with hints of blue and then yellow. She quizzed Lay about it and Lod realized the nerves within her dead eyes could be entwined with the device to detect colour as she once did. For Lay, it was trivial to make the adjustments once Lod isolated the connections. Within an hour, bursts of colour broke before her eyes in a kaleidoscope of beauty as Lay fine-tuned the device. For Julia, it was invigorating to see Anthony's brown hair and blue eyes once again. If anything, seeing colours has encouraged her not to use her extensive vision on transparent mode as she feels almost normal. Reds and greens, yellows and pinks have never looked more radiant to her and, for the first time, she, too, longs for blue skies, lush forests and meadows full of wildflowers. For all their wandering, they are yet to find anywhere as radiant as Earth.

Life isn't what Julia expected it to be. Personally, her life is wonderful, but the life on the various planets the team visits is nothing compared to Earth. As they stand inside their transparent pods, drifting above a world that orbits its red star once every ten days, all she sees is black pond scum clinging to a muddy river bank. Murky water runs down to a dark sea. Slime grows on rocks along the shore.

They drift along, flying easily a hundred feet above the surface of this strange world, following the coastline for miles as Lay makes observations. Occasionally, she descends to take a sample. Were it not for the red sky bathing the rock pools in what looks like blood, this could be the coast of Dorset or perhaps Dover. To one side, chalk cliffs rise above the rocks, only they're ruddy instead of white. Waves roll in from the sea, eroding the shoreline. Rounded pebbles line the coves and beaches stretching away from the headland.

"Where is everyone," Julia asks, drifting above the surface in what to her mind is a soap bubble, only it's far more robust, protecting her from the harsh air and scalding heat on this planet. "I expected more."

"More what?" Lay asks.

"Life."

"Me too," Anthony says. "I thought we'd find other planets with villages—and caravels sailing down the river!"

Lod monitors them from inside the starship as they sweep along through the sky, dropping to barely fifteen feet above the seething, boiling surface of the ocean. Dozens of streams run down from the highlands to meet the black waters. Steam drifts above the surface of the ocean. The wind sweeps it away.

"Oh," Lay says, "Life here is as fascinating and grand as that found on your world."

"But where are the trees?" Julia asks. "The birds and flowers?"

Lay speaks to Lod, saying, "Can you project the image of an oak tree for me just offshore?"

"Sure," is the disembodied reply they've become used to hearing in their ears when exploring new worlds.

Lay brings them to a halt above a beach covered in hundreds of stone columns rising slightly out of the water. They're rough and irregular. It's as though someone began laying the foundations of a pier or a building only to continually change their mind on the location of the footings. On shore, boiling mud seethes out of the ground in the tidal region between the water and the land proper. Bubbles of dark grey mud rise from deep below the beach. The mound of mud moves slowly, forming a dome several feet across before it bursts, releasing a puff of steam. The muddy sides of the bubble plop back to the surface. The residue is as thick as tar and oozes over the ground.

The starship floats several hundred feet above and slightly behind them. Lod projects the ghostly image of a mighty oak tree. Roots extend down and out from the base of the trunk, while limbs as thick as the curved beams that form the hull of a galleon reach out, supporting branches that spread for almost fifty feet around. Twigs and leaves form the dense, outer foliage rising high above them. Lay reaches out, touching the ethereal image, causing it to flicker.

"On all but one world, the life we've found has been related like leaves to twigs to branches to limbs to the trunk and the roots. Often, the direct links are gone, but the common ancestry is apparent from their shared characteristics."

Julia nods, remembering her analogy from several years ago.

"Now if we compare Earth to this red world, what differences do you think we'd see?"

Anthony says, "The tree of life for this world would be smaller."

"Would it?" Lay asks.

"Yes. Our world is teeming with life."

Lay says, "You've seen the harvest we collected from your world, the strange and exotic creatures that frequent every region of Earth, from snakes to spiders, swallows to eagles, giraffes, lions and tigers. And yet here, there's none of that variety."

"So the tree for this planet would be smaller," Anthony says.

"Simpler."

"Simpler, yes, but not smaller."

"I don't understand," Julia says.

Lay soars closer to the ethereal tree suspended within the air on this hostile planet. She reaches out and touches a single branch. She's picked a section in the upper region where the leaves are thickest. Immediately, a thin branch, along with four or five twigs and dozens of leaves light up, glowing yellow.

"On your world," she says. "This is all you actually see. From beetles to ants, oak trees to wheatgrass, chickens to snakes—all of it—all of the millions of species that roam the grasslands or swim in the oceans of Earth would fit on this one, tiny branch."

Julia asks, "But what of the rest?"

"The rest of the tree of life on this world and yours is made up of everything too small to see. The variety is astonishing, well beyond any two creatures you compare on Earth."

Anthony says, "So an octopus and a cat?"

"As vastly different as they may seem, they're all on this one, small branch."

"How can that be?" Julia asks.

"The leap from simple life to complex is akin to Altas carrying Earth on his shoulders. It's rare across ten thousand worlds. Make no mistake, the slime you see here is every bit as remarkable as an albatross winging its way across the ocean or an eel swimming in a stream. If you—"

"Lay, I need you back here now," Lod says, interrupting them. The oak tree fades from sight, leaving the three of them looking along the coastline at the distant, barren hills bathed in red.

Lay says, "I've identified a vast, interconnected colony just ahead of us. Samples would give—"

"Now," Lod says. "I'm picking up subsurface instabilities."

Although Julia doesn't understand the specifics behind the terms

Lod's using, she knows enough to realise there's something dangerous unfolding beneath the ground. She taps the side of her head and peers beneath her feet.

Lod says, "The crust is thin here. There's a pocket of molten rock and gas down there. It's unstable. If it breaches the surface and water gets in—"

"That's not good," Lay says, and with a flick of her hand, the pods rise, returning to the starship.

Julia looks beneath the shoreline, wanting to understand a danger Anthony cannot see. Steam rises from vents that creep below the ground like ivy crawling over a castle wall. She can see heat rising from within the planet. Rocks fracture and crack, breaking under the pressure coming from below.

Ever since she gained the ability to see with strange eyes, Julia's been fascinated by how solid ground floats on liquid rock like the ice on a pond in the depths of winter. All that's firm is a lie. All that seems stable is underwritten by a turbulent swirling layer of rock so hot it flows like molasses. Her father worked in the village smith. She knows metals can melt. They glow before they droop. If a fire is hot enough, metal can be forged, forming any implement before being plunged into a bucket of water to fix the shape. Julia has fond memories of her father dipping plough blades and pitchforks radiating with heat into a trough of water. Steam would billow into the air, forming clouds that dissipated on reaching the roof. It's only now she realises the same mechanics are at play within planets themselves, with their molten cores seething like a furnace.

As they approach the underside of the starship with its thousands of spikes protruding out from the hull at various angles, Julia sees something everyone else misses. The surface of the water below them drops, forming an indentation that lasts barely a second or two as waves rush into the low region, restoring the balance. The depression is easily a mile wide, if not more, and almost directly below the ship.

Julia can see how the sea floor dropped, forming a crater in the ocean that's been filled with a rush of turbulent water. Cracks appear on the land. They splinter through the cliff, causing rocks to crash to the sea below.

A circular hatch opens on the side of the starship, allowing them to enter. Julia's distracted, though. Instead of watching their approach, she turns and looks at dozens of geysers erupting on the distant plain. Jets of boiling hot water rush up, reaching hundreds of feet in the sky. She's dragged backward by Lay but before the hatch can close, a stream bursts through the air in front of the starship. A wall of steaming hot water rushes past, catching the prongs that allow the ship to sail between the stars.

The craft rocks. The hatch seals. The air inside the antechamber is flushed and their soap bubbles dissipate.

"We're good," Lay says, speaking to Lod. "We're inside. Get us out of here."

The three of them slide across the floor as the craft sways, twisting to one side. Julia reaches out with her hands, steadying herself against the wall. Her eyes peer through the hull, through the steam and spray outside at the fractured seafloor.

The starship rises fast, pushing them down as it does so. Beneath the ocean, cracks widen, reaching not hundreds but thousands of feet beneath the rock.

"Hold on to something," Julia says, grabbing onto Anthony out of habit. He knows her well enough not to question her in the moment. He grips the bulkhead.

In a heartbeat, an explosion bursts through the sea. Chunks from the ocean floor are hurled into the air as though they were hay being cast by a farmer onto the back of a wagon. A wall of steam scalds the underside of the starship. Debris strikes the craft, crushing hundreds of prongs. Rocks crash into the hull, having been thrown out of the planet as though hurled by an angry giant. They break through the metal, smashing their way into the hold.

The starship is rising into the sky, but it can't escape the wave of rocks bursting out of the surface of the planet like sparks flying from a log thrown on a fire.

Lay says, "Talk to me, Lod."

"Get them to a storage pod," Lod replies. "We're losing air."

As the starship accelerates, it breaks free of the billowing cloud of debris rising tens of thousands of feet into the air.

"But the craft?"

"She's taken a beating, but she can still fly. There's nothing we can't repair, but it's going to take time to seal the hull. Until we do, we need to isolate them from acids in the air."

Lay turns to them, saying, "Get to the aft deck. There are two empty pods awaiting collection samples. Seal yourselves in there until we can contain the damage."

Anthony starts to reply, but Julia's not waiting for pleasantries. She grabs his hand and drags him out of the antechamber and into the long corridor that leads to the various storage areas within the hold. Julia runs. Even though they're well above the dark, curling cloud rising out of the scar carved into the side of the planet, rocks still impact the hull. These are different, though. She can see them surrounded by steam and glowing with heat. On striking the starship, they shatter into millions of pieces.

The ascent of the craft slows. Lod's not trying to reach the void, probably because of the punctures in the hull. He's taking the ship on an angle, wanting to put some distance between them and the firestorm that's broken through the crust of the planet.

Julia and Anthony reach the aft deck. The storage in this region is tightly packed, with barely any room to move through the aisles.

"Where are the empty pods?" Anthony asks, dragging her to a halt and looking at the thousands of pods packed into the hold. On reaching each pod, the amber surface becomes transparent, allowing them to see the frozen occupants. The creatures here are from neither Earth nor any world they've visited. These must be the samples Lod and Lay collected before the two of them joined the crew. One of the tanks contains what looks like a deer, but the animal has easily a dozen legs reaching several times its body length, making it appear as tall as a giraffe while spindly and elongated. Another creature has overlapping shells forming what looks like a flower, only it's several times larger than either of them.

On they push through the maze of pods. There are trees but their leaves are as fine as needles and jet black. Anthony bumps into a tank with a creature covered in spikes reaching up to form a crest, not unlike that of a pheasant's tail.

Smoke swirls around their legs. On touching their skin, it burns even though it doesn't feel hot, forcing them on. Anthony's struggling to breathe. He wheezes, desperate for clean air. Julia coughs. She pulls her shirt up over her mouth, breathing through the cloth.

"There," she calls out, pointing into the darkness. She can see two empty pods against the far wall.

"I see them," Anthony says. Whereas all the other pods in the hold have different sizes and shapes, having adapted to suit their occupants, these two appear identical, making them easy to spot among the confusion. They're narrow and resemble a coffin made from glass.

As they approach, the pods open. They're cramped, being barely wide enough to fit a single person. Someone as big as Master Dunmore wouldn't fit inside.

The two pods are ready to accept them. It's at that point Julia sees something that causes her to come to a halt. She tugs on Anthony's hand.

"What?"

Anthony may not be able to see the danger ahead of them, but Julia can. Her magnificent eyes reveal the pods are far from identical. The one in front of Anthony has cracks running through its base. The thin lines are as fine as strands of hair, but they're growing, creeping further up the side of the pod.

"Come," Anthony urges, pulling her on, but she can't do it. She can't send him to his death. In that moment, Julia does something she's never done before. Being smaller and lighter than him, it was always he that got a little too rough when they'd play. Back in Westminster, as kids, he could bump her hips while running through the village and send her sprawling into a haystack. After she lost her sight, he was kind, but always far stronger than her, being able to lift her onto the window ledge in front of the apothecary. Now, though, it's her turn to be decisive.

Julia grabs his shirt by the collar and jerks him over in front of her. Anthony's taken off guard.

"Huh? What—"

"Go," she says, pushing him into the pod directly in front of her. She steps sideways, walking into the pod he was heading for.

"What are you doing?" he asks, turning as the pod seals and clean air circulates around his feet.

"Looking after you for once."

"Me?"

"I'm sorry," Julia says, examining the weakened walls of her pod. Cracks weave their way up the back of her tank. Beyond them, she can see a section of the hull glowing where molten rock is clinging to the outer skin of the craft.

"What's going on, Julia?" he asks, pressing his hands against the slick surface of his pod and locking eyes with her.

"I'm saving you."

"Saving?" Anthony says. "I don't understand."

"You should know. I—I have no regrets," Julia says, feeling the heat radiating through the floor of her pod. For her, it's as though Bishop Blaine has finally caught up to her and lit a wooden fagot beneath her feet once more. Tears form in her eyes.

"I don't think I've ever said thank you."

"Julia, you're scaring me."

"I'm at peace, Ant. I've lived more and seen more than anyone in Westminster could ever dream. I've watched as stars burned like bonfires in the darkness. I've seen comets sending streams of light out into the void. I've rejoiced as new worlds were born around fledgling stars."

The wall behind her pod glows in a soft red colour as the hull of the starship melts. Anthony sees it. His hands splay wide against the inside of his pod. Even though the rupture is on the far side of Julia's pod, he must be able to feel the heat.

"No," he mumbles.

Her eyes—or what's left of them after the processing equipment embedded in her forehead has captured the light around her—never leave his eyes. He's all she wants to see. Anthony, though, is frantic. His eyes dart around. His body flexes. He pounds on the inside of his pod, wanting to break free and save her as he once did from the executioner's pyre, only this time there are no chains to shed. A fog swirls around outside the pod. Even if he were to open it, they both know he'd succumb to the fumes before he could reach her. And what then? Would he drag her out into the poison?

"Please," he says. "There must be another way."

Julia hangs her head. Her hair falls around her face. Tears roll down her cheeks, slipping out from beneath the alien mask that gives her sight.

Lay speaks from somewhere else on the starship. Her voice echoes around the two of them, being transmitted by some strange device Julia neither knows of nor understands.

"What's happening? Are you in the pods?"

"Mine's damaged," Julia replies.

She coughs. Cracks splinter through the resin, allowing the foul air to reach her lungs. Rather than feeling pain, her mind grows dull. She feels tired. Her vision blurs. Anthony's voice fades, changing from words to tones. He pounds on his cramped pod, desperate to reach her, but she knows this is the end. It takes all her might to focus and remain conscious.

From the bridge of the starship, Lod says, "Get her into an atmospheric bubble. It won't last as long, but it'll buy us time."

"I'm on my way," Lay replies, but Julia knows it's too late.

"It's not your fault," she says as cramps seize her stomach.

"I'm coming," Lay replies. "Hold on. I'm coming for you."

"I don't know what to do," Anthony says with exasperation breaking in his voice.

Part of the hull melts away, exposing their pods to the air outside. The sky is blood red. Dark clouds billow on the horizon.

"Blue skies," she mumbles, crumpling at the bottom of her pod with her knees up against her chest. Anthony follows her down, crouching opposite her.

"What?"

"I loved it when you used to sit outside the apothecary, telling me about the blue of the sky. Tell me, Ant. Tell me about the sky. What do the blue skies of Earth look like?"

He chokes up. "Blue is cool like a stream. And yet there's warmth there. It radiates but not like a fire. Blue is more like when you warm your hands in woollen mittens on a cold winter's day."

Lay comes running down the corridor. The starship shakes, twisting to one side. The weakened outer hull beside Julia falls away, plummeting toward the rocky ground. Pods fall, tumbling out of the gap.

"Looooood!" Lay yells, holding on to Julia's pod as her feet swing toward a jagged hole in the floor. Burning metal beams fall. In the distance, fiery clumps of rock are flung into the air. Beneath them, boulders slam into the underside of the spacecraft.

"I'm trying," is the reply. "We're almost clear."

Lay clambers over the pod. She works with her hands, trying to reseal the cracks and repair the damage. Sparks fly from her fingertips.

Anthony ignores Lod and Lay. His lips tremble as he speaks. "Blue is somewhere in between everything and everywhere. Yellow is wheat. Red is fire. Green is life. Brown is the ground beneath our feet. But blue is above. It's what surrounds us throughout life. Blue is serene."

"I—like—blue," Julia manages to say, feeling her throat constrict.

"Blue is..." Anthony's still speaking but Julia's past hearing.

Darkness descends on her once more, just as it did in the village when she lost her sight. Rather than being terrified, Julia accepts the calm it offers. Life may be a candle that's easily snuffed out, but for her, the opportunity to shine in the darkness, even if only briefly, has been a privilege. As the pitch-black of the eternal night closes around her, she wishes for nothing more than to be sitting in front of the apothecary once again. She can almost feel the warmth of the sun on her cheeks, the smell of freshly baked bread wafting through the air, the sound of water dripping from the eaves after a storm has passed, and the tenderness of Anthony's voice as he talks about the colour of the sky and its puffy clouds.

And with that, she dies content, knowing Anthony will live.

Act III

21st Century

Cobra

Felix Wilson sits back, allowing a waiter to lay an embroidered napkin on his lap, protecting his William Westmancott from getting stained. It's a suit. That's all a William Westmancott is, but it's a suit that cost twenty-eight thousand pounds to procure from Savile Row. His Westmancott looks like any other dark black business suit in London's financial district, albeit with over a hundred thousand precisely-placed handmade stitches forming the seams. To the untrained eye, his suit is form-fitting with a snug jacket pulling in around his waist, but rather than coming off a machine assembly line, it's been tailored for his figure and his alone. The shoulders are padded, but not overly so, leaving a hint of doubt as to the presence of muscle beneath. The cut of the V in the jacket is sharp, accentuating his tie.

Felix is wearing a red silk tie with a Double Windsor knot. The placement is impeccable, sitting up against his neck and setting off the angles that flow down across his chest in a cascade of triangles being formed between his tie, his collar, his shirt and his absurdly expensive Westmancott. The distinctions are subtle, but the crisp look projects power and confidence, along with unabashed wealth.

"We need to be more... reconciliatory," Ambassador Chenko says, sipping a glass of wine.

Nothing about Ambassador Chenko is haphazard. Her words are

precise, perhaps even rehearsed. The pause as she sips, the lingering moment before she sets her glass down, the careful placement of the glass on the restaurant table: Chenko is sending her own message. This casual dinner in a private section of the *Mauree de Plume* restaurant on the south bank of the Thames has been approved at the highest levels of the Kremlin. Even her dress has been chosen with care. The ambassador is known for wearing drab-coloured dresses. Grey and navy blue are her preferred colours, although Felix has been told she sometimes wears a mint green tea dress to garden parties in summer. Her dresses almost always have a high cut that reinforces the need for business over pleasure. Tonight, she's wearing a light blue dress that accentuates her figure. A pearl necklace and plunging v-neckline direct the gaze down to the pale skin of her cleavage. It's not a *fuck-me* dress, but it's as close as she'll ever wear with anyone other than a lover. It suggests a level of friendship she does not have with the United Kingdom's Secretary of State for Defence.

Felix is brutal in response to her comment, '*We need to be more reconciliatory.*'

"We?"

He raises his glass and sips.

As an avid chess player, for him, these are the opening moves of a game. The wine glass is a proxy for the clock in a competition. After each move, it's the opponent's turn to examine the board.

Felix is being laconic. There's much he could say but won't. The Russian Federation has a sordid history with the West and particularly the United Kingdom, where it has been reckless, to say the least. The poisonings in Salisbury have not been forgotten. Neither has the war of aggression against Ukraine. At the time, Felix was a staffer for then Secretary of State for Defence Ben Wallace, before entering politics at the age of thirty. He remembers the glee with which the minister sought cabinet approval to issue Ukraine with the British NLAW antitank weapons. Although there were considerable discussions about the possibility of the Russians using the NLAWs as a justification to broaden their war, the assassination attempt on Sergei Skripal in

Salisbury wasn't far from anyone's mind. The use of the deadly nerve agent Novichok made this an act of war, but one the Russian Federation quickly denied and the United Kingdom was wary to acknowledge. The Russians could have used any one of a number of means at their disposal against Skripal, from a knife or a gun, or a staged robbery, or even the classic Russian flying school approach where victims are encouraged to take to the skies from a fifth-floor balcony. Novichok sent a message. *We're belligerent. You're nothing to us. We don't care.* It was an insult. It made a mockery not only of the territorial integrity of the United Kingdom but also of its intelligence service. After Salisbury, NLAWs were *always* going to find their way into Ukraine's arsenal.

By replying with just one word—*We?*—Felix is questioning the ambassador's intent. *They* attacked the United Kingdom when they went after Sergei Skripal. *They* attacked Ukraine. *They* sabotaged European energy supplies, destroying their own pipeline in the process. *They* engaged the West with information warfare spanning more than a decade, bringing about Brexit and Trump as a means of destabilizing the body politic at the heart of NATO. The hot war may be over, but none of their acts have been forgotten. '*We need to be more reconciliatory,*' is an insult and Felix isn't going to let it slide, even in an informal, off-the-record conversation over dinner.

Two waiters approach. They're dressed immaculately in black. White gloves hold silver trays. They circle around to the right of each of them, placing an appetizer in front of them.

Ambassador Chenko looks at the gilded plate in front of her.

"Russian caviar."

"On Ukrainian wheat wafers," Felix replies. "Drizzled with Galili olive oil from Israel."

That's the closest Felix will come to any kind of concession, and even that is laced with symbolism. Given his pre-dinner briefing from the Foreign Office suggested the ambassador wanted to discuss the Middle East, he felt it appropriate to include the oil. So much is being said with so few words. And none of it will go unnoticed. The ambassador will be debriefed by the Kremlin as soon as she arrives back at the Russian embassy. Each detail of their dinner will be scrutinised by analysts as they plan their next move.

Felix notices someone enter the restaurant from a side door and whisper something to one of his aides. The aide rushes over. He has his hands held behind his back, which is overly stuffy and formal. Felix knows it's all part of the act.

The aide bends over and whispers, "Daffodils, sir."

Felix has no doubt Ambassador Chenko is wearing an enhanced audio recorder. She, personally, may not have picked up what the aide said, but the mic wouldn't have missed a syllable. The Russians will know *daffodils* is a code word, but they won't know what it signifies. Most of the codes used by the Ministry of Defence change regularly but some remain the same for a protracted length of time. Although it might seem to be an operational security flaw, it's because their use is so infrequent the chance of them being intercepted and understood is low. *Daffodil* has been around since Thatcher, but it's rarely been used. It's a severity warning. Rather than signifying any one threat or type of threat, it indicates the level of importance as deemed by COBRA. *Daffodil* means there's an imminent threat to the civilian population that needs to be addressed immediately.

"You'll have to excuse me," Felix says, daubing his lips with his napkin and pushing his chair back. He gets to his feet, taking time to neatly fold his napkin before placing it on the table beside his cutlery.

"May I ask—" the ambassador says, but Felix cuts her off with a raised hand.

"Perhaps we could continue our meal another time."

"Of course."

He turns and walks away with the aide. Neither of them says anything. They don't rush or show any outward sign of panic.

COBRA is the United Kingdom's emergency response team. It doesn't have a fixed membership, as such, being an interface between senior cabinet ministers and broader government agencies. Normally, any military issues will come directly to Felix as the Secretary of State for Defence. It's then his prerogative to raise them with the Prime Minister or the broader COBRA group. That someone from the standing committee within COBRA has sought to interrupt his meeting with the Russian ambassador means this has a level of severity that is unprecedented. If anything, COBRA would go to the PM first and only to Felix on the PM's orders. Whatever this is, it's big, but British sentiments are nothing if not dignified. Neither man will give the Russian ambassador any hint as to the urgency behind the code.

The aide opens the door to the restaurant, allowing Felix to walk out into the crisp autumn air. Vapour forms on his breath. Being aware he's still visible through the curtains and probably under covert surveillance by the ambassador's outer perimeter team, Felix reaches casually into his jacket pocket and pulls out his phone. He's stalling. He's trying to look relaxed. The screen displays the fact he has several unread notifications but there are no details displayed for security reasons. He could unlock the phone and read them, but he won't.

A Bentley comes around the corner. It's a black SUV with an extended wheelbase. The V8 engine purrs as the car pulls up in front of Felix. The paintwork is immaculate. The chrome wheels have been polished and the tires blackened. To anyone watching, this is just another example of decadence in London's inner city. Dark-tinted windows beg to differ.

The aide doesn't pull the door all the way open. He positions himself so as to obscure the view inside and allows Felix to slip into the back seat.

The Bentley pulls away, leaving the aide standing in front of the restaurant. The car accelerates smoothly while remaining under the speed limit. Apart from two motorcycle police escorting the vehicle, it looks entirely normal.

Inside the Bentley, luxury has been traded for function. Wiring looms and 5G network routers, military radios and satellite equipment line the inside of the roof. Green LED lights flicker with the transfer of information. The leather seats have been removed. The carpet has been ripped up and replaced with a bank of flat batteries designed to power the electronics for up to six days if needed. Felix sits in what looks like the fibreglass shell of a racing seat with a five-point harness. It's cramped and uncomfortable, being designed for safety. Beside him, there's a computer workstation and screen with an in-progress video conference call. The other participants are already talking. He listens, noting his screen indicates he's on mute. Felix removes his jacket and works himself into the seat straps as the car turns onto the main street, joining a motorcade heading out of the city.

The Bentley is part of a fleet of vehicles known as the Mobile Extended Continuity Command Alternative or MECCA. The American President might be able to take to the skies in Air Force One and flee the US capital in the event of an attack, but the United Kingdom is smaller than the state of Colorado. There's nowhere to run to when the country pales in size next to Michigan or Arizona so the plan has always been for the British cabinet to split up and head for the countryside. Although planes and helicopters are faster in an emergency, they're also easier for a foreign adversary to track using radar. The Bentleys are shielded against EMP attacks and designed for the continuity of government in the event of civilian infrastructure failure. They're used to keep the United Kingdom's political leaders in touch with each other and the military at all times.

"What are we dealing with?" Felix asks, loosening his tie.

Although the driver is facing forward, the front passenger's seat has been reversed so it's facing the back seat. An air chief marshal sits opposite Felix, being the equivalent of a full general in the Royal Air Force. He uses a tablet computer to control the screen beside the minister.

The marshal speaks with clarity, wanting to avoid the possibility of being misunderstood. The mute symbol disappears from the screen.

"Air Chief Marshal Mahoney. Broadcasting on COBRA. Summary of threat. Early-warning radar stations in Thule and Fylingdales have detected and independently confirmed a single inbound ballistic missile heading toward the British Isles." He looks at his watch, adding, "Seven minutes out."

"Target?"

"Based on the initial trajectory, either Cardiff or Bristol."

"Wales?" Felix asks, leaning forward and pulling against the straps of his seat in surprise. "Why? Who would target the west country? That makes no sense."

An additional video appears in yet another box cluttering the screen on the conference call. The Prime Minister enters the conversation, picking up on the topic.

"But London's on the same flight path, right?" he says. Like Felix, the PM is in a Bentley being driven out of London, but to a different, secret location. He adds, "I was told we're only a hundred and twenty miles further along the same line."

"What speed is this thing doing?" Felix asks.

"18,000 miles an hour," the marshal replies.

On hearing that, Felix better understands the PM's concern. "So an additional hundred and twenty miles is nothing by comparison. It could cover that in seconds."

"That's correct, sir."

Felix asks, "Do we have confirmation of a launch site? Have we identified a hostile state?"

"No, sir. The Pentagon confirms our data, but even they don't have a ballistic launch location."

The Prime Minister says, "We need targeting response options. I want—"

"Excuse me, sir," Felix says, thinking fast on his feet and realising millions of lives hang in the balance. There's something horribly wrong with what's unfolding.

The Prime Minister does not look impressed with him.

As a leadership group, COBRA is stuck in an East/West paradigm, assuming the usual hostile actors. This wouldn't be the first time Russia has stretched credulity with something that's deniable, but moments ago, Felix was sitting opposite the Russian ambassador. She was relaxed. Is it possible such an attack would be launched not only without her knowledge but with her in harm's way? Even if she was out of the loop, Chenko has eyes and ears everywhere. She hasn't survived for over a decade in Russian politics by being a wallflower. If she had any misgivings about simmering tensions, she wouldn't have been so calm. If she was looking for a backdoor channel to defuse a first strike, she would have jumped out of her seat when he left the restaurant.

And this isn't a first strike. It's a single missile, not dozens of missiles. Even if it does change course and hit London, what will it accomplish? From a civilian perspective, the consequences would be disastrous, but there's no military value to striking the capital. The Russians have to know the UK's Trident fleet won't be sending a single missile in reply. Russia is about to become a radioactive wasteland, so why take only one shot?

Felix asks, "Have we seen any unusual military activity in Russia? Ports? Staging of fighter craft? Bombers? Troop build-ups? Anything in the Bastion Zones?"

"No," the marshal replies. "Besides, it's coming from North America, not Europe or the Arctic."

"Well, the Canadians sure as hell aren't targeting us," Felix says. "Any unusual chatter from China?"

"Nothing."

"I need to know what the hell I'm dealing with," the Prime Minister says. "I will not stand idly by while another 7/7 or 9/11 unfolds around us. Give me options."

Felix's phone beeps with an incoming message. Although the details are hidden, the sender isn't: *Ambassador Chenko*. Felix swipes up, unlocking his phone.

It's not us. You have to believe me. Call me. We need to talk.

One of the other marshals on the video conference addresses the

Prime Minister, saying, "We are at five minutes. I need standing contingency orders in the event of a loss of communication with Cabinet. What are your blackout orders?"

"Are we at this point already?" Felix asks, feeling exasperated, but the marshal ignores him, speaking to the Prime Minister.

"What is the approved response package to a military strike on the United Kingdom? Are we approved for *Twinkle Twinkle, Baa Baa* or *Bingo?*"

"Bingo," the PM replies.

Felix hears this exchange, but it seems surreal. He's speechless. His mind is racing over the conflicting details surrounding the rogue missile. Something is horribly wrong.

The marshal provided the PM with three targeting options for a retaliatory strike on the Russian Federation.

Twinkle, Twinkle, Little Star is a denial-of-function attack where the United Kingdom's nuclear arsenal is used to cripple rather than destroy Russia. It includes two high-altitude EMP blasts that will twinkle like stars as they fry civilian electronics along with probably most of the ageing electrical equipment in the Russian arsenal, but the hardened gear used in missile silos and bombers will probably survive. The challenge for the military, though, would be communicating and coordinating with the broader Russian Federation. Under this scenario, peace talks are held to defuse tension. The plan includes cruise missile strikes on a number of radar and communications centres, but it's designed to force Russia to the negotiating table rather than pursue annihilation, as that would only foment all-out war.

Baa Baa Black Sheep asks, "Have you any wool?" As a package, it includes the EMP strikes but broadens the attack to non-nuclear strikes on key civilian infrastructure such as ports, bridges, radio and television stations, along with warehouse distribution centres. The goal is to bring the war immediately to the forefront of the civilian population and cripple the Russian economy. It's easy to be brave when the battle is over there somewhere. When it's in your own backyard, it's different. Patriotism is a luxury item. Bluster is a pretence for the gullible. When you're in a foxhole, it's no longer about flags and courage. Survival becomes a practical rather than an ideological necessity.

Both *Twinkle, Twinkle* and *Baa Baa* leave the Russians with a way out. Neither is seeking to destroy the state as a whole. Both are intended to cripple any response while avoiding widespread bloodshed. *Bingo* is different. There's no restraint.

The children's nursery rhyme *Bingo* includes the line, "B—I—N—G—O," spelling out the word, but on each subsequent chorus, one of the letters is successively replaced with claps. By the end of the song, all that's left is someone clapping to the beat of the chorus. Under *Bingo*, the Russian Federation is effectively destroyed, starting with military targets, but as most of these are entwined with civilian population centres, no mercy is shown. By the end of the strike, all that will be left is the thunderclap of nuclear explosions ringing out across the land. The emphasis of this scenario is on the speed with which each group of targets is neutralised. The Prime Minister, along with the various cabinet ministers on the COBRA call, is giving the military permission to conduct a full-scale counterstrike.

Felix feels numb. With just a handful of words and in the space of ten minutes, the future of Europe has been forever changed. Millions of people will die. Tens of millions of casualties will suffer over the next few decades. Hundreds of millions of people will be displaced. His eyes glance back down at a new text message from Ambassador Chenko. To his surprise, it's as though she's responding to something that was just said.

This is not coming from Russia

Felix feels confident she's being honest, but how can he convince COBRA of that?

Another couple of messages arrive in quick succession.

Please. You've got to believe me. It's not us.

We've got to work this out.

Don't react.

"It's not the Russians," he says.

"How on Earth could you know that?" the PM asks.

"Because the ambassador's texting me, pleading with us not to respond."

"And you believe that witch?"

"I do."

"Why?"

"Because she's just outed a high-level asset within COBRA itself."

"I don't understand," the prime minister says.

"How else would she know what we're discussing? Someone on this call informed her we suspect the Russians are involved. And she's prepared to hang them out to dry to avoid our countries going to war."

"Fuck," the Prime Minister says. He leans forward within his Bentley, pulling against his seat belt. He taps the screen. "Who is it? Which one of you betrayed us?"

From within a meeting room in Whitehall, on the edge of the camera's vision, a head drops. Felix doesn't know who it is, but someone within the PM's office has been spying for the Russians. A young man with short, black hair finishes typing something and closes his laptop. His guilt is apparent in the tears streaming down his cheeks.

"Arrest him," the PM says. An armed guard already within the room steps behind the man in a dapper, grey suit. He takes him by the shoulder. The man doesn't resist as he's led away.

"Well, that's just fucking great," the PM says, sitting back in his Bentley. "Are there any other intelligence services listening in? Mossad? CIA? DGSE?"

Felix ignores him, saying, "Everything about this is wrong. Not only is this a single inbound missile—the trajectory is back-to-front. If this is a missile, it's a lone missile travelling in the wrong direction. From west to east. It hasn't come from Russia or China or any other hostile state. It's crossed the Irish Sea. It's coming from across the Atlantic toward us. The flight path is all wrong."

The marshal says, "We suspect an as yet unidentified submarine launch off the coast of Nova Scotia."

The Prime Minister reacts with, "Canada? You want me to believe the Russians or whoever are attacking us with a single missile launched from off the coast of Canada?"

No one replies so Felix adds, "We've got this backwards."

"So if we're interpreting this incorrectly, what's right?" the PM asks.

"That's what we need to figure out before jumping to a response."

By this time, his Bentley is racing north along the M40 toward High Wycombe where the steep, surrounding hills provide dead ground from any nuclear detonation over London.

"We've got video of reentry," the marshal says, flicking a tablet screen and throwing up the feed on the conference call video. A brilliant white light cuts through the night sky, leaving a glowing trail behind it.

"It's too shallow for an ICBM," Felix says. "This is a meteor."

He's guessing. He doesn't know that for sure, but he's trying to defuse a European war before it erupts like a volcano.

Although he doesn't have the authority, he says, "Stand down *Bingo*."

"Stand down *Bingo*," the PM says, agreeing with him, and Felix feels as though he can breathe again. Already, his Bentley is off the motorway and heading down the hill toward High Wycombe which, somewhat ironically, is located in a valley. Blue and red emergency lights flash as the motorcycle police clear the road ahead.

As they watch, the glowing ember in the sky curls to one side.

"It's turning," the Prime Minister says.

The marshal says, "A hypersonic cruise missile could do that."

"It's too big for a missile," Felix says. "Look at the glow coming off that thing."

The Prime Minister asks, "What's its current location?"

"The object is over the Celtic Sea, roughly two hundred miles south of Cork in Ireland. It has decelerated to MACH 4 and is in line with the Bristol Channel."

Felix says, "Ballistic missiles don't throw on the brakes."

"No, they don't," the Prime Minister says, rubbing his chin, somewhat lost in thought.

Felix asks, "What do we have in the air? Do we have fighter craft that can intercept it?"

The PM says, "I want everything we've got in the air—armed or otherwise. We need coverage on this thing. We need to know what the hell it is and where it makes landfall within the United Kingdom."

"Understood," a nondescript civil servant says on one of the small boxes on the screen, getting up and leaving his office chair still facing the camera.

Felix breathes a sigh of relief. He has no idea what this thing is, but he's averted World War III over a false positive. In the back of his mind, he knows they're dealing with a UFO but he doesn't think of it in the traditional sense of the word. For him, it's unidentified. It's flying or falling as the case may be. And it's an object, meaning it's something physical. It's real. Whatever it is, it's not a Russian hypersonic cruise missile. If anything, that would have snuck up on them using better stealth technology.

His Bentley comes to a halt outside an unofficial military post near High Wycombe. As they're in the surrounding countryside, the town is a glow on the horizon easily a mile away. Felix gets out to stretch his legs.

The lights are off. The building isn't occupied, leaving the driver to madly call someone in Luton about access codes. Farmland stretches over the surrounding hills. A dark forest dominates the narrow road. The skies are dark. The stars shine like diamonds.

"What are you?" Felix asks the still of the night.

In the depths of his mind, he tries to imagine what's about to come soaring over the trees. If this isn't a lone missile being launched as an unconventional first-strike weapon, then what the hell is it? If the Americans don't know about it, who on Earth does? Should he be thinking about things other than on Earth?

"I've got the access code," the driver says, walking up to him as he rests one of his Italian Brunello Cucinelli business shoes on a wooden farm fence. Mud sticks to the sides of his two-thousand-pound leather shoes, but he doesn't care.

"Sir," the driver says. "We need to get you in the bunker."

"The bunker?"

The term bunker is shocking to his mind. Hitler cowered like a dog in a bunker. What is a bunker, anyway, but an admission of defeat? It's a dead end. What does he have to hide? Technically, he's supposed to be in lockdown to ensure the survival of the government in the event of a catastrophe caused by the inbound object—which is not a missile. Felix will be damned if he's going to shrink in fear.

"No," he says, opening the door to the car. "Take me back to London."

Footage

Stars rush past the Bentley as it races along the highway, only these particular stars aren't natural. They're streetlights. Brilliant yellow/white LEDs have been mounted at regular intervals on the end of metal poles lining the road, forming the constellation *Homo sapiens*. To Felix, it's an indictment of humanity at large. With the best of intentions, humans lit up the night, turning it into day, but at what cost? Actual stars are little more than a blemish in the darkness beyond the motorway. The stars he saw in the countryside have long since faded from view, having been supplanted by these poor imitations. Instead of seeing thousands of stars stretching across the spectacular haze of the Milky Way, all he can see is one or two stars beyond the blinding streetlights. Even then, they're probably planets. He wonders, is this our real problem? Have we blinded ourselves? Are we so insular we fail to see the grandeur that surrounds us as anything more than a pretty picture?

As majestic as the view was outside High Wycombe, the thousands of stars Felix saw in the cloudless sky were but the smallest fraction of the hundreds of billions of stars in this one galaxy alone. For Felix, it was a rare moment of reflection. Wondering what's out there is akin to standing on the shore of the Atlantic and wondering what lies across the ocean. Perhaps now, they're about to find out.

His Bentley races over a bridge, rushing back toward London.

What the hell are they dealing with? This isn't Russian or Chinese or even American—and that doesn't leave them with many other options. The only possibility is one none of them want to consider.

Felix misses the clarity he felt standing by the old wooden fence in rural High Wycombe. The darkened bunker was juxtaposed against the brilliant stars dotting the heavens. There was no way he could head down to the basement. To do that would have been to turn his back on reality. He had to return to London.

The COBRA call is still in progress. Emergency video conferences like these can go on for days during a crisis, and it's not uncommon for people to drop in and out as needed as updates continue to flow.

Politics is the art of projecting certainty where none exists. Felix has fronted numerous press conferences, political rallies, and made enough speeches within parliament to know confidence says more than words ever can. He's always felt more like an actor on stage than a Member of Parliament. At the moment he's running out on stage without a script. Although he's tempted to bluff and project confidence, he knows it would be insulting to those on the video call. Now's the time for rational discussion, not an Emmy Award-winning performance.

Felix isn't sure how fast the Bentley's going as he can't see the speedometer from where he's sitting, but their vehicle is passing cars on the motorway as though they're standing still. To be fair, the motorcycle police up ahead have their lights flashing as does the lead car in the convoy of three. The other drivers on the road on this otherwise lazy Tuesday evening pull to one side to let them pass.

Felix needs to focus. No politician knows the challenges they'll face in office. Oh, they think they do, but they don't. From his first day, there were curveballs but none as sensational as this. The role of the Secretary of State for Defence is largely a policy position. Day-to-day decisions are handled by the military themselves. Never did he think he'd be called on to make life-and-death decisions in real time. He told himself he was ready for this, but it was yet another confidence trick, only one he played on himself rather than the public. Now is the time that tries not only the steel of his spine but his ability to steer toward the future. One day, historians will look back at this event and dissect COBRA's decisions and reasoning. It'll all seem so obvious in retrospect. At the moment, the future is as dark as the night beyond the streetlights.

Felix listens as one of the military officers on the video conference call says, "Air Marshall Coopers confirmed a flight of four Euro Typhoons inbound to London from RAF Coningsby. They're part of the Quick Reaction Force and fully armed. The Americans are scrambling a flight of six F-22s from RAF Alconbury under NATO operational command. They'll coordinate with the Typhoons and link up with a flight of F35 Lightnings coming in from RAF Marham in Norfolk."

"Good, good," the Prime Minister says, but the officer isn't finished yet.

"We have an Airseeker and a Poseidon providing surveillance and reconnaissance. And we'll have a tanker airborne in the next twenty minutes from RAF Brize Norton. Within the hour, we'll have blanket air support over the capital."

Felix asks, "Do we have visual confirmation of what we're dealing with?"

"Negative," the marshal says, flicking an image from his tablet onto the main screen so everyone can see what he's describing. "Radar imaging puts the object at eight hundred meters in length with a leading edge of almost two hundred meters, but there are no straight edges as such. The craft is currently over Wessex. It'll pass over Reading... in a few minutes. It's slowing to a subsonic speed."

"And it'll be visible?"

"Oh, it'll be visible. We've got military personnel standing by to stream images, but everyone and anyone out in Reading tonight will see this thing. It's cruising at a thousand meters so it's low. It's going to be very apparent to anyone on the ground."

"Why is it slowing down?" the Prime Minister asks. "Why enter our skies at a hypersonic speed, drop to supersonic and then slow to something akin to a regular airliner?"

"They know they're being watched," Felix replies. "They want us to see them. It's a case of—we're not making any sudden moves and neither should you."

The PM grits his teeth. His jaw flexes. He's thinking but not speaking, which to Felix is telling. The Prime Minister does not like where this is leading.

"They're telling us not to panic," Felix says, although he's aware he's reading his own hopes and desires into the motion of this object.

"And no one's going to call it?" the Prime Minister says. "No one's going to call this thing what it is?"

Although the answer is obvious to Felix, like the others on the call, he's deferring to the PM. It's not simply a case of calling this a UFO. The real question is intent. Why is this damn thing here? Why now? Where did it come from? Who does it represent? What do they want? And why is it cruising in toward London? For the best part of a century, humanity has not only been looking to the skies for confirmation of intelligent extraterrestrial life—it's been seeing little green men around every dark corner like the boogeyman lurking in the dead of night. This, though, is different. It's loud—for lack of a better word. There's no denying what they've observed. And it's about to go public.

"What are we dealing with?" the Prime Minister asks. "I mean, this is looking a helluva lot like the start of that old Hollywood blockbuster *Independence Day*. Are dozens of these damn things about to pop up all around the world? Is this an invasion? Are we under attack?"

Felix blurts out, "No."

That one word is a reaction rather than a conscious thought. It takes him a fraction of a second to realise he said what he was thinking rather than keeping it to himself.

"Explain."

"We need to keep our cool. And we need to keep our distance. Think of this like a polar bear wandering into an arctic camp. Sure, we've got our finger on the trigger, but now is *not* the time for bravado. The damn thing walked in. Let it walk out."

The PM asks, "You don't think there's hostile intent?"

"No," Felix says with some of the irrepressible misplaced confidence that's seen him elected for a second term in office. "I think it's quite the opposite. Consider this. They can fly between stars. We can barely reach the moon. They know we're down here. Up until fifteen minutes ago, we had no idea they were up there. We had no idea they even existed. Hell, for all we know, they're listening in on this call. We need to exercise caution. They can soar around at tens of thousands of miles an hour, but they're not. They're coming in at what we would consider a safe speed. That's deliberate. They're sending a message. A clear message. We need to heed that message."

"Why are they going to London?" the PM asks from a poorly lit bunker that's somewhere other than in London. He's not rushing back to Downing St.

"We're about to find out," Felix replies. "But regardless of the reason, look at the method. They dropped out of orbit over the ocean—not over land. And not just any ocean. They dropped down over the Atlantic instead of the North Sea. From our perspective, that simplifies the intent equation as we were able to eliminate the possibility of our Russian friends attacking us. But—and here's the real point—they could have dropped down right on London. There was nothing stopping them from coming in hot and hard right on target."

"Why do I feel there's more you want to say?" the PM asks.

"There are two points we shouldn't lose sight of."

"And they are?"

"They didn't go for stealth. I might be wrong, but I suspect that means they couldn't. Even with the technological gap between us, they knew we'd detect them so they didn't even try."

"And the second point?"

"They don't feel they're in any danger. We may be swarming around like ants or bees or whatever, but they're chill. If things go hot, this is going to be a short, heavily one-sided war."

"But," the PM says. "I'm assuming your analysis has a but."

"But they're being polite. They know they're coming down on top of a hornet's nest so they're going slow. They're giving us time to think, time to reason, time to realise what's happening, time to avoid any hotheaded mistakes. And it's time we should use wisely."

"So what's our next step?"

"We need to get out ahead of this thing. We need to send out a press briefing to the BBC, CNN and Reuters saying we're monitoring the peaceful approach of—"

"Of what?" the PM asks, cutting him off. "Of a UFO? You really want your name on that?"

"Of an advanced craft of unknown origin. And the Ministry of Defence is closely monitoring the situation."

"Do it," the PM says, turning to someone sitting beside him. "Using that exact wording."

The marshal interrupts. "We have footage from Reading."

"Put it up," the PM says.

No one speaks as the image appears before them.

The footage has been shot by someone on a phone so the aspect ratio is wrong for their screen. Felix desperately wants to enlarge the image or yell at the person to turn their phone sideways. Houses and trees obscure the foreground, reducing the view. Streetlights cause the camera to shift focus, washing out the image, but there's no doubt about what they're looking at. Whoever's filming this, they're running, trying to get to a better vantage point. They're holding their camera roughly sideways as they head along a narrow street. Dozens of people stand on the footpath pointing, looking up at the spacecraft. It's infuriating to gain glimpses of an alien vessel only to lose it in the branches of an oak tree or behind the silhouette of a council flat.

The only sound is that of heavy breathing and the occasional comment as they pass someone on the street.

"Wut da fock 'mm I looking hat?" a distinctly overweight bald man asks, standing outside in his boxer shorts without a shirt. Vapour forms on his breath in the still, cool air. The cameraman or woman or whoever this is ignores him, rushing further along the street. They reach the main road. The cars have stopped. No one has pulled over. For once, there are no impatient drivers honking their horns. Slowly, drivers and passengers step out of their cars and stand there in the middle of the road looking up into the night, mesmerized by the dazzling display of lights drifting high overhead.

Finally, the camera is steady. It's turned sideways, allowing the image to fill the screen within the Bentley. Felix leans forward. His fingers touch the screen as his mind tries to decipher the sight before him.

The man holding the camera says, "Lef-Tenant Charles Barlow, Army Reserve."

By *Lef-Tenant* he means lieutenant, but his west country accent suggests he's from further afield than Reading.

"It's 8:17 Tuesday evening, November 18th. I'm standing on the B3350 Church Road in Reading, looking south. From what I can tell, the vessel is heading east toward Windsor."

Another voice speaks over the audio. Presumably, someone within MOD, the United Kingdom's Ministry of Defence, has set up the video call with Lieutenant Barlow, knowing he lived on the flight path. In the rush of the moment, it's the best they could do.

"We copy you monitoring the incursion. Please continue to transmit until the vessel has passed out of sight."

"Yes, sir."

Barlow walks slowly down the street, improving his angle as the alien spacecraft crosses the M4 in the distance.

Felix says, "It's going to pass over Heathrow."

"Fuck," the PM says, swinging around to face another aide. He points at the woman's chest, barking instructions. "Everything is either on the ground or diverted, is that understood? Nothing takes off. Nothing lands."

"Sir," she says, peeling away from him with her phone already raised to her ear. Like him, she barks orders at whoever's on the other end of her call.

If there was any doubt before, there's none now. The alien spacecraft is otherworldly and unlike anything ever seen. By the time Lieutenant Barlow reached the main road, most of the vessel had passed out of sight, being obscured by the rooftops. Tens of thousands of spikes protrude from the vessel at all angles. They're chaotic. They're so densely clustered it's impossible to see the hull of the craft. The tips glow like stars while the various shafts roll through the colours of the rainbow, causing patterns to appear on the vessel reminiscent of a kaleidoscope.

Felix isn't sure who is speaking on the COBRA call as all the thumbnails have been minimised to provide them with the best view from Lieutenant Barlow.

"It's like someone crossed a porcupine with a cuttlefish."

"I need options," the PM says, snapping Felix back into his bucket seat at the rear of the Bentley as it rushes back toward London. For a moment there, he felt as though he was standing on Church Road along with everyone else.

"We let this play out," Felix says. "We may not know what's happening, but they do. This is intentional—all of it. None of it is haphazard. We're in the process of First Contact with an advanced extraterrestrial alien civilisation. Right now, our number one priority is to not fuck this up."

"Agreed," the PM says, "I want Air Marshall Coopers to maintain an outer perimeter at a hundred miles. We'll show them we're watching but that we don't feel threatened. Issue orders that no one is to engage without expressed permission from COBRA."

"Sir," the marshal says. "The flight of Typhoons is inbound toward central London. They're timing their run to coincide with the arrival of the craft."

"Pull them back."

"It's not that simple. Operational command is out of Brize Norton."

"Make it that fucking simple! I want ground units, not airborne. They're heading to London for a reason, we need boots down there ready to respond."

"Yes, sir."

Someone else asks, "Shouldn't we have a reception committee? You know, scientists, civic leaders, religious leaders, authorities like the police?"

The PM is sarcastic. "And would you like to organise that in the next few minutes?"

"No," is the reluctant reply.

"I'm five minutes out," Felix says, sitting in the back of his Bentley and rushing along with his police escort. He's the only one heading into rather than out of London.

"Leave this to the professionals," the Prime Minister says.

"We are the professionals," Felix says. "We're the ones duly elected to represent the people. We need to be there."

"You know what I mean," the PM says. "COBRA needs you and that means I need you. Alive."

"And I need to know what we're dealing with," Felix says, staring out the window at the massive spacecraft as it drifts across the London skyline. "I can see it. It's out over the Thames and heading this way."

"Which way?"

"Toward Westminster."

Sex Toys

A red neon sign glows in the window of the apothecary. A single fluorescent tube winds its way through several words. Black sections block the light at various points as the tube twists and contorts to spell out:

XXX

Sex Toys

Adults Only

Lucy leans on the counter inside the apothecary. She rests her forearm against the worn veneer beside the cash register. It's Tuesday night and the night is dragging. The street outside is quiet. A couple walks past ignoring the tasteful but scantly clad mannequins visible through the window. Lucy watches them with idle curiosity. The woman's looking forward. The man's also facing forward, but his eyes dart sideways. Is he thinking about her in the black lace negligee? Or is he thinking about someone else?

Lucy goes back to staring at her phone. She's bored. There's only so long she can scroll through Instagroan, Snapclap and Twatter, or whatever they're called these days. Once, social media was heralded as the coming of a new age of public participation. The internet was to be a global village. Long-lost friends could reconnect regardless of where they lived. Holiday photos could be shared. Grandma and grandpa could get to see the kids getting ready for their first day of school from the comfort of their own toilet seat—although no one would ever admit that. Reality, though, was cruel. It wasn't the trolls that ruined the internet for everyone else, it was the execs. *'Free speech,'* they cried, drowning out all but their speech and that of big-spending corporations. Lies replaced reason. Brands replaced opinions. Indoctrination replaced debate. *'Respect others' opinions,'* they'd say as they shit on civil rights in the name of free-dumb. Lucy isn't impressed.

Far from giving individuals a voice, social media has become a megaphone for the rich, allowing them to drown out everyone else. The problem with the rich is they only care about money—not people. If a conspiracy theory will line their pockets, "*It's worth considering both sides.*" But no one considers both sides of chemistry vs alchemy. Or reason vs superstition. Or physics vs witchcraft. If someone wants to understand black holes and supernovae, they need to learn about astronomy, not astrology. Blood tests and MRI scans are far more accurate than a crystal ball at predicting the future, but if there's a buck to be made scamming people, life becomes a game of poker—the rich will bluff from behind a weak hand. And Lucy hates them for that.

It's the damage that's done that bugs her. If the indifference of the rich was benign, she could accept that, but lies cost lives.

Vaccines save lives—how that was ever spun otherwise is a testament to how easily people can be misled. When the public buys into misinformation, they're like Inuits buying ice from a cheerful, smiling, travelling salesman. Climate change is destroying the planet, but in England, it leads to summer at the beach and warmer winters, so what's the big deal, the media pundits ask. For India, it leads to poverty, premature death and millions of people being displaced each year when the monsoons strike. But the shareholders of British Petroleum still have their air-conditioned holiday homes in Spain so all is good with the world. The only collateral damage the rich care about is a drop in share prices. It's then—and only then—they care about civil rights. Selfishness isn't so much of a blight on humanity as a design flaw.

A fighter jet roars overhead. There's no sonic boom, but the damn thing is flying so low it shakes the roof, startling Lucy. In the distance, several car alarms sound, having been set off by the pressure wave washing down from the jet. Every muscle in Lucy's body goes tense, clenching tight as she grimaces. Lucy relaxes only to cringe as three other jets roar past hard on each other's heels.

"What the hell," she yells, ducking again even though she's inside the apothecary and the jets have already roared into the distance.

At first, her assumption was that a commercial airliner was in distress and about to crash, but then she realised she's heard this particular scream before. The Royal Air Force conducts flyovers several times a year in flights of four to eight military aircraft. Normally, they're on show for the king, with the flights being conducted over Buckingham Palace, which is just down the road from the apothecary. Sometimes, the flyovers coincide with festivals held on the Thames. This flyby, though, seemed to buzz the Houses of Parliament. Someone's showing off with high-tech toys. It wouldn't be the first time the Secretary of State for Defence flexed some muscle to make a political point. Perhaps Parliament is sitting late and he wanted to wake everyone up.

"Fuck you, asshole," Lucy yells at her empty shop. "Next time, give us some warning."

Her phone chimes with an incoming message.

"Ah, and here's the SMS warning. Late as usual."

Ministry of Health Advice:

Please make sure your COVID vaccinations are up to date so you're protected against the latest hyper-variant Upsilon-Tau. The NHS is providing boosters free to everyone over the age of 12.

"Oh, not even an apology," she says. Normally, if the RAF is conducting flyovers or anti-terror manoeuvres they'll issue a statement.

To be fair, letting terrorists know when and where you're conducting live field training probably isn't that smart. Any adversaries in London—and there are plenty—can just sit back with binoculars and learn.

She sighs, re-reading the message.

Wasn't the pandemic declared over several years ago?

"Mission Accomplished," she mumbles to herself, echoing US President George W. Bush back in 2003. After barely a month at war, Bush declared victory in Iraq even though the occupation would go on for almost nine years and cost the lives of a million civilians. More British and American troops would die from suicide after deployment concluded than from the actual insurgency itself. Lucy's always felt a strange affinity with the Iraq war because she was born on the day Bush landed on the USS Abraham Lincoln aircraft carrier to deliver his supposed victory speech. She'd like to think her birth was the most notable event on that day but the history books disagree.

For Lucy, the parallels with the pandemic are all too real. There's spin and then there's reality—and, as Rudyard Kipling said—*never the twain shall meet.*

Hyper-variant is the latest term for how fast the virus is mutating, but Lucy understands the real reason. It's not the virus that's at fault. Humans are giving the damn thing *millions* of opportunities to adapt every day. On the counter beside her, a small HEPA filter hums, cleaning the air. Lucy doesn't understand why more people don't have them—even if only for allergies like hay fever. She loves her little air filter with its soft blue LED light.

The annoying car alarms reset and quiet descends on her beloved apothecary again.

Another message pings on her phone. She's supposed to have notifications turned off while she's at work, but it's hardly busy within the apothecary.

BBC World News: Read our latest OpEd on the importance of

individual responsibility in The Age of Change.

Aren't all ages times of change? Was there ever a time when humans weren't undergoing societal change for one reason or another?

In the back of her mind, Lucy knows stone axes remained largely unchanged for several million years, spanning several genera of hominids prior to the rise of *Homo sapiens*, but since the agricultural revolution, there's been nothing but change. Empires have risen and fallen. Each and every one of them looked unassailable at the time—and yet they're all gone. Empires don't die, they moult, shedding their former trappings. They morph, but not always for the better. Regardless, change has been the only consistent characteristic of humanity for thousands of years.

Lucy's index finger hovers over the hyperlink. Deep down, she knows this is yet another soon-to-be-ignored article about how we should be doing more to combat climate change—because walking to work instead of catching the bus will offset a rockstar's private jet, *amiright*? She smiles at her heretical thoughts.

Lucy swipes the article away without looking at it. To read it would only result in one of two things: anger or depression. And Lucy's got good reserves of both.

Yet another message arrives. It might be a quiet Tuesday evening in the apothecary, but her phone doesn't agree. This message is an invitation to a protest march through the streets of London on Saturday. What are they protesting? The title of the march doesn't make it clear: *One Last Chance*. Chance for what? Does it matter? Whether it's the land war in Eurasia, the ice-free North Pole or child labour in the cobalt mines of Africa, the grievances of her generation are all linked. Greed has replaced ideology.

Protests might seem ineffective, but without them, no one knows whether anyone else actually cares. Without protests, it's too easy for politicians and corporations to ignore injustice. And that's all they want to do. Ignoring problems is a policy position for conservatives. Lucy's parents argue that protests make no difference as nothing changes, but that's a lie. Everything's changing. Always. And everywhere. It's just whether that change is for the better of someone's bank balance or humanity as a whole. To protest is to reject the distractions of modern life. Capitalism is a shot glass full of Tequila. Android tablets and iPhones, streaming services and social media, fancy clothes and gourmet fast food—they all provide a sense of revelry that defies reality. Protesting is the least she can do. It says, '*No. I won't be quiet. I won't be content. I won't sit here playing Candy Crush as the world burns.*' It's not that Lucy doesn't play games on her phone. She loves crushing a little candy. The problem is all that's being lost.

Lucy pities her parents. Once, they had the fire of youth. They protested against everything from nuclear war to hunting whales for swanky Japanese restaurants. What is it about adulthood that steals the passion of teens for something more out of life? At what point does protesting become too much of a bother? When does money become more important?

Less than a minute later, Lucy's best friend Deloris sends her the same link, asking the question, "Are you going?"

Lucy hits reply and types, "Yeah, I'll be there."

She should look at the hyperlink.

The door to the apothecary opens.

A small bell on the top corner of the door frame rings as the door swings. The sound of steel ringing against brass announces the arrival of a customer. Lucy watches with interest, looking for a reaction. The bell is divisive. Her dad hates it. The apothecary is his store but he's rarely here. Ever since Lucy tacked the bell onto the timber frame, she's been amused by its impact on customers. Technically, she shouldn't be driving away business, but as she has a degree in psychology, she can't help herself. She loves conducting impromptu experiments on the unsuspecting public. As far as she's concerned, any new customers walking into the apothecary are part of a randomised trial. She considers regular customers her control group. Anyone wanting to sneak in quietly and browse without drawing attention to themselves quickly gets scared away. Apparently, it's disconcerting when heads turn to see who else has walked in. Often, new folk will turn around and leave as though the act of walking into a sex shop was an inadvertent mistake.

Lucy keeps a tally on a sheet of paper. She's drawn up a matrix that notes the approximate age group, gender, ethnicity and a few clothing styles. To her surprise, sand shoes are the biggest predictor of whether someone will continue inside while business shoes are least likely to continue. Couples are eight times more likely to continue than a guy with a crisp haircut in a smart suit. She even had one embarrassed teen ask her if she sold milk before backing out and heading into the 7/11 next door. Yeah, milk. That's what he was after, she thinks, smiling to herself.

Why are people embarrassed by sex? It's natural. What's unnatural is bigots telling everyone else how to live their lives. The key is *everyone else*. All too often, they themselves get exposed in the very acts they supposedly eschew. How many drag queens have been caught with child porn? Priests, politicians and sports coaches, though, now that's another story—and yet these groups are revered while drag queens are reviled. It makes no sense, but since when have humans been logical?

So far, Lucy's logged over six hundred unique entries, giving her a fairly decent sample size. Eventually, she'd like to publish an article on her findings. She's not critical of those that back out of the store. They wouldn't have entered if they didn't want something, but it seems they need a little more introspection. Perhaps her article can provide that.

Ironically, sex sells everywhere but in a sex store. Lucy figures it's the implications that sell more than the act. People like to be teased. Her sister has three kids under the age of five and, at Christmas, it never ceases to amaze her how they're more interested in wrapped presents than whatever it is they just tore open. Her psychology lecturer calls it the anticipation bias. We're more interested in what *could* happen than what *has* happened. It's the same effect that gets gamblers to push one more coin in a slot machine. She's seen her nephew Timmy rip open the wrapping on an electric tricycle only to move on to a present no larger than her phone. It's the allure of the unknown. Until it's unwrapped, it could be anything. On that occasion, it was a packet of cards for playing *Happy Families*. He wasn't disappointed, though. He just moved on to the next present without taking the time to enjoy what he already had.

In Lucy's mind, the same is true when it comes to sex. Her dad likes hanging explicit posters around the apothecary. Tits and ass sell, he says. Only they don't. Well, he thinks they do. In her experience, a see-through, lacy camisole stirs the imagination far more than a topless picture.

Lucy loves sex, and yet she hates the missionary position. To her, it's lazy. It's bland. She likens it to cooking without any seasoning. Sex should be vibrant, not embarrassing. It should be interesting, not repetitive. It should be exploratory. She wants to be celebrated, not ignored. In her past relationships, whenever sex has degenerated to the point where she might as well be a blowup doll, she's walked away.

The young man that enters the apothecary is handsome. He looks up at the bell, surprised to hear it ring. Lucy waits. Is he going to walk out? Based on his profile and her matrix, she puts his odds at staying somewhere around 20%. He's not wearing a suit, but he is ostentatious. He's making a statement with his clothing but she's not sure what that statement is. The young man is wearing a puffy white shirt beneath a tight leather tunic with polished brass buttons. His hair is straggly, sitting just off his shoulders. His pants have the biggest pleats she's ever seen while his boots are rough and scuffed. The leather doesn't look as though it's ever been polished. His boots make a distinct clomp on the wooden floor. There's no need for a bell when this guy enters.

"Do you need any help?" she asks, and immediately she regrets asking. She's broken the first rule of shop attendants. Don't say anything. Leave them alone. Let them browse. If they need help, they'll ask.

"Ah," he says, waving his hand at the five rows of sex toys and leather paraphernalia hanging from clothing racks. "This is…"

"This is?" she replies, unsure what else he thought he'd find inside a sex store.

"Unexpected," he says. "What happened to the apothecary?"

"What happened to it?" she replies, screwing up her face in surprise at that comment. "It's been a sex shop for decades."

"Why?"

"Why what?" she asks, finding his manner amusing.

"Who would..." He shakes his head. "I mean. This is what you sell?"

"Yes."

"This is all you sell? No herbs? No spices or oils?"

"We've got lube," Lucy says, wanting to provoke a reaction. She's had enough of his bewildered puritan act. "Listen, buddy. There's a chemist down the road if you want something more discreet."

"Lube?" he says as though it's a term he's never heard. "Discreet? As in separate or intelligent?"

Lucy leans on her elbows, asking, "Are you okay?"

"Oooh?" he says, followed reluctantly by a lengthy, "Kay?"

That's not the response she was expecting. Before she can reply, he says, "Does that mean well? If so, then yes, I am well."

Lucy lowers her phone, setting it out of sight on the shelf below the counter. Without making it obvious, she dials 999 for the emergency services but she doesn't press the call button. Lucy's had enough weirdos in her store to know when someone's unhinged. It doesn't take a degree in psychology to realise this guy is a live wire. She's unsure whether she should humour him or simply ask him to leave. Technically, he hasn't done anything wrong. He hasn't insulted her or threatened harm. It seems he's just a little eccentric. For the moment, Lucy decides to play along. Her right hand, though, still grips the phone. Her thumb is poised over the call button.

"Is the circus in town?" she asks.

His eyes narrow, but not out of anger. He's confused by her

comment. She's trying to backtrack and offer a playful critique of his clothing. She's looking for an explanation, but he's silent. He looks at her as though she's speaking French.

"Did you come from a fête or something?" she asks. "Is there a medieval faire I've missed?"

He ignores her. His hands reach out, touching a black latex gimp suit.

"This is the apothecary, right?"

"Right," she says, thinking that's obvious given the name is plastered on the door.

He nods and walks away from her, heading down one of the aisles.

Lucy's assessment of him is he's a little simple but not a threat. She tried to be chatty on a slow, boring night, but he looks uncomfortable with the conversation. Given his partner probably sent him down here to grab some condoms and lube, she's probably being too friendly. She resigns herself to playing the role of unassuming shop attendant and returns to her phone, swiping away the emergency call. It'll still be there as a background app, but she doesn't think she's going to need it.

Lucy goes back to her WhatsApp group chat. Although she's staring at her phone screen, she keeps her eye on him. There's something off about him—something wrong. He doesn't fit in, and not just here in a sex shop. He looks and sounds as though he doesn't fit in anywhere on Earth. Perhaps she's being too harsh. He seems overwhelmed by the posters strung up on the walls. A quick look and he averts his eyes and continues on.

The apothecary is over six hundred years old. It has changed hands dozens of times over the centuries. It's been used as a tollbooth for trade from the countryside, a jail, an abattoir, a shipping office and a restaurant. The basement doubled as a bomb shelter during World War II. Lucy's not entirely sure about its original purpose. As far as she knows, an apothecary is an old-fashioned pharmacy, but does that mean it included alchemy? Was someone melting down lead in a crucible in hopes of turning it into gold? Sometimes, on rainy days, she wonders about the tens of thousands of people that have walked through the front door over the centuries. She's curious about what they saw. She wonders what they'd think of the apothecary today.

As the apothecary has been listed with the English Heritage Trust, there are strict restrictions on what can and cannot be altered within the building. Lucy's allowed to hang pictures on the drywall installed in the 1970s but she can't alter any of the original, exposed stone walls. In practice, that means she can only hang specials and signs on the north wall. Occasionally, she'll use a bit of Blu Tack to stick a poster on one of the stone walls. The Blu Tack never lasts, though. It's as though the apothecary detests her and rejects her efforts. She's never had one of those signs stay up for more than a day or two. There are a few rusted screws on the stone walls, but most of the signs on the stone are hung from the drop ceiling using fishing wire.

The young man halts beside a barrel full of discounted dildos reduced to clear. Behind the barrel, a sign peels from the stone wall, threatening to fall on the floor. The faded text reads, "*Five pounds each or three for a tenner.*" That special has been running since she was a little girl. It seems sex toys are inflation-proof. Either that or their value is dropping.

The weirdo picks up one of the supersized pink dildos with a suction cup on the end. Lucy watches with fascination as he turns it around in his hand, examining it with what can only be described as astonishment. His eyes look like they're about to fall out of his head. Lucy's on the verge of laughing. He jiggles the dildo slightly, watching how it flexes in his hand. His fingers run over the fake rubber veins and the scrotum. Has he never seen a dildo? He turns, looking around as though he wants to ask her a question about it. Lucy lowers her gaze. You're on your own, kiddo, she thinks. Bring it up to the counter if you really want to talk about it. Otherwise, just hand over your credit card and we'll both pretend it's nothing more than a loaf of bread or a can of coke from the 7/11 next door.

The peculiar young man puts the dildo down and wanders along, running his fingers along the edge of a shelf full of classic magazines. Although most porn is online, there's a market for *'the discerning gentleman'* who's looking for something retro. Playboy did a limited reprint of magazines from the 80s and their glossy magazines are surprisingly popular. Lucy's not sure why, but men young and old buy them. This guy, though, isn't interested. He's not browsing. He's distracted, but not by tits and ass. What's his angle? Why is he here?

Keeping her phone out of sight beneath the counter, Lucy swipes sideways, double-checking the call to the police is still sitting there, waiting for her to press the green call button. It is. She knew it was, but she felt she had to check. There's something about the renaissance fair guy that leaves her feeling uneasy.

The Churlish Dalcop Fopdoodle

The door to the apothecary opens again.

After three hours with no customers, Lucy's got two in the space of two minutes.

"Hi," she says, waving politely and wondering if the bell is going to scare this guy off. She's glad to see another face. Creeps tend to back off when there are other people around. She's reasonably sure her medieval cosplayer isn't actually going to buy anything. Maybe the presence of this other guy will get him to move on.

The new guy is muscular. He comes across as confident, perhaps a little cocky. He's wearing denim jeans, a black t-shirt and a baseball cap pulled down low above his ears. Normally, a nondescript black cap like this would be a red flag for Lucy as it obscures the view of the surveillance cameras set around the store, but she's happy for some additional company on this quiet night. His jeans are halfway down his ass, exposing his Calvin Klein's. At least his underwear is clean. A steel chain hangs from his belt, forming a loop reaching halfway down his thigh. He's probably got a set of keys attached to one end. Not only does it look cool, it means they can't be snatched by a thief. It's a classic street look, but that doesn't mean he's a hood or that he has bad intentions, rather that he's part of the crowd. Lucy bumps into this stereotype a dozen times a day out in the alleyways and backstreets of London. They think they look hip. They think they're being rebellious, that they're breaking stereotypes, but they're simply shifting from one norm to another. His choice of clothing might not be a suit and tie but it conforms to the expectations of his social circles as much as any businessman's attire.

Anyway, she's glad for a bit of company beyond the would-be goth loitering at the back of the store.

"You got skins?" the new guy asks.

"French letters are in the next aisle," she says. Both of them avoid naming condoms for no other reason than to sound cool.

He looks around the store but not at the second aisle. It's at that moment, Lucy knows. He's going to rob her. It's the way he glances everywhere but at the condoms. He's assessing who's in here and if they're a threat. The court jester at the back of the store has a puny build. He's not going to cause this guy any trouble. He'll hang back and probably whip out his phone to take some useless photos and then blabber to the cops for an hour and a half about how if he'd had more time he would have taken Mr. Muscles down himself.

 Lucy keeps her eyes forward. She fixes a smile on her lips, only it's fake. To anyone watching, it would appear comical rather than relaxed, but he won't notice. He's too damn nervous. She can see that in the way he fidgets with his hands. He's still talking himself into this extremely dumb idea.

Lucy's got to buy herself some time. She keeps her phone out of sight and she doesn't look down at it. She doesn't want to tip her hand. She swipes sideways, hoping she's on the correct screen, hoping her finger is hovering over the call button as she waits for him to commit to the robbery before she presses down on the slick, glass surface.

Without making it obvious, Lucy edges back from the counter while he's still distracted and looking around. She's trying to make sure there's as much room between her and the blade of the knife he's probably carrying. The counter is three feet wide and well over ten feet long. The area behind the counter is narrow. If he is going to rob her, he'll lunge over the counter rather than rush around it, at least, that's what she suspects is going to go down. If he does run around the far end of the counter, she'll vault over it and rush out the door, leaving him to raid the cash register. Although that's her preferred option, she doubts he'll do that. The last thing he wants is someone screaming into the night while he's grabbing handfuls of cash.

Within a fraction of a second, he's satisfied he can pull this off. His eyes narrow. He's committed.

And there it is.

The downlights in the apothecary catch the edge of a polished blade. Brilliant, bright white LED lights glint off the shiny, smooth metal.

He turns to face her. "Empty the till, darling."

Lucy presses her finger firmly against the glass on the screen of her phone and slides the phone onto the shelf below the counter. She raises her hands to show him she's no threat. Sweat breaks out on her brow. Lucy doesn't dare look at her phone. Her fingers shake, knowing how important that seemingly mundane act was while also knowing how easy it would be to have swiped to the wrong screen or pushed the wrong section of the glass panel and missed the call button. For all she knows, her phone is currently displaying Candy Crush or a list of contacts and recent calls. She wants to look down at the phone but she can't.

"Easy," she says, keeping her back to the wall as she edges sideways over to the cash register. She speaks for anyone listening on the call. "Take whatever you want. I don't want to get hurt."

"No tricks," he says, raising the point of the knife in case she had any doubts about his willingness to use it. "Keep your hands in sight. Don't you dare hit a panic button."

"I'm not hitting any buttons," she says, lowering her voice and speaking softly.

Lucy's never been robbed before but she's been trained in how to respond during a robbery. Her brother is a bobby in the Metropolitan Police. Although she didn't want to attend, he dragged her along to a course at Scotland Yard. The focus of the training was on ending the interaction as soon as possible. The longer a robbery goes on, the worse the outcome. The last thing the police want is for a robbery to deteriorate into a hostage situation. The police would rather catch someone on the run than corner them in a store along with innocent bystanders. Their advice was: *give them what they want and let them go.*

Her instructor said when a criminal is in the act of committing a robbery, their senses are heightened. The smallest perceived slight can provoke violence. Don't be a roadblock, he said. Never corner a robber. Give them an out. Give them everything they want and show them the door. Let them leave. They want to get out of there as fast as they can so help them do that and let the police do their job afterwards. Don't be a hero. Insurance can replace things, not lives. They won't get away. 99% of armed robberies end with a conviction. Don't tell them that, but remember, they might get out that door but they won't get away.

Even though Lucy knows all this, her fingers shake uncontrollably.

"We don't carry much cash," she says, which is true. The float in the till is set at two hundred and fifty pounds but most of that is in small denominations.

"I'll take all of it," he says, not even bothering to ask how much there is even though he's risking a prison sentence for a bunch of paper and a few coins. He dumps a crumpled plastic shopping bag on the counter.

Lucy opens the cash register.

"One hand," he says, waving the knife before her. Apparently, he thinks her register might have some kind of built-in silent alarm that operates if money is pulled out in a hurry using two hands at once. Oh, she wishes that were the case but her father is too much of a tightwad for anything more than a few cameras. The shopping bag has been scrunched up in his pocket so it's not easy to unfold. With one hand, she starts with the twenties and then the tens, pushing them down into the bag with her other hand.

Lucy can't help herself. She has to know. She shouldn't look but she has to be sure. Her eyes glance sideways, peering at the phone several feet away from her on the shelf below the three-legged, battery-powered "*alien massagers*" (which is a name that provides plausible deniability for a vibrator should the kids find it in the bedside drawer). Her phone screen shows an active call with the distinct red button to end the call displayed near the bottom of the glass. Somewhere, someone's listening. Lucy tries to recall the conversation so far, wondering if there's enough context for the emergency services operator to distinguish between a robbery-in-progress and someone butt-dialling them by accident.

"*You fucking bitch!*" the robber yells, seeing the motion of her eyes. "Phone. Give me the goddamn phone."

Lucy stalls. "Take it. Take the money. Take all of it. Just take it and go."

She grabs handfuls of coins and notes, dumping them into the bag.

"I will cut you," he yells, lunging forward over the counter and grabbing her by the collar of her shirt. Lucy tries to pull away, but she can't. The tip of the knife presses against the soft skin of her throat, drawing blood. A thin trickle runs down her neck.

The medieval stranger in the puffy shirt is standing behind the robber. He yells, "Unhand her, you rascal!"

"What?" the robber says, still leaning across the counter. Although he's got a good hold on Lucy, he's vulnerable to attack from behind. He releases her and wheels around to face the stranger.

"Be gone, scoundrel. Take your ill-gotten gains and flee before I make a mockery of you."

The robber looks confused. He keeps his knife out in front of him, holding it in a clenched fist.

"What the fuck?"

Even Lucy's perplexed. She leans to one side, wanting to peer past the robber at her would-be knight in shining armour. She runs her finger across her throat, trying to indicate to him that he should back off and let the robber leave. The robber grabs the bag of money. Coins rattle as it falls to his side.

"Run, you coward," the stranger says. "Run and hide like the churlish dalcop fopdoodle that you are!"

It's at that point Lucy realises the stranger's holding two pink dildos, one in either hand. He's holding them by the head of the penis so the plastic ball sack hangs out on either side of his hands. If she wasn't so scared, she'd laugh. What on Earth does he think he's going to do? Assault an armed robber with a pair of plastic cocks? Is he going to get him to bend over and thrust in two at once?

The robber laughs. "Get out of my way, fool, or I will skin you alive?"

"With a child's toy not worthy of a butcher's block?"

The robber waves the knife before him, stepping forward and threatening to attack. The stranger stands his ground, holding his arms out wide with the dildos hanging from each hand, inviting the robber to strike.

"I am going to carve you up, asshole."

"I've been chained to a fire, condemned to burn at the stake, and you think I would trifle before a razor not worthy of a man's head?"

The robber lunges at him.

Lucy yells, "No!"

The stranger dances back, avoiding the strike. The blade of the knife catches the edge of his vest but pierces no further. He steps on the balls of his feet, pushing off with his toes rather than the flats of each foot. He shuffles as though he were wielding a sword. To Lucy's astonishment, the stranger swings inward, striking the head of the robber with the dildos. Thick, heavy, plastic ball sacks complete with suction cups slap at the robber's ears, whipping over his head. The stranger strikes with such force, the dildos make a wet, squishing sound.

The robber drops both the knife and the bag, grabbing at his ears in pain. Welts form on the soft red cartilage. Blood runs from his right ear. He staggers, making for the door.

The stranger drops the dildos and grabs the knife.

The strike to his ears causes the robber to sway, having upset his balance. His right hand strikes the wooden lintel. He steadies himself as his left hand seizes the door handle. The stranger grabs the robber's arm, holding his hand in place as he plunges the knife through his wrist and into the door jamb beside the colour-coded sign identifying the height of a fleeing criminal.

The robber screams in agony. He tries to turn, but his hand is pinned to the wood. Blood squirts across the stone beside the door.

The robber grabs at the knife, trying to wrench it free, but it has been driven into the wood. He slips. The glass within the door shatters as his shoulder collides with the pane and his weight shifts. Shards of broken glass fall, digging into his trousers and tearing his legs. He shuffles with his feet. His boots skid on the linoleum floor as he struggles to take the weight off his impaled hand. Tears stream from his eyes. Blood runs down the wood and onto the floor.

The stranger turns to Lucy, asking, "Would you have that I dispatch him, m'lady?"

"What?" she replies, understanding each of the individual words he's used but not the meaning of his question. And m'lady? Who is this guy?

"He would have taken your life. Would you I take his?"

"No, no," she yells holding out her hands and rushing around the counter to get to him. "God, no."

Outside, blue and red lights flicker over the surrounding buildings as police cars pull up, coming from both directions. The robber crouches in the doorway. As the glass is broken, he has his feet on either side of what's left of the door, with his back against the wood and both arms up over his head. He's in agony, holding his right arm in a feeble attempt to reduce the pain. Blood drips from his elbows.

Flashlights illuminate his face. Police officers with batons drawn close in on the apothecary, yelling, "Come out with your hands in the air. Everybody out on the street! Now!" But for Lucy, that's not possible without climbing over the robber.

"Who are these people?" the stranger asks. "Their uniforms. Are they part of a royal detachment?"

Lucy looks at him as though he's from Mars. She shakes her head. That she needs to state the obvious is alarming to her. Her eyes go wide. "They're the police."

"And who or what are the pol-lease?"

"Who *are* you?" she asks as several of the police officers lean down to get a good look at how the robber has been impaled on the inside of the door. Radios crackle with words spoken in haste.

"I am Anthony of the Meyers of Westminster South. I used to work here in the apothecary."

"Listen," she replies, sensing an interview with the police could go horribly wrong for this eccentric fellow. "Let me do the talking, okay?"

"Oooh—"

"It means, agree with me. Just follow my lead. Okay?"

"Okay," he says, somewhat awkwardly.

"Be quiet about what just happened. And whatever you do, don't tell them you were about to kill him."

Outside, an ambulance pulls up. Medics rush over to attend to the robber.

"Are you okay, miss?" one of the police officers asks, shining his blinding flashlight inside the apothecary and trying to understand the dynamic between her and Anthony.

"Yes. Yes. I'm fine. We're fine." She points at the robber. "He attacked me with a knife. My friend, Anthony, stepped in to stop him."

After having assessed the threat, one of the police officers steps through the broken glass door and inside the apothecary. He's wary, keeping a close eye on the robber, but the street thug is in no state to do anything other than moan in agony. The officer is followed by a medic, who attends to the robber.

"Tonight of all nights," the officer says, shaking his head. He looks up at the ceiling within the apothecary as though he has X-ray vision and is staring at the night sky beyond. "Well, I needed something to snap me back to reality."

"Reality?" Lucy says, confused. Her heart is still racing at a million miles an hour. The blood smeared over the floor is more than enough reality for her.

"Quite the mess," the officer says, trying not to step in the hundreds of blood droplets surrounding the thief.

He walks over to Lucy, adjusting his body cam and speaking for the record as he says, "On top of everything else, we have an attempted armed robbery in the sex shop on the laneway leading from Barton St to Tufton."

Lucy has no idea what everything else entails. Right now, the apothecary is her whole world. For a moment, the officer ignores her, turning around and taking in the whole of the store with his body camera.

Outside, several officers point away from the apothecary along nearby Cowley St. One of them calls out, "Over at the Abington Street Gardens. They want any spare hands down there to cordon off the area."

Lucy's not sure why the apothecary doesn't have the undivided attention of the police. She knows the gardens. They're not gardens at all but rather a section of grassy lawn that's remained largely the same over the past five hundred years. Once, it acted as a market, hence the name '*gardens*.' The Abington Street Gardens are opposite the House of Lords. Just up from there is Westminster Abbey and the House of Commons. If anything weird happens up there, the anti-terror squad goes hard. Lucy was having lunch in the garden one day when the bomb squad turned up to defuse a black plastic bag full of rubbish that had been dumped beside a bin.

A helicopter flies low overhead. From the sound of its engine, it, too, is heading toward the gardens.

The officer standing beside her looks utterly distracted. She wants to ask, "Are we boring you?" But she's too polite. He sways, making sure his camera captures both Lucy and Anthony. To help—and to show she and Anthony are on the same side—Lucy steps closer to her strange, goth saviour. She takes his forearm. He looks down at her fingers in surprise. She holds on to him gently so he doesn't react. Lucy feels this evening is weird enough without her new-found friend confusing things any further so she takes the lead.

A medic comes over to her, examining the nick on her neck. "You got lucky, lass."

"That I did," she says, but she's thinking about Anthony, not the cut on the side of her throat. The medic applies some cream and a bandage. He wipes away the fine trickle of blood running down to her clavicle.

"All yours," the medic says to the officer.

Lucy's waiting for the officer to ask her what happened, but he looks befuddled. He's looking at the pink dildos lying on the ground. One of them has a smattering of blood on it, begging the question—*how?* This isn't going to be easy to explain.

"Ah," she says, straightening her hair with her other hand. "I was getting ready to close for the evening when that guy over there came in and threatened me with a knife. Anthony stopped him."

"That he did," the officer says, raising an eyebrow. He runs his flashlight over the floor in front of the counter even though the interior of the apothecary is well-lit. He makes sure subtle details are caught by his body camera. His shoulders move with the flashlight, directing the camera across the floor and taking in the aftermath of the fight. He stares at the pink dildos lying on the ground again but doesn't ask about them. In a sex shop, it seems anything goes.

The officer returns his gaze to the two of them, asking, "And you are?"

"Lucy Bailiwick. I work here. My father owns the store."

"And your father? Is he here?" the officer asks.

"No, he's at home."

"And you live with him?"

"Yes."

"And where's home?"

"2024b Uxbridge Road, West Ealing."

"And you?" the officer asks, looking up and down at Anthony and taking in his unusual clothing.

"Anthony's my cousin," Lucy says before the stranger can reply. "He's visiting us from Portsmouth. You have to understand—he's socially awkward. Shy."

Lucy's not sure why she's rushing to defend Anthony. Perhaps it's that he just defended her from an armed robber. Perhaps it's that she has a sense he's not only in the wrong place, he's somehow in the wrong time.

She sees the look of disbelief on the officer's face and adds, "And he's been at a medieval fair all day."

"Is this true?" the officer says, addressing Anthony.

"Eye, 'tis true," Anthony replies.

"No need for role-playing now, boyo. There's been more than enough silly business tonight. I want to see some ID. From both of you."

"Umm," Lucy says, leaving them and walking around the counter to get her purse. "Sure. Here's my driver's license."

After handing it to the officer. She picks up her phone. The phone call is still active. She holds up her phone, showing it to the officer.

He says, "You can hang up now."

Lucy speaks into the phone, saying, "Hi. Hello. This is Lucy."

From the tiny speaker, a woman's voice says, "You're with Emergency Dispatch Officer Susan Holloway. Is that the police you're talking to?"

"Yes, it is," Lucy says. "I'm in good hands."

"Great," the dispatcher says. "It's been a crazy night. Tuesdays are supposed to be quiet, you know."

"Tell me about it," Lucy replies, happy to draw the conversation out a little longer as she knows the officer is listening in. Anything that diverts attention away from her weirdo friend is a good thing.

"Okay, I'll let you go," the dispatcher says. "The emergency response system has been swamped with calls tonight. Finding actual emergencies among all the panic calls has been difficult."

"I bet," Lucy replies, unsure what the dispatcher is talking about but wanting to be agreeable.

"You take care of yourself, Lucy."

"You too," she replies, ending the call.

Lucy walks back to the officer. From her perspective, finishing the call was a delaying tactic. She's pretty sure Anthony doesn't have any ID on him. His demeanour alone suggests he's an oddball and is probably homeless, but she feels she owes him something for coming to her rescue. By talking briefly with the operator, she's hoping she's distracted and somewhat disarmed the officer. After all, she and Anthony are the good guys, right?

"Here you go," he says, handing her ID back. Several other police officers examine the scene of the fight. Photos are taken of the chaos around the door. The bloody knife is dropped into a plastic evidence bag.

"And you?" the officer asks, addressing Anthony. "Have you got a driver's license or some other form of ID on you?"

Anthony looks confused. "Eye? Dee?"

Lucy takes his arm again, squeezing his bicep gently and nudging up to him as she speaks to the officer, saying, "He's my cousin."

"You've already said that," the officer replies.

Anthony turns toward her asking, "Driver? Of what? Sheep? Cattle?"

Lucy raises her eyebrows, looking for some compassion from the officer as she says, "He's a little…"

"All right," the officer says. "Well, I'm going to need you two to come with me to the station and we'll get a statement from both of you." He points at the surveillance cameras, asking, "And these were running during the incident?"

"Yes, sir. They're backed up in real-time to the cloud so I can give you a copy of the file. You can view any time period from tonight."

"Good, good," the officer says, turning and gesturing to the door. The robber has already been taken away on a stretcher.

First Contact

"It's chaos down here," Felix says, holding his phone out flat in front of him, wanting those gathered around him on the road to hear every word of this conversation. It's a risky play. It could backfire on him, but given what they're dealing with, pride isn't an option. He needs clarity. They all do.

Felix stands beside his Bentley on Abingdon Street in Westminster.

"I've got you on speaker with the various units on the scene. They're using JESIP, the Joint Emergency Services Interoperability Programme to feed information to COBRA, but I'm concerned about confusion in the command structure. The Met are saying they have jurisdiction under the anti-terror rapid-response legislation. They've got their Counter Terrorism team onsite. I've got MI5 telling me the Home Secretary told *them* to take the lead, while the MI6 liaison officer is saying he spoke to the Foreign Secretary and *he* has the lead."

"This is ridiculous," the Prime Minister says. His voice carries on the wind.

"Tell me what you want, sir."

"I want you on point. I want you over MI5. MI6. Metro Police. Whoever's there. I don't care. You're in charge. Leave Mark and Jules to me. I'll talk to them once I'm off this call."

"And I'm acting in my capacity as the Secretary of State for Defence?" Felix asks. His voice wavers. "Stationing soldiers outside parliament might send the wrong message."

"It might just send the right message," the PM counters. "That thing is gone. It's what happens next that's important. COBRA is telling me the UFO reached orbit somewhere over Birmingham. After that, we lost it. But me? I think you're right. I think none of this is haphazard or random. That thing came in over international waters and flew into our airspace. Then it stayed inside our borders. I don't think that's accidental. It could have departed in any direction it wanted. The North Sea was on its flight path but it avoided Europe. It's almost as though they were trying to avoid an international incident."

Felix nods even though the Prime Minister can't see his response. He's lost in thought. He asks, "And Defence? What do you want our role to be?"

"We're not playing to an extraterrestrial audience," the PM says. "We're playing to a global one. We need the rest of the world to see we're competent. That we're handling this with an appropriate level of security and oversight. This is a global event, not a local one."

"Understood."

"Take me off speaker."

"Yes, sir," Felix says, hitting the button and raising the phone to his ear. The police commander and officers from MI5 and MI6 take their leave. It's nothing personal. They all know that. They're professional. They understand the stakes. It's only natural they'd have confidence in their own abilities and departments and internal procedures, but Felix agrees with the Prime Minister's assessment. The initial incident might be over but the ramifications are global. They'll ripple outward for days, weeks, months and possibly even years. The game has changed. Humanity is no longer alone—and no one's quite sure what that means in practice. The questions that haunt him are, *"What the hell just happened?"* and *"What's next?"*

The Prime Minister says, "I've got the Americans breathing down my neck. President Blackwell has already called *twice* and I've just been handed a note asking me to call him back. The US Ambassador is waiting outside in the lobby. I've got General McCallister telling me the Americans at Lakenheath and Fairford are mobilising."

"Against what?"

"Who knows? Does it matter? You know the Yanks. Logistics is their jam. They're already loading M1 Abrams in Poland and Germany onto transports and sending them here."

Felix shakes his head. "We don't need tanks. We're not fighting a land war. We're not fighting any war at all."

The PM replies, "You know that. I know that. But the American President is spooked. If a war is to be fought, he wants to win it."

Felix raises his eyebrows. "With tanks? Against an interstellar spacecraft? That could drop down anywhere on Earth?"

"I understand his position. If we're attacked—"

"Which we weren't," Felix says, cutting him off.

"If we are," the Prime Minister says. "We need to throw our best into the fray—and sooner rather than later. At least, that's the American position—overwhelming power projected at the tip of a spear. They are *not* taking any chances. They're ready to fight a war if need be but this is our show, not theirs. This occurred over our territory. We will determine our response."

"Understood."

"I don't want the Americans to get too pushy. And the only way to keep them at bay is to show them we're making progress."

"Progress with what?"

"Anything."

Not for the first time in his political career, Felix feels flustered. Once again, he's being asked to perform the impossible. What the hell can he do? He stutters, "B—But the spacecraft is gone."

"Blackwell made the point it could be back as quickly as it came. He wants us to learn everything we can about them before they return."

"If they return," Felix says. "Panicking isn't going to help anyone."

"Precautions will," the PM says. "For now, that's all it is. I'm hosing things down with Washington, but I need answers. I've got to give them something tangible. That thing could have gone anywhere, but it didn't. It came here. They want to know why. And I want to know why."

"So do I."

"Good. That's what I want you to do. Figure out why they came here. What the hell is so important about the House of Lords that they'd burn the grass outside? I'm counting on you, Felix. Figure this shit out and keep me in the loop."

Felix replies, "Understood."

The Prime Minister never hears him. He's already ended the call, probably because he has yet another incoming call from the US President.

Felix calls the Chief of General Staff, General Sir Patrick Wordsworth. No doubt he'll be expecting this call and will recognise the incoming phone number. If anything, he's probably wondering why Felix hasn't called earlier. The chief's subordinates on the COBRA call represent each of the various armed services individually. There's no doubt they would have kept him abreast of developments. That he didn't join the call is a sign of the confidence he has in them and his need to coordinate things more broadly without getting bogged down. Wordsworth doesn't suffer fools lightly, even if they're members of parliament. Felix has worked with him for five years now. He knows Wordsworth would rather sit back and take in the big picture rather than get stuck in soul-sucking meetings.

"Minister."

"Pat. We're in a pickle," Felix says. His mind is rushing along at a million miles an hour as he fights to unravel dozens of conflicting thoughts and ideas about the next steps.

"I've got your back," the general says. "The Armed Services are on high alert. We've got a combat air patrol circling London out of earshot but close enough to engage any threat."

"I don't think we're facing a threat."

"I agree. I heard the thing touched down in the gardens. At the moment, I'm thinking containment is what's required. On the ground, B Company 4th Battalion Paras are inbound from their Notting Hill barracks. I've got them on standby on Vauxhall Bridge, not more than five minutes away, awaiting orders. Sixty soldiers in four trucks."

"Good. Good," Felix says, knowing it would have taken a colossal effort to mobilise armed troops this quickly.

"The SAS Counter Terror team are hot. They're waiting just outside of earshot on two Eurocopters we've put down in Hyde Park. They're two minutes out if you need them."

"Okay," Felix says, knowing Wordsworth probably has a dozen other contingency operations underway as well. Felix trusts Wordsworth. He doesn't need to know all the details, just those that are immediately applicable to him. "Bring in the Paras. I want Metro Police on the outer perimeter and the Paras forming a second, inner cordon. Keep the SAS on standby, but I don't think they're going to be needed. Once the area is secure, they can stand down after a period of two hours."

Felix has only ever dealt with the SAS once before during an armed standoff on Tower Bridge. Metro Police managed to talk down the hostage-taker and it turned out the incident was related to domestic violence, not terrorism. No one informed the SAS the situation was resolved. Not officially. They saw the incident had been defused on the news, but the SAS does not operate on assumptions. As three people were stabbed and in hospital, they remained on high alert in case Metro Police misread the situation and there was a second attacker on the prowl. It was twelve hours before someone with MOD Operational Command approached Felix asking for permission for the SAS to stand down. Felix knew of the SAS involvement, but like everyone else, he assumed they'd gone back to their barracks. Ever since then, he's had nothing but respect for their dedication. When dealing with the SAS, it feels only appropriate to be specific and avoid assumptions.

Wordsworth says, "Understood. Is there anything else you need?"

"What I really need is some structure around what we do next here at the point of contact."

"What is it, sir? What are we dealing with? I heard the craft burnt something."

"I'm still not sure what happened," Felix replies. "I'm staring at a patch of ground in the Abingdon Street Gardens that looks like it's been hit with a massive blow torch. The pavement. The grass. It's been burned. It looks like a blast crater, minus the crater. The scorch marks form a circle maybe two or three meters in diameter. Right now, I need to make sure no one gets within fifty yards of this spot. Then… I don't know. There's no playbook on this."

Wordsworth says, "I can get our nuclear containment team in there to collect samples. They'll be decked out in NBC suits. They're adept at containing contamination—both ways. Not bringing anything in. Not taking anything out that isn't secure."

"I like that," Felix says. "Bring them in, but have them talk to me. I don't want anyone to approach this spot without my express permission. An alien spacecraft just hovered over London and no one knows why. These burn marks are the only clues we have."

"Understood."

"And get someone to wake up Oxford and Cambridge. The universities. They've got to have someone that knows what the hell we're supposed to do with First Contact, right? The way I see it, our priority is: secure the area, bring in the experts."

"Agreed. I'll make it happen," Wordsworth says as Felix walks up to the police commander outside the House of Lords. Felix hangs up without replying. He doesn't mean to be rude. The adrenaline surging through his veins has him hyped. He hasn't been this pumped up since his university days when he'd cram all night before end-of-year exams, drinking bucket loads of coffee to stay awake.

The police commander has a paper map spread over the bonnet

of a police car. Up ahead, at the parliament square roundabout, the Metropolitan Police have set up barricades in front of their cars. Blue and red lights flash across the surrounding buildings. Already a crowd is forming. Although the police are unarmed in the United Kingdom, those assigned to protect the Houses of Parliament carry MP5 submachine guns. The commander has assigned them to form a second cordon behind the officers on the barricade.

Several army trucks pull up. They're waved through by the police. Soldiers jump from the back and jog to take up positions north and south of the Abingdon Street Gardens. Even at a glance, it's clear they've been well-briefed. An army captain joins Felix by the police car.

"Sir," he says, but he doesn't salute. Felix respects that. Salutes are only for active military officers.

"What's the plan?" Felix asks, pointing at Abingdon Street Gardens. "How do we seal this place off?"

"It's a nightmare," the police commander says, addressing everyone around the vehicle. "Of all the spots they could have touched down on within London, this has got to be the worst. I've got Parliamentary Protective Services locking down the grounds, but we've got a park to the south and the Thames to the east. The approach from the southwest is worse as there's no open ground. There are lots of side streets and alleyways. Hell, we've even had reports of an armed robbery only a couple of streets away from here." He points at the map, adding, "At a place called *The Apothecary*."

"Huh?" Felix says. It's a name he's vaguely familiar with but he doesn't know what it means. Wasn't the apothecary the old-fashioned name for a chemist or pharmacy?

The police commander sweeps his hand over the southern part of the map.

"This whole area is porous. It's too easy for someone to slip through the net. And it may not be malicious. People get curious. Some are simply oblivious."

"What do you recommend?" Felix asks.

"I've got police cars blocking traffic on Great College Street, but my guys are going to be right on top of your soldiers," the commander says, looking at the captain, who's staring intently at the map.

"The real problem," the police commander says, "is this area to the west and north-west of the gardens. It includes Westminster Abbey, Lady Chapel, the cloister, a school, a college, an underground car park and various excavated historic sites. And get this, there's a secret garden. The whole place is over 900 years old. It's riddled with nooks and crannies, tunnels, open drains and alleyways. I've got two dozen constables in there already. They've found homeless people, rats and broken sewer pipes. It's just not possible to lock it down."

"In practice, what does this mean?" Felix asks.

"It means I can give you an outer cordon. The army can give you an inner cordon. But neither of us can give you any guarantees. As it is, the wall of the Abingdon Street Gardens is probably the best point to restrict access, but it's within twenty feet of the scorch mark. I'll do all I can to make sure no one makes it that far, but it's a nightmare to administer."

The captain says, "It's going to be a long night."

Felix nods.

No amount of bullish bluster or unreasonable demands from him or anyone else is going to change the position on the ground. He may want a clear exclusion zone around the site but it's not happening. Even if the Metro Police had the resources to go street by street and clear out the dozens of buildings and hundreds of rooms surrounding the Abingdon Street Gardens, it would be pointless. In the dark, it would be easy for someone to slip past unnoticed. It might give him a false sense of assurance, but his job is to get answers, not drive both the police and the army mad with ridiculous requests.

"I trust your judgment," he says, knowing that now is the time for certainty. "I need you to keep the area immediately around the Abingdon Street Gardens secure until we can get scientists on site. What that means in practice, I will leave to you."

"Thank you, sir," a clearly relieved police commander says.

"Oh, and I want your team to be on the lookout for anything unusual. At the moment, we think this is the only point of physical contact, but we don't know that for sure. We have no idea why they came here instead of New York or Paris, so if you see anything out of the ordinary—no matter how small or insignificant it might seem—let me know. Treat this as a crime scene. We have to preserve the evidence and unravel what happened here and—most importantly—*why* it happened here."

"Understood," the police commander says. The captain nods.

"Um," a police sergeant says, standing slightly behind and beside the commander. He raises his hand above chest height. It's as though he's in primary school asking for permission to use the bathroom. The commander notices. He looks concerned but doesn't say anything. Felix suspects he'd rather his subordinate brief him before potentially wasting the time of a Member of Parliament.

"This is an open forum," Felix says. "We're all here to do a job. If you've got something that might help, go right ahead. The floor is yours."

Technically, there's no floor as they're standing in the street around a police car and not in the House of Commons, but he hopes his poli-speak translates.

The sergeant says, "Protective Services caught the incident on camera."

"Okay," Felix replies, not seeing anything significant in that comment. On the drive back from High Wycombe, he saw multiple views of the spacecraft uploaded to social media. Everyone and anyone with a cell phone hit record during the sixteen seconds the craft floated above the Houses of Parliament.

The sergeant points up and down the street. "This whole area is under constant surveillance. Everyone else had their cameras pointing up, but the security system looks down at the street. It caught the thing touching down."

Felix raises an eyebrow. "And you've seen the footage?"

"It's mostly washed out," the officer says. "The light was too bright. But you said anything, right? Anything that looked strange, no matter how small or insignificant?"

"Yes."

"Well, after the craft left, there was a man there—in the gardens."

"Where?" Felix asks, pointing down the street toward the stretch of lawn backing onto the 11th Century stone wall lining the college courtyard.

"He was on the south side of the scorch mark. Maybe ten to fifteen feet away."

Felix nods as the sergeant continues, saying, "Only he wasn't there beforehand. At the time Protective Services showed me the footage, I assumed he was a tourist or a drunk. I thought maybe he came out of the underground carpark, but he wasn't there before the light washed out the image."

"I need to see that footage," Felix says, walking around the car toward the sergeant.

"This way, sir."

They jog to a security checkpoint in Old Palace Yard. The police officer stationed there waves them through. Inside, several of the Protective Service detail are waiting. If anything, it seems they're surprised it's taken anyone this long to reach out to them. They lead Felix downstairs and into a control room. Dozens of screens line one wall, having been stacked four high and eight screens wide. Every possible vantage point around the Houses of Parliament is covered, including the approaches from the Thames.

Felix asks, "What have you got for me?"

A young woman sitting at the centre console jogs the video from a camera mounted on Victoria Tower on the south side of the complex.

"Oh, you want to see our teleporting man, huh?"

She switches displays, putting her view up on the large monitor in the middle. The view is partially obscured by tree branches, but they're denuded at this time of year. Several of them have been pruned, probably by security services as each year's spring growth attempts to thwart their view of Abingdon Street. The focal point is on the road, but the gardens are visible in the background. Low-lying shrubs line the footpath. Beyond them, a flat grassy stretch opens out before the ageing stone wall enclosing the college square beyond. Even at this distance, the weathering of the stone is visible, leaving them rounded and exposing the grout between them.

"And in three, two, one," the woman says. She's clearly watched this dozens of times and knows the exact moment the alien craft appears overhead. For a second, the image darkens slightly. She pauses the video and points at another screen. It's only then Felix realizes all the screens are replaying the event from their various perspectives.

"See this here," she says, reaching up and tapping one of the other screens. "That's from a camera on St Margaret's church on the other side of the road, up by the roundabout. It provides us with a reverse-angle view, allowing us to see the approaches to Parliament. And there, in the top left corner, is one of the prongs of the spaceship as it hovered overhead."

Felix nods. As tempting as it is to say something, now's the time to listen. Injecting his opinion isn't going to help. She's worked with this security system for years and it shows.

"Now if we roll forward, we hit the whiteout."

All of the screens go blank.

"Masters was on the front door at the time. He said there was no light, as such. No spotlights or anything like that. Nothing visible to the naked eye, but they hit us with some kind of interference as we couldn't capture anything for twelve of the sixteen seconds the damn thing was overhead."

She swivels in her seat to face him.

"I was freaking out. I'd never seen one camera go down, let alone all of them at once. I thought we were facing a sophisticated, coordinated terrorist attack. I grabbed the phone. Dead. Picked up the radio. Dead. Looked at my cell phone. Dead. I thought we'd been hit by a nuclear EMP or something. I've got to tell you, my heart was pounding out of my chest. I was expecting the building to collapse around me. Chase stayed on the desk while I ran outside. Everyone was looking up. It was like standing under a gigantic Christmas Tree. People had their phones out, but this close to the spacecraft, they were dead bricks, just like mine."

She shakes her head.

"And then it was gone. The damn thing moved so fast. No one knew quite what to do next. Everyone stood around still looking into the sky. I returned to my post and the cameras were all operating again.

"Our standard operating procedure is to review any incident frame by frame. I went back through every blank screen on every blank camera, watching carefully as the images slowly resolved, looking for anything unusual."

"And that's when you saw him?" Felix asks.

"Yes. Given the time we were blind, I figured he was just some random. He could have easily walked down from Jewel Tower or out of the carpark during that time. There was no reason to think he was related to the incident."

"But?"

"But he wasn't looking."

"I don't understand," Felix says.

"I went back through all the footage four or five times, looking for anything that might represent a security threat and everyone else was looking up. Not him. He was the closest person to the scorch mark on the grass and he was looking away from it. I counted twenty-seven other civilians in our operational area and, immediately after the vessel left, they were all looking up, but not him. They all loitered. Not him. He headed south toward Milbank House."

"Good work," Felix says, patting her shoulder. "Exceptional work."

He turns to the police sergeant beside him. The police commander has joined them in the security control room. Felix isn't sure how long he's been standing there, but he seems to have caught most of the conversation.

Felix says, "I need you guys to contact Scotland Yard. I need them to comb through CCTV footage from here south for at least two miles. I've got to know who this person is and where they went. I want them brought in for questioning."

"You really think there's something to this?" the commander asks.

"That thing came here for a reason. And I think we may have just found it."

"On it."

They walk out of the control room, up the stairs and back into the lobby. Felix hits the speed dial on his phone, calling the Prime Minister, letting the others walk on ahead of him out into the night.

"This had better be good," the PM says. "I just put the Secretary General of the United Nations on hold for you."

"They dropped someone off."

"WHAT?"

"That's why they were here. They set someone down."

"Jesus..."

Felix says, "We have an extraterrestrial on the ground."

The Prime Minister is blunt. "Find him."

McDonald's

Once all the police officers have walked out of the apothecary, Lucy pulls down a roller door and padlocks the handle in place, locking the store. In the distance, multiple sirens sound. At the end of the lane, she can see blue and red flashing lights coming from somewhere north of them, from up near the Houses of Parliament. So much for a quiet Tuesday evening. More jets roar across the sky, but they're not as low as they were before.

A police officer fixes bright yellow tape on the steel door that says, "*CRIME SCENE. DO NOT ENTER.*"

"How long will that be in place?" she asks, pointing at the wording.

"Once we've completed our preliminary investigation, forensics will come by to collect physical samples and do blood swabs. They'll give you the all-clear to reopen."

"Okay."

Anthony mimics her with a distinctly unconvincing, "Ooh-Key."

The officer looks sideways at him for a moment before opening the back door to his police car. Lucy slides in, shifting to the far side. Anthony stands there examining the car before joining her in the back seat. He whispers, "No horses, huh?"

"No," she replies as the officer closes the door and walks around to the driver's side.

"How long has this been the case?"

"What?"

"How many years have you had metal carts with no horses?"

"Umm. I don't know. Over a hundred, I guess."

"And the stars?" he asks, pointing out of the police car window at the darkened sky. "Have you reached the stars?"

"Me?" Lucy says, pointing at herself. "No."

"Anyone?"

"Ah, no. But we've walked on the moon."

Anthony smiles. "So have I."

Lucy shifts in her seat, feeling awkward and unsure how to respond. She's sitting beside a renaissance cosplay nutter that wields dildos like nunchucks. What is there to worry about?

The police officer puts on his seatbelt and starts the car. Lucy puts her belt on but Anthony sits there oblivious to what's happening. He's fascinated by the Perspex barrier behind the driver's seat. His finger rests on the plastic as he looks at the computer and radio mounted on the centre console next to the driver.

Lucy whispers, "Put your belt on."

Anthony looks down at his waist.

Realising he's somewhat of a lost cause, she releases her belt and sits forward. Lucy leans around him, which surprises him, causing him to sit back in his seat. She pulls his belt forward and secures it before putting her own belt on again. None of this goes unnoticed by the police officer, but he doesn't say anything. His eyes, though, meet hers in the rearview mirror. There's an unspoken agreement between them, a recognition that Anthony is not normal. The officer drives off, but he adjusts his mirror to keep an eye on Anthony. Lucy can't blame him for being suspicious.

After a short journey, the officer pulls into a secure parking garage beneath the police station and escorts them in an elevator up to the second floor. Anthony is like a child. He examines the thick elevator doors as they open and close automatically. He smiles as he feels the floor of the elevator rise beneath them. When the doors open, he stands back, letting Lucy and the officer exit first. He steps over the crack between the elevator and the floor as though it were a boobytrap.

"Portsmouth, you say?" the officer says, looking sideways at Lucy.

All she can say in reply is, "Yeah, he's not from around here."

Technically, that's not a lie.

"No, he isn't," the officer agrees, signing them in and leading them to an interview room.

Lucy's surprised to see the station is packed with police officers, many of whom are still in the process of donning their uniforms. Shirts are unbuttoned. Radios and utility belts are slung over various shoulders. Tactical vests have been dumped on tables. The wall of noise means she can't hear any one conversation. Given Tuesday should be a quiet night, it looks like most of them have been called in at the last minute, probably because of whatever happened at Abington Street Gardens. She's tempted to ask the officer escorting them, but given how flakey Anthony is, it's probably best they get in and out as fast as possible. Now's not the time for idle chit-chat.

The officer closes the door to the interview room behind them, blocking out the commotion. He opens a laptop and places it on the table. Yet again, Anthony is fascinated. He leans forward with his elbows on his knees, looking intently at the computer screen. He's quiet. At least he's following her advice to remain silent.

"Have you seen a computer before?" the officer asks.

"No. Not like this," Anthony says. So much for being quiet and letting her take the lead. Lucy nudges his foot beneath the table, but he doesn't take the hint.

The officer says, "But you've seen a computer before, right? An iPad or a smart phone?"

"The rectangle," Anthony says, smiling with delight and pointing across the circular table at Lucy. "She spoke into it."

"Yes, she did."

"And it's not magic. It uses waves beyond the reach of our eyes to transmit knowledge through the open air. Is that correct?"

"Yes, it is," the officer says, raising his eyebrows at Lucy, who shrugs, unable to come up with any more wild yarns about Portsmouth, at least nothing that will in any way sound credible.

The officer positions the laptop against the wall so they can all see it, even though that means he's sitting side onto it. He opens an incognito browser tab and gestures to her, saying, "Can you sign in and retrieve the video logs from the apothecary?"

"Sure," she replies.

As Anthony's sitting in the middle, he watches with intense interest as she leans over and uses the mousepad to move the cursor around the screen. She types in the URL for her security system and enters her username and password. Seconds later, her phone pings with a two-factor authentication code. She doesn't try to explain it to Anthony. The officer knows what she's doing as she checks her phone, and that's enough for her. She feels as though she's sitting in front of someone from centuries past. Anthony isn't dumb, but how has he lived his whole life in isolation so as to have never been in a car or seen a laptop?

Lucy downloads the video feed.

There's a knock on the door of the interrogation room. A face appears at the glass. A split second later, the door opens.

"Victor!" she cries aloud, rushing to her feet.

Lucy's brother enters the interview room. He waves at the police officer a mere fraction of a second before she wraps her arms around his neck and hugs him tight. He's also only partially dressed in his uniform.

Victor asks her, "Are you okay?"

"I'm fine. I'm okay."

"They said someone was strung up on the doorframe with a

knife."

Lucy steps back, straightening her hair as she summarises what happened. "Ah, yeah. I was robbed, but Anthony was there. You remember Anthony—from Portsmouth."

Her eyes go wide, seeking agreement from him.

Victor looks at her with suspicion but he says a cautious, "Sure."

"Anthony fought off the robber."

"You shouldn't have," Victor says, addressing Anthony. "Just leave it to the professionals next time, okay?"

"Ohhh-Key."

In the meantime, the officer has opened the video file and jogged the timeline controls to the point the robber lunged at Lucy.

"Damn," Victor says, taking a seat along with Lucy and looking at the screen.

The video has audio but the words are muffled. The video quality, though, is 8K so the images are crisp and clear. From the bottom of the frame, Anthony steps up behind the robber holding two bright pink dildos in his hands.

"There! 'Tis me," Anthony says, pointing at the screen with a sense of childlike amusement at seeing himself from above and behind. "Me!"

"It is you," Lucy says with a grin on her face, knowing what's about to unfold.

The two police officers watch as the robber turns to face Anthony, threatening him with the knife. Words are exchanged, but only fragments are picked up by the camera microphone. The audio is scratchy. It's as though the video was recorded in a tin hut during a hailstorm. Lucy's complained to her dad about this before, but he's said the store's cash flow was too tight to justify replacing all three cameras. She pointed out only one is needed for sound, but he ignored her.

The robber lunges at Anthony. Instead of stepping back, he seems to prance around, darting on his feet and holding the dildos out wide on either side of him. The police officers lean in, watching intently.

The robber lunges again and Anthony strikes.

The slap of two dildos simultaneously hitting the robber's head is the only clear sound on the whole video. Both officers sit back, letting out an elongated, "Ooooooh," as the robber staggers to one side following the strike. They watch as the knife clatters to the floor followed by the dildos. The robber makes for the door but Anthony moves with the speed and agility of a cat. He grabs the knife and springs after the criminal, impaling the man's hand against the door.

The officer pauses the video, saying, "What the hell did I just see?"

Victor says, "Just when I thought this day couldn't get any weirder."

"I know, right?"

Victor laughs. "Self-defence with dildos. Now I've seen it all!"

"Oh, this is going to go viral when it's released."

"It'll have some stiff competition from that flying rainbow hedgehog."

The officer taps the screen, laughing as he says, "Honestly, I think this beats that."

"I mean, it's excessive force on the takedown—"

"—but no jury is going to convict," the officer replies. "Hell, after seeing dildos wielded like mafia blackjacks against a knife, no judge is going to let a motion from the defense stand."

"They'll be too busy laughing at the defendant."

Victor rests his hand on Anthony's shoulder, chuckling as he says, "In fifteen years on the force, that's the funniest goddamn thing I've ever seen. I don't know which prison our robber is going to end up in, but he'll *never* live that down."

The officer fills out some paperwork and gets Lucy to sign it. When he hands it to Anthony, the young man looks at the paper as though it were blank. He doesn't seem to read it at all.

"This is your statement," the officer says. "Basically, it's a summary of what you both testified to in the store along with a summary of the video evidence, corroborating your version of events."

The officer taps the page, indicating where Anthony should sign. Lucy slides the pen a little closer. Anthony picks it up. He examines the nib.

"Right here," the officer says, encouraging him. "I know this is a bit overwhelming for you, but it's okay. You're not in any trouble. You acted in self-defence. I just need your signature to confirm that you've read this."

"Signature?" Anthony says, looking at Lucy.

"Write your name," she says, smiling warmly at him.

With meticulous care, Anthony writes his name. The characters slope backwards. They look disjointed. When he's finished, he hands the paper back to the officer who looks at it and says, "Well, that's a little unorthodox, but hey, that's you, right?"

Anthony nods.

The officer gets to his feet and escorts them out of the interview room and along the corridor to the exit. He speaks to Lucy, saying, "I'll be in touch tomorrow. If I need anything more from you, I'll let you know, but I doubt it. The evidence is airtight."

"Thank you."

"Oh, and keep your buddy in town for a few days, okay? Don't let him go back to Portsmouth or wherever quite yet."

"Sure."

"It's been a crazy night," Victor says, giving Lucy a hug. "Do you want a ride home?"

"No," she says. "My car is back at the apothecary. It's a nice night. We'll walk back there and get something to eat along the way."

"Are you sure? I mean, after all that's happened."

Lucy rests her hand on her brother's chest. "I'm fine."

"It's not you I'm worried about," he says. "A lot of people are freaked out at the moment."

"Well, I'm not."

"Okay. I'm just looking out for you, sis. You had a rough time tonight. I just want you to be safe."

"I know. Thanks."

As they walk out of the secure area within the police station and into the reception room, Victor calls out, joking with the two of them, saying, "Oh, and keep your friend away from dildos!"

Lucy and Anthony walk down the stairs and out into the crisp cool evening air.

Once they're away from the station, Anthony asks, "Dildos? That's a penis, right? But they're not real. They're fake."

"Yes," Lucy replies, not feeling comfortable with his line of questioning.

"What are they used for?"

"Oh, no," she says, raising a finger and gesturing for him to be quiet. "We are not going there. Don't you—"

"I don't understand," he says. "What purpose could such a thing serve?"

"No."

"And there were so many of them in that crate."

"No, no, no," she says, not wanting to be drawn into the issue.

They walk along in silence for a few minutes. Whereas most people look ahead or watch the fall of their steps as they walk, Anthony looks around as though he were at the fairgrounds trying to take everything in.

"Where are you from?" she asks.

"London. Well, I was born in Dorset, but I lived most of my life here. We would visit the south coast for the holy days, but London was home, only..."

"Only what?"

"Only London was much smaller back then. Everything here is so big."

Anthony looks up at the street light they're passing beneath. A bus rushes past barely an inch from the curb, causing him to jump in alarm.

"There's a lot to take in, huh?" she says.

"Are they always so close? So fast?"

"Oh, the double-deckers will run you down," Lucy says. It's a joke, and yet it isn't.

Anthony looks behind them, wanting to see the oncoming traffic. Most of the cars are in the centre lane with only the occasional bus on the outside.

"How long has it been?" Lucy asks. "I mean, since you were last here? You're what? Twenty-five? Thirty years old? London hasn't changed that much in thirty years."

"It has been many years," he says. "Far more than you could imagine."

"Try me," she says.

"Who is the monarch?"

"The monarch? You mean, the king?"

"King," he says absentmindedly. "Are the Tudors still on the throne?"

Lucy comes to a halt. She swings around to face him. Her eyes go wide. "The Tudors? What? Like Henry the Eighth?"

"I was last here during the reign of Mary."

"Oh, boy," she says, turning and walking on. Anthony rushes to keep up with her.

"I would like to know. I need to know what has happened since then."

Lucy shakes her head. "You want to know what's happened in the last five hundred years? A lot. Okay? A lot has happened."

"Five hundred?" he says, coming to a halt. "It's been that long?"

She stops not more than ten feet in front of him. "You're not serious, are you? I get the whole medieval look is chic and you play the part well, but you can't tell me you were around in the time of Shakespeare."

"Shake spear?" he replies, narrowing his gaze. "Who was he? A minister? A prince? A king?"

"He wrote plays."

"Plays?"

"Yeah, you know. Someone walks out on a stage in front of an audience and recites lines from a script."

"I know of plays."

Lucy lowers her gaze. "And you've never heard of Shakespeare?"

"No."

"Everyone's heard of Shakespeare."

"I haven't."

Lucy opens her phone and brings up the browser. She holds it up for him to read.

William Shakespeare
English playwright, poet and actor
Born 26th April 1564
Died 23rd April 1616

"This first number," he says, pointing at the screen.

"That's the year Shakespeare was born."

"I would have been twenty-two."

"Would have?"

"I left Earth in the Year of Our Lord 1558."

"Wait?" she says, trying not to laugh. "You're telling me you're actually from the Renaissance?"

"I'm from England," Anthony replies, not being familiar with the term.

"And you knew Queen Mary."

"I did not. But I was her subject. Hers was a reign of terror."

Lucy shakes her head. She gestures around her, saying, "So all this is new to you?"

Anthony nods.

She asks him, "Where have you been all this time?"

He points at the sky.

"You're going to have to do better than that," she says. "Where have you been for the past five hundred years? You're telling me you've been in outer space all that time?"

"It has not been five hundred years for me," he replies. "I experienced less than ten years."

"How is that possible? Were you in suspended animation or something? No. Nope. I don't believe this. You're delusional."

"I know not what you asked of as suspension seems naught. 'Tis time and the void of space itself that bends. We think they're fixed, but they're akin to water rushing through a brook. Rates and speeds differ."

"What are you talking about?" Lucy asks.

"The Thames," he says, pointing at the dark water ahead of them as they walk through Jubilee Gardens and come out on Queen's Walk by the river. "You've sailed here, no?"

"I use the bridges."

"But you've seen the current."

"Yes," she replies, unsure where this is leading.

"Close to shore, a boat will move slower. The sails fail to full and the current is slight over the mudbanks, but out in the channel... Out in the depths, the water flows and the wind is unimpeded. Out there, you make much more of your journey."

"Ooooh-kay."

"And 'tis the same among the heavens. Here on Earth, you're close to shore."

"But you," she says.

"I was in the depths. I was carried along further. I sailed on while you drifted near the rocks."

"Relativity?" she asks him, waving her hands in the air as she talks. "Are you talking about Einstein's Theory of Relativity?"

"Too many words," he says, looking up at the London Eye as they walk beneath the oversized Ferris wheel. "You oft use terms with such speed and clarity but I know not from whence they come. The sounds are similar but the meaning eludes me."

"There was this guy named Einstein," Lucy says. "He figured out that the speed of light was equal to something. $E = mc^2$. I don't know, but there were all sorts of weird things he understood, like time dilating and light bending."

"Waves," Anthony says, pointing at the wake of a barge moving up the river.

"Waves?"

"Waves always move at the same speed. 'Tis the distance between the peaks that differ, not the speed of the wave. Like these waves rolling to shore, light rolls to us from distant stars."

"I guess so," Lucy says. "I dunno."

"I've been among the stars. I've seen planets and moons. They're not small. They look small to us, but they're not. They're—"

"Hold on there, Professor Brian Cox," she says, interrupting him. "I know what planets and stars are, but no one has ever been to them."

"I have."

"You have not."

"I've seen Saturn. It is not as you would imagine. It's golden. And it has rings. Tens of thousands of rings curling around each other. They are the most majestic—"

"Like this?" Lucy asks, having brought up an image of Saturn from one of the NASA missions. Far from being impressed, her response is droll.

Anthony is excited. "Yes. Yes! That's it. That's what Saturn really looks like! 'Tis not just a yellow speck in our night sky. 'Tis an entire world, but one of clouds. I've—Wait. How is this possible on your rectangle? You said no one has been there."

Lucy's voice is as dry as the cool autumn air around them. "We have space probes."

"I don't understand. So people have been there?"

"No. We've sent machines to Saturn. They take photos and send them back."

"But I've been there."

"Sure, buddy. Sure."

They walk up a set of stairs and onto Westminster Bridge.

"What about this bridge?" she asks. "Was this here back in your day?"

"No." Anthony stops and looks over the edge at the footings of the bridge, watching how the water flows around them.

"What about Big Ben? Surely, you had Big Ben?"

"Who is Big Ben?"

Lucy points.

"The tower?"

"The clock."

"No."

"What about the Houses of Parliament?"

"Ah, yes. We had the House, but it was much smaller. It was a…"

"A what?"

"A house."

She laughs as they walk on.

"What's the M?" Anthony asks, pointing up at a light on the side of a building on the other side of the bridge. The smooth, curved yellow arches are familiar to her.

"It's McDonald's," Lucy replies.

"The Scottish clan?" he asks, coming to a halt. "Here? In

London? What business do the Scots have with the English? Did Mary give them an advantage? She was of the Scots, you know."

"Ooooh, boy," Lucy says, dropping her gaze and staring at the cracks in the pavement as they walk on. "McDonald's is from America."

"Oh, I know about the Americas," Anthony replies as they continue on.

"America—singular. It's just America now."

"It's all just one?"

"Ah, actually, no," Lucy says, screwing up her face a little. "Kind of. It's like made up of a bunch of states. Lots of states. United States. And then there's Canada. And Mexico. And South America."

"Canada? Mexico?" Anthony says, intrigued by these words. They sound exotic falling from his lips. "But the Americas were explored by the French and the Spanish, not the Scottish. When did the McDonald clan seek its claim?"

Lucy looks lost. "Umm."

"The Scots had no conquest of the seas, no navy to fly their flag."

"Ah."

"Wasn't it *de Soto* that explored the interior of the new continent? He was a conquistador. He discovered the Father of Waters in the Americas."

"The Father of Waters?" Lucy asks, furrowing her brow.

"Yes, yes," Anthony says, clicking his fingers and trying to jog his memory. "Ah, there was a native name for it—*Messipi*."

"Mississippi?" Lucy asks.

"That has more vowels and consonants than I remember, but after almost five hundred years, yes, yes. That must be it. Please. Tell me more about these Americas. Are they dominated by the French, the Spanish or the Portuguese? Or was it the Dutch that finally settled the New World?"

"Oh, well. America has Americans."

Anthony's eyes narrow as he tries to discern the meaning of her words. To him, such logic must seem circular.

She goes on to say, "They're kind of their own thing now."

He squints. "Their—own—thing?"

"They're a big deal."

"A—big—deal?"

"Yes, America and Americans are everywhere now."

"Everywhere?" he asks, becoming ever more confused. "So not in America?"

Lucy points at the McDonald's fast food restaurant as though its mere existence is proof of her point.

Anthony joins her, also pointing at the store, but he says, "Scottish. Not American."

Lucy hangs her head and walks on toward the restaurant, laughing.

"So do you want some?"

"Food?"

"Yes, food. Are you hungry? Do you eat in outer space?"

"We eat in the void," Anthony replies, feeling a little indignant at losing an argument he clearly didn't think he'd lost on logic alone. He's defiant. "But I won't be eating haggis."

"There's no haggis in McDonald's," Lucy replies. "I promise."

They walk inside. It's quiet. Normally, even on a Tuesday, McDonald's is buzzing with customers, although a lot of them tend to be students using the free wifi. A television screen near the toilets plays a science fiction movie. Lucy doesn't recognise it. She figures the footage must be from the trailer for a new release. There's nothing she loves more than a good summer blockbuster. A multi-coloured alien spacecraft hovers over Parliament. The view is from the other side of the Thames, looking back at Westminster. Thousands of spikes reach out of the craft at different angles. One appears to touch the spire on top of Big Ben. If anything, it looks like an oversized Christmas tree with waaaay too many lights. Given the outlandish production values, she wonders if it's an ad for the Doctor Who Christmas Special. She's half expecting to see the Tardis materialise on the bridge beneath Big Ben.

Lucy pauses for a second before the screen, waiting for the cliched shot of a death ray bursting out of the massive spacecraft, splintering the tower. Destroying famous landmarks is an overworked trope in sci-fi but she doesn't mind. It seems Guy Fawkes may have his day after all. Or will he? Perhaps this movie plays on that particular historical event but with aliens destroying the government instead of a disgruntled Catholic. Oh, it's definitely a Doctor Who plot, she thinks, imagining the Doctor defusing gunpowder set by alien imposters. That's a storyline she could get behind after sinking one too many glasses of eggnog on Christmas Eve. She watches, willing the attack to unfold, but the spacecraft rises high over the city and then, in the blink of an eye, it's gone. For a fraction of a second, there's a streak on the screen and then nothing but stars.

"Boring," she says, wishing the sound was up so she could have heard the narration.

"What is this," Anthony asks, still looking around at the inside of McDonald's. He seems fascinated by the plastic tables and swivel chairs.

"Well, it's not Scottish," Lucy replies, getting in one last dig.

Anthony stays close beside her as she walks up to the counter. He whispers, "Is this a tavern without ale?"

"That's probably overstating things a little," she says, tapping on a flat screen and ordering two quarter pounders. Anthony watches with intense interest.

"These glass panes, they're the passage, but to where?"

"The kitchen," she replies, pointing. "They take the order here and cook our food there."

"Everything is so bright in the future," he says, touching a screen acting as a sign. "I mean, everywhere. You've turned the night into day."

"We have," she says, picking up their order. She hands him a burger as they walk out into the night.

Sovereigns

A double-decker bus drives past them. There's only one person on the upper deck. A couple snuggles on the lower level, being seated just behind the driver. Other than that, the huge bus is empty.

"I don't understand," Anthony says, pointing at the bus as it goes down the street. "It's so big but only for three passengers?"

"Oh, wait till rush hour," Lucy replies. "Then it's standing room only."

"Rush? Hour?"

"Yeah, it's when people go to work."

"Why does everyone rush in a single hour? That does not make sense."

Lucy points at him. "I'm gonna give you that one, caveman."

"Cave?"

"It's a joke."

"Oh."

Lucy's still not sure what to make of Anthony but he saved her life—with a pair of dildos no less. The whole *I'm-from-another-time* shtick might make for a great romcom but it's wearing thin. At what point does her obligation to him end? Is she even obliged in any way to help him? She's tired and grumpy and not thinking straight. And he's following her like a lost puppy.

They cross the four-lane road and walk along the pavement surrounding Parliament Square, which, somewhat ironically, is a roundabout. Lucy's not one for politics, but that something even vaguely associated with parliament is entirely misleading seems appropriate to her. Her cynical nature finds the contradiction in a round square humorous.

Ahead, police cars block the main road running down between the Houses of Parliament and Westminster Abbey. Lucy sighs. Her five-minute shortcut back to the apothecary has just been turned into twenty minutes of drudgery down Victoria Street and then along various back roads and laneways to the garage where her car is parked.

As the apothecary is in a narrow laneway, there's no parking out the front. The alley is still paved with the original roman cobblestones dating from the second century. Only two of the police vehicles responding to the robbery were able to squeeze down between the narrow brick walls. The ambulance was blocked in by additional police cars out on the main street. They'll all be gone by now, but the location of the apothecary means Lucy has to park her vintage Morris Minor in a private garage about a hundred meters further down the road. Her father bought a tiny one-car garage almost a decade ago—not the adjacent house or even one of the seven flats spread throughout the three-story Edwardian home—just the goddamn garage. There's barely enough room for her to squeeze her car in past the rotting wooden doors. The front bumper rests against cardboard boxes full of merchandise being rotated through the apothecary. It's mainly seasonal items, like Easter Bunny butt plugs and Santa lingerie (which is surprisingly popular). From where she's standing outside the Houses of Parliament, it's a straight line through to where her car is parked, but the police aren't going to let them through. They'll probably send them on a U-shaped detour around the area. Whatever happened here is clearly long over, but bureaucracy must be worshipped.

She sighs.

Lucy knows the side streets leading to the apothecary are poorly lit. They can be dicey this time of night. She's tempted to joke with Anthony about needing a few more dildos for self-defence. Although it's a torturous route, the London School of Bollywood is on the way and she wonders what Anthony would make of Indian film culture in England. Her best friend, Deloris, is a Bollywood tragic and even goes to Indian dance-aerobic classes to exercise while swaying to a hot and heavy Mumbai beat. What would her renaissance hero think of that?

They walk along the edge of Parliament Square, making their way toward the small crowd that's formed on the other side of the street. Curious onlookers have gathered on the corner of Abingdon Street, beside St. Margaret's Church. Beyond there, police cars sit idle with their emergency lights flashing over the buildings. A couple of army trucks have been parked across the road. Soldiers have taken up what she guesses are sentry positions along the pavement. They don't seem to be protecting anything in particular. Why the hell are they here? Has there been some kind of terrorist attack?

"Look! Cavalry," Anthony says, pointing at two police officers riding horses.

Lucy counters his point with "Mounted police."

The horses saunter out of the shadow of the trees on the far side of Parliament Square. Rather than being part of the blockade, the mounted police are behind the crowd on the large grassy lawn that makes up the square. Lucy wonders about their position. It's not accidental. She doubts they're here for the good of the horses. It's probably strategic as it gives the police a better view of the forty to fifty people that have gathered near the Houses of Parliament. Rather than looking out at the crowd from behind the barricades, they can see any agitators that might be lurking on the fringes. Lucy doubts there will be any trouble. It's Tuesday night. No one's protesting anything, they're just curious. But about what?

Anthony seems befuddled. "You have horseless carriages and carriage-less horses."

"Yeah, doesn't make a lot of sense, huh? Especially when the police have motorcycles."

"Motor what?"

"See the cars? The horseless carriages? They have four wheels. Motorcycles have two wheels and a seat, but no doors."

"Ohhhh," he replies. She has no idea what image she's conjured up in his mind, but he looks horribly confused. He's probably not thinking about two wheels in line but rather side-by-side.

They cross the road and join the crowd.

"What's going on?" Lucy asks a stranger holding up his phone above the crowd. He's recording the police and army doing precisely nothing. They look bored.

"It's the alien spaceship."

"What's *the alien spaceship*?" Lucy asks, trying not to laugh as the man seems entirely serious.

"You know, the Christmas Tree."

"The Christmas Tree?" she replies, remembering the footage she saw in McDonald's. "Oh, the movie trailer? Are they filming that here? Is that why they've closed the road?"

She looks around for the quintessential equipment truck, props table, portable tents, camera crews, lighting rigs and extras milling around. London is *always* being used for films and especially during quiet times, like on Sunday mornings or, as is the case now, a lazy Tuesday night.

A couple of months ago, Lucy got to see Chris Hemsworth and Tom Hiddleston over by the Tower of London. The film crew supporting them was quite small. She watched with fascination as a single scene was filmed over and over again. '*Action,*' was called and a bunch of taxis and cars drove forward as Chris and Tom darted across the road behind them, joking with each other. '*Cut,*' was yelled out and the vehicles all came to a simultaneous halt and then reversed to their starting positions. The camera crew repositioned itself and '*Action,*' was called again. And again. And again. Chris and Tom smiled, making as though each take was the first. They repeated their jovial laughs. Lucy stood there for almost half an hour. After watching nine repeat takes she got bored. Movies might be interesting, but making movies is monotonous. Lucy thought acting was easy, but Chris and Tom had to look fresh and vibrant and excited regardless of the sweltering heat during take number ten. Each time, they had the same explosive energy. Their enthusiasm never wavered. And when she finally saw the movie in the cinema, that particular scene lasted barely twenty seconds.

The stranger stares back at her with a blank face.

"Oh, you're serious," she says. The idea that this isn't a Hollywood blockbuster or a BBC dramatisation hadn't occurred to her, even though she's spent the evening with someone who claims to be from medieval London.

She pushes through the crowd and waves her hand, wanting to talk to one of the police officers. A well-built young man walks over with a bulging tactical vest. His radio squawks with seemingly meaningless codes.

"My car's on the south side," she says. "Down on Gayfere Street. Is there any chance of—"

"No chance at all," he says, cutting her off and directing her gaze sideways along Broad Sanctuary Road. "Best you head toward Storey's Gate and go south from there around the exclusion zone."

"Exclusion zone?"

"Yes, ma'am. The police commissioner has declared a public safety exclusion zone extending around the Houses of Parliament and surrounding buildings, including the Abbey."

"Umm. Okay, thank you," she says.

Lucy walks off along the northern road with Anthony beside her. For a few minutes, there's silence between them. As they pass the Shrine of St. Edward the Confessor, Lucy asks him, "Was that you? The spaceship, I mean. Is that how you got here?"

"Aye, 'twas."

Lucy can't believe what she's hearing and yet it's undeniable. "Aliens brought you here from the 16th Century?"

"From 1558," Anthony replies with a deadpan voice.

"I don't understand. Why would they do that? Why would they take you forward five hundred years? Is their spaceship like a time machine? Something like the TARDIS?"

"Tardy?" Anthony replies, confused by the term.

"You know, like in Doctor Who? Oh, no. You don't know Doctor Who."

"Doctor who?" he replies, but there's a hollow ring to his words. There's no sense of recognition in his voice at all.

Her phone chimes several times in rapid succession.

OMG. Lucy. You've gone viral.
Sooooo funny. Hahahaha.
Only you could upstage a UFO.
You're famous! Or is it infamous?
What are you going to do with your fifteen minutes?

Lucy sends back a quick reply, asking Deloris what she's talking about. Barely a second later, her phone chimes with another series of replies. Deloris must be sitting at a computer typing as there's no way her fingers could move that fast on a phone screen.

The dildos.
Who was that guy?
He looks rough but kind of cute.
#dildo is the no. 1 hashtag on Mastodon.
You're a legend.

Anthony is fascinated by the way Lucy's thumbs dance across the virtual keyboard at the bottom of her phone. He leans in, looking at the screen and not watching where they're going. Lucy steps down from a curb as they cross a side street. Anthony stumbles. His foot falls further than he expected. It seems to shock him back into the moment.

"Is it all well?" he asks, pointing at her screen.

Lucy shakes her head. "I don't think so." She sends a text asking Deloris how she knew about the robbery in the apothecary.

Someone leaked the video.
Must have been a cop.
Personally, I think they've done us a favour.
Not sure I'll ever look at a dildo the same way again. lol.

Lucy sighs. This is all she needs.

They walk past the historic Church House Bookstore with its high, arched windows and dozens of novels on display. To her, the ornate Victorian-era building with its white marble and stone facia is a glimpse of yesteryear, but this place wouldn't have been built for hundreds of years after Anthony departed Earth.

"Madness," she says, shaking her head.

Anthony asks, "Do you refer to the letters on your rectangle or the streets on which we walk?"

"Both," she says. "None of this was here when you last walked these laneways, was it?"

Anthony looks around, but at what? He's trying to get his bearings. As they head around the corner of a T-junction, taking a side street back toward the apothecary, he points further down the main street, saying, "This was a farm. This road followed a stream, but it was made from dirt back then, not rock. Wild flowers grew in the middle of the lane, being sustained by horses dropping their load. Beyond—over yonder—there was a forest leading down to the estate of Lord and Lady de Brooke. Theirs was a grand home with orchards lining the drive."

Lucy feels overwhelmed. What is she doing? What the hell should she do? Deep down, she knows she should turn Anthony over to the authorities, but she can't. He hasn't done anything wrong. If anything, he's done everything right. He saved her life. She's pretty sure the government would be pretty damn interested in someone that's spent their life on an alien spacecraft. Given London is covered in CCTV cameras, the police must know Anthony was dropped off by the UFO. Do they think he's an alien? What would they think if they knew he was human, but that he originated in the age of the Tudors? What would they do with him?

She asks Anthony, "Why did you come back to the apothecary?"

"My master," he replies. "He kept his earnings hidden. I know not, but I think he may have left them. 'Twas common in my day for those without wife or child. A stash once hidden could be lost for a time. Depending on what transpired. If the pox took hold or pleurisy, he may have neglected his collection."

"Buried treasure?" Lucy says, raising an eyebrow as she turns to look at him. "You mean, like pirate's treasure?"

"Nay, 'tis the honest earnings of a righteous man."

Lucy leads him down a side road. She pushes open an old wooden door leading to a narrow alley between two houses toward the rear entrance to the apothecary. The path is barely wide enough for one person to pass at a time. From the street, there's no way of knowing this alley leads to the rear of the apothecary. It's mostly used by the homes on either side to access their gardens.

"Close the gate," she says.

Anthony pushes it shut, saying, "The courtyard. It's gone. Once, we grew thyme and rosemary here. Lavender and sage."

"This is London," Lucy replies. "If a scrap of dirt's not on the heritage trust list, it'll become part of someone's home or their driveway."

She unlocks the door and walks into the back of the apothecary. Rather than turn on the lights, she uses the light on her phone. She's not sure why she's being secretive. She hasn't done anything wrong, but she feels as though she's breaking the law.

"Where's your treasure buried?" she asks. For Lucy, this is an opportunity to dispel any last doubts. If there really is gold or diamonds or coins or whatever hidden in her store, it proves his story's true. Even if the stash is empty, that he could find a secret cavity would be enough for her.

"Ah, 'tis back here," he says, leading her through the store. He pauses in front of a door beside the barrel of dildos. The pink, red and black rubber phalluses are poorly illuminated by the tiny light on her phone.

"Don't even think about it," she says, looking down at the dildos and joking with him.

Anthony laughs.

Lucy opens the storeroom door. There's a bathroom at the top of the steps and a musty, sunken basement down below. The room is divided by shelves. Dust rests on ageing cardboard boxes. Plastic has been draped over a clothes rack with a dozen black faux-leather gimp suits hanging on a steel pole. To Anthony, they must seem like medieval torture devices. Perhaps they are.

Anthony paces. He's measuring the layout, trying to recall the exact position of the stash. Lucy watches with keen interest as he taps the sheetrock wall. After a few minutes, he points at the unfinished stone floor in front of the wall.

"Here."

"Show me."

Anthony looks around for something to pry the wall loose. Lucy hands him a box cutter. He looks at the plastic handle, confused as to how this flimsy device is supposed to help him.

"Push up the black handle."

"Oh," he says, seeing the stainless steel blade protrude from the end.

Anthony kneels and scores the board. Lucy waits for him to cut deeper, but having marked the wall, he slips his fingers into the gap between the board and the floor, where flooding has softened the material, and yanks it away. A section of sheetrock comes off in his hand, revealing the old stone behind the sheetrock wall. Anthony is rough, tearing more sections away and widening the hole. Lucy grimaces. Her father is going to kill her for breaking up the wall. She figures she'll dump a box in front of it and, hopefully, he'll never notice.

"The light," Anthony says.

"Oh, yes. Of course," Lucy replies, crouching beside him and shining the torch on her phone at the wall. The stones are held in the wall by some kind of old-fashioned grout or concrete. There's a stain on the floor. Although the basement has flooded a few times in the past, it's clear that water has found a way out at this point as water has dried, leaving irregular rings on the floor. She's never noticed them before, but Anthony points at them.

"Here," he says. "Master Dunmore kept his excess hidden above an old drain."

Anthony works the blade of the box cutter over the grout. The fine powder comes away easily. If he goes a little wider, it's clear the grout on either side is thicker and stronger than around this one particular stone. It's as though concrete dust has accumulated there rather than been set. Once Anthony has scraped it away, he uses his fingers to edge the stone out of the wall. It's heavy. Lucy's heart is racing. This is real. Regardless of what they find, she knows there's no possible way Anthony could have known about this without actually having been in the apothecary hundreds of years ago.

The stone is roughly half the size of a loaf of bread. It's no wonder no one's ever pried it loose before. Once it's out, Anthony reaches inside the cavity. His hand disappears into the shadows. Lucy drops to her knees. She leans forward, shining the light inside the opening, desperate to see what lies in the darkness.

Anthony pulls out several items. He hands her a scroll covered in dust along with several loose-leaf pages. The parchment is yellow and brittle.

Lucy mumbles, "We need to get this to a museum."

She's gentle, laying each page on a cardboard box beside her. And she's grinning. She can't help it. She's never felt such a rush of life surging through her veins. The writing before her is pristine. To her eye, it looks like calligraphy. She doesn't recognise the words or types of currency, but she realises this is some kind of ledger or record of transactions.

>   *Llywen doughe* . . . . *15 d v(3)*
>   *Rose narsh & tyme.* . . . . . . *7 d*
>   *Castor of Myrrh* . . . . *3 d (fore his Lordshipe)*
>   *Cardeamon* . . . . *4 d 2 f*

"This is... oh, my. This is real."

"You doubted, m'lady?" Anthony says. He leans over and flicks through a few pages before pointing at one of the entries. "This one. This one here. It's the last entry I ever made."

>   *Lday* . . . . *4 g s*

"I remember the day I wrote this. It was after the execution of two men at the stake for heresy."

Lucy's quiet. It's insane to hear Anthony talking about people being burned alive as though it happened yesterday.

"Lady de Brooke," he says. "She took pity on me, but I spelt *lady* wrong. I knew it at the time, but the ink was already on the page. I wondered who would read this entry. What I never imagined is *when* it would be next read."

"Five hundred years later," an astonished Lucy says, shaking her head.

Anthony hands her one of several leather pouches covered in dust. He pulls the drawstring open and reaches inside. Lucy feels her heart beating out of her chest in excitement. Coins clink together. Anthony holds up a tarnished coin for her to examine. She's never seen an irregular coin before. All the coins she's ever seen throughout her life have been perfect, coming from the Royal Mint. The die which cast this coin, or perhaps the stamp that sealed it, was slightly off-centre, leaving the coin misshapen. She examines the coin in the light of her phone.

"I'm just... I'm speechless... All this has been here all along?"

"Yes."

"For centuries?"

"Yes."

Anthony hands her a gold coin. Unlike the other coins, this one looks as though it was minted yesterday. There are no scratches on the surface, no tarnish on the metal, no imperfections in the design.

"And this is?"

"M'lady. Do you not have sovereigns in your time? 'Tis the most valuable of our coin—issued by the Queen herself."

"How many of these do you have?" she asks with her eyes going wide.

He rummages around in another purse, saying, "Looks like the master kept his daily taking separate from his savings. I count nine, along with dozens of shillings, farthings and pounds. Will these suffice for trade in this day?"

"Will they?" she asks. "I dare say they're worth more today than they ever were back then."

"Then we can use them."

"Ah, not in a store."

"No?" he asks, confused.

"You're going to have to change them for modern money, but one of your pounds is probably worth, I don't know, a hundred of our pounds? A thousand?"

Anthony raises his eyes at her comment.

Lucy says, "You can't use these to buy anything from a store like mine, but collectors will pay a fortune for pristine coins like these."

"Then 'tis good," Anthony says, putting the coins back in the pouch.

"It's really good," Lucy says, nodding and unable to wipe the grin off her face.

Her phone rings. The sudden noise breaking within the darkened, quiet confines of the basement storage room causes her to jump. She looks at the caller ID. It's her brother.

Anthony counts out the coins on a cardboard box before gathering them together in the largest leather pouches.

"Victor," she says with a rush of excitement.

"Lucy," he replies, but there's something about the way he says her name. There's caution, perhaps reservation. Given how close they were growing up and the laughter they just shared over the dildos, it seems misplaced. Something's wrong. "Is he still with you?"

Lucy's silent. She hesitates.

"If you can't talk," Victor says. "If something's wrong and you can't speak freely then cough."

"He's gone," Lucy blurts out, feeling brash. Anthony looks up at her. He knows she's talking about him and that she's lying. Although he doesn't know her well, the look in his eyes speaks volumes. He knows he's vulnerable and she's protecting him.

"Where?"

"Why?" she asks. "What's wrong?"

"I don't know."

"Victor!"

"I don't. I swear."

Lucy knows her brother well enough to know he wouldn't lie to her like she just lied to him, but he would withhold the truth. There's a painful silence.

"It's a madhouse here," he finally says. "That—that spacecraft. It's got everyone spooked. The police commissioner is here. The assistant commissioner for met ops and special ops. It's eleven at night and they're all here."

"And?"

"They've all watched your video."

"And?" Lucy asks again, feeling there's more he's holding back.

"No one laughed." Victor sighs.

"I don't get it. Why do they care?" she asks.

Anthony is on his feet, holding the bag of renaissance coins and standing by the stairs. He mouths the words, "We should go," pointing at the door. Lucy holds up her hand, wanting him to wait.

"Your guy. The guy from Portsmouth. They've got him on CCTV at the point the alien spacecraft lowered some kind of platform. The footage is grainy, but after a bright flash of light, he's standing there in the background."

"How clear is the video? How do you know it's him?"

"I don't. We don't. The footage is a mess, but the tracking isn't. They never got a good shot of his face, but ops were able to follow him to the apothecary. It's him, Lucy."

"How do you know he's involved? He could have been walking by when that spacecraft flew overhead."

"We've got CCTV from before the incident. He wasn't in the underground carpark. He wasn't on either of the approaches on the street. He wasn't there at all until after the cameras came back online."

Lucy's quiet.

"He's there with you, isn't he?" Victor asks. "Where are you?"

"I left him at the Abbey," she says. There's a rustle in the background over the phone. Someone is hurriedly scribbling something or doing something. Lucy knows she's not on speakerphone as the sound of Victor's voice would have more resonance, but he could be using his AirPods. If he is, he could have given one of them to someone else so they could listen in. Knowing that, she's quite deliberate. She says, "I don't know what he wants, but he said he needed to speak to the King. Last I saw, he was heading toward St. James's Park."

"Thank you, Lucy," her brother says. "You've been a great help."

To her surprise, he hangs up before waiting for a response from her. Lucy feels bad about lying to Victor and sending him on a wild goose chase, but she feels she has to protect Anthony. He's got no one in this world. She doesn't mean to be dishonest, but she's not one to blindly trust the government. She'd like to know their intentions and have some assurances before turning Anthony over to them.

St. James's Park is huge. It covers easily fifty acres, if not more, and has a lake dividing the commons in two. In summer, once daylight savings has started, Lucy loves catching up with friends in the park and playing frisbee football after work. There are two other adjacent parks linking up with Buckingham Palace in the middle. If the King is in residence, they'll be whisking him away. Scouring the park at night is going to be a logistical nightmare. She feels bad, but if they focus their search there, she can slip away with Anthony and buy herself some time to think.

"Is trouble brewing?" Anthony asks.

"Oh, *double, double toil and trouble; fire burn, and cauldron bubble*," she says, jogging up the stairs as she quotes Shakespeare's Macbeth. Anthony's eyes narrow. Lucy shakes her head. "Never mind. Yes, there's trouble. We need to leave."

Lucy sends a quick WhatsApp text to Deloris, knowing it's encrypted end-to-end.

Meet me at the McDonald's on the A23 in Croydon.

It takes a few seconds for a reply. While she's waiting, Lucy searches through the settings on her phone for the factory reset option.

What? Why?

Please. I need your help.

And with that, Lucy enters her PIN and sets her phone to reset itself and wipe her data. She's unsure how effective the process is. A progress bar runs across the screen. To be sure, she drops her phone in the toilet bowl once it's finished. The screen flickers and goes dark.

They walk back into the apothecary. Although she pulled a roller door down over the storefront, there are thin slits in the sheet metal, allowing the wind to pass through. Blue and red lights flash from somewhere further up the lane. A police vehicle is out there.

"Quick," she says, taking his hand and leading him out the back door.

At the end of the narrow walkway, the lights of a car sweep along the road. Even though the wooden door to the street is closed, the bottom few inches have rotted away, allowing the light to seep through. Car tyres crunch on loose gravel on the edge of the road. At this time of night, there's no way in hell that's one of the locals. Although she can't know for sure, she figures it's a police car out looking for them.

Lucy slaps the wall beside her, saying, "We need to jump this." She cups her hands in front of her so she can help Anthony step up but he ignores her.

Anthony moves like a jackrabbit. He springs off the muddy ground, pushing one leg against the brick wall to his right and launching himself to the left. Lucy hasn't had time to blink, let alone think, and he's up. He crouches on top of the wall and reaches down, offering her his hand. She accepts. Before she can push her shoes against the bricks, he hauls her up with uncommon strength, grabbing under her armpits and pulling her onto the wall. Given he has a thin frame, he's surprisingly strong.

"Thanks," she says in a whisper.

From the top of the wall, Lucy can see the roof of the apothecary on one side and a row of joined townhouses on the other. Boots scuff the ground at the end of the walkway. That's got to be a police officer on foot. The door leading out to the street has a stone surround, meaning the only way someone could see them is if they climbed up. A flashlight flickers across a nearby wall.

"Quick," she says, dropping down into the courtyard of one of the townhouses. Before she can say anything, Anthony has scaled the next wall. He has his hand out, grinning. He's done this before—hundreds of years before. He probably thinks her means of escape is quite quaint. He lived in a time when a night in jail probably came with a flogging, not an embarrassed dad escorting his wayward daughter before a judge the next day.

They pass through three yards in utter silence, crouching under citrus trees and avoiding garden sheds.

"I'm parked on Gayfere St," she whispers, pointing across the road. "Just down there. You wait here. Watch me. I'm going to the house with the green garage."

"They all look grey," he says, and under the dull yellow streetlights, he's right.

"British Racing Green," she says, pointing again and then realising he has absolutely no idea what she's talking about. "Dark green."

"The fourth one?" he asks.

"The fourth one," she concedes, realising that's a much better description. "Wait here. I'll go and get my car—"

"Your horseless carriage?"

"Yes, my horseless carriage. It's white. I'll unlock the doors. You jump in the back."

Anthony points at himself. "I climb in the back."

"Well, not the back-back, that would be the boot. You climb in the side door."

"The side door, not the back door."

"There's no back door," Lucy says, waving with her hands and realising what a mess she's made of this.

"The door on the side?" Anthony says, looking at her with a sense of confusion washing over his face.

"All the doors are on the side, some are in front, some at the back."

"But you said there's no back door."

"Not at the back-back."

"So there's a door at the back, but it's not at the back?"

"Yes," she says, feeling as though she's made some progress.

"Is everything this confusing in this century?"

"Okay. There are two doors. Well, there are four doors. They're all on the side. But there are only two doors on each side."

"Like a carriage."

"Yes, like a carriage. I'll be in the front of those doors. You get in the back of those doors, but not the back-back or you'll be climbing in the boot or the trunk or whatever it was called in the 16th century. I need you to remain out of sight. Understand?"

"I think so."

With that, she peers either way down the street and drops to the pavement. Lucy jogs across the road and down Gayfere St with her keys in her hand. She unlocks the garage and pulls the heavy wooden door open.

Lucy grabs a permanent marker from the shelf and alters her license plates. She kneels down and changes the number 5 to 6 by colouring in the gap. From a distance, it's believable. Up close, it's comical, but it's all she can do to try to disappear. London is notorious for its surveillance. Closed-Circuit TV cameras, traffic cams, anti-vandalism cameras, and anti-loitering cameras that allow the police to move the homeless along are located everywhere, and that's before factoring in security cameras on private homes, dash cams, and cameras on businesses.

Someone somewhere is probably already weaving together footage and figuring out she lied about Anthony heading up to St. James's Park. Like Hansel and Gretel, they'll follow the breadcrumbs. Hopefully, by jumping through half-a-dozen backyards, crossing a street and hiding behind trees, she's thrown these electronic sleuths off the scent.

Once she's out on the road, traffic cameras will use optical character recognition to track vehicles going in and out of the area. A human might recognise the similarity between G52 HKU and G62 HKU but machine learning algorithms focused on resolving grainy images in poor lighting at various angles won't. Oh, someone will have set a watch for her license plate, but the sophisticated computer system will never see the correct number. Hopefully, this will buy them some time.

She starts her car, backs out onto the street and then leaves the engine running while she shuts the garage door. Lucy drives up to the T-junction and looks for Anthony. He's gone. He should be on the second-to-last stone wall, perched next to a fir tree. Her heart races.

She leans over the back seat and struggles to open the far door. She flicks the lever and it comes loose but doesn't open. Lucy doesn't want to stop and get out. She's hoping he's seen her and will come running to the rear door. Her eyes scan up and down the street. She checks her rearview mirror and side mirrors, muttering, "Where the hell are you?"

From behind her seat, a soft voice whispers, "The back door on the side, right?"

Lucy has to twist around in place on her seat to see Anthony crouching in the footwell behind the driver's seat.

"How did you? Never mind."

She reaches over the back and closes the far rear door. He must have snuck in while she was closing the garage. She expected him to wait for her to return to the street, but he had other ideas. Well done, Lucy, she thinks, reprimanding herself. Once again, you've overcomplicated the simple. And yet somehow, everything's okay.

She drives off with Anthony remaining out of sight.

"Lucy?"

"Yes."

"Thank you."

Deloris

"Okay," Lucy says, walking down the narrow, carpeted stairs in the rundown south London flat. "He's set for the night."

Deloris is in the kitchen making a pot of tea. Under her breath, she asks, "And this is really him? I mean, this is like *ET phone home* or something, right?"

"He's not an alien, Dee."

"That's what they're calling him on the TV."

"Well, they're wrong."

"What is he then?"

"Human. Just like you and me. Only he's five hundred years old."

"Five hundred years!" Deloris replies, struggling to keep her voice down. "How is that possible? And you think that's easier to believe than him being from Alpha Centauri?"

Lucy slumps into a vinyl seat at the table.

Lucy met Deloris at the Croydon McDonald's. By that time, Anthony was asleep in the footwell behind her. Lucy wasn't sure how that was possible as it must have been uncomfortable, but he was snoring when she parked next to the dumpster behind the fast food restaurant. She left her car with the window half down. Deloris said she was mad. *'What if someone steals it?'* Deloris asked, to which Lucy replied, *'Maybe I should leave the keys in the ignition as well. Or do you think that makes it too obvious?'* Since then, Lucy has helped Anthony settle for the night upstairs in the flat.

Deloris lives with her brother Frank, who's roughly the same height and build as Anthony. As Frank's away in Southampton for the week on training, Anthony gets his old clothes and his bed. Lucy showed Anthony how to work the shower and left him to rest for the night.

Deloris puts a ceramic teapot down on an embroidered tablecloth, letting it rest. She grabs some teacups and saucers from the cupboard. Her home is half a flat, which in itself was originally half of a home. Subdividing an ageing Edwardian house into four sections doesn't result in a lot of living space. Her combined washer/dryer is nestled in between the bar fridge and the oven within a tiny kitchenette. The dining room is an alcove set between the kitchenette and the lounge. The bedrooms upstairs are the size of a shoebox that's been crushed at the bottom of a shipping container. Even with a single bed, there's barely enough room to open the door and squeeze in beside the dresser.

Like so many places in Greater London, the rent is exorbitant in Croydon, while the blood-curdling scream of foxes at night makes it sound as though someone's being murdered outside the window, but Lucy knows that shouldn't be confused with the hellish scream of a train braking on approach to the nearby station. Poor Anthony probably thinks he's in a war zone. For now, though, he's safe.

"What's your plan?" Deloris asks, retrieving a carton of milk from the fridge and placing it on the table.

"I don't know. For now, to get some sleep. Maybe things will be clearer in the morning."

"Hah," Deloris says, pouring them both a cup of tea. She adds a teaspoon of sugar, stirs, and then adds a little milk. Her process is deliberate, not haphazard. She doesn't want to scald the milk proteins and needs to avoid the cream fat separating with the heat. Anywhere else in the world, no one would care, let alone notice the difference. In

England, though, a cup of tea isn't a refreshing drink, it's an act of sacrament. Once she's satisfied, she hands one of the cups to Lucy, having selected the tea she deems closest to perfection.

"Thanks."

"I mean, for a spaceman, he's kind of cute."

"Dee," Lucy says, trying not to laugh as she sips her tea.

"You need a plan."

"I know I need a plan."

"Listen, my cousin is a cleaner up at Oxford."

"A cleaner?" Lucy replies. "Seriously, that's your plan?"

"Don't underestimate us cleaners," Deloris says. "We have access everywhere. I mean. Every. Where. Number Ten, Downing Street. The Tate Art Gallery. MI5. Cambridge University. Oxford. No one cleans their own office. Absolutely no one. We cleaners do. And we're invisible. So long as it's a familiar face, no one bats an eyelid where we go or what we do."

"And?"

"And they're not going to stop looking for Anthony. They're going to use every trick they have to find your medieval guy."

"And you're thinking..."

"Negotiate with them—while you can."

"What do you mean?"

"I mean, we can leave messages with the Head of Astrophysics at Oxford, or at Cambridge, wherever you want. Or I could introduce you to them. We get *them* on our side and slow this whole thing down. At the moment, the public is going nuts. The press is calling this the greatest manhunt in history. I suspect Bin Laden would disagree, but the media is nothing if not hyperbolic. And behind the scenes, the police and army and MI-whatever will be going hard on this. And they're not subtle. But we can take the initiative away from them. We can defuse this whole mess."

"Defuse it how?"

"By telling your side of the story."

"My side?"

"You're the one that says he's not an alien."

Lucy sips her tea, lost in thought.

Deloris asks her, "Who can you trust?"

"No one."

"And yet you're here."

"You know what I mean."

"I'm serious," Deloris says. "Think about it. Who can you trust?"

"I—I don't know. Friends? Family?"

"Scientists."

"Scientists?"

"Well, you sure as hell can't trust the police, or the army, or politicians—or even the news media. They *all* have an agenda. That doesn't mean they're bad, but even your brother Victor's got a duty to perform. What you need is someone that's impartial. Someone that wants to get to the truth."

"And you think that's a bunch of scientists up at Oxford?"

Deloris says, "The only thing that stands between you and me and the Stone Age is a bunch of scientists figuring shit out!"

"I'm not sure they can figure this shit out."

"If he's a spaceman or a medieval man or whatever, he's better off in *their* hands than sitting in an isolation cell on some army base while the British Cabinet freaks out about a bunch of overblown security concerns."

"That's a fair point," Lucy says. She likes the idea of taking charge of the situation. Deloris is right. They can't run forever. At some point, the authorities are going to catch up to them, and then what? At least, this way, she can steer things to a positive outcome.

A fighter jet roars overhead. It's a long way off, but it's a less-than-subtle reminder that the military is still overreacting to the presence of a spacecraft that has long since vanished from British skies.

"Okay," Lucy says. "Tomorrow, we'll head up to Oxford and see if your cousin can get us in front of the professor of astrophysics."

"Oh, he'll get you in. Don't worry about that. Just be ready with what you want to say."

Lucy finishes her tea. She knows she won't get much sleep tonight. She'll spend the quiet hours rehearsing her speech time and time again.

She asks Deloris, "Do you have a spare tablet or a computer I could use?"

"Frank left his phone here," she says, picking up an old iPhone with a cracked screen from the counter and handing it to her. "The passcode is all ones."

"And he won't mind?"

"He won't know. I doubt he even realises he left it here. Now, if he'd forgotten a novel, it would be different. He'd be messaging me, asking me to mail it down to him even though he's due back on Friday."

"Okay," she says, unlocking the phone and looking at the front screen. Her phone was packed with mobile apps she barely used, spanning eight screens. Frank's phone has almost no apps. There are icons for email, a browser, the phone's camera and a dictaphone app, but that's it. Everything else has been dumped in a folder called *Useless Crap*.

"Just like old times, huh?" Deloris says, rinsing but not washing the teapot. To clean the inside of a teapot is sacrilege. To maximise the flavour, a teapot needs to be nurtured like a baby. Deloris wipes the inside of the teapot with a tea towel, saying, "Sleepovers were always my favourite part of the holidays."

Lucy laughs. "Oh, I think our beds were bigger back then." She lingers by the door, asking, "Do you want some help with—"

"No," Deloris replies, cutting her off. "Go. You get ready for bed. I'll clean up down here and be up in a second."

Lucy nods. She places her empty cup on the sink and heads up the stairs.

Alone

As Lucy walks down the narrow corridor past the first bedroom, she hears a slight whimper.

"Hey, what's the matter?" she asks, pushing open the door and peering inside.

The light from the corridor spills onto the darkened floor. Anthony is seated on the bed with his legs crossed in front of him. He should be asleep.

"I am well," he says, but the tremor in his voice betrays a lie.

Lucy pauses at the threshold of the room. Doubts crowd her mind. The unlocked phone glows in her hand. She knows she shouldn't, but she can't help herself. She needs proof of Anthony's existence. She opens the dictaphone app and hits *record*. With a deft motion, she turns off the screen and slips the phone into the back pocket of her jeans. To Anthony, it'll seem as though *'the rectangle,'* as he calls it, has been shut down even though it's still recording. Lucy doesn't mean to be deceitful, but she feels she needs to record at least one of their remarkable conversations. If Anthony is legit, and everything seems to be pointing that way, then she owes it to herself and the public at large to record his comments. Technically, she's invading his privacy, but she's aware of the significance of his life, even if he doesn't think he's important.

She pushes the door wide. Anthony looks up at her with tears streaming down his cheeks. Lucy walks in and sits next to him on the spongy mattress.

"Do you want to talk about it?"

"Talk?" he says, trying not to laugh.

"Talking can help."

"Nothing can help."

Damn, there's no comeback she can offer for that other than to be there for him. Lucy feels her heart sink. This isn't Deloris whining after being dumped-by-text on her second date with some hotshot banker from Canary Wharf.

Lucy rubs Anthony's back. In her lifetime, she's only ever seen one other man cry like this—her father. On the evening her mother passed away from a heart attack, her dad was stoic. He had to be strong for the kids, or so he said. Lucy was eighteen. Her brother was twenty-two. Neither of them were children. Both of them bawled at the loss of their mother in a nondescript hospital room that was seemingly one among a million other identical, sterile rooms on a million other identical, sterile wards in the rabbit warren that was London's St George Hospital, but not her dad. He blotted tears from the corners of his eyes. His lips trembled as he held his dead wife's hand one last time. But he didn't cry. Later that night, once they'd returned home and succumbed to exhaustion, Lucy heard him sobbing from her room. She remembers creeping into his bedroom and offering him hollow comfort as he finally grieved. What is it about men and emotions?

Anthony, it seems, has reached a breaking point. He sobs. His chest heaves. Lucy can feel his ribs expanding and collapsing through her fingers, which brings back the loss of her mother and the grief of her father. She can't imagine what has stirred Anthony so deeply. Men don't cry. Oh, they do, but the stereotypical macho bullshit in Western culture says they don't. From what she's observed, men hide their tears. Being open about emotions doesn't come easy for most men. Too many of them have been raised on a diet of *Die Hard* and chants of *yippee-ki-yay motherfucker!* Emotional men are gay, or so the myth goes. And if men do cry, they don't bawl their eyes out *'like a girl.'*

Lucy hates how fucked up modern social conditioning has become. It started out innocent enough. Chivalry was sweet. Daring knights dressed in shining armour were said to rescue a damsel in distress. They were strong and brave. And so the facade was built. Thinking they're tough, they cower behind the illusion of strength, not realising that only makes them weaker. Anthony, though, is from another time. Although he has his own mountains to climb, it seems he's avoided the assault of Hollywood on masculinity.

As Lucy's studying psychology at university, she feels as though she can help Anthony if given the chance. In the back of her mind, though, she senses a deeper meaning to his comment that nothing can help. Now is not the time to play Sigmund Freud.

"If you want to talk, I'll listen," she says.

He sighs, releasing the air in his lungs and sagging under the weight of the burden he's bearing. Lucy has no idea what could have hurt him so deeply. He's safe—for now, at least.

"I am nothing."

In the darkness, his words cut into her soul. She wants to contradict them, but she understands this is how he feels. Telling him he's someone would be insulting. He already knows that. The problem is, he doesn't feel that. And what is life without feeling?

"All that I thought I was is but a mist drifting over a pond in the early morning light, damned to vanish from sight as the sun rises over the trees."

Lucy has tears in the corner of her eyes. His eloquence touches her. Anthony speaks in otherworldly tones. Whereas modern language is clipped and short, he is drawn to analogies. By painting a picture with his words, he's laying bare his heart and soul.

"I looked for answers, but from whence do they come? Answers are not found in libraries or churches, not in the song of birds on the wing or an ox pulling a plough through a fallowed field.

"What are these lives we live? From whence do we find meaning when all that surrounds us is sorrow? We are but the scurry of ants swarming over the ground, rushing to get somewhere without going anywhere. We meet by a rock, bumping into each other and exchanging words as we glance off each other. Time cannot be wasted. Time is too precious. And we rush on to meet the next ant crawling over the mud and grime. All the while, we feel like we're accomplishing something when it is but for nought.

"Then the ploughman comes. He stomps through the field, looking for shade so he can rest awhile from the heat of the noonday sun. He's ready to eat his lunch of mouldy cheese and stale bread. Without a thought, he steps on the pebbles and crushes the ants. And with that, he steps on again, and they are nothing. All their toil has passed without reward or recognition. There are none that care. What gain has there been from their fatigue? What meaning to their frantic motion? Has it not been all for nought? And the ploughman? He seizes his chest, choking on a piece of crust lodged in his throat. He gasps his last and joins the ants in their misery. He too has become nothing."

Reluctantly, Lucy nods, appreciating the depth behind Anthony's words. In her psych course, this would be labelled as an example of an existential crisis—the definition of which is simple: *the feeling life has no meaning*. The solution is elusive. No one answer satisfies everyone. Some find meaning in religion. Others find solace in science. Still others feel the need to lighten the load of their friends or the world at large. Problems arise, though, in the lives of those that ignore the ache and focus only on themselves. They don't see outward, only within. For them, there is no crisis, only more money to be made and junk to be purchased. Lucy knows that at some point, they'll realise being selfish is vain, but not before they, too, have trodden on ants like the ploughman. And then, one day, they too will choke on some bread.

Lucy wants to tell Anthony he's something other than nothing. She wants him to feel a sense of worth, but this is his journey to take, not hers.

"I'm alone."

The utter simplicity of his words leave her stunned. They break like thunder within the cramped room.

Yet again, Lucy doesn't reply. She leaves his two words hanging in the air. If there's one thing her psych course has taught her, it's the importance of listening without responding. As a psychologist, she's tempted to hear a problem and solve it with some pearl of wisdom she read from Locke or Wollstonecraft. It's easy to give advice, but empty words solve nothing. Anthony's right. When he scoffed at the notion of talking to her, his scepticism was justified. On their own, words are hollow.

It takes all her might not to say anything in response. The temptation borders on overwhelming. The words of her senior mentor flood her mind: *if you're talking, you're not listening*. When she conducted her first therapy session, Lucy was told to repeat things back to her client for two reasons. First, it lets them hear what they said, and that gives them the opportunity to reflect on what they meant. Second, it slows *her* down, allowing her to really think about the issues rather than rushing to a solution. Even with three years of theory and fifteen practical placements, she feels inadequate sitting next to Anthony. It's the weight of the moment. This is real. Nothing could have prepared her for sitting with someone from the 16th century, someone that's ventured into the depths of space with an advanced alien race. If he says he's alone, he's right.

Lucy's lips move, but no words come out. She remains true to her convictions, halting before her tongue utters a single syllable.

"We live in villages," Anthony says, speaking softly as he explains himself. "But why? 'Tis because we need each other. Even the hermit needs more than birds in the trees. What king rules over an empty castle?"

Lucy nods. She's aware she's gaining unique insights into the mind of the past. She wonders how many generations lie between them. The scale of change over the past five hundred years must leave him feeling as though he's landed on an alien world—and in many ways, he has. What for her seems commonplace for him is overwhelming. Reality is catching up to her renaissance-era spaceman.

"You've been kind," he says. "And I thank you for your gentle nature, but there's nought here to assuage my hurt."

Anthony sits back, leaning against the wall. Lucy lowers her hand to her thigh. She turns side on toward him, tucking her legs up on the bed as she faces him in the darkness. Whereas at first, she wanted to speak, now she longs for nothing more than to listen to this stranger from another time, from another world. Far from helping, she understands she has nothing to offer beyond being here for him. This moment is something he needs to work through for himself.

Anthony says, "We're alone even when we aren't. Whether we're in the quiet of the forest or lost in a crowd, we are but one and separate from all others, despite what we may long for. 'Tis strange, but from the womb, we are separated, and once separated, all our longing cannot forge otherwise."

He wrings his hands together.

"Perhaps it is time that makes my soul ache. Such change as has been wrought over the centuries has left me stripped naked. I see buildings and machines so grand and wondrous, filled with lights and sounds the envy of which my age could not even begin to dream, and yet there is all that has remained unchanged. For all that has advanced, so much has stayed the same."

He looks deep into her eyes.

"In your world, it seems as if you're never alone, and yet you're as a beggar in the Lud Gate, sitting on paving stones laid by the Romans themselves. Try as you may, you cannot join the throng of the crowd pressing past to reach the markets.

"To me, you seem as a princess on horseback or gentry in a carriage, passing through the town, pretending the stench of horse shite and piss does not fill the streets and lash at your nostrils as it does mine. All the trappings may have advanced, but the facade remains the same. We fool ourselves into thinking we're not alone because we're afraid of being found short and being seen for who we are."

The phone in Lucy's back pocket is stiff and unyielding, constantly reminding her she's betraying him. She had no idea what he was going to say when she walked into his room. She never meant to record him baring his soul. She wants to pull the phone out and hit *stop*, but not only would that distract him, it would shatter his trust in her. Sitting there in the darkness, Lucy feels like a heel.

And he's right. She may have dumped her smartphone in the toilet back at the apothecary, but less than an hour later she's found a replacement. She can sign into any one of her social media apps through a browser and instantly connect with friends all over the planet. And yet, like him, she too is alone. Lucy's never thought about life in these terms before. Being connected is an illusion—a distraction. She wouldn't consider herself afraid, but in the quiet times, her phone is always within reach. The glowing rectangle of glass provides refuge from loneliness—only it doesn't. At best, it's a placebo.

"What about love?" she asks.

"Love, till it is lost, is like a bonfire in the darkness, giving us warmth and light against the bitter cold."

"But?"

"But love too has bounds no one can cross."

It's then it strikes her.

"You lost someone."

"I did."

"Someone close to you."

"Close enough to stave off the dread of night."

"Out there," she says. "Out in space."

Anthony hangs his head and cries.

"That's why you're here. That's why you returned."

"To a world I know not," he says, wiping away tears. "To a world in which I don't belong. To a world in which I will forever be a stranger. And they warned me. They told me I could never return to my world. And they were right. I could return to the planet, but my world is forever lost in time."

Lucy can feel the depth of anguish clinging to his words. She wants to ask him about his grief, but out of respect, she remains silent.

After a few seconds, Anthony says, "We seek connections we can never have. We love, we laugh, we commune, we care, we chat, we jostle and banter—and for what? To mask the loneliness that cannot be supplanted."

Lucy breathes deeply. She reaches out and takes his hand in hers. After a few seconds, she says, "I won't leave you."

"Hah," he says, being animated out of his lethargy by her ridiculous comment. "That's a promise you can make but not one you can keep."

"Wait here," she says, getting up off the bed and rushing out into the hallway.

Wait? Lucy scolds herself. As though he's going anywhere in the middle of the night. All Anthony can do is wait in a world he barely understands.

She charges downstairs. Deloris is in the process of turning off the lights in the lounge. The diminutive five-foot-two woman looks horrified as Lucy comes rushing around the corner. In the quiet of the night, she's expecting calm, not panic.

"Is everything okay?" Deloris asks. With one hand, she grabs the keys to her car. With the other, she grabs a 12-inch butcher knife from the counter. It's clear she thinks something has gone horribly wrong and they need to bolt from the apartment. Her fingers tighten around the wooden handle of the knife as she tries to assess where the threat is coming from.

"Oh, I'm sorry," Lucy says, holding her hands out in front of her. "Nothing's wrong. I got over-excited, that's all."

"Get excited playing an Xbox," Deloris says, laughing as she rests the knife back on the counter.

"Wait. Why did you grab a knife?"

"This is south London," Deloris says. "Things don't go bump in the night down here, they go, '*Hand over your fucking money and you won't get cut.*'"

"Do you have an AirTag?" Lucy asks, ignoring her comment. "You know, the small silver discs you can track almost everywhere?"

"Yep. I've got one in my bag. I left my backpack under a seat on the tube a couple of weeks ago and the AirTag led me right to it. Why?"

"Can I have it?"

"My AirTag?"

"Yes. Can you reset it and sync it to Frank's phone?"

"Ah, sure. Why? Wait, do I want to know?"

"I want to give it to Anthony. That way, he'll know he's never alone, that regardless of what happens, we'll know where he is, and we can find him."

Deloris screws up her face. "I'm not sure that's the intent behind these things, but sure, here you go."

Deloris hands Lucy a small metal disk the size of a coin and follows her back upstairs and into Frank's tiny room. Unlike Lucy, Deloris is less than subtle. She switches on the light. Anthony grimaces with the sudden influx of brilliant white light. He shields his eyes. He's not used to dawn breaking in a fraction of a second in the middle of the night.

"Sorry," she says, turning off the light.

"You're not alone," Lucy says, sitting sideways on the bed and facing him. She takes his hand again. "Whatever happens, I will not leave you. I will not abandon you."

Anthony looks down at the AirTag she's placed in his palm.

"And this coin?"

"Ah, 'tis not a coin," she says, giggling slightly. "Sorry, I just really wanted to say 'tis and sound like you."

Deloris shrugs in response to the confused look on his face. "Language changes."

"This is an AirTag," Lucy says. "If we get separated, I can find you with my rectangle—my phone."

Deloris fiddles with her phone. She addresses Lucy, saying, "Try syncing to the tag now."

"Got it," Lucy says. She turns her phone around so Anthony can see the map on the screen. She points, saying, "This is you. Right here. Wherever you go, I can find you, as long as you have this on you."

Anthony examines the AirTag. One side is tacky. If he pushes his finger against it, the tiny device sticks to his hand.

Deloris says, "I'm not sure it'll work everywhere. I think you have to be in range of some kind of Apple device or wifi and stuff, but that's pretty much all of London these days."

Lucy says, "If anything happens, hide this in your shoe or stick it behind your ear. Your hair will cover it from sight. And you won't be alone. I promise. Okay?"

Anthony smiles. "Okay."

Politics

Felix is tired. There's only so long he can run on adrenaline and crappy tea served in disposable cups. Although the support officer assigned to him means well, a tea bag dunked into a sickly mixture of low-fat milk and tepid water might as well have been drained from his bathtub. He needs a glazed ceramic pot with a knitted cozy, full-cream milk, a freshly opened pack of Gorreana Broken Leaf Black Tea and a handful of golden tea buds added for good measure. Let the whole thing sit for six minutes—not five, not seven—and then sieve the tea only as it is poured into fine china. Ah, he thinks, now that would get him through any crisis on this world or any other.

Sir John Leighton, the Commissioner of Police, escorts Felix into the Metropolitan Police Major Incident Room. Like most of the other staff in the control room this late on a Tuesday night, he's dressed casually. Speed and accuracy are more important than uniform etiquette at the moment, although the commissioner does have his formal jacket draped over his shoulders, hiding his t-shirt and gym pants. Felix doesn't know where he was when all this went down, but like the rest of the team, he scrambled to get in here.

At first glance, the Major Incident Room looks like something from NASA's mission control in Houston. Dozens of desks curl around an amphitheatre, all facing in the same direction. Felix doesn't count the screens mounted at the front of the room, but there are easily twenty or so of them arrayed across the vast wall. Every possible approach to the Houses of Parliament is displayed on the various screens.

He casts a quick glance at the central image of twenty soldiers in full chemical suits walking slowly forward with collection kits, atmospheric samplers, full-spectrum cameras and radiation detectors. Being part of the highly trained NERG, or Nuclear Emergency Response Group, they're methodical, moving in unison. They've been trained to dissect a chaotic scene with the intent of recreating the events that led to a destructive incident at civil or military nuclear facilities. They shuffle rather than walk, pausing when anyone on the line stops to collect something off the ground. At this rate, it'll take them about two hours to cover the gardens, which are only fifty to sixty yards in length. Soil samples are taken at regular intervals along with concrete scrapings. Everything is sealed, labelled and handed off to the support team walking along behind them.

Sir Leighton leads Felix through the maze of desks toward the stairs at the back of the amphitheatre leading up to a mezzanine floor above the Major Incident Room. No one looks up from their desks. Police officers point at screens, talking with each other in hushed tones or speaking over wireless headsets with officers in the field, coordinating their efforts.

The mezzanine level is divided into a reception area, an executive office, a boardroom with glass walls opening out onto the Major Incident Room, a kitchenette and a bathroom.

Sir Leighton opens the door to the office, saying, "You'll have full use of my—"

"No," Felix says, walking in and looking around. There's a broad mahogany desk with a computer, along with a round table and chairs and a plush leather couch. The rear of the office is a floor-to-ceiling, wall-to-wall bookcase full of legal books and binders. The spines of the books are all dull, being either brown, black or cream in colour, with identical embossed titles and volume numbers. It's a reference library in an age where everything should be digitalised and searchable online.

Before Felix can explain himself, a woman sticks her head through the open doorway behind him, saying, "I've got the PM on line one for you, sir."

Felix raises his hand. "I'll take it in a minute."

She disappears. Sir Leighton looks confused.

"I need you, John."

"Of course, sir."

"No need for sirs between us. Besides, you're the one with a knighthood. Please, call me Felix."

"Yes... Felix. Ah, the Prime Minister is waiting."

"He can wait," Felix says. "I need you, but not as a delegate. I need you as an equal. It's not enough to simply coordinate our response. We have to read between the lines. I need you to understand the intent of the government's position and communicate that to your staff."

"Understood."

The woman appears at the open door again, saying, "The US President is on line two."

"Tell him, I'll be with him in a moment."

Sir Leighton's eyes go wide.

"They think they're important," Felix says. "And they are, but you and I are the lynchpins in this operation. We're the ones with boots on the ground. We're the ones that make things happen. We're the interface. It's important that we're on the same page. I want you in here for these conversations."

"Okay."

Rather than sitting behind the commissioner's desk in his chair, Felix hoists himself up on the desk, sitting next to the phone. He gestures to the couch and the commissioner takes a seat. Felix hits the speaker button and switches to line one.

"PM?"

"Felix. Have you spoken to the American President yet?"

"He's on the other line."

"Okay. I just got off the phone with him."

"And?"

"He's being pushy."

"No surprises there."

"Listen, I won't keep you," the prime minister says. "Here's how I want to play this. You, me and Sarah will be on point for the next forty-eight hours. I've informed COBRA we'll cover the leadership role in eight-hour shifts. I'll take over from you at eight tomorrow morning. Sarah will pick up the mantle at four in the afternoon. You'll be back at midnight, and we'll reassess based on where we're at. If the state of emergency continues, we'll rinse and repeat. Any escalation, and it's all hands on deck."

"Got it," Felix says.

"All right, I'll let you arm wrestle the President. I'm going to get some sleep."

"Night," Felix says, grinning.

Although it sounds fair splitting the leadership responsibility between the three of them, Felix has already been deeply involved in this since around eight in the evening. And now he's got the graveyard shift. He suspects the Prime Minister offered this spot to the Deputy Prime Minister, Sarah Armitage, but she's astute. She would have politely pointed out that Felix was already in the groove. Besides, who wants to be dragged out of bed to babysit the police and army through the night?

That there's a level of trust between the PM, Deputy PM and him is reassuring. Micromanagement is leadership by doubt—and it never ends well.

Felix ends the call and switches to line two.

"Mister President. Are you there?"

"Please hold for the President," a distinctly American woman's voice says. There's clicking on the line for a few seconds, followed by a beep that repeats every thirty seconds, indicating the call is using a secure, encrypted channel.

After just over a minute, a jovial voice calls out, "Felix. How are you doing?"

Before Felix can respond to the entirely insincere question, the President continues. "Sounds like you've had one helluva night over there. My boys tell me your team is tracking a goddamn certified U—F—O."

Felix doesn't reply. The President has already been briefed by his national security team, and he's spoken to the Prime Minister directly. If anything, the Americans have a far better idea of where the craft came from and where it's gone than he does. Their surveillance satellites and NATO assets will be running hot. This is small talk chit-chat. The President is being politically polite. Felix waits for him to get to the point.

"Listen, Jimmy tells me y'all are willing to sign a Memorandum of Cooperation on this event so we can both share our intel fully and without reservation."

Only the US President could get away with calling the Prime Minister of the United Kingdom, Sir James Vespasian Pritchard the Third, by the name *Jimmy*. Other than his mother, Felix doubts anyone has ever gotten away with calling him that for at least forty years.

"That's correct," Felix says, knowing the special relationship between the United Kingdom and the United States of America is unique. It's an informal alliance that has lasted since the Second World War. That there are no written statutes or legal requirements makes it all the more remarkable, allowing both countries to assume their shared heritage and common interests reach beyond the politics of any given day.

"I've got two things I need you to consider," the US President says.

Felix nods but doesn't reply, waiting for the President to continue. For a moment, the President pauses, probably because he's in the White House Situation Room with a bunch of generals and other advisors. Felix suspects one of them has pointed out that he has the

President on speakerphone. What seems like a private conversation is anything but that when there's no indication of who else is listening in. To be fair, that's true for both sides. Felix is tempted to assure the President it's okay to continue. After all, he's a sworn minister of the Crown and has been personally selected by the Prime Minister to head up the initial investigation.

The President clears his throat.

"When it comes to Europe, keep your cards close to your chest. I—we—don't want the Russians or the Chinese picking up on any details that may influence future operations."

"Understood," Felix replies.

Although Felix doesn't share the President's distrust of the European Union, he appreciates that intelligence has a half-life of value. The closer any piece of intelligence is to the moment it occurs, the greater its importance. From there, it drops away quickly as time transpires. Eventually, everything will come out, but delaying that release can give both the UK and the US some tactical advantage.

There's whispering on the line.

Felix asks, "And the second point?"

"My boys at DARPA tell me there's a lot we can learn from combining data from different sources. For example, radar imaging and gun camera footage from your aircraft combined with video footage could reveal the use of... meta-materials. Now, don't ask me what the hell that means, I'm reading it off a sheet of paper, but they say it's pretty damn important. They want the opportunity to review all the footage and flight data before anything is declassified."

"Agreed."

"We've got a team on their way over the pond to liaison with you and yours. Wheels are already up. They should be down in about six hours."

Liaison is not a verb, but Felix lets that slide.

"Now, they're telling me you think someone hopped off this damn thing. Is that correct?"

Felix looks at the Police Commissioner sitting opposite him. That was a detail Felix tried to keep from going public, but someone on the front line let that slip in an innocuous comment before a reporter. The indiscretion was innocent enough, but for the media, it was like dumping bloody chum in a bay full of sharks.

"It's a line of inquiry we're investigating," he says, measuring his words with precision. "We have to be careful about speculation. Sir John Leighton is the Commissioner of Police. He's working with his team to identify and track down the individual observed near the point of contact. At this time, we have no reason to believe they are anything other than a bystander. Once we've contacted them and debriefed them, we'll provide you and your team with the details. I suspect this will be a dead end, but it is something we're pursuing."

"Hmmm," the President says, seemingly impatient and wanting more detail.

"Our most pressing concern is the analysis of the physical evidence from the scene. We have specialists in NBC suits combing the area, recording everything."

"Good. Good. And that will be available to us?"

"The results will be available to you. It may take some time to collate, but we will be sharing all the data."

The woman from reception appears at the window to the office holding up a hastily written sign, saying, "UN Secretary-General on line three. President of the European Union on line four."

"Good. Good," the US President says. "Well, I won't keep you. I know you're a busy man. If anything new arises, I expect you'll keep us informed."

"That we will," Felix says.

The President ends the call.

Felix has only ever met the US President once during a state visit, and only during a dinner held in his honour at Buckingham Palace. Before tonight, Felix has only said one or two words to him. Although the President is intimidating, Felix understands that comes with the role. Being Commander-in-Chief of the world's largest, most powerful army, navy and air force, he needs to project absolute authority.

Sir Leighton is sitting on the couch beside the desk, not more than six feet away from Felix. He leans forward with his elbows on his knees and his hands pressed together.

"Fun times, huh," Felix says.

"Oh, yeah."

Felix switches to line three. "Madame Secretary-General."

"Ah, Felix," a warm, kind Spanish voice says. Felix has never met the UN Secretary-General, but no one would know that from the way the elderly woman speaks to him. "You're a hard man to track down."

"It's been a busy night."

"Indeed. Indeed."

Felix tips his head sideways, raising his eyebrows. Sir Leighton smiles. He gets it. Felix is dancing the tango with the UN Secretary-General, whirling around and shuffling his feet while avoiding getting too close.

"You understand my concerns," the UN Secretary-General says without actually having voiced any concerns. It's right about now Felix wants to yell at Sir James Vespasian Pritchard the Third, saying, *'Jimmy, you utter bastard!'* The Prime Minister has gone to sleep, leaving Felix to wander through the international political minefield, knowing this buys him time and gives him deniability. Depending on what eventuates over the course of the night, the PM can either support any comments made by Felix or deny that Felix ever had the authority to make them. It's a clever play—or it would be if it wasn't Felix in the firing line.

"Madame Secretary-General," Felix says, knowing a whole host of analysts and diplomats will be listening in on the call both now and in the hours and days ahead. "Please be assured that the United Kingdom is acting in good faith to gather what data it can on the event that occurred over the Houses of Parliament earlier this evening."

"And you agree with my concerns?" the UN Secretary-General

asks, still not having actually expressed any concerns to him. She's shrewd, manoeuvring politically for whatever gains she can squeeze out of Felix. She, too, must know the Prime Minister is using Felix as a shield to deflect and buy the UK government both time and plausible deniability. Hindsight is easier than foresight.

By dumping the US President, the UN Secretary-General and the European President on Felix, both the Prime Minister and the Deputy Prime Minister are distancing themselves from any potential mistakes. Tomorrow, they'll have the luxury of reviewing the phone transcripts, the results of the investigation conducted in the gardens and any interviews conducted with the mysterious *Mr X*, as the Metropolitan Police are calling the suspect. Armed with that knowledge, they'll be able to carefully craft the official response of the United Kingdom. If Felix has done well, he'll be commended. If he trips over his feet, they'll override his decisions with an official position. It's smart—for everyone other than him.

Felix doesn't bite at the UN Secretary-General's question. As difficult as it is, he remains silent. He points at the phone, looking at Sir Leighton as he mouths the word, "*Snake!*"

Sir Leighton nods. Right about now, he's probably relieved he wasn't given overall operational command. It's one thing to manage a major incident spanning various agencies, including the intelligence community. It's entirely another to meddle with international politics.

It's a full fifteen seconds before the Secretary-General breaks the impasse. Whether that's because she's deeply considering her point or reading something that's been handed to her, Felix is unsure. He doesn't need this. He's supposed to be focusing on the response, not babysitting political egos.

"This is an event of global historical importance."

Felix sits there, nodding his head in agreement while knowing he has to go through all this again with the President of the European Union, who will, no doubt, be sharing the conversation with the Germans, the French and the Italians.

The UN Secretary-General sounds as though she's reading a

speech to him. Perhaps she is. Perhaps this is a dry-run rehearsal of what she'll later read to the UN General Assembly.

"The significance of what has just happened cannot be measured strictly in terms of the event itself. The passage of an alien spacecraft through the skies of southern England and its appearance over the Houses of Parliament may, as yet, be unexplained, but the significance cannot be overstated. We are not alone.

"Here on Earth, we are the only sentient species capable of escaping the bonds of gravity and yet, for us, the Moon has been our only destination. Beyond that, we've sent rovers to Mars and probes to all of the planets, even venturing beyond the reaches of our solar system, but we're still in our infancy. We've looked out into the cosmos with the most sophisticated, sensitive equipment ever devised, being capable of detecting the fall of a single snowflake. We've imaged the transits of exoplanets and the accretion discs of black holes, but we have never seen any signs of life beyond Earth—let alone intelligent life. Now, though, our perception has changed. Rather than spotting life at a distance, life has visited us here on Earth."

Felix and the Police Commissioner look at each other as the UN Secretary-General speaks. Her words stir his soul, but Felix isn't naive. He knows she's softening him up, wanting to gain concessions from him, only he's in no position to make them. Goddamn it, Jimmy—Sir James Vespasian Pritchard the Third—has set him up royally. The PM knew this was what would happen. He knew premature overtures would be made. He knew the United Kingdom would not be ready to accept or reject advances until it had time to properly assess what had happened, and so he sent out Felix as a decoy.

"The passage of the spacecraft over the United Kingdom represents a global event. We may have divided our planet into countries, but no intelligent alien species would recognise our borders from space. They'd have no knowledge of our maritime boundaries or airspace. To them, this is Earth and its inhabitants. To them, we are one species. Countries, cultures and races are irrelevant."

And there it is, Felix thinks. The UN Secretary-General is

wanting to dissolve any sense of sovereign entitlement over the passage of the spacecraft. And she's got a point. If this craft had appeared over Berlin or Paris, the United Kingdom would lend its voice to the call for transparency, but it didn't.

"Madame Secretary-General," Felix says, thinking carefully about his response and knowing it'll be in the morning papers all across Europe, the United States and the world at large. "This is indeed an event of global significance—and yet it occurred not only over the United Kingdom, not only over our largest city, our capital, but directly over the seat of our government.

"Although the craft did not display hostile intent, we must assume its actions were deliberate and with purpose. Until we can properly assess the nature of this incursion, we must proceed with caution. At this point, we are still gathering, collating and analysing the data associated with this incident. As you can imagine, we need to compile a comprehensive, cross-referenced timeline of observations made by the public, by civil aviation authorities and by our military. We will, in due course, provide access to this information as appropriate, but I cannot commit to a timeframe just yet.

"It's also important to note that it is an assumption this incident is over. We had no prior knowledge of the appearance of the spacecraft. We need to give the scientific community time to review existing research, such as the Near-Earth Object survey and our digital sky scans, to see if the vessel showed up but was misidentified. Although the craft has left our airspace, it may return elsewhere.

"Our advice to others in the international community is, should the spacecraft appear above your cities, show restraint and observe its motion from a distance. For now, that is all the information and advice I can provide."

Felix takes a deep breath. He's gambling on the fact that everyone on the call is focused on them. They should be thinking about where the spacecraft is now. For all anyone knows, it could be about to pass over Moscow, Beijing or Washington DC. By pointing that out, he's deflecting attention away from the United Kingdom and buying his team some time to figure out what just happened and—importantly—why. It's the why that troubles him. There has to be some logical explanation for why creatures from an entirely unknown advanced, intelligent alien civilisation flew over London—and it isn't because they were sightseeing.

Somewhere out there, someone that's walked on another world is walking around London. Why?

Good Morning

Lucy wakes with a hand groping her breast through her t-shirt. It's not intentional or sexual. Deloris is still fast asleep. She's cuddled in beside Lucy in the single bed, resting her arm on Lucy's chest. Birds chirp outside the window. Somewhere in the distance, a siren sounds, but it's faint and moving away from Croydon.

Lucy's lying on her back, pushed up against the wall and staring at the ceiling. Sunlight slips through the gaps around the curtains. Gently, she nudges Deloris. Lucy raises her friend's hand and rests it on the pillow. She sits up and stretches, trying to shake a crazy dream from her head, only it wasn't a dream. Her heart races at the realisation that reality has resumed.

Anthony is from another time?

Is he still here?

She assumes he is but she doesn't know for sure. He could have fled in the dead of night. They're strangers. There's no reason for him to trust her. As far as he's concerned, she's a stepping stone. She got him out of central London. Now he needs to flee further afield. He said he felt alone. Perhaps he thinks he'll be better off on his own. Maybe he would.

Lucy climbs over Deloris, trying not to squish her as she struggles to get out of the twisted bed sheet and crumpled duvet.

Deloris groans. She never was a morning person.

Lucy pulls on her jeans. She hops on one leg and then the other as she slips her socks on followed by her shoes. Vapour forms on her breath. Like so many Londoners, Deloris doesn't leave her central heating on overnight. Lucy grabs her coat and Frank's old phone. She wanders out into the hallway. The door to Frank's room is ajar. Quietly, she edges it open and peers inside.

Anthony's gone.

Lucy panics. She thunders down the stairs, catching her heel on the worn carpet. She trips and tumbles forward. It's all she can do not to cartwheel to the bottom of the stairs. Lucy pushes her hands against the walls on either side, trying to prevent herself from crashing into the landing by the front door. Her body falls faster than her feet can move and she ends up colliding with the shoe rack and sprawling out on the mat by the door.

A confused-looking Anthony rushes out of the lounge.

"You're not well," he says, crouching beside her and offering her his hand.

She looks at him with a misplaced smile, laughing as she shakes her head, saying, "Oh, in so many ways."

Deloris appears at the top of the stairs, still wearing the t-shirt and knickers she slept in. Although Lucy is on her feet and picking up the scattered shoes, Deloris asks her, "Are you okay?"

"I'm fine... I was rushing, that's all."

Deloris means to be helpful, but all she can say in response is, "Be careful."

"I'll remember that next time," Lucy replies, looking at the folds of carpet on the stairs and noting the patches where the steps have been worn threadbare.

Anthony takes her by the elbow. He assists her to the kitchen as though she were an invalid.

"I'm okay. Really," she says, but she doesn't want to brush him off. His concern is quaint. There's an old-world charm about the way he treats her with kindness and dignity.

"Would you like some water?" he asks, presenting the stainless steel kitchen sink to her as though it were a marvel of human ingenuity. It is, but she's never thought about it that way before.

"Ah, sure."

"The pump," he says, taking a glass from the drying rack and putting it under the tap. "It is inexhaustible. And one of the pumps is hot. And clear. There's no sediment whatsoever!"

He fills a glass and holds it up to the light streaming in through the kitchen window.

"Everything is so clean in your future," he says. "Your homes. Your glass. Your water. Even the windowsills are devoid of dirt."

He's excited. He gestures to the couch in the lounge, saying, "And soft. This seat over here. When you sit on it, you feel as though you're floating on a cloud."

Lucy tries not to laugh.

"And your books," he says. "I must confess. I know not all of the words, but those I do speak with clarity."

He pauses, thinking before continuing.

"And the drawings, they're far too detailed. This is some kind of new knowledge for capturing what is seen. Is that correct?"

"They're pictures," Lucy says. "Images. We have devices that can capture a picture with just the touch of a button."

"Your images are horrific."

"Um, what have you been reading?"

"History," he says, pointing to an old book lying open on the table. Without losing his spot, Lucy closes the book so she can read the cover: *A Concise History of the Western World*. If this is concise, she'd hate to see the comprehensive version. As it is, it's thicker than the medical textbooks her mother had in her office. This must be one of Frank's books, as Lucy can't imagine Deloris using it for anything other than a doorstop. Or perhaps a cure for insomnia.

Lucy leaves the book open on the page Anthony was reading, which was about the Rwandan genocide in the 1990s. It's not the most pleasant subject. There's a photograph of aid workers unloading a helicopter in a grassy field.

"A lot has changed, huh?" she says, tapping the image of a pilot wearing an oversized helmet with the dark visor pulled down, obscuring his face. To someone from the 16th century, the pilot must look like a knight in armour. If anything, Anthony's probably wondering why the protection starts and stops with the man's head as he's wearing baggy trousers and has his sleeves rolled up.

Anthony taps another part of the picture, saying, "And yet a lot has stayed the same."

Lucy leans down, taking a closer look at the image. The skids of the chopper are resting on crushed skulls. A bare ribcage protrudes from the grass.

"Oh."

In another photo, dozens of bodies lie wrapped in straw mats along the edge of a gravel road. Villagers walk past. Trucks drive on. The loss is ignored. Regardless of what Anthony is able to read, these images are unambiguous.

"Why all this change?" he asks, pointing at a photo of a C130 Hercules sitting on the tarmac with its ramp lowered and its propellers turning in a blur. Refugees have formed four lines, waiting to board, carrying what little remains of their belongings in bundles balanced on their heads. "Why change everything about your world but heartache?"

"I—I don't know."

"You live in paradise—to me, at least. Your progress is beyond my dreams, but not my nightmares. The time has come when this hurt could have been banished from Earth, and yet still it remains as bitter and as vile as under Queen Mary herself."

Lucy lowers her head.

"The marvels of your age," he says. "They leave me longing for more, but the bloody past I witnessed still clings to the future."

"I know," she says, unsure what else she can say.

Deloris walks into the kitchen wearing an old, scruffy dress. Her eyes are immediately drawn to the water splashed over the counter and across the floor. She looks at Lucy, who smiles. Lucy shakes her head slightly, indicating she should let this slide.

"Ah, and 'tis Lady Deloris," Anthony says, offering her a slight bow with the wave of his arm across his chest.

Deloris smiles. "Well, aren't you a gentleman?"

"Me? Gen-tee-al? Oh, no, ma'am. 'Tis not my station."

Lucy steps between Anthony and Deloris. She's picked up on a subtle distinction in his comments. She waves her hand between Deloris and herself, asking, "Who do you think we are? Not as people. As in society?"

"Why you're ladies."

"We are, but perhaps not in the sense you think."

"You're not part of the aristocracy?" he asks, gesturing at the flat around him.

"As in lords and ladies?" Deloris asks, raising her eyebrows.

"But all this..."

Lucy laughs. "This is normal. We're the peasants of your day."

"Peasants?" Anthony says, stepping back in shock. "But no. In my day, we lived with the most meagre of possessions and in all of one room. You—you live in luxury."

Deloris points at her narrow lounge room. The couch has been pushed hard against the wall, leaving only a few feet between the seat cushions and the TV cabinet.

"You can't swing a dead cat in here," she says.

"You would kill your cat?" Anthony asks, screwing up his face at the notion.

"She's joking," Lucy says. "It's our way of saying there's not much room in here."

"Oh. To me, this is a palace!"

Lucy says, "Well, it beats sleeping on the streets."

"All right," Deloris says, clapping her hands and changing the subject. "I'm hungry. Let's make some breakfast."

The bushes outside the window move in response to the sound of her clap. At first, Lucy assumes it's a bird being scared by the sudden noise, but she catches a glimpse of dark clothing. Someone's been crouching there. Whoever it is, they dart out of sight. Lucy rushes to the window, wanting to see them.

Deloris lives in a tiny flat that's part of a larger, subdivided house with a shared driveway. Someone in a grey tracksuit jumps the low hedge and jogs along the pavement heading toward the main road.

"Who the hell was that?" Deloris asks.

"I think they're on to us," Lucy says.

Anthony asks, "Soldiers?"

"Probably the police," she replies. She turns to Deloris, saying, "They won't mobilise the army, will they?"

"SAS?" Deloris asks. "God, I hope not."

Lucy looks both ways down the street. There's a British Telecom van at the end of the cul-de-sac and a bright red Royal Mail van on the corner by the main road. Neither van has a driver. The back of each panel van is obscured by a lack of windows.

Deloris lives halfway down the cul-de-sac at the point the road widens to form a circle allowing cars to turn around with ease in the dead-end street. There's a roundabout with a maple tree in the middle of a concrete circle. Tyre tracks line the grass where lazy drivers have ridden up over the tapered edge of the roundabout while turning.

"BT, I get," Deloris says, referring to British Telecom. "The internet here is shit. They're always cleaning out the flooded junction box, but the Royal Mail? They never stop. They drop off a package and then they're on their way again."

"Okay," Lucy says. "So they're watching us, but they don't know Anthony's in here. If they did, they'd have stormed us by now."

"Or they *didn't* know," Deloris says, "until that guy did a runner.

Now, they're probably waiting for backup."

"Damn it. They must have staked out every friend I have," Lucy says, realising she wasn't quite as clever as she thought. She covered her tracks but not her contacts. If anything, the two of them should have moved on to Oxford last night.

Anthony is quiet. The intensity on his face suggests he understands at least the basics of what they're discussing.

Deloris grabs a trench coat from the hallway cupboard. She tucks her hair beneath the collar and swings a scarf around her neck before pulling a golf cap low over her ears.

"I'll draw their attention," she says. "You two go out the back. If you jump the fence, you'll find yourself in the rear car park of the local kindergarten. From there, you should be able to get back to your car at McDonald's."

"If it's still there," Lucy says.

"I'll meet you at the Cafe de Luna in Oxford," Deloris replies. "Good luck."

She throws open the front door and runs out onto the street with the coat pulled tight around her. Deloris sprints for the main road. The side door on the British Telecom van slides open. The Royal Mail van pulls across the road, blocking the exit from the cul-de-sac. Black-clad men rush after her. Deloris dodges one of them, but two more sprint up from behind her. She's crash tackled on the grassy strip between the pavement and the road. Her hat goes flying across a driveway.

"We've got to go," Lucy says, grabbing Anthony's hand and dragging him to the back door. She throws the flimsy door open. Loose glass panes rattle in the door. She's about to run down the concrete stairs into the backyard when several ladders are pushed against the brick wall from the far side.

Someone on the other side of the wall yells, "Go! Go! Go! We're breaching!"

The ladders are long, reaching several feet beyond the top of the wall. Black gloves grab at the rungs. Lucy's unsure whether these are regular soldiers, SAS or tactical police. All she knows is that they're terrifying. Black helmets appear. Dark eyes peer out from behind the glass visors of gas masks. Bulky tactical vests contain stun grenades and ammunition clips stowed in pouches. MP5 machine guns are levelled at them.

"Stop where you are," someone yells.

"Back, back," Lucy calls out, pushing Anthony behind her and slamming the door. She flicks the switch on the deadlock. The panes within the door are made from frosted glass. They offer no protection. Their attackers will be able to see their motion in the hallway. If they want to shoot them, they've got easy targets.

Lucy's desperate. She's never felt the terror of being hunted before. Each step on the ageing carpet leaves her with a sense of increasing helplessness. She wheels around, yelling, "Front door!"

Glass breaks behind her. A gloved hand reaches through to grab the lock from the inside.

Ahead of her, a dark shadow passes over the front door before the glass is smashed with the butt of a machine gun.

Instinctively, Lucy rushes back into the kitchenette.

The glass window in the lounge shatters. A grenade tumbles across the floor. Lucy's confused. This isn't the classic round, baseball-like grenade she's seen in the movies. Instead, it looks like a can of fly spray with the label removed. Yellow letters have been stencilled on a grey cylinder. She starts to yell at Anthony to retreat back into the hallway when the world around her goes white. The table, the chairs, the couch, and even the walls disappear, being absorbed by the most brilliant, blinding white light she's ever seen. It's as though she's staring at the sun.

Barely a fraction of a second later, the air around her compresses, rattling her chest and causing her arms to shake. Her legs feel like jelly. The *bang* that echoes around her sounds like a thunderclap breaking inside the flat itself. The noise is overwhelming, leaving her feeling disoriented.

Lucy squeezes her eyes tight, but even from behind her eyelids, all she can see is that one brilliant point of light radiating outward, blurring her vision and blinding her. She shakes her head. Her ears feel as though they're blocked. It's as though she's descended too fast in an airplane and not had time for them to equalise. There's yelling around her. Male voices call out to each other, but they're not frantic. To her, they sound distant, but she realises that's because her ears are ringing and still struggling to recover from the deafening blast.

As her eyesight returns, she finds her back pressed up against the narrow strip of wall between the table and the lounge. Broken glass lies shattered on the carpet. Smoke billows through the air.

At least one of the black-clad figures has the word POLICE on his tactical vest, but it's written in charcoal on black. At a distance, it would be invisible. Most of the officers don't have any identifying insignia.

"On your knees," one of them yells, pointing an MP5 machine gun at her.

Lucy's already got her hands up. It's an instinctive reaction. The sheer amount of force being used against them is overwhelming, leaving her feeling defeated. The speed and violence that's been unleashed on them is like nothing she's ever experienced, leaving her utterly disoriented. The only thing she can do is comply. *'Fight or flight'* has been reduced to *'Cower in abject terror!'*

Anthony has backed up into the lounge. One of the officers faces him with a TASER drawn.

"On the ground! Get on the ground," he yells from behind his gas mask.

Anthony, though, fights like a wild boar being cornered in the forest.

Another officer grabs him from behind. A fraction of a second later, that officer has been flipped on his back. He lands on the kitchen table beside Lucy. His momentum causes him to somersault out of the already broken window, shattering what's left of the glass panes.

The first officer fires his TASER.

Metal barbs strike Anthony in the chest. Fifty thousand volts rush along the thin electrical wires and into his muscles. Anthony's body convulses. Foam appears in his mouth. His knees buckle, but he manages to grab at the wires and yank the TASER from the officer's hand. Anthony tears the barbs from his chest. Blood spots his t-shirt.

The officer rushes him, looking to take him down with what amounts to a rugby tackle.

Anthony has the agility of a monkey. Lucy got a glimpse of this back when he took down the robber and again when they were jumping over the backyards stretching away from the apothecary. He's light on his feet. It's as though gravity has no hold over him. He springs up, kicks off the wall behind him and then the wall beside him, moving more like a gymnast than a 16th-century refugee. He grabs the electrical cord hanging from the ceiling. The light bulb breaks as he uses the cord like an acrobat at the circus. He plants his feet on the walls, using them to run around the officer while holding onto the central electrical cord. Within barely a second, he's behind the bewildered officer. He grabs the gas mask, wrenching it up. Although Anthony can't pull it off, the off-centre mask leaves the officer effectively blinded. As the officer struggles to correct the fitting, Anthony kicks him in the small of the back, sending him careening into several other officers coming in through the other door to the lounge. With that, Anthony leaps out of the window and onto the grassy lawn outside. Lucy's barely had time enough to blink.

The officer holding her by her upper arm shoves her into the wall and scrambles up onto the kitchen table, wanting to follow Anthony outside. A fraction of a second later, he's tossed back into the lounge. He lands on his back and rolls to one side, groaning as he clutches his tactical vest.

Lucy scrambles onto the table and through the window. Broken glass digs into her palms. Blood drips from her fingers.

Outside, Anthony has one of the officers in a stranglehold. The officer's body is limp. He's alive, but he's not struggling. Anthony has a shard of glass held to his neck. He holds the man's head to one side with the point of the glass pressed against the jugular.

Several officers have them surrounded. They've got MP5 machine guns, handguns and TASERs drawn. They're yelling at Anthony. Fingers tighten on triggers. Anthony walks forward, carrying the dead weight of the officer with him.

"Drop the glass!" one officer yells, followed by the others yelling, "Let him go!" and, "Get on the ground!"

A helicopter flies low over the house. The beating of its rotors is deafening. Lucy doesn't have to look to know this isn't a regular police helicopter. It's far too loud and obnoxious. A dark shadow passes over them. A voice calls out over a bullhorn.

"It's over. Surrender. No one has to get hurt."

There are several officers lying on the floor inside that would disagree with that sentiment.

Lucy steps between Anthony and the officers. They yell at her to get out of the way. Her body shakes. Staring down the barrel of numerous guns has her on the verge of wetting her pants.

"Please," she yells with her hands held up in a sign of surrender. "Don't shoot. Let me talk to him." Tears well up in her eyes as she adds, "He doesn't understand."

Lucy turns her back on the guns. The officer held hostage looks at her with wide, bloodshot eyes. A trickle of blood runs down his neck as the glass bites into his skin. He's terrified.

"Anthony," Lucy says, wanting to calm him down as she steps toward him. "You can't do this. Please. Let the officer go."

"They'll kill us," Anthony yells at her.

Lucy speaks with a soft, calm voice. "No. They won't. They're scared. I'm scared. You're scared. We're all scared. They don't know who you are. To them, you're an intruder into our world. Please. Trust me. You've got to let this man go. There's no other way this ends."

"They'll take me," he says. His hand trembles.

Tears run down Lucy's cheek as she says, "I won't leave you. I won't. I promise you—you won't be alone. You have to trust me."

Anthony releases his grip on the glass. A torrent of blood runs from his palm, rushing down his forearm and onto the lawn. As he loosens his hold, the trooper breaks away to one side, scrambling toward several other officers.

The rest of the officers advance from all sides. Barrels are pointed at Anthony's face. There's yelling, but all Lucy can hear is Anthony's quiet voice. He falls to his knees and stares at the grass, saying, "Please, don't leave me alone."

Military Intelligence

Felix leans back on a towel laid out on a deck chair in Cala Llamp Bay, just outside of Port d'Andratx in Majorca. The idyllic Mediterranean island is barely a two-hour flight from London and less than a hundred miles from Spain.

Damn, Felix needs this. Stress has been eating him alive. Holidays are a time to recharge. He sighs, letting the air escape from his lungs and imagining all his worries going with it.

The rim of a broad, straw hat lies tipped over his face, shielding his eyes from the glare. Sunlight warms his body, radiating through his skin. The smell of SPF 50 coconut-scented sunscreen wafts through the air.

The beach is rocky rather than sandy, which he likes as it means sand doesn't get between his toes or down his swimming trunks. At high tide, water washes across the flat rocks to a depth of half a foot. There's a submerged shelf leading to deeper water, but the bay is more reminiscent of a pool than a beach. The waves are gentle.

As he lies there on his back, he lets his fingers dip into the water washing up around the legs of his chair. It's soothing to feel the ocean swirling beneath his fingertips.

Gulls squawk overhead. Teens play nearby. They're excited, shouting as they jump from a rocky cliff into the depths, but their enthusiasm doesn't bother him. Waves roll into the shore with a steady rhythm. He breathes in time with the surge of water sweeping over the low-lying rocks and then draining away.

"Sir?"

A hand rocks his shoulder.

Reluctantly, Felix wakes. Darkness surrounds him. He's groggy. He sits up, feeling disoriented. Light spills in from the hallway outside. Dozens of people are talking over the top of each other somewhere just beyond the meeting room. A set of blackout blinds have been drawn over the floor-to-ceiling windows. The boardroom table has been turned on its side to make room for half a dozen cots. Police officers lie beneath itchy woollen blankets, resting their heads on flat pillows.

"If you would come with me," an aide says.

Felix would much rather lie on the beach in Majorca but reality demands his presence in London. His mind replays the events of the past evening. The unthinkable has happened, only it's not a doomsday scenario. First Contact has occurred between humanity and some advanced alien species capable of traversing the stars. What it all means is still cryptic, but Earth wasn't attacked. That alien spacecraft could have chosen to appear above the Houses of Parliament while the government was in the chambers, but it didn't. It waited until the quiet of night. Felix is unsure why the strange craft chose London over Paris, Beijing or New York, but it didn't pull doughnuts in a cornfield in the American Midwest. There was no secrecy. But then it left. What the hell is going on?

Felix grabs his jacket and walks out onto the mezzanine landing. He looks out over the Major Incident Room. The aide closes the door quietly behind him, letting the other officers sleep.

"What time is it?" he asks, checking his phone and answering the question for himself.

8:27 am

He's been asleep for less than half an hour.

"Eight-thirty," the aide says, seeing him still looking at the lock screen on his phone.

"What's going on? Why did you wake me?" Felix asks. He feels as though he's been in a deep sleep for hours, not mere minutes.

He leans on the hand railing, looking out across the sea of heads toward the display screens on the far wall. Try as he may, he can't discern any meaning from any of the metrics or graphs so prominently displayed. Traffic cam images of the street outside Parliament show the army trucks and police barricades. There's no urgency to the motion of the soldiers or police milling around. The crowd is still there. It's grown to several thousand people even though there's nothing to see. The roundabout is impossible. Out on the fringe, mounted police move through the scattered crowd milling around on the street. McDonald's appears to be doing a roaring trade as there's a queue out the door. Felix smiles at that one irrelevant observation. Even in a crisis, British sensibilities demand orderly lines. What would ET make of such civility? Do aliens queue?

"They've got him, sir."

"They?"

"SAS Counter Terrorism Unit."

"And him?"

"The stranger visible in the Abingdon Gardens—as seen from the Victoria Tower CCTV camera."

Felix nods. He loves nothing more than precision.

"And we're sure it's him? We haven't run down some random?"

"No, sir," the aide says, leading him down the stairs onto the floor of the Major Incident Room. Someone hands him a cup of tea. It looks like dishwater. The drawstring of the teabag hangs over the rim. For now, it's perfect.

Felix uses a wooden stirrer to squish the teabag against the side of his cup before he drops the bag in a bin. His mind is still waking.

"And we're sure we're not going to be sued for wrongful arrest or excessive use of force?"

"We've matched him to the footage from the sex shop," the aide says, ignoring his question like a true political bureaucrat. This officer won't be quite so glib when called before a magistrate to explain himself, but Felix understands. So long as it's their party in power, the means justify the end. Pesky side issues such as human rights and due process can be left to lawyers to debate long after the fact. The interpretation of laws by the government of the day always leaves room for flexibility in the courts. Add terms like *National Security* and *Potential Terror Threat* to a court submission, and the presiding judge is likely to rule in favour of the government.

Felix nods. "Who is he?"

"We don't know, sir. Fingerprints don't show any match against our records or with Interpol. Facial recognition hasn't pulled any positives. The Americans have checked their records and nothing. They're asking for a DNA sample."

"Huh. It's almost as though he's not from here?"

"Yes, sir."

Felix blinks, rubbing his eyes. One of the screens gets his attention. A small monitor on the bottom right-hand side of the wall is displaying the BBC Morning Show.

The aide says, "The Prime Minister has asked for you—"

Felix cuts him off with a wave of his hand. Something's wrong. Rather than rushing to pat himself and his team on the back for a job well done, he's looking for blind spots. It's the details that get overlooked in the hubris of the moment that tend to bite one in the ass. Most of the screens in the Major Incident Room are meaningless to him, but he's curious—why is the *BBC Morning Show* up there? Someone else has spotted something significant in the broadcast and he wants to know what worries them before he pops the cork on the champagne to celebrate.

"What's that?" he asks, pointing.

One of the senior police officers tasked with escorting him says,

"The BBC have rolling coverage of the incident."

"But it's over."

"They say they've got an exclusive interview with her."

"Her?" he asks, raising an eyebrow.

"The woman from the apothecary. She negotiated the suspect's surrender."

"And you let her go?"

"Ah," another officer says, flustered. "I don't think she did anything wrong. He was the target, not her."

"You could have detained her for 36 hours under the anti-terror legislation. Hell, get her in front of a magistrate and we can hold her without charge for 90 days."

A second officer looks confused. He says, "But she wasn't involved in a terror incident."

Felix shakes his head. "Wasn't she? We still don't know what the hell we're dealing with."

They don't get it. At the moment, the biggest problem facing the government is the flow of information. Felix spent most of last night putting out spot fires. Misinformation and unfounded rumours have raced ahead of the facts. And now, they've got someone that's spent at least twelve hours with the suspect and they just let her walk. He sighs.

His phone rings. It's the Prime Minister. He answers. Before he can say anything, he's greeted with, "We got him! We bloody well got him, Felix! He was in Croydon. A goddamn alien in Croydon! Who would believe it, huh?"

"Sir," Felix says, still looking at the screen. The sound is turned down, but subtitles display the conversation unfolding between two anchors and their guest, a young woman in her twenties. She's not wearing any makeup, which makes her face look washed out. Scratches line her cheeks. There's bruising below her right eye. One of her hands is bandaged. Blood seeps through the cotton mesh. This is not a good look for the government. The woman leans forward on the glass production desk, clutching at her shaking fingers. Bandages have been wrapped around her wrist and her upper arm. The subtitles beneath the image read:

...wasn't necessary.

Anthony wasn't going to hurt anyone.

Sending in the SAS was a gross mistake.

The Prime Minister distracts him, saying, "They found the car at the local McDonald's. I guess he wanted *'fries with that,'* or something."

The PM laughs.

Felix doesn't.

On the screen, the anchor addresses the young woman in the pretty floral dress:

We're talking to Lucy Bailiwick,

Who was working down the road from

the Houses of Parliament

When the spacecraft appeared last night.

She's the first person to interact with the alien.

Lucy, what can you tell us about Anthony?

The Prime Minister is still talking over the phone but Felix isn't listening. His eyes track the discussion on the TV, willing it to proceed faster. Lucy pleads with the interviewer. Even with the sound turned down, the anguish in her voice is apparent from the pained expression on her face.

He's not an alien.

He's human.

Just like you and me.

He's not from another world.

He's from another time.

—

What time?

"What time?" Felix says in perfect unison with the BBC

Presenter.

"What?" the Prime Minister says. It's only then Felix realises he cut off the PM mid-sentence while the old man was talking about NATO readiness shifting in case there's a second incursion.

1558

Anthony lived during the reign of Bloody Queen Mary.

He was tried for heresy, tied to a stake and set to be burned alive.

—

But he survived?

"But he survived?" Felix again says in unison with the presenter.

"Who survived?" the PM asks.

Several miles away on a BBC set, Lucy has tears in her eyes. The studio lights capture the glistening beads before they trickle down her cheeks.

He escaped to the stars.

Felix feels compelled to ask the same follow-up question as the BBC presenter.

Where is he now?

"Where is he now?"

On the other end of the phone, the Prime Minister asks one of his aides, "Where have they taken him?"

Felix isn't expecting a reply from the PM. His eyes are set on the screen. He's not sure why, but he understands Lucy knows far more than she's letting on. Lucy speaks with slow deliberation.

In a cruel twist, Anthony was taken to London's Queen Mary Hospital.

They took him to the emergency department to treat his injuries,

including TASER burns and numerous lacerations.

Then they took him to radiology for full-body scans,

And held him in the MOD Unit within the hospital.

"Lance is saying they took him to the hospital for some checks," the PM says. "Apparently, he was injured during the takedown. Nothing serious, but he needed stitches and—"

"And they wanted full body scans," Felix says, interrupting the Prime Minister.

"How did you know that."

"Switch on your television, sir. BBC One."

"What?"

"He's in the Queen Mary Hospital, right?" Felix asks.

"Um, ah. I think so. I'm not sure where they took him. Why?"

"Because it's all over the news."

"What???" the Prime Minister says. In the background, Felix can hear a television being turned on as the PM barks orders at those around him.

"We have a serious operational security breach," Felix says, pointing at the screen in front of him and knowing the officers beside him in the Major Incident Room can hear what he's saying. Several of them scramble to their desk phones in response to his comment.

"You need to move him," Felix says. He's missed part of the television interview, but the next few words catch his attention.

"Already on it," the Prime Minister says. "Apparently, he's already been moved. They're taking him to—"

MI6 headquarters

"MI6," Felix says.

"How does she know that?" the Prime Minister asks, clearly watching the same show. "Lance is saying they only just moved him in the last ten minutes. He would have only just arrived."

"This is not good," Felix says. He notes that a few seconds before Lucy mentioned MI6, another woman of a similar age stepped into view and whispered in her ear. She was holding a phone, but the screen was turned away from the camera. As best he understands it, she was feeding information to Lucy, but who is she and how did she know where Anthony was being taken?

The Prime Minister says, "This is a goddamn PR nightmare. What are we going to do? Bust into the studio and arrest her? We could detain her on the basis of national security."

"No," Felix says. "That'll only make things worse."

"We need to contain this."

Felix counters with, "We need to talk to him."

"The suspect? What? No. Lance says he's feral. He tried to scratch out the eyes of a nurse. He won't talk to anyone."

"He talked to Lucy," Felix says.

"That was different."

"Was it?" Felix asks. "Ask yourself why. It may just be that assault troopers firing stun grenades isn't the greatest way to open dialogue with someone from outer space."

"We did what we had to," the Prime Minister says, sounding annoyed at the need to justify his decision to capture the suspect. Felix, though, won't let the point go.

"Fifty thousand volts rushing through two metal prongs sticking into your chest sends the wrong message."

"What would you have done?" the Prime Minister snaps.

"I would have walked up to the front door and talked to him."

From the other end of the phone, there's a huff. Felix has known Sir James for over a decade. Felix didn't get the portfolio of Defence by being a yes-man. The Prime Minister may not like the way he's speaking to him, but Felix knows the mutual respect between them gives him the latitude to speak his mind.

Felix says, "Once Anthony was boxed in, there was no need to escalate. As soon as the house was surrounded, it was clear he wasn't going anywhere. There was no danger. This wasn't a hostage situation. There was no need for the SAS to storm the place."

"That's an easy call to make in hindsight," the Prime Minister says. "We had no idea who or what we were dealing with. We had to go in hard."

Felix sighs. He bitterly regrets being out of the loop when they found Anthony. He knew seventeen locations were under surveillance based on Anthony's association with Lucy Bailiwick, but they could have all been dead-ends. If the two of them were smart, they would have splashed some cash and hunkered down in one of the thousands of bed and breakfasts scattered throughout the countryside. If they'd done that, they would have been invisible to the security services. Going to stay with a known associate was always going to be a mistake. Confirmation must have come through just after eight in the morning as Felix laid down his weary head.

What would Felix have done differently? He would have stressed to COBRA the need for caution. He would have been the cool head in the room calling for calm.

As the Secretary of State for Defence, Felix knows better than anyone that the military is a blunt axe. Even the proverbial '*surgical strikes*' the US and the UK are so fond of undertaking in the Middle East are anything but precise. The military can pinpoint a specific building with GPS-guided munitions fired from a ship or a submarine hundreds of miles offshore. They can ensure that the detonation causes minimal damage to any surrounding houses. They can even watch it all unfold in real-time on a satellite feed, and still, they'll miss a supposed meeting between warlords by a day or two, striking a kid's birthday party or a wedding instead.

Prior to launch authorisation, military analysts will swear the target is legit. They'll throw up a dozen slides, point to converging intel, talk about their '*eyes-on*' and yet, almost without fail, a couple of days later, the newspapers will invariably report that a nurse working for *Médecins Sans Frontières* was assassinated or some other innocent civilian was killed. '*Warlord, my ass,*' is the exact wording Felix wrote across the top of that particular internal MOD investigation. To make sure it wasn't missed, he used a red marker with a thick tip. Those in the chain of command were embarrassed. Felix reminded them that was a better alternative than being dead because of some dumb mistake made in a boardroom thousands of miles away.

As the only civilian authority overseeing the United Kingdom's military, Felix preaches restraint whenever he can. His position has always been: *if the military is needed, something has gone horribly wrong somewhere along the way.* He's not a peacenik, but he's not a war hawk either, which is precisely why Sir James appointed him to the role.

"You're worried," the Prime Minister says, apparently reading his mind.

"MI6 aren't known for their tact."

"You want to talk to him?"

"Yes."

"Mmmm. Tread carefully," the Prime Minister says. "Chris is flying back from Pakistan. Reception can be patchy in flight, but I'll get a message through and let him know you want direct access. You know he's going to protest about separate jurisdictions, right?"

"Leave it to the professionals," Felix says, mocking what he anticipates will be the reaction of Chris Davis, the Foreign Secretary. "But no one's a professional when it comes to First Contact. We're breaking new ground."

The Prime Minister is blunt. "Try not to piss him off."

"My worry is how long it'll take for any of this to filter down through the ranks."

"Go," the PM says. "See what you can do. And keep me in the loop."

"Understood."

Felix ends the call, but he doesn't put his phone away. He turns to one of the officers, saying, "I need you to drive me across town."

"No problem, sir."

As they walk out into a secure carpark, Felix brings up the live feed from the BBC. He leaves the stream on mute, preferring to read the subtitles. Although they're automatically generated, they're reasonably accurate. He only catches one point at which there's clearly a blunder by whatever AI program's generating them.

"Where to?" the officer asks, leading him to an unmarked police car. Two uniformed motorcycle officers ride up on either side of the car, preparing to escort the vehicle.

"The MI6 building. Just off the Vauxhall Bridge. Over on the embankment."

"Yes, sir."

Felix sits in the back of the car and puts on his seatbelt, still watching the *BBC Morning Show*. Lucy is passionate, appealing to the camera.

This isn't us.

This isn't Britain.

This isn't who we are.

They pull out of the carpark and onto the main road. The motorcycle police ride ahead of them with their lights flashing, clearing a road that's already largely devoid of traffic.

Something incredible happened last night.

We were visited by a spacecraft from another world.

They returned one of our own to us.

And what do we do?

We panic. We react. We launch fighter jets.

We send the SAS to take down a single, unarmed man,

Someone who saved my life.

He's a hero, and yet we're treating him like a war criminal.

The roads are empty. The streets of London should be bustling with rush hour traffic. Instead, the roads are deserted. The only other time Felix has seen so few cars in the city is on Christmas Day. Hundreds of pedestrians clog the pavement, though, sometimes spilling onto the street, but there are very few cars or vans.

Is this who we really are as a nation?

Whatever happened to the old spirit of the Blitz?

So much for **Keep Calm and Carry On***.*

Whatever happened to **You'll Never Walk Alone***?*

Or is that only for football games?

I'm calling on everyone in London.

Make your voice heard.

Come to central London.

Fill the streets.

Demand the government releases Anthony.

Felix is torn between watching the broadcast and looking out the window of the car at the growing crowd. Everyone's walking in the same direction, which indicates a rally forming. Normally, protests are limited to a subset of the population, like nurses striking for better pay or teens calling for action on climate change. The people he passes, though, come from all walks of life. There are mothers with strollers, businessmen in suits, and teens with placards tucked under their arms. Almost every second person has their phone out, looking at the screen as they walk. They're all watching the same broadcast.

Even though Lucy has only just called for a march, it seems the British population was already on the move. Her cry has only reinforced their resolve.

Remember, they're OUR government.

They answer to us—not us to them.

So make them answer.

Tell them, no more lies.

Tell them, this is wrong.

Tell them, no more fear in politics.

Tell them, it's time for change!

Felix is fascinated by how an obscure attendant working in a sex shop can be catapulted onto the public stage and speak with such authority. Last night, he read some background research on the apothecary and its owners. They've been active in the LGBTQ+

community and have supported AIDS research and trans rights for over a decade. The apothecary itself barely turns a profit. Lucy's father owns a cabinetmakers workshop in Slough, competing with cheap imports from Southeast Asia. He employs forty people. He doesn't need the apothecary. He seems to keep it running as a hobby.

Lucy is passionate.

I don't care if someone's come from

another country,

another world,

or another time.

This is not the way we treat people.

It's time to embrace what it means to be British.

We call ourselves Great Britain, but what makes us great?

We invented physics, antibiotics, jet engines,

electronic computers and photography.

We were the first country in the world to establish a modern democracy.

But what really makes us great

Is our ability to come together and create change.

We've made mistakes along the way,

Let's not make another one.

Let's show the world who we really are.

I'm calling on you to flood the streets.

I'm call—

The screen goes blank. At first, Felix assumes his phone has run out of battery, but the black screen is quickly replaced with a BBC logo and a message saying, *"Please be patient. We're experiencing technical issues."* Felix wonders if these are technical, political or judicial issues.

The police wouldn't have the power to shut down the broadcast directly. Such an order would have to come from a magistrate. Damn, he thinks, the Prime Minister must have called in a dozen favours to swing this. To Felix, silencing dissent is a mistake. He'd rather Lucy didn't have a platform, but once she was on it, he felt she should be left to run her race. Shutting down the broadcast is like putting out a fire with gasoline.

The Prime Minister is moving fast. He had to convince a judge that stopping the broadcast was in the public interest and then had to get the police to execute that order. By shutting down the BBC, he's gone nuclear. PMs have been rolled out of office for far less than this. Felix knows there's going to be some major recriminations in the days ahead, but for now, they have some breathing space.

His car pulls up at the sprawling monstrosity of a building complex that is MI6 headquarters on the Thames.

"Thanks," Felix says, getting out of the car and walking to the main doors on the north corner of the complex.

Inside the lobby, a security guard stops him with an outstretched hand.

"I'm sorry. Access is currently suspended. MI6 is under lockdown."

Felix pulls out his ID and shows it to the guard. Several other guards working on the security checkpoint come to the aid of the first officer, backing him up.

Felix is undeterred. "I'm the Secretary of State for Defence."

"I'm sorry, sir. I can't let you through security."

Felix feels his blood boil. At least this time, he got a sir from the officer. As much as he doesn't want to admit it, Lucy's right to doubt the intentions of the government and demand transparency. For all his speeches in the House of Commons about governing by consent, he's seen far too many instances in his career where the overriding concern was bureaucracy and not what was in the best interests of the country or its people. Once again, he's seeing blind obedience prevail over common sense.

"I don't think you understand, Officer Payne," he says, reading the guard's name tag. "I am a Minister of the Crown, serving in the

Cabinet at the pleasure of the Prime Minister, having been appointed to the portfolio of the Defence of the Realm by the King himself. On what grounds are you preventing me from entering this building?"

The officer swallows the lump welling up in his throat. Somehow, he manages to respond.

"With respect, sir. The Secret Intelligence Service falls under the Foreign Secretary."

That's a statement of fact, not a reason. There's no logic there, only a defensive reaction to being challenged. Felix fingers the phone in his pocket. He's tempted to call the Prime Minister, but what means would these guards have of verifying the identity of someone on the other end of a phone?

He looks at the men flanking the lead officer. They're all wearing tactical vests and carrying sidearms, including a Glock and a TASER, which is unusual for the front-line security service. Someone in a position of authority has raised the threat level. The officers themselves are nervous as hell. Felix can see the sense of conflict in their eyes. Like all good public servants, they want nothing more than to do their duty. The problem is—what defines that duty? Is it unquestioning obedience to the commands issued by their immediate superiors, who are probably acting on similarly vague instructions, or is it to do what's right based on their loyalty to the Crown?

"You, Officer Davis," Felix says, reading the name tag of the stony-faced man to the right of Officer Payne. "Do your duty to this country and not this department. Arrest this man."

Davis swallows hard. His eyes go wide. He grits his teeth. It seems his mind is racing at the implication of what he's been asked to do and the sheer audacity of the Secretary of State for Defence to call upon him in this manner. What's the right thing to do? Does the minister even have this kind of authority? Felix can see the anguish on his brow as he struggles with what he can and should do in this situation.

Officer Davis is easily six foot four inches in height and has a chest like a rugby player. Payne is equally muscular but not quite as tall.

Both men are wearing shirts that look too small for them. Their bulky shoulder muscles pull the cotton tight. At a meagre five foot seven inches, Felix is tiny by comparison. His narrow shoulders and slim arms made him the last pick in gym class back in high school, but the power imbalance between them is not related to physical strength. Felix is not intimidated by muscle, and that makes him intimidating—to Officer Payne, at least, as he steps slightly back, retreating. Officer Davis, in contrast, seems genuinely impressed by the prowess of the minister.

Officer Payne turns to look at Officer Davis. His fingers are shaking. Regardless of whatever camaraderie they have, their duty is being called into question. Neither man is a fool. Neither wants to obstruct justice. When they took their oaths of office, neither of them would have ever considered turning against their own, but they're being challenged to think rather than blindly obey.

Fractions of a second pass like hours. Felix is stone-faced. He could speak, but he won't. Now is the time for them to decide where their allegiance lies.

Without looking down at the thick leather belt around his waist, Officer Davis unclips the strap over his holster. His hand rests on the butt of his Glock.

"Now, hold on," Officer Payne says, putting his hands out and appealing for reason. "I just think we need to talk to our superiors—that's all."

Officer Davis says, "Our superiors will need to reach out to senior management. And they'll need to reach the director. And the director will need to reach the minister. Someone like him. But we don't need that. The answer is literally standing before us, telling us what to do."

Felix addresses Officer Payne. "You can chase all the command authority you want, but do not stand in my way. Time is of the essence. I'm not going to wait for you to reach the ministerial level because *I am* at the ministerial level. And I will not stand by as we torture an innocent man. The damage we are doing cannot be undone."

Officer Payne steps to one side. It's subtle, but his lowered head says, I will not stop you.

Officer Davis addresses Felix, saying, "Secure holding is down on B3."

"Take me there," Felix says, marching forward.

The debate is over. None of the other guards interfere with him. Officer Davis leads Felix to the elevators as the others remain at their post, frantically talking among themselves.

"Are you willing to use that thing?" Felix asks, looking down at the gun on the officer's hip.

"Yes, sir."

"Good."

Officer Davis pulls out a plastic card attached to his belt by a chain. He swipes it over the control panel for a nondescript service elevator in a corridor behind the main elevators. Seconds later, the doors open and they step inside. He swipes his card again, punches a button and they descend to Basement Three.

"There's an internal checkpoint down there," Davis says. "It's a mantrap designed to catch unauthorised personnel between two bulletproof doors. Beyond that are the holding cells."

Although they came in on the ground floor, the elevator descends far more than three floors. It seems the designation B3 is deliberately misleading.

Davis speaks into his radio, saying, "Checkpoint Echo. This is the Northeast Security Desk. Come in."

"This is Echo, go ahead Northeast."

"I am en route to you with Felix Mason, Secretary of State for Defence, requesting access to B3 holding cells. Over."

"Negative, Northeast. I cannot allow access without authorisation."

Like everyone in the United Kingdom, Officer Davis must have seen the rolling coverage of the extraterrestrial incident above the Houses of Parliament. He may not understand the specifics, but he must know Felix is here dealing with something related to the appearance of the UFO. He has no problem pushing back on the guard on the other end of the radio. "The presence of the minister here in person is the authorisation you need."

The doors to the elevator open. A narrow corridor leads to interview rooms on one side and a glass sliding door on the other. Then there's a security desk followed by a second set of glass doors. The glass is so thick it gives the neon lights above the security guard a green tinge. The officer on Checkpoint Echo speaks into his radio, still in the process of replying to Officer Davis, saying, "Negative." Felix can hear him through a security grill in the glass.

Officer Davis walks up to the first door. It remains shut. He stops with his nose barely an inch from the thick bulletproof glass. Felix stands slightly back and to one side, holding up his ID. He smiles, trying to be friendly—as though that will help.

Officer Davis speaks in a deadpan tone of voice. "Open the door, John."

"You know I can't do that," John says, picking up a desk phone and dialling a number.

Officer Davis rests his hand on his holster. As John is behind bulletproof glass, it's an idle threat, but a threat nonetheless. Davis is making it clear this is not a social visit.

After a muffled discussion on the phone, John says, "I'm sorry. This is a restricted area. You'll have to go through formal channels to gain entry."

"Who was that?" Felix asks, pointing at the phone on the desk. "The person you were just talking to?"

"SM Intelligence Agent Williams."

"Does Agent Williams have a first name?" Felix asks, sounding far too calm and informal.

"Ah, Jackie."

Felix leans forward, peering through the glass at the officer's name tag. "And you're John Kelly."

Officer Kelly looks nervous. Felix is relaxed. In contrast, Officer Davis hasn't moved from where he's positioned himself in front of the sliding glass door. Felix walks around the lobby, examining the elevators with idle curiosity. There's no music, but he steps as though there were, looking at the various fixtures and emergency evacuation plans with fake interest, talking as he feigns being distracted.

"Do you know what power is, Officer John Kelly?" he asks with his back momentarily to the officer.

Officer Kelly doesn't reply.

"It's not this," Felix says, coming full circle and wrapping his knuckles on the glass. His eyes dart around the security room, looking into the corners of the ceiling. "Power comes from institutions, not people. Now, people make up those institutions, but the power comes from the structure and not any one individual or even a group of people. It's the process that's important—the way people are organised."

He steps around Officer Davis.

"I mean, look at this," he says, pointing at the gun on the officer's hip. "Power doesn't come from a gun. It comes from the authority to use a gun. And in our society, all authority comes from the government."

He curls away, turning his back on Officer Kelly again. Felix throws his arms wide, saying, "By itself, a gun is useless. Use it for the government, and you're a hero. Use it against the government, and you're a villain."

Felix taps his fingers on a Health and Safety sign beside the elevator. It's colourful, with cartoon characters encouraging MI6 staff to keep their vaccinations up to date. His motion is peculiar and unsettling, and he knows it. He wants Officer Kelly to feel uncomfortable.

Felix turns to face the officer, saying, "People mistake brute force for power all the time. They think *might makes right*. It doesn't. Might is powerless against any group of people that are organised and disciplined.

"The public doesn't understand. They've seen too many god-awful Hollywood movies where the good guy comes charging in with guns blazing, but power isn't about muscle. It's not about bullets or bombs. No, it's more subtle than that. I'll give you an example."

He taps the glass again.

"You. You think you're safe behind this glass, but you're not. You think this provides protection, but it doesn't."

Felix points into the corner of the ceiling behind Officer Kelly. The officer turns, following Felix's gaze. A black dome hides a security camera.

"That's power, right there. And that, my friend, gives me power over you."

The officer looks confused.

"Take a good look at it," Felix says. "Because in the coming days, you're going to be seeing yourself staring up at that camera, and this one over here, and that one way down at the end of the corridor. They'll all be used to exercise power over you in a way you cannot begin to imagine.

"I want you to think about what you're going to say once you're sworn in. The judge will listen intently to your recollection of this moment. If you're lucky, you'll get a civil trial with a jury, but I suspect the government's lawyers will invoke the Armed Forces Act and try you in a court martial. What you need to think about, though, is how the prosecution will present its argument."

Officer Kelly's face goes pale. Felix feels bad for him. Felix shouldn't be enjoying this quite as much as he is, but this is the only avenue he has open to him. Truth be told, he's not actually that confident in his legal assessment. There are provisions in the Armed Forces Act for disobeying lawful commands and failing to perform one's duty, but whether these could be applied to obstructing a Minister of the Crown is debatable. The law was drafted with the intent of applying to the chain of command. Ultimately, that chain leads beyond the military to the government, but Felix doubts such a case has ever been tried in British courts before. There's no clear precedence, but the

Secretary of State for Defence represents civilian control over the military. It would be a brave lawyer that would argue otherwise.

Part of him would like to see the case tested in court as, even if it failed, it would lead to the formation of new laws to prevent situations like this from occurring in the future.

Regardless of the actual legal ramifications, which need to be thrashed out in court, Felix knows he's got to get Officer Kelly to think beyond here and now. As long as Kelly has a narrow focus, he'll keep that door shut. Felix has got to get him to see beyond the moment.

"The prosecution is going to make the case for the willful obstruction of justice and press for a sentence of hard jail time."

Felix turns away from the security desk, raising his voice as he stares the other way down the corridor, still pacing within the lobby in front of the elevators.

"Now, your lawyers, if they're smart, will go for the classic obedience defense—*you were only following orders*. They'll say you felt compelled to obey your immediate superiors. Although it should be noted that defense didn't work all that well at Nuremberg."

As Felix reaches the fire exit, he turns back, returning to the security desk as he continues.

"The prosecution will call me as a witness. Hell, they'll probably replay this exact conversation, admitting it as evidence in the trial. The jury will watch the video closely. They'll examine your facial reactions, like that one right there when your eyes narrowed! The prosecution will say your reaction reveals an awareness of guilt, that —regardless of orders—you were conscious of right and wrong. They'll say you knew—at this exact moment in time—that you were making a mistake. They'll press you to explain why you acted as you did. Your defense team will object, saying, '*Your honour, inaction is a reasonable default when faced with uncertainty.*' But the judge won't let that stand. The prosecution will counter, saying, "You had a choice. Your delay—"

The glass door slides open.

Officer Kelly hangs his head.

Officer Davis marches forward, getting inside the security zone before the door has fully opened. He pats Officer Kelly on the shoulder, saying, "You did the right thing, John."

Felix walks up to the forlorn security officer. Their eyes meet. Officer Kelly is still conflicted—that much is clear from the furrow of his brow. He's still processing a decision that was as simple as pushing a button.

Felix doesn't have the luxury of explaining all the details. He speaks with authority, saying, "With me."

Officer Kelly gets up and opens the inner door leading to the holding cells. "He's in room sixteen."

There's a distinct change in the nature of the building in this subsection of the MI6 security complex. Whereas out by the elevators, the decor could be mistaken for any other office tower in London, now there's no mistaking the function of the basement. It's a prison. Sheetrock walls give way to rendered brickwork, not only to confine suspects but to reduce noise from adjoining cells.

The generic, industrial office carpet ends just beyond the inner glass door. Polished concrete extends across the floor. Felix is wearing business shoes. His heels make a distinct chatter on the floor in contrast to the soft squelch of the officers' boots. The door to each "*room*" is made from quarter-inch plate steel. A tiny window with thin, reinforced wires running through the glass provides a narrow glimpse inside. Beside each door, there's a video screen showing four camera views. Felix quickly realises the doors hide an anteroom outside the interrogation room itself. From there, officers can observe suspects through a one-way mirror. Should a suspect get out of their cell, they'd find themselves trapped in the anteroom. Metal grates cover the neon lights on the concrete ceiling.

"We're here," Officer Kelly says, coming to a halt beside a large black **(16)** painted on the wall beside the door. He inserts an oversized key into the bulky lock and turns it. His keys jangle like wind chimes. On the screen, Felix can see someone panicking in the anteroom. They rush to the thick steel door, but it opens outward before they can secure it with a deadlock.

"What the hell are you doing?" the agent inside the room says. She's in her forties. She's got her hair pulled back in a ponytail, but her most notable characteristic is the vomit splatter on her white blouse. Her shirt is soaked. Chunks of partially digested food and stringy bits of stomach acid cling to her clothing. From the direction of the spew, it's not hers. Someone has vomited on her.

"SM Intelligence Agent Williams?" Felix asks, extending a hand in mock friendship.

"You shouldn't be here," she says, ignoring his gesture.

Felix pushes past her, noting, "And you should be ashamed of yourself."

He peers through the vast one-way mirror. Anthony is in handcuffs. He's been chained to the centre of a steel table that's been bolted to the floor within the interrogation room. Bloody rings line his wrists, marking where he's pulled against the steel cuffs. The chair behind him has been knocked to the floor, leaving him on his feet, leaning over the table, still pulling against his restraints. Spew drips from the edge of the table.

There are two intelligence officers in the interrogation room. One of them has a split lip. Blood seeps down his chin. The other has a bruise under his right eye. The swelling is causing his cheek to sag. They both keep their distance from Anthony. They're shouting at him. Spittle flies from their lips as they point at Anthony, accusing him. The soundproof room prevents more than a whisper from reaching Felix in the anteroom.

The intelligence agents gesture to a silver Apple AirTag that's been placed on the table in front of him. At a guess, Felix figures this is how Lucy has been tracking Anthony's location, but it seems these guys suspect something more sinister. One of the officers leans forward, tapping the steel table immediately in front of the AirTag. Felix wants to yell at them, saying, "Idiots!" They're not thinking clearly. What use would an alien or someone from the past have with 21st-century technology? It's clearly been given to him by someone else, someone tracking him and exposing the machinations of the secret service. He smiles. He's got respect for Lucy. Planting that was some smart lateral thinking on her part.

Felix glances at the controls on the table in front of the one-way mirror and the screens showing the various angles being recorded. A pair of headphones lie discarded on the desk. Felix doesn't have time for games. This has to end now.

Officer Kelly looks shocked by what he's seeing. He grits his teeth. His nostrils flare. It seems he's disgusted to realise this is what he was defending.

"Get him out of there," Felix says.

Officer Davis draws his gun and throws open the door.

Officer Kelly charges in behind Officer Davis with a ferocity Felix can only admire. The time for fucking around is over.

SM Intelligence Agent Williams steps toward Felix, protesting and wanting to enter the room as well. Felix plants his hand in the middle of her chest and shoves her back into an office chair. She falls, landing on her ass on the cushioned seat. Her momentum causes the chair to swivel. It rolls away, racing across the floor before colliding with the far wall.

Felix points at her, talking to her as though she were nothing more than a trained attack dog.

"Stay!"

He walks into the room. Davis has his gun drawn. He's pointing it at the intelligence agents. They raise their hands and back up against the wall. Kelly moves swiftly, cuffing their hands behind their backs against their vehement protests.

"Silence," Felix says. His presence commands respect.

Anthony, though, growls like an animal.

Felix looks at the strange young man with disbelief. Given all Anthony's been through over the past twenty-four hours, Felix doesn't know what to say to him. Felix hasn't thought about anything beyond reaching their celestial visitor.

He does the only thing he can.

He lies.

Felix doesn't mean to be deceitful, but he's thinking on his feet. He can see what's happened here. Whatever orders were issued by the Prime Minister to the Foreign Secretary, they've cascaded as they've descended the chain of command. It's not fear so much as uncertainty that's driven an overreaction from the security services. No one knows if the spacecraft will be back again or what its intentions are. For all these agents know, they have just minutes to extract useful information before some *Independence Day*-style attack unfolds over London. To be fair, Big Ben got blasted by an alien warship in that movie, or was it the sequel?

Officers Davis and Kelly lead the two intelligence agents over to the door. Neither of the captive men offers any resistance. Felix understands their motives, but they've been shown as hollow. Now, they're ashamed. They avoid eye contact with Felix, staring down at their feet. These agents thought they were the good guys. They were just doing their duty. They didn't want to be the ones that let the country down. From their perspective, they were doing what they need to in order to protect not only the United Kingdom but Earth itself from an alien invasion or something. From there, the situation spiralled out of hand. Whatever resistance Anthony put up was misinterpreted as defiance. These men have been trained to deal with terrorists, not extraterrestrials or someone from another time. They acted as if they had mere minutes to find and defuse a nuclear weapon hidden beneath parliament, only that was a fabrication of their own fears.

Felix has built his career on reading people and situations. His strength comes from anticipating reactions and understanding intent—sometimes to a degree that's better than his political opponents realise about themselves. He intuitively knows Lucy is right. If he was asked to explain how or why, he couldn't articulate a reason, but there's something genuine and uncontrived in her testimony, and that assures him that everyone else is wrong about this damn thing that appeared in the skies over Westminster.

He holds his hands out to show Anthony he means no harm.

And then he lies.

"Lucy sent me."

The mention of Lucy's name is disarming, which was precisely what Felix intended. Instantly, Anthony softens, but Felix can see the turmoil in his eyes. Is this real? Or is it yet another trick?

Officer Davis bundles the two intelligence agents out into the anteroom while Officer Kelly walks over beside Felix with a small key held up for all to see.

Felix says, "Uncuff him."

Kelly reaches in from the side, wary of Anthony with his torn, bloody clothing and vomit sticking to his chin. He releases the cuffs, allowing them to fall to the metal table. Anthony springs back away from them. He pushes his back against the wall.

"If Lucy sent you, where is she?"

Felix has been around long enough to know this is the basic problem with lies—it's far too easy for someone to call his bluff. For once, he's not being malicious or manipulative. He's trying to help, but what can he say to give Anthony confidence in him? The poor guy has been assaulted by the SAS and dragged into this hellhole. From what Felix can tell, he vomited on SM Intelligence Agent Williams—probably because his body was in shock after being tasered. He has no reason to trust anyone on Earth other than Lucy. She's the only one that hasn't betrayed him.

Felix reflects on the BBC broadcast, wanting to pick up on the subtleties of what she shared. He's searching for something that might resonate with Anthony. He takes a punt, turning his hands outward as he says, "You'll never walk alone, right?"

That was something Lucy emphasised in her interview with the BBC. Felix can see how that idea would resonate with someone that's been displaced in time by roughly five hundred years.

Anthony lowers his hands. His shoulders stoop. He's exhausted, but he's heard what he needs from Felix.

For his part, Felix isn't working an angle. He genuinely wants to bring this episode to a constructive conclusion. He understands that what humanity needs is allies, not enemies, among the stars—and Anthony could be the key to that.

Felix pulls out his phone, holding it up so Anthony can see the lock screen.

"You know what this is, right?" he asks, unlocking the phone and hitting a speed dial number along with the button for the speakerphone.

Anthony nods.

"Felix. What's happening?" is the gruff answer coming from the tiny speaker in his phone.

"Prime Minister," Felix says, not taking his eyes off Anthony. "I've found him. Anthony's safe. I'm with him now. I've got you on speaker so he can hear you. I've told him I'll take him to someone he trusts—Lucy Bailiwick."

"Well, you won't have far to go," the Prime Minister says. "She's leading tens of thousands of people across the Vauxhall Bridge as we speak. It's the only thing any of the broadcasters are showing on TV."

Felix says, "Can you have her meet us by the main entrance?"

"Oh, that won't be a problem. She's leading a BBC film crew to MI6, demanding access to Anthony. Our injunction was limited to the morning program so they simply switched to another slot and restarted their broadcast. The judge has refused to broaden the injunction, citing public interest and safety concerns. Everything's going out live. Be careful, Felix. We want to end up on the right side of this mess."

"Understood."

Felix ends the call and beckons to Anthony, reaching out his hand in an offer of friendship. Anthony accepts. Far from simply shaking, Anthony grabs his hand. It seems he has no intention of letting go. In the 21st century, it's strange for a man to hold the hand of another man, but Felix feels Anthony's pain. The comment about not walking alone unlocked Anthony's trust. Hearing he'd be reunited with

Lucy has given him hope. For someone that's been isolated from human society for five hundred years, everything he sees around him must be disorienting. Touch transcends time.

"It's okay," Felix says as Anthony grips his hand. They walk out of the interrogation room.

"What about us?" SM Intelligence Agent Williams asks.

Felix says, "I'm going to leave you intelligence agents to think about how utterly unintelligent you've been."

With that, he turns his back on them and walks out into the corridor.

Your Choice

Officer Kelly takes the lead while Officer Davis brings up the rear, walking behind them as they leave the secure basement within MI6 and step into the lobby. Anthony seems to visibly relax with the change in decor. He's free. He's really free.

"These metal boxes," Anthony says, stepping cautiously into the elevator beside Felix. "They're everywhere now?"

"Elevators," Felix says, still holding Anthony's hand. "Yes. They allow us to move between floors."

"And it's a pulley system? Like those used in the stores? But it's mechanical rather than being pulled by a horse?"

"Yes," Felix replies. He's only vaguely aware of how elevators work. There's a cable or something similar and an electric engine somewhere. Does that pass for a pulley system?

The doors to the elevator open on the ground floor. Anthony squeezes his hand.

"It's okay," Felix says, seeing dozens of soldiers in the lobby. "They're with me."

Polished combat boots reflect off the dark marble floor. These aren't the SAS. They're not dressed in black, with their faces covered for anonymity. These soldiers are wearing camouflage—and that does *not* work in central London. Several police officers and the MI6 security team are talking with the army captain. Felix walks forward with Anthony. The soldiers form a perimeter around them in the empty lobby, moving with them. Radios chatter with discussions about security.

"This way," Officer Kelly says, directing them through the sprawling lobby. He leads them away from the northeast security checkpoint and over to the main entrance.

As they approach the vast glass doors, Felix spots Lucy with a camera crew. A dark lens peers in at them from the marble stairs outside the building.

The MI6 building is surrounded by a courtyard with a twelve-foot-high concrete wall, topped with a black privacy screen and vertical bars that reach up and out over the road to deter anyone from breaching the perimeter. Even so, protestors have climbed up. They cling to the bars, peering through them much to the concern of security services. Felix is curious about what they thought they'd see, but they seem content to look at the austere building itself. Behind them, the street is a sea of heads bobbing as the crowd surges. People have climbed lampposts and trees to gain a better view of nothing in particular. Hundreds of people have clambered up on top of the raised railway on the far side of the road. That's got to be causing someone major headaches. Their presence there will have shut down the trains. It seems everyone wants to see Anthony. Only what is there to see? At a distance of a hundred yards, or even for those on the street immediately outside the building, he'd be nothing more than a vague figure moving in the shadows.

The crowd is boisterous. Even from within the building, they can be heard with clarity. Roughly a hundred thousand people sing in unison, with voices raised as one.

You'll never... walk alone...

The sound of their singing echoes off the surrounding buildings, providing a natural sense of harmony.

The senior police officer addresses Felix, saying, "You should know. We do not have effective crowd control in place. Things could get ugly out there. I can't guarantee your safety."

"It's okay," Felix says. "I understand."

Outside, Lucy pushes past a guard. She runs through the open door, sprinting across the marble floor toward them. Felix lets go of Anthony's hand, allowing him to run to meet her. They embrace each other with a hug. Lucy's sobbing. Anthony's crying. Felix wipes tears from the corner of his eyes. He's getting soft.

The BBC camera crew follows close behind Lucy, capturing the moment and transmitting it around the United Kingdom and out to the world at large.

"Are you okay?" Lucy blabbers. She flicks her hair behind her ears, stepping back and looking at his blood-splattered clothing and the sick still sticking to his shirt. "What have they done to you?"

She peers at Felix with hatred in her eyes.

"Not him," Anthony says. "He freed me."

She glances around at the soldiers, but they've fanned out. Felix notes the look of surprise in her eyes. She was expecting them to be facing Anthony, but they're not. It's apparent they're here to protect him.

Anthony and Lucy step out into the warm sunshine. The soldiers ready themselves to follow through each of the side doors, but Felix raises his hand, wanting them to hold where they are. He says to the captain, "Keep your men in reserve. If the crowd gets violent, drag us out but do not engage with civilians. No weapons are to be used. Not under any circumstances. Leave them in here. Is that understood?"

"Yes, sir," the captain replies, swallowing a lump rising in his throat. Felix has asked him to do the impossible, and if it comes to it, he will. As Secretary of State for Defence, Felix has seen this countless times before—the dedication and devotion of the armed services to do whatever it takes, regardless of personal consequences. If things go bad—and Felix doesn't think they will—he has no doubt the captain and his men will give their last ounce of courage to save them. And they'll do it without firearms.

Felix walks out onto the broad portico overlooking the steps. The main gate is partially open. Police helmets are visible, pressing against the swell of the mob, trying to maintain order on the fringes of the crowd. On seeing Anthony, people cheer. Thousands of smartphones are raised in unison, all wanting to capture the event on video. They'll be broadcasting live, which to Felix, is redundant. The BBC has both the best and the closest camera, and they're already live.

The singing swells in volume, echoing around them. The crowd enters a reprise where the chorus of the song is sung as a refrain, growing in intensity as the song reaches an extended climax.

You'll...

Ne...ver...

Walk...

A...lone!

"How do you want to handle this, sir?" the police commander asks Felix, struggling to be heard over the noise. He looks as nervous as hell.

Felix needs to defuse the situation. The only way to do that is to satisfy the crowd. It's at that point he realises the smartphones scattered throughout the crowd can help. They can send *and* receive. And that means they can act as a substitute for a PA system.

"Have a seat," Felix says to Anthony and Lucy. "Right here on the steps. Sorry, it's not as comfortable as a television studio, but you need to talk to them."

"To the crowd?" Lucy asks, somewhat perplexed by his comment. To her, it must seem impossible and yet both she and Anthony sit on the top step, looking out over the sea of people.

Felix walks down a few steps and talks to the police commander, saying, "Get the word out to your officers. Tell them to tell the crowd to stream the BBC. Tell them, forget about recording this—watch it live instead. And tell them to spread the word and tell the person behind them. Tell them Anthony's about to speak to them."

"Yes, sir," the commander says, jogging down to the main gate.

The camera crew positions itself lower on the steps, preparing a shot that looks up at Anthony and Lucy. One of the police officers walks over, handing them both bottles of water.

"Thanks," they reply, accepting the kindness of a stranger. For them, there's no pretence. Felix notes their humility is genuine. He sits down beside them, feeling better about the ambling chain of decisions that brought them all to this point in time.

"Are you going to take us somewhere else?" Lucy asks.

Her question is innocent enough, but it assumes the overbearing nature of the government is still in full force. Given that she's surrounded by police, with the army on standby inside the building, that's a fair assumption, but from his perspective, all this is out of necessity and not by design. Felix didn't intend for any of this, and certainly not a crowd growing into the hundreds of thousands. He's heard over the police radio that the march extends back to Whitehall in the north and Hyde Park in the west. Both Lambeth and Westminster bridges have been blocked by protesters. Like water running through a flooded house, the marchers have backed up and are now flowing across Waterloo Bridge. By all accounts, the protesters are peaceful, but they've overwhelmed police resources.

"No," he says, sticking to his initial resolve and being very aware his comments are being broadcast live across the country by the BBC film crew. "You're free to go. You can do whatever you want."

"You don't want anything from us?" she asks, raising an eyebrow.

"No," he says, talking to both of them. "All this was a mistake. You have to understand. We were taken by surprise. We reacted. We felt we had to protect our citizens, but we were clumsy and heavy-handed. Governments are good at governing. They're lousy at being flexible, thoughtful and agile."

"So we can just leave?" she asks.

"Yes," he says. "We'd love to talk to both of you, but you're not under any obligation to talk to us. You have an opportunity right here and now to have your voice heard, but the choice is yours. The official position of the UK government is simple. We'd love to sit you down with our scientists and researchers, but it would be—and it was—a mistake to try to force you to cooperate with us."

A group of rowdy protesters near the barricade calls out, "Tell us about the aliens! Tell us!"

Felix gestures toward them, saying, "They're waiting."

Anthony points at the crowd, saying, "But how can I talk to them? They can't hear me."

"Ah, but they can," Felix replies. Over the course of a few minutes, the sea of smartphones subsides as the crowd watches them on the BBC live stream. Instead of holding up the cameras on their phones and recording the event, people in the crowd are looking down at their screens. Felix can see how word of the broadcast is spreading like a wave through the crowd as people further back respond to the admonition and lower their phones. Even Anthony seems to realise the change as he looks at the reaction of the crowd.

"You're not alone," Felix says, leaning forward on his knees. "All of this is for you. They're listening—all of them. What do you want to say to them?"

"I—I..."

"Tell them who you are."

"Tell them who you really are," Lucy says.

Felix says, "Tell them how you managed to live in outer space for five hundred years!"

Forget about aliens and UFOs—this is what he really wants to know.

Anthony seems flustered. "For me, 'twas mere years, not centuries, just shy of a decade. Time is like the eddies and currents in a river. Out in the deep, the water moves faster than in close to shore. And yet sitting out in the channel, you barely notice yourself drifting along."

Felix has no idea how this is possible, but he's content to learn if Anthony wants to explain further. Felix figures somewhere nearby, a bunch of scientists are nodding in agreement with Anthony's comment.

They'll know what he means. Felix is happy to wait for the one-page summary in the daily cabinet briefing paper.

Felix is aware of the optics of the interview. MI6 fucked up by going hard on what they saw as an existential threat to the United Kingdom. The presence of the Secretary of State for Defence in this impromptu live broadcast should help negate the public relations damage to the government. Viewers will see the cuts and bruises on Anthony's face and the way he rubs his wrists, but they'll also see a senior minister sitting beside this stranger from another time.

Felix has never had aspirations for party leadership or the role of Prime Minister, but after this, he knows his team will look closely at the numbers. Sir James isn't dumb. He'll do all he can to keep Felix on his side, but all politicians pass out of favour. It's inevitable. Being in government turns even folk heroes into villains. When the public tires of Sir James, Felix will play this particular card showing him as *'a man of the people.'* Perhaps. Maybe. As usual, the ruminations of his mind are getting ahead of him. For now, this is enough. Freeing an innocent man from another age may just be the highlight of his political career.

Anthony doesn't elaborate any further on his comment. It doesn't matter how much anyone else may want him to explain his remarkable statement, he chooses to remain silent. Lucy holds his hand, gripping it tight as he rests his arms on his thighs.

Felix wants to keep the conversation rolling. "What can you tell us about them? The aliens?"

"Aliens?" Anthony asks. It's only then that Felix realises how much the English language must have changed over the centuries. Here's a term that has dominated the modern consciousness for the best part of a hundred years, but it's entirely obscure to someone from the 16th century.

"Foreigners," Felix says. "But not to our country, to our world."

"They're kind," he says. "Compassionate. They didn't have to bring me back here. For them, my passage meant forgoing the exploration of another planet before their kind converges to share what they've learned from this world and dozens of others."

Felix swallows the lump rising in his throat. For all his bluster about being a minister of the Crown, for all his fancy suits and expensive ties, nothing compares to the importance of interacting with an intelligent extraterrestrial species. A million questions rush through his mind, but he remains silent. Now is the time to listen.

"They warned me. They told me nothing would be the same. They said I'd be an outcast, that nations would fight over me—and all for nought."

Felix nods. He feels guilty. He can't maintain eye contact. Anthony's right. Even within the United Kingdom, fractures splintered through the government in less than twenty-four hours. It's as though the presence of the alien spacecraft was a hammer striking glass. He looks down at his highly polished shoes. The sense of pride he takes in his appearance is utterly meaningless in the face of someone that's walked on another world.

"The first thing I learned from them was how we fool ourselves."

The term *'them'* gets everyone's attention. Felix leans in, wanting to hear more.

"Oh, 'tis not on purpose, but we surround ourselves with things that don't exist. We mean not to lie to ourselves, and yet we do—time and again—often without realising it"

"I don't understand," Felix says, not meaning to interrupt but feeling compelled to ask for clarification. To him, Anthony is speaking in riddles.

"Look into the distance, and what do you see?" Anthony asks, pointing down the street. "You see the horizon—only the horizon doesn't exist. There's no horizon. There's only the limitation of our own eyes. And we know it's not true, but still we believe it. I've ridden from London to Kent. I've crossed grassy meadows and muddy tracks and trotted through forests and along riverbanks. At each point, the horizon lay before me, just out of reach. It lay over the next rise, across the next field. On reaching the crest of a hill, I'd see it lying further afield again. Only it didn't. It never existed. Only I existed, and the horizon was within me."

There's a beauty to Anthony's words that resonates like poetry. Felix could listen to him talk for hours, but it's the substance that's important. Felix would have never believed he or anyone else in the 21st century would stand to learn anything from the ignorance of a medieval peasant. The difference in their education is so extreme it seems absurd, and yet such arrogance is blinding—and that realisation has him listen with more intensity, wanting to understand Anthony's points with clarity.

"Just as we sail the oceans in caravels and galleons, so too do they sail the dark of night in ships, only these are made of iron rather than wood. Stars guide them as they guide us, allowing them to navigate vast distances with ease. To them, planets are as the islands of the Caribbean. Some are little more than rocky shoals. Others teem with life and beauty.

"But the horizon. When we first ascended into heaven, rising out of the Bay of Biscay off the coast of France, I watched as the horizon retreated. The higher we climbed, the more I could see as the horizon fled like the imposter that it is. Spain was hidden to us while sailing on the ocean, but we knew it lay not far off to the south. From the skies, though, we could see the forests along the shore and then the mountains further inland. All the while, that liar that is the horizon retreated further until it was gone.

"And what was it that remained in its place? An orb more beautiful than the royal jewels. What had seemed flat when riding a horse through the countryside was as round as a ball. The mariners were right when noting the tip of the mast appears first as ships sail over the horizon. Earth itself curls like clay spun on a potter's wheel.

"And 'twas then I realised Earth was not everything and everywhere as it had seemed from Westminster or the heights of London. Instead, it was just another planet like that of Mars or the Moon. Its horizon wrapped around on itself with no beginning and no end.

"Oh, the beauty of this world from the void. To see the blue of the ocean, the green of forests, the jagged outline of mountains and the swirling white clouds carrying life-giving rain. These are a rarity beyond that of silver or gold. Out there, in the dark of the night that never ends, Earth is a treasure beyond compare.

"And so 'twas then I learned how readily and easily we fool ourselves. I was sure Earth was large and the stars small. I was certain it was Earth that dominated the heavens, and the sun was but a fiery orb that did circle overhead. Like the horizon, these misgivings were a deception with which I fooled myself. And like others—both then and now—I believed the lies formed by my own eyes. I saw grandeur where there should have been humility."

Felix would not have thought it possible, but with tens of thousands of people clogging the streets around MI6 and hundreds of thousands more on the roads and bridges and parks surrounding central London, there is nothing but silence. Birds can be heard where before, there was the roar of trucks, the clatter of trains and the incessant chatter of people on the streets.

"Beware of your own intelligence," Anthony says. "To be smart and wise is the lot of both men and women, but 'tis easy to think that our corner of the world is all there is when it is but a trifling under heaven. No doubt we're smart. But to flatter oneself is folly. Ignorance comes from ignoring all that should be embraced. Think not, '*How smart am I?*' but rather think, '*To be smart is to learn more.*'

"Where does your horizon lie? What reaches past all you see from one day to the next? What's more important, the land over which you ride from village to town or all that waits to be discovered beyond the horizon?"

Anthony takes a sip of water from his bottle.

"And this time in which you live, 'tis marvellous! In what other age could there be cool, clear, clean spring water in a vessel such as this? In your world, there is genius in the mundane.

"For me, 'tis interesting to see what has and has not changed over the centuries. I find it fascinating to observe the things you overlook."

"Like what?" Felix asks, genuinely intrigued by his comments.

"Your toilet. Is that the correct term?"

"Yes."

"Ah, 'tis simple. 'Tis wondrous! To you, though, it is unremarkable. You use the toilet every day. Several times a day. Such an invention would be a luxury in my time. But for you, it's not worthy of note. Each and every house has a toilet—even among the poor. Some homes have two, three or four of them, and yet they're an embarrassment. They're used quickly and quietly and then ignored. But me? I lifted the lid on the cistern. 'Tis not a bucket of water being emptied into the bowl. No. There's a device in there. A contraption. There's a tap, a valve, and a float. There are rods and chains and screws. All intertwined and connected. The complexity is hidden by a button but 'tis there nonetheless. It's merely out of sight."

Felix furrows his brow. This is not what he expected from Anthony. Where's the discussion about alien anatomy or strange worlds in orbit around distant stars?

"Your rectangles, are they not the same?" Anthony asks. In response to his comment, Lucy hands her phone to him. He holds it up, but he's got it upside down. The screen rotates to compensate for the unusual orientation. If Anthony notices, he doesn't care.

"Who among you knows?" Anthony asks, showing the phone to the crowd and mimicking the way they recorded him earlier. He leans forward, turning and making eye contact with Felix as he continues. "Dost thou know? Thou art a minister of the government, serving the King, but can you tell me how the plunger works within a toilet? Can you list for me the parts inside this rectangle and explain each function?"

"Ah, no," Felix says, shaking his head.

"Can anyone?" Anthony asks, turning and looking out over the crowd. He holds Lucy's phone high overhead. "And yet you're smart. And you all have one. Someone must know, for someone built this, but you know not what it is you possess."

Felix nods in agreement.

"And this is what worries them," Anthony says. Yet again, the term *'them'* gets everyone's attention. "You're smart and yet ignorant. You know not that ignorance leaves you vulnerable. Ignorance invites lies, for it cannot distinguish between truth and error. Ignorance relies on ego for answers, not accuracy. Ignorance thrives on feelings, not fidelity.

"It's not that everyone needs to know everything, but that ignorance should be acknowledged rather than overlooked and ignored. And when ignorant, we should listen to those that know, not to those that are also ignorant but happen to be the loudest among us.

"As for them? They've studied our world from afar. You may have only seen them yesterday, but they have observed this world for hundreds of years.

"It took more than eighteen months for them to return me to Earth, during which voyage, they could see the messages you encode in the waves that radiate through the void."

Lucy says, "Like television? Radio?"

Anthony says, "Yes. They've seen our strengths and our weaknesses. They see us in ways we fail to recognise in ourselves. In my day, ignorance was the norm. Now, with your devices, ignorance is a choice. And they know that. They understand we choose our direction in life. They see in us the things we *refuse* to see in ourselves."

He lowers the phone, looking carefully at the dark screen.

"In my day, we feared magic. You, though, live in a time where magic is commonplace. Perhaps not the magic of wizards and witches in defiance of scripture. Perhaps not where superstition curdles the mind. But your science is as magic. Your science harnesses nature the same way a horse ploughs a field, but without knowing how science works, it might as well be sorcery to you.

"They see all this, and they lament. '*Why?*' you may ask. 'Tis not that they would begrudge you your toilets or your rectangles or your metal birds that soar through the air. 'Tis not these that bother them. No, rather, 'tis that for each advance, your morals remain firmly in the past. They sorrow that you cannot advance both of these in stride.

"You rely on things you don't understand. But you're smart. And being smart, you flatter yourselves. You fool yourselves. Instead of exercising your intelligence, you surrender to your impulses. When you should be informing yourselves, you cling to superstitions and fables—those lies that itch the ears and salve the soul.

"In my day, we suffered Bishop Blaine. He was no fool. He burned many a man at the stake. Heresy was the charge, but that was a lie. He was lazy. Arrogant. Selfish. He wanted not for doctrine or purity. These were but an excuse for his cruelty. He wanted power. He used the systems around him, exploiting them to crush us."

Felix swallows the lump rising in his throat. Although Anthony isn't singling him out, it's clear he's less than impressed by the way authority is wielded in modern day England. And he's correct. All too often, *might makes right*—only it doesn't. *Might* makes for oppression. The UK government may not be burning anyone at the stake, but there have been plenty of incidents where *might* has blurred what it means to be *right*.

Anthony points over his shoulder, saying, "Blaine sought to burn me in chains on the other side of the Thames, on the hallowed grounds of Saint Paul's. Were he here today, he would be among those that grabbed me from that house. He would be the one hitting me with cruel blows in that gaol cell.

"And for what? Why would he be so cruel? Because he could. Because power is a drunkard's tankard. 'Tis pewter silver with an ornate handle, yet it might as well be a swill bucket for feeding swine. Such as Blaine drink to excess and are never full. For Bishop Blaine, there was never enough blood washing over the cobblestones. Nay, unchecked authority is but a bulwark to excess. Hate is an excuse for the cruelty that lingers in the dark heart of a coward. All other reasons are hollow.

"And which lie is worst? Which deceit is cruelest of all? 'Tis the lies we tell ourselves. And Bishop Blaine told himself he was righteous. He told himself he was honest. And yet honesty is akin to the title of a knight. It must needs be given, not taken. It cannot be inherited or granted at the whim of one's self. No, it must be bestowed out of honour.

"And this is your problem. After five hundred years, this is what has not changed. You think yourselves as pure as the snow, but you see not the fine flakes drifting toward the mud in the gutter. You think you are as clean as the rain falling from the heavens, not realising it will wash through the sewers. You flatter yourselves, but they are not fooled. They see what you fail to see—all that you don't want to see in yourselves."

He holds up the phone again, saying, "Your love, your hate, your kindness and anger, your reason and your lies, these all come from different places within your soul. One is born out of cooperation, the other out of selfishness. One looks to take, the other to give. One would carry you forward, the other drags you back.

"The speed with which you have progressed since my day is breathtaking—if only your morals kept pace. Your machines may not be far from the stars, but you squabble like pigeons fighting for crumbs. There's no debasement that cannot be assuaged with power. And so power is what they would deny you. They will give none of you the secrets they possess lest another Bishop Blaine arise. For it is Blaine they fear. It is the havoc he could cause with a starship.

"I have read your history. I've seen images of the wars you have fought. Power should not be a license to persecute. Power should be metered for all. It should curb excesses, not encourage them. 'Tis not right that law binds some but not others. 'Tis not right that law is used as a club against the downtrodden but not the wealthy. You should strive to live in peace with one another and not force your misguided unity on a stranger.

"So build your spaceships, build your toilets and your rectangles and your metal birds, but fail not to build society as well. For there is nothing more important than ridding the world of hypocrisy. Let no amount of gold buy your soul. No horseless carriage is worth dishonesty. No glowing screen is greater than harmony between your houses. If you can do this—if you can improve both human and machine—then they invite you to join them among the stars. The choice is yours."

There's an awkward silence as Anthony falls quiet.

The camera shifts from Anthony to Felix, leaving the minister feeling as though he needs to say something in the affirmative, but what can he say to what this stranger from another time has said? Words are the problem. Hollow, empty promises have plagued humanity for thousands of years. Felix has no idea who Bishop Blaine was back in the 16th century, but he's sure he had all the best words. From what Anthony has said, it's clear Blaine could spin lies to look as though they were made from the silk of truth when they were but a cheap imitation.

Felix reaches up, wanting to adjust his tie. Loosening it will allow him to breathe, only it's not there. It's been scrunched up in his jacket pocket since last night. His fingers touch at his neck, pressing against the open collar of his shirt. He swallows the lump in his throat.

Anthony gets to his feet, saying, "I wonder if they have more black pudding."

"What?" Felix asks, confused, feeling as though he's missed something crucial in the conversation.

Lucy gets to her feet. She follows Anthony down the stairs toward the crowd. The police cordon parts, allowing Anthony through. Lucy turns back to Felix and the camera crew, calling out, "He means McDonald's. He gets the Scottish and the Americans mixed up. I think he wants a hamburger. He says the patties taste like black pudding."

"I'm sure they do," Felix mumbles to himself, shaking his head and laughing.

"If you need us, we'll be at the apothecary."

The End

Afterword

Thank you for taking a chance on independent science fiction.

If you've enjoyed *Apothecary*, please tell a friend and leave a review online as stories like this tend to be ignored and quickly slip into obscurity. You won't find *Apothecary* on the shelves of your local bookstore. You won't find it dominating the bestseller charts alongside Andy Weir's *Hail Mary* or Martha Wells' *Murderbot Diaries*. If others are to enjoy this story, it'll be because you were kind enough to tell them about an obscure science fiction author from Australia writing about the possibility of First Contact in 16th-Century England.

As I write several books a year, it's easy to think these stories run off the end of my fingers as I type, but they're the result of years of thoughtful consideration. Back in early 2016, I was in Adelaide, Australia, on business and caught up with a super-fan down there, Jason Pennock. The two of us went to see *Arrival* at the cinema. Afterwards, we headed to a small bar called *The Apothecary* and talked about what it would be like if First Contact occurred in medieval times. Although numerous other stories came to the forefront of my mind during the intervening years, I continued to make notes on what it would be like if intelligent aliens arrived when we were still burning people at the stake. It's taken a while, but I think *Apothecary* has some really interesting themes. I hope you've enjoyed this novel as much as I have.

As with any historical novel, there are bound to be inaccuracies, but to the best of my ability, I've tried to ensure this story is grounded in realism.

Language

One of the challenges of writing *Apothecary* was to find the right balance between modern English and English in the mid-16th century. Rather than labouring in the old English of the day (which was pre-Shakespearean and would be largely unrecognisable today), I chose to use modern English for readability. Anthony and Julia speak in a slightly archaic tone to convey a sense of life in those times but without resorting to words, phrases and terms the modern reader wouldn't recognise.

At times I've used archaic terms for effect, but these have been sparing to ensure the book flows. I've relied on etymononline as a resource because it lists the way words have changed over the centuries.

Historical Accuracy

As much as possible, I've endeavoured to keep the novel historically accurate. As an example, Queen Mary's marriage to Prince Phillip of Spain opened up trade with southern Europe, so I wove that into the opening scene with Anthony being fascinated by a Spanish caravel sailing down the Thames. The sailing terms and techniques described in this novel were taken from Historic Naval Fiction.

Looking back at the history of London, it's easy to think of historic landmarks and old buildings as being static and essentially unchanged over the centuries, but that's not true. When describing St. Paul's Cathedral, I avoided any notion of its iconic dome as that wasn't built until the 17th century, well after the period covered by this novel.

Language drifts, changing over time. Words such as '*okay*' are extremely common today, but they simply didn't exist in the 1500s, making it hard to convey that particular meaning within this novel. I referred to several online resources on Shakespearean language while developing this story but didn't want to douse the book in the language of the period. Instead, where practical, I adopted similar words to help anchor the story in that time. For example, I used '*Are you well?*'

instead of '*Are you okay?*'

Although the vast majority of my readers are American, I used British English spelling within this novel for a few reasons. First, the story is set in England. Second, any discomfort readers get from the spelling of words like colour, manoeuvres and demeanour only further establishes the story's unusual setting in a different time/place. For those in the United Kingdom, Australia and New Zealand, it's normal, but for North American readers this spelling must seem anachronistic.

Apothecary is set during the brief reign of Bloody Queen Mary the First. It's important to note, though, that the historical moniker *Bloody* is somewhat misleading. All of the Tudors were bloody. They all used public executions for their own convenience. If anything, Mary pardoned more people than she killed, but she did focus her ire on religious dissent. Being a Catholic, she sought to turn England back to what she considered the true church. Roughly three hundred people were publicly executed in the space of barely three months for trivial, religious doctrinal issues, earning her the title '*Bloody Mary.*'

The depiction of London in this novel is based on Anthony Stow's *A Survey of London from* 1598, while details of Queen Mary's murderous reign have been lifted from *Foxes Book of Martyrs (Actes and Monuments)* from 1563, a mere five years after the time covered in the novel. Far from the bustling metropolis of today, London was spread out along the river and surrounded by farmland. Back then, Covent Garden was an actual garden!

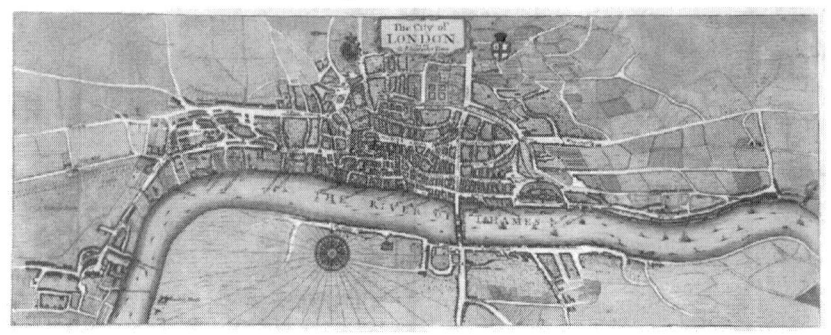

Looking at the map, the apothecary would be located at the bottom left corner in the village of Westminster.

Even though this story is fictional, details such as the execution in front of St. Paul's are accurate, with the words and events being drawn from the historical account of the executions of Dr. Ridley, Mr. Latimer, Dirick (Derek) Carver (who was a brewer), Anthony Philpot and William Flower (a teacher). Some may ask why I would include such gruesome details. The answer is because it happened! This is our heritage. This is the pedigree from which western civilisation arose. To ignore our bloody past, regardless of the form in which it came, is to whitewash history. We must be honest with our past if we want to forge a different future.

Bishop Blaine is a historical figure from this time. He perpetrated much of the slaughter during the reign of Queen Mary. For me, he's symbolic of everything that's wrong with humanity, while Anthony, Lucy and Felix typify everything that's right. Blaine was arrogant, entitled and self-righteous. He used his authority to terrorise those he despised. Hate is a long-range emotion. It rules the minds of people with an iron fist, demanding they act to satisfy its need for vengeance. In recent memory, the Rwandan genocide showed the extremes to which such hatred can run when left unchecked. Anthony sees this in a history book while staying with Deloris, and it informs his view of the modern world—flash cars and nice clothing are often used to hide the ugly side of modern life.

The descriptions of the Rwandan genocide in this novel are taken from accounts published in Time Magazine and The History Collection. In 1994, within the space of three months, a million people were brutally murdered in Rwanda. On the surface, it was Hutus killing Tutsis. In reality, it was fratricide, with humans slaughtering humans because one group didn't conform to the expectations of the other. The Tutsis were called cockroaches, rats, animals—everything but human as there's no other way to justify such bile and hatred. The lesson is clear: whenever one group demeans another, violence comes next.

Julia's character is based on Joan Waste (1534-1556) from All Hallows, Derby, who was blind but loved to hear the Bible being read aloud. When the local catholic mass was made compulsory under the reign of Queen Mary, Joan refused to attend. She was dragged before the local bishop and questioned about her beliefs. Joan turned the bishop's questions around on him, wanting him to defend himself. He refused to answer her, and she used that as justification for her refusal to reply to him, saying, '*If you won't answer me, then why should I answer you?*' In any civilised society, that would have been the end of the matter, but religious zealots are nothing if not bitter, spiteful and cruel. A week later, they burned her at the stake.

For me, Joan's life is an example of the kind of injustice that pervades so much of human history. Far too often, justice is defined by those in power and not by principle. As a species, we can and should do better. Joan deserves better than to be forgotten.

America

Today, it's easy to see America as a land of skyscrapers and interstate freeways, mountain ranges, deserts, canyons and wheat fields. Its origins as an English colony that fought for independence in 1776 is legendary, but prior to that, the fate of America was far from settled. Before the Revolutionary War and the Louisiana Purchase, it seemed as though America might develop like Europe, splintering into a variety of different countries. The thirteen original colonies may have been united, but the French south and Spanish conquest in what would eventually become the American southwest suggested otherwise. The New World was fragmenting like the Old.

Europeans had no practical knowledge of the American continent prior to 1492 when Columbus first reached the Bahamas. For the next century, the exploration of the New World was undertaken by the French and Spanish. The British didn't attempt to establish any kind of colony until 1587—several decades after the events in this novel—but their settlement on Roanoke Island failed. It wasn't until 1609 that Jamestown was settled, a hundred and seventeen years after the Americas were discovered by Columbus. As Anthony is from 1558 England, he would have no knowledge of America being settled by the English, let alone that the English would saturate the land and bring about a uniquely American culture. To him, the idea that the English would dominate North America would have been absurd. The English were late to the party, and yet now...

Cost of Living

Calculating the value of money in the 1550s isn't easy. I've used a number of online resources, including Castellogy. As an example, one gold sovereign was equal to 20-30 shillings or roughly a pound. In the buying power of the day, that equated to about £450. When Lady de Brooke offers Master Dunmore five gold sovereigns, she's giving him an advance of roughly £2000.

The Twin Paradox

The central scientific premise of this novel is that once Anthony and Julia leave Earth at relativistic speeds, they can never return to their world. Oh, they can physically return to the planet but not to their time/culture as time dilation sees them flung into the far future. In science, this is known as the twin paradox and was first discussed by Einstein. In its most basic form, two twins are separated from each other. One travels for eight years out into space at close to the speed of light relative to his brother on Earth. When he returns, his twin has aged by ten years due to the way spacetime has to flex to remain consistent with the speed of light. Basically, the astronaut's passage through space is traded for the brother's passage through time.

Apothecary takes this to the extreme, but it's the same basic principle.

Sex Shop

My ex-wife laughed when I told her I needed to visit a sex shop for research. "Sure," she said, putting air quotes around the word, "Research." I had to remind her it was her idea to turn the apothecary into a sex shop when I first pitched the story to her several years ago.

Never Forget

Although it's only a passing comment in this novel, it is true that during the Global War on Terror almost four times as many soldiers died at their own hands than in combat in both Iraq and Afghanistan. As a society, we have memorials for fallen soldiers, but these tend to focus on patriotism and pride. We celebrate battles and heroics. We say, "*Never forget*," and yet we fail to remember that war is hell. The suicide rate among veterans should tell us something profound about the misery that is war. Contrary to the impression given by flag-waving devotees, war is not something that should be glorified. Also, the devastating impact on civilians is rarely mentioned. There are times when war is thrust upon us as a brutal necessity, but most of the time, war isn't justified. Never forget, the cost of war is far greater than we dare imagine.

COBRA

COBRA is the colloquial name for COBR the United Kingdom's emergency coordination and decision-making committee. Originally formed in 1972, the acronym stands for Cabinet Office Briefing Room. In practice, it functions much like the Situation Room in the White House although it is not confined to a single room, allowing politicians access to key operational people within the military and government.

MECCA, though, the Mobile Extended Continuity Command Alternative, being a vehicle-based control and evacuation system for politicians is entirely fictitious.

Chris and Tom

This is a throwaway paragraph within the story, but when Lucy describes seeing multiple takes of Chris Hemsworth and Tom Hiddleston filming in London, that's based on an actual event I witnessed. One of the *Thor* movies was filmed here in Brisbane, Australia, and I got to watch them film and re-film the same scene over and over again while munching on a sandwich during my lunch break. It was fascinating to see how much attention goes into what was nothing more than a passing scene within the overall movie. Perhaps one day I'll get to see them making one of my stories into a movie.

Modern Democracy

The earliest modern democratic institution was that of the British House of Commons, established in 1265 to ensure local representation of the common people before the king. Over time, the Commons addressed the excesses of the Crown and even impeached some of the king's ministers. By 1610, Parliament was able to curtail royal decrees and ensure the king could not change common law by decree, essentially ensuring that the laws that governed the people were those laws established by the representatives of the people. For the most part, these "representatives" were wealthy landowners in the United Kingdom, Europe and America, but over time, this matured into the modern voting system we have today. Democracy has been a torturous road traversed over almost a millennium—and it's far from perfect—but, to paraphrase Winston Churchill, it's the best of the worst forms of government.

Colours

As crazy and counterintuitive as it seems, there is no colour. Red exists only in our perception of the world.

The visible light we see is only a tiny fraction of all the light on the electromagnetic spectrum. The difference between red, green and blue is a difference in frequency, not a difference in the type of light itself.

You've probably heard terms like infrared and ultraviolet to describe colours that lie just outside what we can see, with *infra* meaning under or below what's visible to us and *ultra* meaning above and beyond what we can naturally see. The light we see each day sits between violet/blue at ~400nm and red at ~700nm. It seems bizarre, but the difference between green and yellow is the difference in how fast a particular electromagnetic wave is oscillating back and forth. There is no colour of itself. Colour is an interpretation of the world around us by three different receptors in our eyes.

The implications of this are quite fascinating. It suggests that one colour could turn into an entirely different colour simply by changing its frequency—and that's precisely what we observe in astronomy. When astronomers look at distant galaxies, they speak of them as being *red-shifted* when moving away from us or *blue-shifted* if they're moving toward us. It's the visual equivalent of hearing an ambulance race past with its siren blaring. As the vehicle approaches, the sound is high-pitched. As soon as it passes, the pitch drops and the sound changes— only it doesn't. If you were sitting in the ambulance, you'd hear the same siren the whole way to the hospital. When we see a red-shifted or blue-shifted galaxy through a telescope, we're seeing colours slide back and forth along the visible spectrum.

No two species see exactly the same colours. Oh, closely related species, like humans and chimps, probably see similar colours, but there's no guarantee two people see the same two colours, let alone two different animals. As astonishing as it sounds, colours are subjective to each species. Not only do bees see flowers differently, they see patterns we miss entirely. While someone that's colour blind sees the world as it actually is!

Colour is beautiful. As I sit here writing, I'm staring out the window at a brilliant blue sky. Green eucalypts are swaying in the nearby forest. A red car just drove by. And yet, all these colours are a freak accident of evolution. Our sensitivity to light predates our species by hundreds of millions of years. The origins lie somewhere in how plants enticed insects to visit and pollinate their flowers. From there, the ability to distinguish between ripe fruit and poisonous berries conveyed a survival advantage. And now, we get to enjoy Monet and Picasso playing with colours on canvas.

Seeing the Sun at Night

When discussing Julia's alien-enhanced sight, the point is made that she can see the Sun at night by staring down and looking through the entire planet. This is based on a remarkable image developed by the physics department at the University of Louisiana using neutrinos rather than visible light to peer through the core of our planet at the core of our local star. The image was so faint it needed to be developed over five hundred days, but it worked!

Thank You

Thank you for supporting independent science fiction. I know I say that in all my novels, but I mean it. Without you, none of these stories would exist. By buying this novel, you're investing in my next book. You're giving me the privilege to write, so I thank you for your generosity.

Writing is a lonely process, but one of my favourite parts is when beta-readers get involved. They're hard-core fans with a passion for excellence. They love these quirky stories and enjoy ferreting out bloopers, so thank you Didi Kanjahn, Chris Fox, Terry Grindstaff and David Jaffe. In particular, John Stephens went through this novel several times to help polish the contents.

British science fiction author Ralph Kern was kind enough to read an advanced copy of *Apothecary* and help me with contemporary accuracy. Being a frontline police officer in the United Kingdom and having served in the British Army Reserves and as an RAF instructor, he was able to help me ground the novel in realism. If you enjoy military science fiction or sci-fi thrillers, be sure to check out his catalogue on Amazon.

If you'd like to chat about this or any of my novels, feel free to stop by my virtual coffee shop.

If you'd like to learn more about upcoming new releases, be sure to subscribe to my email newsletter. You can find all of my books on Amazon. I'm also active on Facebook, Instagram and Twitter.

Peter Cawdron
Brisbane, Australia

Printed in Great Britain
by Amazon